Desire's End

Maricca Wood

Copyright © 2026 by Maricca Wood

All rights reserved.
No part of this book may be reproduced, distributed, or transmitted in any form or by any electronic or mechanical means, including information storage and retrieval systems, without written permission from the author, except for the use of brief quotations in a book review and certain other noncommercial use permitted by copyright law.

This book is a work of fiction. Any resemblance to actual persons and things living or dead, locales, or events is entirely coincidental.

DESIRE'S END:
Cover Design: Books and Moods
Editor: The Havoc Archives

ALSO BY MARICCA WOOD

Desire Series
Desire's Curse
Desire's Blessing
Desire's End

Brothers of the Red Sky
A Healing Love

TRIGGER WARNING

Dear Wicked Readers,

Before immersing yourself in this roller coaster of emotions, please be aware that this book is indeed a dark romance. Our characters find themselves up shit creek without a paddle as they try to survive a couples retreat that was intended to celebrate love. This will bring the couples from books 1 & 2 together for one last thrilling, suspenseful adventure. If you haven't read Desire's Curse and Desire's Blessing, I suggest you do so to familiarize yourself with the characters and their stories.

This book contains conversations, actions, or situations that might be triggering and unsuitable for some readers. 18+ is advised. Some triggers include explicit sexual scenes, graphic violence, guns, miscarriage, PTSD, kidnapping, murder, attempted suicide (briefly mentioned), military funeral, child death (age 12, briefly depicted on page), death/dying, and bodies/corpses.

With all that being said, there may be some triggers within the book that I have not listed. Things will not be easy for all our couples, so strap in for their crazy and twisted journey.

-Enjoy

*To those who've lost the other half of their soul
and/or a baby that they never got to meet.*

PLAYLIST

Rock You Like A Hurricane - Scorpions
Addicted – Saving Abel
In Too Deep – Sum 41
Outskirts – Sam Hunt
Porch Swing Angel – Muscadine Bloodline
Still Into You - Paramore
In the End – Linkin Park
Wild Thing – Tone-Loc
Now That We're Dead – Metallica

CHAPTER 1

The house alarm chimed three times, pulling Serenity Jinx from her TV show as her head swiveled toward the massive dark oak front door. Rays of afternoon light filtered through numerous windows, flooding the open-concept main floor with natural light. Her vision softened when they landed on a familiar figure.

Hunter walked through, locking it behind him as he kicked off his boots and crossed the spacious living room. The simple crimson T-shirt and blue jeans he wore framed his tall stature, accentuating his sculpted muscles and broad shoulders. A physique that could only be achieved after years of rigorous military training, sending her bottom lip disappearing between her teeth at the sight of her fiancé.

"Hey, Angel." He kissed her on the lips as he laid stomach down on the couch, wrapped his arms around her waist, and nestled his head in her lap.

Warmth ignited within her chest, as it always did whenever he was near. Though his woodsy-scented cologne had dimmed throughout the day, faint hints clung to the fibers of his clothes as if refusing to drift away with the passing breeze. She didn't bother stopping herself as she took a long, slow inhale.

Home. That was what home smelled like to her. It didn't matter where in the world they were, what structure sheltered them, or who they were with. As long as this man was by her side, she was happy.

"Hey, sweetie. How was work?" she asked as she removed the elastic tie from his hair, letting his shoulder-length brown strands fall loose as she began to massage her fingers against his scalp.

A groan of pleasure slipped past his full lips as his ice-blue and hazel eyes slowly drifted closed. "Long." He released a heavy breath. "Send me behind enemy lines with nothing but a rock and I'd be like a kid in a candy shop, but paperwork…" He groaned again. "I hate paperwork. How was your day?"

Hunter Gatlin was a former Navy SEAL, but after leaving the service, he founded his own security company. Red Sky Security provided short-term bodyguard services for affluent clients for a variety of occasions. She knew that since he didn't have protection duty today, he was in the office most of the time, responding to emails and sorting out paperwork, invoices, and things of that nature.

She couldn't help but laugh. She knew better than anyone that her fiancé wasn't the kind of man who could sit behind a desk for hours each day. He'd go stir crazy two days in. Thankfully, she knew that Phoebe Vega, his receptionist, tended to handle the bulk of the paperwork for him, which he compensated graciously with a healthy salary for all her hard work. But some things were beyond Phoebe's control, requiring the owner's attention.

"It was good. Addi and I did some shopping and had lunch. We mostly discussed wedding plans."

A part of her had feared planning both her and Addi's wedding at the same time would get crazy, but it's been surprisingly fun.

Addison Thatcher was her best friend. They'd met five years ago at the bank they still work at and grew as close as sisters. Last year, Serenity found herself in need of a new date for Addi's first wedding after she found her long-term boyfriend, Noah, in bed with another woman.

Addi had suggested using the dating site, Desire, to try a type of speed dating in hopes of finding a new date. Luck was on Serenity's side, and after a few questionable dates, she'd met Hunter. It was nearly love at first sight for them both and they'd been inseparable ever since.

Hunter burrowed his head further into Serenity's lap. "Sweeney keeps giving me shit at work about him being the favorite, because out of everyone, I picked him to be my best man."

She laughed and shook her head as she kept massaging his scalp. There was no malice in his tone. She knew he loved Sweeney and all the men he worked with like brothers. "I think he'll be gloating about it for the rest of his life."

"Probably. The man has the maturity of a twelve-year-old boy."

"Ah, but you can't help but love him."

She smiled, and her mossy gaze shifted to the diamond ring that now adorned the finger on her left hand. Her mind transported her to the past. To a day she'd never forget, even if she lived to be a hundred. A few months back, Hunter had surprised her with a spontaneous trip to the mountains, where they got snowed in at a beautiful cabin. He'd proposed, and they spent the rest of the weekend in a mess of tangled limbs in front of a roaring fireplace.

"Oh, I checked the mail earlier and there was a letter from Desire," she said, snapping back to the present.

Serenity reached over and picked up the rectangular, cream-colored envelope that rested on the end table next to the couch, handing it to him as he propped himself up on his elbows.

"Really?" he questioned as he removed and unfolded the piece of paper. "What do they want?"

> Dear Mr. Gatlin and Ms. Jinx,
>
> We at Desire love to see success stories like the ones both of you experienced while using our dating site. It is our mission to help as many people find the other halves of their souls as we can. As a gift, we've chosen a handful of couples who've had success just like you two. We want to celebrate you all with an all-expenses-paid vacation to our island resort in the Bahamas for a week of relaxation and fun. If you have any questions, please, don't hesitate to reach out. We hope to hear from you soon and to see you there.
>
> Sincerely,
> Patrick Grundy – Marketing Director

He remained quiet as she watched his vision move over the letter again, slower this time.

"Sounds like a scam." He snorted and passed the paper back to her.

"Don't be so pessimistic." She slapped his shoulder lightly as she shook her head incredulously. "It could be real."

Companies entice new and existing customers with trips as marketing tactics all the time. Hell, the bank she worked at just did something similar last year, allowing anyone who opened a savings account with them to be entered for a chance to win a three-day cruise for two to Mexico.

"I don't know, something seems off."

"You have to admit, it does sound amazing." She couldn't stop the sigh of joy that escaped her parted lips. "I'd kill for a vacation to a tropical island."

Though Hunter frequently traveled around the world for work, she couldn't tag along for numerous reasons. All of which she completely understood. However, that meant that the only trips she got to take were few and far between, when they both could get away from work for a few days.

"Have you forgotten what happened the last time we vacationed on an island, Angel?" He arched his thick, scarred brow at her.

She knew he was referring to what had happened at Addi's wedding last year. Hunter was even more of a saving grace after Addi and Serenity found themselves kidnapped by Jack, Addi's ex-husband. Apparently, he'd been infatuated with Serenity and was only with Addi to get close to her.

Jack had orchestrated an off-the-wall plan that sounded like an insane plot for a thriller movie. He was a criminal defense attorney and, after observing his client's mistakes and taking notes, had formulated what he thought was an airtight plan that would allow him to get away with murder.

He'd taken a huge life insurance policy out on Addi and hired a couple of criminals to murder her the day after their wedding so he could collect the money and live the rest of his life with Serenity in a large home he'd bought in Hawaii.

After both women were kidnapped by Jack, Hunter and Sweeney came to their rescue and brought them home safely. Several months went by as Addi and Sweeney's relationship blossomed from roommates to best friends, then to lovers when he helped her heal over the loss and betrayal Jack had put her through.

"That was different," she tried to protest, but sounded doubtful herself.

His deep chuckle filled the quiet room around them. "Was it?"

Serenity opened her mouth but closed it again, unsure of how to respond. She hated it when he spoke rationally. Sound logic wasn't what she wanted right then. She wanted a beach vacation surrounded by sun, sand, and all the umbrella drinks she could get her hands on. Her face contorted into a pout and she felt her shoulders deflate.

A languid sigh slipped past his lips, and she knew he hated to see her with anything but a smile on her face. "I'll have Einstein look into this for us. If it's real, we can talk about it more."

That instantly perked up her spirit.

"Really?" She beamed.

She knew he'd never tell her no. He responded with a slight nod before resting his head back down on her lap. She resumed the massage of his scalp, nearly putting him to sleep as she continued her TV show.

The following morning, Hunter pulled his blacked-out Harley Sportster into the parking lot of Red Sky Security. A single-story, standalone brick building with bulletproof windows lining the front. Two crotch rocket motorcycles, one black and green, the other black and red, and a powder-blue Volkswagen Beetle were parked out front. After resting his bike on the kickstand, he stood and entered through the front door.

It was unlocked. Phoebe was usually the first one here in the mornings, unless Einstein pulled an all-nighter, but none of his men were on any dangerous assignments at the moment, so Einstein's constant monitoring wasn't needed.

"Good morning, Boss." Phoebe gave him a beaming smile, her colorful-framed glasses popping against her creamy skin.

"Good morning, Blue," he greeted back with a smile that would most likely never be as bright as hers.

That's the kind of woman Phoebe Vega was. Heart of gold, soft-spoken, always happy. She'd worked for him for nearly three years now, and she was the glue that held all the men together around there, though they'd never told her that. Not that it was some big secret, but rather because they weren't the kind of men who openly shared their feelings like that.

The first receptionist he'd hired put more effort into trying to sleep with them all than doing her job. It was a nightmare. He'd given her multiple warnings, but she never listened, which resulted in him firing her. Phoebe walked into the conference room for an interview to fill the position, and after one look at her, he knew she was the right person for the job. Thanks to his previous profession in the military, he'd always been a good judge of character.

Phoebe had never once crossed the line with any of them, and she quickly became a little sister they all looked out for and would kill for. Since she was a member of their family, it was only fitting that she had her own nickname. Blue, because of her hair—long, light blonde strands with baby-blue highlights throughout.

He walked down the hallway lined with all their offices, entering the last on the left. After placing his helmet and keys atop his desk, he made his way back into the open and airy lobby, through a set of double doors that led to a conference room with a massive table and enough chairs to seat twenty comfortably. He kept walking through another set of double doors that led to the fully stocked armory and a room tucked away on the right-hand side.

That was Einstein's office. Hunter had tried many times to offer the guy an office next to all of theirs, but he kept refusing, saying he liked his privacy. Which was understandable. Hunter was the same way, but that didn't stop him from keeping an office by theirs empty in case Einstein ever changed his mind.

With a quick glance, he found the room empty and knew the men must be in the gym. He kept walking back, passing through one last door that led to a fully stocked gym equipped with cardio machines, circuit machines, and a massive free-weight section. In the back of all that, the concrete floor was covered with black mats. That was where they grappled and practiced fighting each other to keep their skills honed and sharp, in case they were ever needed while on an assignment.

If they had a meeting with a client, they would show up to work dressed in a nice shirt, slacks, and dress shoes to help look the part. To show they can look professional but still protect at a moment's notice. If they didn't have any meetings, they arrived in workout clothes and hit the gym. Then they'd spend at least an hour or two sparring with each other, and once they were done, everyone was free to leave for the day.

Hunter had four really good guys who worked under him. Each was given their own call sign that was unique to them. Doc was a skilled sniper and gun enthusiast, named after the infamous gunslinger, Doc Holliday. Fuse was an explosive expert and pyro enthusiast. Sweeney preferred knives over guns, so he was named after the fictional serial killer from the mid-1800s, Sweeney Todd, who killed people with straight razors. And Einstein was the brains of their operations—a computer genius, skilled hacker, and avid gamer.

As suspected, Hunter found Einstein and Sweeney had already

started on their workouts. Einstein was in the middle of a rep of squats and Sweeney was using the bench press to work out his chest. Fuse was on an assignment and Doc had left for a week-long vacation. After a quick greeting to the guys, Hunter slipped in his headphones, turned on his music, and lost himself in a killer back and bicep workout. By the time everyone was done, they were layered in sweat.

They took to the mats and began sparring, first Hunter and Einstein, then Einstein and Sweeney, and last, Hunter and Sweeney. Though Einstein never went out on assignments, he still worked out with everyone and somehow had one of the best ground games Hunter had ever seen. The kid was tall, lean, and lightning-quick, making wrestling with him a good challenge and always fun. Everyone called him a kid, but only because he was the youngest amongst their family at twenty-three. Well, besides Phoebe, who was the same age.

After everyone was exhausted and dripping sweat come lunchtime, they hit the locker room, showered, and changed into casual clothes. After bidding goodbye to Sweeney, Hunter followed Einstein into his cyber cave.

A large, wooden L-shaped desk filled the left side of the space. Numerous monitors of various sizes were mounted on the wall above. A large flat-screen TV was mounted on the opposite wall with a sofa positioned in front of it. Einstein, clad in his usual style—a dark hoodie, jeans, and a beanie—pulled out his black gaming chair and sat down.

"You mentioned you'd found something?" Hunter inquired.

"Yeah, Bossman, I looked into the letter you sent me, and from what I can tell, it's legit." Einstein turned to face him.

His shaggy black hair stuck out like wings beneath the worn

grey beanie, his deep blue eyes popped against his pale skin, which was free from any tattoos or piercings, and he always had his fingernails painted. Today, they were dark blue.

Hunter was given the call sign Boss. Though the explanation is self-explanatory. However, each man had a different variation of the name. Einstein always called him Bossman, Doc and Fuse addressed him as Boss, and Sweeney, the adult-sized child, referred to him as Big Daddy.

"The company, Desire, owns an island in the Bahamas. They purchased it almost a year ago and started construction on the resort immediately. Patrick Grundy, the guy who signed the letter, *is* a real human being and *is* Desire's marketing director. They've sent out the same letter to three other couples across the country. One couple is from Rhode Island, another is from Georgia, and the last is from Washington. They also sent one to a woman, however, hers was an apology letter, offering the same week-long vacation. I remember seeing the story in the news last year. Apparently, this woman had met a man on the site who turned out to be a stalker and kidnapped her. He was a real creep, and she put him six feet under."

"Good for her," Hunter responded.

He knew all too well the damage a stalker could inflict on a woman. Jack had stalked Serenity in the weeks leading up to his wedding to Addi. Serenity was a wreck about the whole thing, to say the least. But he was glad that whoever this woman was, she was strong enough to end her stalker. That's one less sicko in this world and this planet is better off because of it.

"Well, Angel will be happy that the offer's real." He couldn't help but laugh lightly, knowing his fiancée would want to start packing, even though it was a few weeks away.

He'd asked how Serenity felt about it, but how did *he* feel about the whole thing? He was skeptical at first, thinking it was some elaborate hoax, but after Einstein's research, he believed in the legitimacy of it. He'd believe just about anything the evil genius told him. The kid always seemed to know way too much for his own good.

Do we go? Do we stay? A vacation did sound pretty good to him. Though he traveled around the world a lot for work, he rarely did it for pleasure. The last vacation he took was months ago, when he proposed to Serenity. A memory tugged one side of his lips up. The look of shock across her angular features when he'd popped the question, the love that filled her mossy eyes, the way her body felt beneath him after she said yes and they made love.

However, that was months ago. They were well overdue for a vacation, just the two of them, filled with relaxation, fun, and sex. Lots of sex. *Damnit*, he sighed to himself. Just like that, he'd talked himself into it.

"Thanks, man. I appreciate it."

"Anytime, Bossman." Einstein smiled and twisted back toward his monitors.

Hunter watched as Einstein clicked a few buttons on his keyboard, and one of the large screens changed to what looked like a video game. A man dressed in a blue and yellow jumpsuit appeared to be exploring a decrepit town many years after an apocalypse. Hunter shook his head and chuckled to himself. Although he'd told Einstein numerous times not to play video games while at work, none of his men were currently on dangerous assignments, so he often let it slide.

CHAPTER 2

Hunter Gatlin lounged in his office later that morning, craving a much-needed distraction. He was up to his elbows in invoices. He'd been staring at numbers for so long that his vision had begun to blur and sting. A groan slipped out as he closed his aching eyes, rested his head back against his chair, and pinched the bridge of his nose.

I despise office work...

He had half a mind to walk into the armory, grab a pistol, and shoot his computer. Though that wouldn't solve his problem. It would only cost him money he didn't want to spend to replace the monitor. He wasn't made to sit behind a desk for hours on end. It was as if his body were an hourglass, and once the sand stopped flowing, he became antsy. His leg would begin bouncing erratically, and his mind would be begging for any kind of movement.

He was never like this in the field though. Hell, as a SEAL, he lost count of how many days he spent hiding out in a foreign country, patiently biding his time until his team got the go-ahead to move forward with their missions. He could camp out in tall grass, lie prone for hours like a statue, waiting for the target to arrive, and be perfectly content, but sit him behind a desk, surrounded by four constricting walls, and he was in hell.

He'd lost count of how many times he'd have to break after so long and enter the gym just to walk on the treadmill for a few minutes to get his body and mind to settle down. Thanks to Phoebe helping out with the majority of the responsibilities, he only had to occupy the prison cell he called an office once or twice a week.

He'd never take that godsend of a woman for granted. Without her, the company would be in a constant state of disarray and the relationship between him and his men wouldn't be nearly as strong as it is now. She was the overly joyful, love-distributing little sister who kept their chosen family together like glue.

Doc had left on vacation a few days ago, heading to a resort his family owned in the Bahamas, where his little brother was getting married later that week. Decades ago, Doc's father had taken a leap of faith, sinking what little money he and his wife had to purchase a run-down resort. Over the years, with a lot of elbow grease, hard work, and unwavering dedication, they now have multiple locations all over the tropics.

Hunter hadn't heard a word from Doc since he left, and he wanted to check in. He picked up his phone from atop his desk and shot off a quick text in the group chat he shared with all his men.

Boss: How's paradise?

Doc: I'm here with my family, so... it could be better.

Einstein: I'd figure the girl you brought with you would've made it more bearable.

Hold the fuck up? The men, though they were all as close as brothers, liked to keep certain aspects of their lives private. They all respected each other's boundaries and never pushed. For reasons unknown, Doc doesn't date. Ever. For him to bring a woman on vacation with him and his family was a huge curveball that no one saw coming.

Fuse: Girl? What girl?

Sweeney: Wait… You're straight? (Crying face emoji)

Doc: Sweeney, fuck off… Einstein, how the hell do you know I'm here with someone?

Einstein: I know everything. (devil smiley face emoji)

Sweeney: Well, that's not creepy at all, evil genius.

Fuse: That's unsettling…

Hunter couldn't help but sigh aloud and shake his head. He'd had countless chats with Einstein about respecting other people's privacy. He knew the kid didn't mean anything nefarious by it. That's not the kind of man Einstein was. He simply was the kind of person who made it his business to know as much as possible. Whether it was a defense mechanism or he was simply a nosy person, no one knew.

Though he kept most of what he knew to himself. Which they were all thankful for. The last thing the guys needed was Einstein spouting the shadows they all kept locked away in the closets of their souls. Though Einstein would never do that. He'd take their secrets with him to the grave.

Boss: Do we need to have another talk about boundaries, Einstein?

Einstein: I'm just looking out for you all. You're welcome.

Fuse: Back to the topic at hand. Doc, what girl?

Sweeney: Send a picture! I need proof.

There was a moment of pause in the chat while everyone, including Hunter, waited with bated breath. A minute later, a photo came through of Doc standing on a boat with a beautiful woman with straight chocolate hair and pale grey eyes wrapped in his arms. The way the rays of the falling sun reflected against her skin made her glow.

Sweeney immediately sent a GIF of Bugs Bunny with his eyes popping out of his head in the shape of hearts. Though he could be immature at the most inappropriate of times, they all loved his crazy, charismatic ass.

Boss: She's beautiful. I'm happy for you, Doc.

Fuse: Damn! Good job, man. I didn't know you were seeing anyone. I thought you didn't date.

Einstein: He doesn't. She's a hired date.

Doc: WTF, Einstein! There's no way you could possibly know that!

Einstein: (Knowing grin face emoji)

Fuse: Wait… What?

Boss: I'm confused. You paid a woman to go on vacation with you?

Sweeney: Damn! I knew your game was bad, but I didn't know it was that bad...

Doc: Again, Sweeney, fuck off! We're not together. I hired her to pretend to be my girlfriend to get my mother off my back.

Boss: Yeah, this won't implode horribly. (Palm face emoji)

Fuse: I second that, Boss.

Einstein: Third, Bossman.

Sweeney: Fourth, Big Daddy! Doc, do you at least get to sleep with her?

Doc: Dude... Your lack of a filter is alarming.

Sweeney: (shrugging shoulders emoji) I am who I am. Love me or hate me. (kissy face emoji)

Fuse: But... Do you??

Doc: No! She's not an escort or some shit.

Sweeney: Explains the testy attitude. A hundred bucks says he'll have sex with her no later than tomorrow.

Fuse: You're on! My bet is for today, though.

Boss: Thursday.

Einstein: Friday.

Doc: Hhh, I think it's time for a career change...

Boss: Sorry, Doc! No can do. I'll have Einstein forge a document that traps you at this company for life if need be.

Fuse: Yeah, we're all stuck in this cult for good.

Einstein: Who says I don't already have blackmail folders on each of you for such an occasion? (devil smiley face emoji)

Doc: I've had all I can take from y'all today.

Sweeney: Have fun, you crazy kids! (winky face emoji) And don't forget to use protection! No glove, no love!

Fuse: Take more pictures and keep us updated! We're invested now.

Einstein: If you don't send them, I'll put them in the group chat for you, Doc. Mwahahaha!!!

Hunter's deep laughter echoed off the walls of his office as he placed his phone back atop his desk. He knew Einstein wasn't bluffing. If Doc didn't keep them updated, Einstein would. Every man there was now deeply invested in this new turn of events in their brother's life. Heels clacking against the hardwood floors drew Hunter's eyes up. A few seconds later, Phoebe appeared, her mossy sundress hugging her slender frame, stopping at her knees.

"Hey, Boss." She greeted him with a beaming smile, causing her rounded cheeks to slightly shift her colorful glasses up. "I'm going to order some lunch. Do you want anything?"

Oh, thank God!

He was on his feet a second later, tucking his phone into the back pocket of his jeans and reaching for his keys. "No worries, I can go get it."

This is just the break I need to clear my head before getting back to those damn invoices.

She crossed her arms over her chest and hiked a brow at him. "Avoiding responsibilities, are we?"

His grin was cocky as he shot her a playful wink. "Twenty minutes tops, then I'll get back to it. Promise." He placed his hand over his heart as if taking an oath.

She stepped aside, allowing him to exit his office. He was halfway down the hallway when she called after him. "Those invoices aren't going to process themselves, you know."

He could hear the laughter in her tone. She knew him so well. Hell, Phoebe seemed to know all the men better than they knew themselves sometimes. But that's what it's like with family, and that's what they were at Red Sky Security.

"I promise, I'll have them done by the end of the day. Text me everyone's food order." He called over his shoulder, a smile playing on his lips. He didn't slow his steps as he exited the building and took a deep breath of fresh air as he swung his leg over his bike and roared the engine to life.

CHAPTER 3

With their fingers intertwined, Liam and Amarah strolled down the dirt path. An extra-wide, well-loved path broken in from leading dozens of hikers daily wound its way through the woods at an uphill angle. Despite the intense heat, the thick green foliage provided much-welcome shade from the unforgiving sun, and a gentle breeze brushed past, helping to cool the group down during their hike.

"We should be nearly there," Travis called out from behind the couple, where he walked side by side with his wife, Sandra.

Travis Patterson, Amarah's older brother, has been Liam Godrik's best friend since they met in their junior year of high school, when the two were seventeen. After graduation, they joined the Navy, and together, after years of rigorous training and various lengthy schools, became SEALs. Their friendship continued to strengthen when they were stationed together in Virginia.

After Travis and Liam had separated from the military and moved back home, the group of four often found themselves exploring Mother Nature. Whether it was hiking or camping in some long-forgotten forest utterly untouched by civilization, scaling the sides of a rocky cliff, scuba diving in the tropics, or snowboarding down mountains, it didn't matter. They were always up for new adventures and exploring the vast beauties this world had to offer. This explained why, after nearly a five-mile hike, in the dead heat of an Oklahoma summer, not one of them was winded in the slightest.

"I heard the view is stunning," Sandra practically sighed with anticipation, her fiery hair braided into pigtails so the humidity wouldn't have it sticking to her creamy neck.

Twenty feet up the path, they finally broke the tree line. The ground, rocky beneath their boots, came to an abrupt stop about fifteen feet in front of them, where the edge of a cliff gave way to a picturesque view one would find on an inspiring photographer's Instagram. Miles of hills and valleys were exposed before them as far as the eye could see. The sun soared high above, lighting up a breathtaking cloudless sky so blue that it would put the Mediterranean Sea to shame.

Liam heard a breathy gasp escape Amarah's lips. He would agree that the view was stunning, but it paled in comparison to the woman standing at his side. He peered to his right, admiring the woman he'd secretly loved for years but couldn't have because his best friend's little sister had been a no-fly zone. That is, until the events of last summer finally brought the truth of their feelings for one another to the surface.

Amarah's hair, as bright as the sun, was pulled into a high ponytail, allowing an unobstructed view of her angular features and a slender neck that he loved pressing his lips against any chance he got. Her deep sapphire eyes were wide as they darted over the valley as if she were trying to take in everything the view had to offer at once.

He'd had her all to himself for an entire year, yet he still struggled with the idea that she was all his. A woman he'd known since she was eleven, but after years away in the military, when he came home and saw her all grown up, something inside of him shifted. Even after two more years and thousands of miles away, her enticing beauty held him in its snares. A woman who'd saved herself just for him, because for whatever reason, out of all the men on the planet, she decided that he was the most worthy of giving that special part of herself to.

This woman, who went from being his best friend to his lover and then his wife. Still, to this day, he's uncertain of how he ever deserved such a blessing. A month after she'd moved into his house, he'd proposed to her on a beach in Hawaii, and she'd said yes. Five months after that, they were married, deciding that after knowing each other for over a decade, there was no point in waiting a year or more to plan some extravagant wedding.

They were confident in their feelings and knew they'd be devoted for life. Although he had more money than most ever thought possible for someone to accumulate in one's lifetime, Amarah kept their ceremony small and intimate, surrounded only by family and close friends. The image of her walking down that aisle toward him, her eyes glassy with joyful tears, her dress, simple but elegant, forming around her slender body like a glove, flashed through his mind, causing warmth that had nothing to do with the summer sun to spread through his chest.

Their wedding had been nothing short of magical. He would've dropped millions on their special day if that was what she had wanted. Anything to make the love of his life happy. However, that's not the kind of woman Amarah was. She's down-to-earth, kind, gentle-natured, and always has a smile lighting up her face so contagious that everyone around can't help but join in. A smile that he thought he'd never see again... Not after the events of last summer.

Liam nearly lost her to the clutches of a psycho who was obsessed with her. He quickly pushed those dreadful events from his mind, not wanting to spoil the moment by allowing anger to consume him. He'd lost count of how many times he dreamed about resurrecting Derick Watland, just so he could kill the man all over again for everything he put Amarah through.

His height easily allowed him to shift his gaze over her head to see Sandra standing next to Amarah, a similar look of amazement filling her eyes. Travis came to a stop on the other side of his wife, and Liam watched as he withdrew his phone from a pocket of his cargo pants. Travis twirled his wife around, planted a kiss atop her lightly freckled cheek, and snapped a photo with the perfect backdrop behind them.

Good idea. A grin spread across Liam's face as he did the same with Amarah. Except he claimed her lips for their picture, causing his heart rate to spike. *God, I'll never tire of kissing this woman.*

"Eww! Get a room." Travis groaned but couldn't hide his smile that was surrounded by a full light brown and blond beard he kept trimmed close to his face. His straight, shoulder-length, sunny hair was secured beneath a black ball cap. "I didn't give you permission to marry my sister so you could make out with her in front of me."

"Fuck off." Liam laughed.

"Technically, he never asked for permission," Amarah clarified as she shot her husband a wink that sent blood rushing to a certain extension of his body.

Sandra patted her husband's muscular bicep. "She's got you there, honey."

The group perched atop some large rocks next to the cliffside to further enjoy the view while they took a twenty-minute break to rest and refuel. Afterward, they began making their way back down the worn path through the woods. Another five miles later, they exited the thick forest, reentering the gravel parking lot they had started at.

"You know, for a local hiking spot, that view was breathtaking." Sandra smiled as she handed her backpack to her husband, who placed it along with his own in their truck.

"I agree, although that one spot we found last year, high atop the mountains of Colorado, is a pretty close contender." Amarah laughed as Liam took her pack from her and stowed it in their vehicle.

"Though, neither comes close to a few years back when we went to Japan in time to see the cherry blossoms blooming." Sandra sighed.

Amarah mirrored her sister-in-law's dreamy expression. "There were no words to describe that level of elegant beauty. That photo you took was my screensaver at work for months."

Liam stepped up behind his wife, wrapped his arms around her middle, pulled her flush against his front, and rested his chin atop her head.

"I'll look at our calendar, but I say next time, we take a boat out on Lake Eufaula or maybe Tenkiller?" Travis offered as he came to a stop beside his wife, draping an arm over her slender shoulder. "That way, we can bring the kids."

Travis and Sandra were high school sweethearts. She'd supported his passion to join the Navy and stuck by his side through every deployment and mission, waiting with open arms and an understanding mindset that he might not come back as whole as he had left. Fourteen years later, they've welcomed three beautiful kids into this world—two girls and a boy—and are still madly in love, as if they were still teenagers back in school.

"Oh, I second that idea!" Amarah beamed. "That sounds like so much fun."

"What'll be fun is seeing how long they can stay on the inner tube before I can throw them off." A wicked grin slid across Liam's bearded face, and he felt his wife's body shake with laughter.

"Hundred bucks says I can toss them from the tube higher than you can." Travis gave his brother-in-law a sly grin.

Liam mirrored it. "Prepare to pay up!"

"Ugh, my poor babies," Sandra said as she shook her head and laughed. "If anyone ends up in the emergency room, I'm going to kick both of your asses," she warned both her husband and Liam, causing the group to burst out in laughter. Not because they thought she was bluffing. No. Redheads had a stereotype for a reason, and Sandra was one crazy woman, especially if it involved the safety of her babies.

After everyone said their goodbyes, Liam held the truck door open for Amarah. When he climbed in and turned the engine over, he couldn't help but chuckle when he heard his wife sigh as the cool AC began blasting through the vents, decreasing the stuffiness of the cabin. However, his good mood was short-lived when he noticed her usual golden complexion was gone, replaced by a paler shade. Which didn't make any sense, given the fact that they'd been in the sun, hiking for the majority of the day.

"Are you ok, Cupcake?" Years of learning how to mask his emotions in the Navy helped to keep his voice even, though concern was settling heavily in his chest.

"Yeah." She nodded, sparing him a quick glance. "I think I just got too hot out there." She must've observed the look of concern that sparked through his vision because she quickly added, "I'll be ok, I promise."

"Buckle up." He tipped his head toward her seatbelt. "I'll get us home quickly so you can relax."

The entire forty-five minute drive back to their house, he couldn't stop his eyes from shifting between the road and his wife. She'd remained quiet, her gaze trained out her window and leaned back in her seat with an arm wrapped tightly around her middle. By the time he pulled through the wrought iron gate and parked in the garage, her complexion had grown ashen. She barely waited for him to put the vehicle in park before she threw open her door and jumped out.

"Amarah!" he shouted, but she had already disappeared into the house.

Muttering a string of curses beneath his breath, that feeling of concern further tightened around his heart. He grabbed their backpacks from the back seat and stepped into the large mud room, dropping them atop a wooden bench meant for putting on shoes. He'd worry about unpacking them later. Right now, he needed to find his wife and figure out what the hell was wrong with her.

He crossed through the open-concept kitchen and living room, passed his home office, and turned down the hall, heading right for their bedroom. The moment he entered, the sound of Amarah retching in the attached bathroom sent him sprinting, the plush carpet quieting his approach.

The sight before him nearly broke his heart. She knelt on the cool tile, hunched over the white porcelain toilet as she continued to throw up everything that was in her stomach.

"Go," she groaned, trying to wave him off, but he ignored her futile attempts. "I don't want anyone to see me like this."

Liam squatted next to her and began rubbing soothing circles across her back. "I'm not going anywhere, Cupcake. In sickness and in health, remember?"

"I think that's meant for cancer and other terminal illnesses." She tried to give a weak laugh, but another round of nausea worked its way out instead.

Despite the worrisome vision in front of him, the memory of their wedding tugged a corner of his lips up. He knew she would say the words without hesitation, but hearing her say "I do" ranked top three on his list of greatest life moments. Right behind the first time she'd voiced those three little words, and the first time they'd had made love, when he claimed her virginity.

Another long, painful groan slipped out when she'd finally thrown up everything her small body had to offer. She quickly flushed the toilet before sitting back against the wall. Without being asked, he retrieved a rag, soaked it in cold water, and handed it to his wife as he sat next to her, his heavily tattooed forearms resting atop his bent knees.

"Were you feeling unwell on our hike?"

His jaw clenched as he waited with anticipation. She's never been one to complain, and if she were feeling unwell, she wouldn't have mentioned anything until after, not wanting to ruin the hiking trip or that stunning view for anyone. That's just the kind of woman she was, always putting others first.

"No." She sighed as if the cool rag against her heated skin felt euphoric. He released a breath of relief before she continued. "It hit me when we were saying goodbye. It's either a stomach bug or food poisoning from breakfast."

They'd stopped at a small diner they'd been wanting to try for months before they met Travis and Sandra at the hiking spot.

"I'm praying for the former."

However, another option slowly crept into his mind. Could she be pregnant? She's been on birth control, and they've never used protection the entirety of their relationship. The chances of an accidental pregnancy were low but never zero. That theory was unlikely though, because she'd just gotten her period the other week, and morning sickness didn't usually hit until a month or so in. They were on the same page when it came to children. They both wanted kids, but not right away, wanting to wait a few years so that they could enjoy just the two of them.

A small part of him, though, hoped it would happen unexpectedly and sooner rather than later. To watch his wife's belly swell with life, knowing his child was in there, to kiss her growing stomach each night before bed. But he kept that admission to himself.

The more he thought back, the more he realized the possibility of it being a stomach bug was more plausible. They'd babysat their nieces and nephew the other day so Travis and Sandra could have a date night. Caroline, the youngest, who had just turned six, had been battling a nasty stomach bug, and she begged her Aunt Amarah to stay in bed with her the whole time, forcing her to read story after story. Caroline had said that each one helped make her feel better, and Amarah, being the wonderful woman she is, happily conceded.

"Well, come on. Let's get you cleaned up and in bed so you can rest."

He rose and extended a large hand toward her. Though her smile was shaky, she accepted. Electricity shot up his arm from their simple connection, heating his body and accelerating his pulse. He'd never tire of the feeling of her smooth, delicate skin against his. He effortlessly pulled her to her feet and held her steady when she began to sway. Once she was stable, he crossed the space and started the shower.

"Arms up," he instructed as he came to a stop in front of her, gripping the hem of her tank top.

"I can undress myself, you know." She gave him an exhausted laugh but obeyed, raising her arms.

"I know." His grin turned sly as he continued. "But I'll use any excuse I can to take your clothes off."

She rolled her eyes as he removed her shirt and sports bra. He then hooked his fingers into the waistline of her leggings and began to tug them down her long, toned legs. She helped by stepping out of them, and he had to force his hands to stay at his side, no matter how much they were itching to touch every inch of her.

Liam held the shower door open as she stepped in and didn't miss the small moan that escaped when the hot spray connected with her clammy skin. He laughed to himself before he stripped out of his clothes and tossed everything into the hamper. He climbed into the shower behind her and grabbed the bar of soap. Though he wanted to take his time with her, he knew she didn't feel good and needed to get to bed. Instead, he made quick work of soaping up her body.

"Man, this sucks." She released a tired sigh. "I wanted to go with you tomorrow on your trip."

After he left the military, Liam took over his father's company and has been the CEO of Godrik Enterprises for the last few years, growing the real estate and architectural firm into a multi-billion dollar corporation.

His work required him to travel frequently, whether it was to discuss business with a potential client or to check in with existing ones about ongoing projects. Because Godrik Enterprises employed a handful of some of the most renowned architects, people from all over the globe would reach out about homes, hotels, businesses, or resorts they wanted designed and built.

Amarah had begun working for him last year as his personal assistant before they'd started dating. Shortly afterward, he started bringing her along on his business trips, making him more than happy for numerous reasons.

One, because even though they've known each other for over a decade, the thought of being away from the other, especially after upgrading their relationship from friends to lovers, was pure torture. Two, because they've always been outdoorsy people. So, traveling and seeing the world with her while he worked was a dream come true. Tomorrow, he was heading to Bali for four days to close a deal on the design of a luxury resort.

"I want you there with me too, Cupcake." He placed a small kiss against the back of her shoulder as he continued washing her. "But you can't help it if you get sick."

"I want pictures, ok?" She twisted after he was finished and placed a quick kiss against the black scruff across his cheek before stepping out of the shower.

"I'll send so many that you'll be sick of hearing from me." He laughed.

"You can bombard me with messages every minute, and I'd never tire of hearing from you."

Though her face was turned away from him, he could easily hear the love she held for him in her voice and knew, without a shadow of a doubt, that she was smiling. Just as he knew the Earth would continue revolving around the sun. He washed himself off as she dried herself and handed him the towel as he stepped out.

Her vision slowly dropped down his front, and his heart started to race, trying to send his blood racing south.

"You can't look at me like that, Cupcake." Mischief laced his deep tone as he accepted the towel, and he relished the look of disappointment that flashed through her deep sapphire vision when he wrapped the soft cotton around his waist, concealing half his body from her.

"Ugh! Getting sick is so stupid," she pouted as she brushed out her blonde strands and braided them back into a loose French braid.

"I agree." He laughed as his gaze followed her naked retreating form as she entered their bedroom in search of pajamas.

By the time he exited the bathroom, she was already tucked into their king-sized bed, sound asleep. Liam quietly slipped into a pair of boxers and dark blue pajama pants. He entered the kitchen and gathered a few items he knew his wife would be searching for when she woke, returning with a glass of water and a sleeve of saltine crackers that he placed atop her nightstand.

Then he retrieved the small trash can from their bathroom and placed it on the floor beside their bed so Amarah could easily get to it if needed. If it was the stomach bug she had gotten from their niece, he knew she'd be utilizing it for at least a day or two. Unfortunately, this was going to get worse before it got better.

After placing a quick kiss atop her clammy forehead, he made his way into his home office, having a bit of work to get done before he could crawl into bed and pull her into his arms as he fell asleep.

CHAPTER 4

Amarah Godrik glanced toward the bottom right corner of her computer screen, propped her elbows atop her desk, plopped her chin in her open palms, and huffed out a frustrated sigh. Two minutes had passed since she last checked. That's it? Only two? The minutes were ticking by like hours, and she was losing patience. Her husband was due back at the office any minute, and the anticipation was killing her.

A man she'd secretly crushed on since she was eleven and had the privilege of watching him grow from a boy into one hell of a man. Even though they'd been married for six months now, the reminder that such a strong, powerful, and dangerous man was all hers still pulled a blinding smile across her angular features, and wings erupted throughout her belly.

For the last four days, Liam had been in Bali on one of the most exquisite beaches she'd ever seen. She sighed when he'd texted her several photos of the area, wishing more than anything that she could be there with him. Pure white sand as far as the eye could see, clear blue water that called to you like a siren's song. She knew that once the resort was constructed and open for business, it would become an instant hotspot.

She made a mental note to ask her husband to book them a room the moment the resort opened. Instead of being laid out on a beach, tanning, she was lying in bed, throwing up anything she tried to eat or drink.

She hadn't suffered a stomach bug of that magnitude in years and wouldn't wish it on her worst enemy. Not since her senior year of high school, when her lab partner unknowingly passed the virus to her. She'd been forced to miss their senior class trip to Six Flags amusement park. A part of her never forgave the boy, even though she knew it was completely unintentional.

Thankfully, she woke up feeling much better yesterday, and she'd finally been able to keep food down and wasted no time in flushing tons of fluids into her body. She swore she had downed at least three Liquid IVs, and her body thanked her by allowing her to wake up this morning as if she'd never been sick in the first place.

This had been the longest period they'd been apart since they started dating, and she hated every minute of it. Sure, they texted periodically throughout the day and talked on the phone every night while he was gone, but it wasn't the same.

The faint ding of an arriving elevator sent her spine straightening and her leg bouncing beneath her desk. She tried hard to listen for footsteps, but thanks to Liam's background, if he didn't want his presence known, you'd never hear him coming until it was too late. Instead, she busied herself with a new email that just came through, a potential client inquiring about getting on the schedule for a meeting with Liam and one of their architects.

Though her eyes were glued to her dual monitors, she felt the moment his gaze reached her, and she had to bite back a moan of relief that he was finally home. As casually as she could manage, she glanced toward him, and her lungs momentarily forgot how to function. The man was devastatingly handsome in his dark blue suit, tailored to fit his six-foot-two, lean frame. The expensive fabric was pulled tight, professionally accentuating his mouthwatering muscles.

His bright green eyes popped against his tanned skin, and a hunger filled them that mirrored her own. After having sex constantly with someone—as in, almost every day for a year—and then going four days without it, was pure agony. Good thing they only had half the workday left before they could go home, and she could have her way with him.

He flashed her a devilish smirk as if he were reading her thoughts and liked every one of them. His full black beard looked freshly trimmed close to his skin, and he ran a hand through his short black hair, brushing back the longer strands on top in the most delectable way that always sent heat warming her core.

He didn't slow his long strides as he came down the hallway lined with offices of the other higher-ups: the head of HR, the CFO, and an office for each of their architects that resided on the top floor of Godrik Enterprises. A modernly designed, stand-alone, ten-story building in the heart of downtown.

"Cupcake." His voice was low and deep as he shot her a wink and flashed her a devilish smile.

She watched with bated breath as his eyes dipped, tracking the movement of her thighs as she pressed them together before they shifted back up in time to witness the flush trying to creep its way up her neck. He'd always been freakishly observant like that due to his years in the Navy, and she equally loved and cursed it. It made surprising him *exceptionally* hard.

He'd had that nickname for her for as long as she could

remember. She never understood why, of all names, that one stuck until last year when he finally told her. *It's because you're as sweet as one.* The memory of her and Liam in the shower after the horrors of last summer flashed through her mind. He'd told her that he loved her for the first time moments later, and if she had died right then, she would've died the happiest woman on the planet.

"Liam." Her lungs still refused to work, causing his name to come out as no more than a breathy whisper.

He didn't stop to greet her, to kiss her hello, to tell her how much he missed her. They always kept things professional at work, at least when they were in the presence of other company. Behind closed doors, however, they couldn't keep their hands off each other, and within the first month of dating, they had christened every inch of his office, the conference table, the elevator, and numerous other locations throughout the building.

He pushed through one of the double doors that led to his office, where Amarah's desk resided just outside, knowing that he had a meeting to prepare for in half an hour. Only after he was out of sight and a wall separated them did her lungs begin to function properly again.

An hour later, Liam's last meeting of the day was wrapping up. Amarah gathered the papers off the printer and put them inside a manila folder before heading toward his office. Her black heels clicked against the marble tile floor with each step. She knocked on the double doors as a courtesy and waited for her husband's response.

"Come in," Liam's deep voice flowed through the dark wooden door.

She stepped inside, and though she'd been working there for a while, she never got over the beauty of his office. From the dark hardwood floors to the bloodred area rug and the modern white furniture that filled the space. Her favorite thing, however, had and will always be the floor-to-ceiling windows that line the left wall, overlooking the downtown area. She'd lost count of how many evenings she'd spent on the white leather sofa that sat in the corner, simply watching the setting sun light the sky on fire as he finished his work for the day.

Liam's presence dominated the space as it always did, no matter where they were or who they were with. Her gaze clashed with a pair of bright green irises that didn't waste a heartbeat before raking down her front. He sat behind his large desk, which was free of clutter aside from the bare necessities, looking like a god about to pass judgment. The client, an older bald gentleman, resided in a cushioned armchair in front of his desk, an ankle crossed over a knee as if they were old friends catching up after years apart.

"I've got the paperwork you requested." She crossed the space, giving the client a kind smile and a nod.

She rounded the desk and placed the folder atop the pristine surface, bending slightly in a way she knew made her legs and ass pop in a teasing manner only her husband would be able to notice. Liam's quiet groan was confirmation that her teasing had its desired effect. She straightened and turned toward him with a satisfied smirk as she clasped her hands together in front of her.

"Is there anything else you require, Mr. Godrik?"

She didn't miss the way his fist tightened around his ink pen, and her vision flicked to his lap, where a bulge was now clearly visible beneath the fabric of his suit. The look that swam in her husband's heated gaze promised retribution for her teasing, further extending her enjoyment.

"No, that's all. Thank you, Amarah."

The hint of strain she caught in his voice nearly made her laugh in satisfaction. *Oh, how I love teasing this man.* The client, however, seemed oblivious to their connection and the sexual tension sizzling between them.

Amarah gave them each a small smile before turning and leaving Liam's office, swaying her hips as she walked, knowing her husband's eyes would be glued to her until she was no longer in sight. They always were. Never once had he made her feel unattractive or like she wasn't the most important person in the room to him. They could be standing in a room full of supermodels and Playboy bunnies dressed in skimpy lingerie, but Liam would only have eyes for her. It was empowering in a dangerously addictive way.

She returned to her desk and got back to work responding to emails. After a while, the client opened one of the office doors and stepped out, closing it behind him.

"Have a wonderful day, Mr. Browning." Amarah smiled as she typed away at her computer.

"You too, ma'am." He returned her smile before striding toward the elevator.

Liam's deep voice nearly scared her half to death as he paged her through the phone resting atop her desk. "Amarah, can you come here, please?"

"Of course, Mr. Godrik." She answered with a knowing, wicked grin.

She pushed back from her desk, straightened her black pencil skirt, and entered his office again. No sooner did the door close and she turned, one of her husband's hands snaked through her loose blonde strands as his lips claimed hers in a hot, hungry, and desperate way that sent her toes curling in her heels.

Her mouth instantly parted as their tongues fought for dominance and her hands freely roamed beneath his unbuttoned suit jacket, loving the feeling of his lean, chiseled torso beneath her touch. A torso she knew was covered in beautiful dark ink that she'd traced with her tongue too many times to count.

"Always the tease," he growled as he broke the kiss, gripped her shoulders, and quickly spun her around.

A gasp of surprise left her lips as one of his hands gripped her hip, and the other was placed against her back, forcing her to bend over the side of the white leather sofa.

Her body became an inferno as she heard him unzip his suit trousers, and anticipated breaths slipped past her parted lips. His large hands hastily bunched up her skirt around her hips as he reached beneath, only to freeze when he was met with heated, slick flesh instead of cotton.

"No panties?" His deep voice sounded of desperate hunger, causing more need to slicken her center.

Amarah peered at him over her shoulder, flashing a sensual smile.

"No," she whispered, a wicked twinkle in her eyes.

"God, I missed you," he groaned in satisfaction as he lined his swollen head at her drenched entrance.

Ditto. Pure desire rendered her voice useless and with a single thrust of his hips, he was buried inside of her. They both groaned with pleasure at the feeling of being one, and he didn't give her time to adjust before he began moving inside of her. She didn't protest. Her need for him was just as desperate, like a fish on land craving the sanctuary of water.

"Fuck, Cupcake," he groaned. "Your pussy is Heaven's gates."

Amarah bit down on her lips to muffle herself. She didn't need every person on the top floor to know what they were doing in there. Although it was nearly impossible to stay quiet anytime her husband was inside her or touching her in general.

"Yes," she moaned as she felt a familiar tightening that would soon send her over the edge. "Just like that, Liam." She panted as she arched her back more and pushed her ass further into him, loving the roughness of his movements.

"Say my name again," he demanded.

"Liam," she moaned, her eyes fluttering closed.

His name on her lips seemed to drive him crazy as his thrusts became more erratic. "You better come for me, Cupcake. I'm not going to last much longer. Not with the sight of your sexy, round ass bent over like this."

A quick smack landed against her right ass cheek, forcing out a gasp that quickly turned into a deep moan. As she reached her hand beneath her skirt so she could begin rubbing circles against her swollen clit, one of Liam's large hands cupped her breast over the silk fabric of her blouse and bra.

She was so close, and after a handful of hard thrusts, her finish exploded through her like a grenade, causing her vision to go white. Her husband's hand left her breast as he covered her mouth, muffling her cries of pleasure.

"Shh, we can't have the entire floor knowing that you're coming around my dick right now," he whispered devilishly in her ear as he continued his rough movements, further extending her orgasm with each thrust until he spilled deep within her.

CHAPTER 5

Amarah Godrik felt her husband approach from behind her as he placed a soft kiss on the top of her head. "Something smells amazing."

"I hope so." She chuckled as she opened the oven and removed the glass dish, setting it atop the stove to cool down. "I'm attempting homemade lasagna."

She loved cooking, always searching for new recipes to experiment with, and her husband never turned down being a taste tester. He usually went in for seconds with the excuse that he needed one more bite to make sure he got the full experience.

Liam crossed the kitchen, withdrew a beer from the fridge, popped the top, and took a sip. "Do you want one?"

"No, I've got a slight headache." She chuckled lightly. "Alcohol, especially beer, would only make it worse."

She had to watch which ones she consumed. Though she was more of a mixed drink type of woman, sometimes she craved a good old bottle of cheap beer. However, some brands gave her some of the worst migraines she'd ever experienced. And the dark bottle her husband clutched in his hand was among the list of culprits.

He hiked a thick, dark brow toward her. "The orgasm I coaxed out of you earlier didn't help?"

Heat scorched her cheeks as she shook her head and opened an upper cabinet. Memories of earlier that day, when he had bent her over the couch in his office, danced through her head. And just like that, her body had come alive again.

"I guess not," she laughed as she removed two plates and closed the door.

She felt his presence consume her, as she always did anytime he was near. His strong arms snaked around her middle as he pulled her back flush with his hard front.

"Mmm, shall I try again?"

His lips brushed the sensitive skin of her neck, and his warm breath and husky tone caused a delicious shiver to roll over her body.

"You're insatiable," she giggled as she set the plates atop the counter and tilted her head back against his chest.

"What I am, Cupcake, is determined."

"You, giving me another orgasm to help my head? How did I ever get so lucky to be blessed with such a thoughtful, kind man?" She feigned a dreamy sigh.

His shoulders shrugged. "What can I say? I'm selfless."

His humor vibrated against her flesh, causing goosebumps to sprout down her arms as he kissed her softly before releasing her and walking to the stack of mail resting atop the counter a few feet away. She watched as he took one more sip of his beer, set it down, and began flipping through the various envelopes before returning her attention to their dinner.

"Have you had a chance to look through the mail yet?" Liam inquired.

After knowing someone for over a decade, you learn so much

about them, you'd swear you knew them better than you knew yourself. Like the cautious tone of her husband's voice that sent numerous alarm bells sounding through her head, causing her to slowly turn and peer over at him.

"No, why?"

"There's a letter here addressed to you." He held up the creamy envelope. "The return address says Desire Headquarters."

Amarah's body instantly locked up, despite dozens of therapy sessions over the past year. Something about that single word, that one name, made her stomach churn, the hair on the back of her neck stand on end, and made her skin feel as if hundreds of spiders were crawling over her. *Desire.*

Her sapphire eyes widened with fear. After having zero success with dating, she allowed her sister-in-law to talk her into trying online dating. Desire was the dating website where she'd unknowingly met her stalker last summer. Everything seemed magical at first. She'd met Derick Watland, a man she thought was one of the good ones, and quickly began to fall for him, until he let his true colors shine. He turned out to be controlling, possessive, and psychotic. When she had tried to break up with him, he refused to let her go.

She attempted to handle the situation herself, going as far as filing assault charges against Derick after he tracked her down at her old job. He cornered her in her office and tried to force himself on her, but she managed to get away and call building security. Unfortunately, Derick had quit his job and packed a bag, leaving his home and lying low, causing the cops to be unsuccessful in locating him.

Somehow, Derick found where she lived and was waiting inside her home one night. He'd attacked her, and they fought, but he was faster and stronger, overpowering her before she could get to the gun she had hidden in her bedroom. He'd violated her, but thankfully, Liam had heard the commotion and kicked in her front door before things went further with his assault. Derick took off through her back door before Liam could catch him and disappeared into the woods behind her house.

That's when Liam found out about her stalker situation. Needless to say, he was pissed that she kept it from him. He's always hated secrets, saying secrets are what get people killed. She finally found herself agreeing with him. He'd made her pack a bag and stay with him at his house until Derick was either caught by the cops or killed. During that time, the truth of Amarah's and Liam's feelings toward each other was brought to light, and their relationship blossomed from friendship into something more beautiful. Something you only read about on the pages of romance novels.

However, while on a double date with Travis and Sandra, Derick cornered her in the restroom of the restaurant and threatened to hurt her nieces and nephew if she didn't leave with him quietly. She wasn't about to risk calling his bluff, not when it came to the people she loved, so she left with him. Liam had come for her, and together, they were able to put the psychopath six feet under.

Amarah had reached out and gotten professional help, and even though a year had passed, she still had nightmares now and again about everything Derick had put her through and the violations he'd done to her. Her story had made national headlines, but she'd never heard from the company.

Until now…

"What…" The word came out shaky and uneven, so she took a calming breath, cleared her throat, and tried again. "What does it say?"

Liam opened the envelope and was quiet as his green irises quickly skimmed over the letter. Then he reread it. She tried to study his face, but the man was skilled in shielding his emotions. He could be experiencing the true depths of sorrow or relishing in pure happiness, but if he didn't want anyone to know, you'd think he was simply bored or unimpressed. Seconds passed by like minutes as she waited for him to speak, forcing herself not to bounce nervously from one foot to the other.

"It's an apology letter." His words were clipped as if he were struggling to contain his anger. She watched the sharp lines of his jaw tick once, twice, before he growled in a low and dangerous tone, "A little fucking late, if you ask me."

She snorted in agreement but remained quiet as she walked over to his side and read the letter for herself.

> Dear Mrs. Godrik,
>
> We're terribly sorry to hear about your experience using our dating site. Words cannot express how horrible it is that someone used our site for something so malicious. In a few weeks, we're hosting a gathering for a handful of couples who've found success with our site. We know your experience was a bit different, but we'd love to offer you the same week-long, all-expenses-paid trip to our resort. If you have any questions, don't hesitate to reach out. I hope you'll accept this gift as a sincere apology, and we hope to see you soon.
>
> Sincerely,
> Patrick Grundy – Marketing Director

"Wow, that's rich." She couldn't help but roll her eyes, her tone filled with heavy skepticism. "After everything I went through, they offer me a free trip?"

Now she was beyond pissed. She'd gone through a hell she wouldn't wish on her worst enemy, knowing the dating site wasn't to blame. They had no way of knowing someone was using their site for such evil. However, after it made national news, Amarah knew the company was more than aware of what had transpired. Still, she heard not a damn word from them. Not that she expected anything in return, but she knew they had her email from when she registered her account. They could've at least attempted a bullshit quick apology.

Twelve months later, they offer her a free seven-day trip? It sounded too good to be true. She walked over to the lasagna and began to plate the food, maybe a bit too forcefully, but she couldn't help it.

"Is it even real?" she called out as she continued to fill their plates, her back turned toward her husband.

"I'm not sure. Seems a bit odd to me. They've been paying attention though, because they know you're married now."

That got her attention. She peered over her shoulder, her face scrunched up in confusion.

He held up the paper and said, "They addressed it to Mrs. Godrik." His brows were pinched in thought. "If it were real, would you want to go? It's a week at a resort on a tropical island in the Bahamas."

"I..." She paused, unsure of how exactly she felt at the moment. "Honestly, I'm not sure."

After being stalked, assaulted, and kidnapped by Derick, she wanted nothing more than to put the entire incident behind her.

To pick up the pieces Derick left and move on with her life. Being surrounded by couples who credited their relationship to Desire would be like reopening an old, nasty wound. She was happy for those who had much happier experiences with the dating site and wished them nothing but a lifetime of love, but she was unsure about being around it all.

She chewed the inside of her cheek nervously as she pondered the idea before asking, "What do you think?"

He set the letter down and pulled her into a tight hug. "I've got a friend I can call. Let me speak to him about this, check out the legitimacy of it, and then we can decide."

"Ok." She wrapped her arms around his waist and leaned her head against his chest, letting the beat of his heart play her a soothing melody that never failed to relax her.

CHAPTER 6

Hunter Gatlin pressed his boot down on the brake pedal, his Jeep Wrangler rolling to a stop at a red light. The cloudless sky and the warm summer day allowed him to roll his windows down, causing a soft breeze to flow through the cabin. His gaze shifted from the road to the time on the screen mounted in the middle of his dashboard.

A breath fell from his lips, thankful that he wouldn't miss his and Serenity's wedding cake tasting appointment. As if on cue, his stomach rumbled in agreement. All he'd had was a cup of coffee this morning. To say he was hungry was an understatement. His six-foot-three, bulky frame required a few thousand calories daily to function properly. And though cake isn't the healthiest thing to put into his body, he was looking forward to sampling every last piece the baker had to offer.

He'd just left the airport terminal where his client's private jet landed. He had spent the last three days accompanying four politicians on a deep-sea fishing excursion. After having Einstein dig into the captain's background, making sure the man wasn't a threat, Hunter knew the only real protection the men would need would be during transport from the jet to the boat, and from the boat back to the jet.

Normally, politicians were self-centered snobs with a severe god complex. Thinking that they were above the law and nothing on this earth could touch them, but these men were different. All four of them were well into their sixties and, to his surprise, were some of the most laid-back guys he'd ever met.

The trip was filled with coolers of cheap beer, a few boxes of cigars, and food that Hunter was positive wasn't allowed in their diets. The men, though, had made him a bargain. If he didn't snitch them out to their wives, then there were a few beers and cigars with Hunter's name on them.

With a knowing smile, he swore that whatever happened on the boat, stayed on that boat, and every night, the men included him in their surprisingly competitive poker games. The group of old friends had so much fun that they scheduled the exact same vacation next year with Red Sky Security, wanting to make it a yearly ritual now that they were getting older and didn't have as much time left on this planet.

When the light turned green, he continued toward MoneyFirst Bank, where his fiancée worked. Her lunch break was coming up, and though they planned on meeting at the bakery, his flight landed earlier than expected, so he figured he'd pick her up at work instead. Anything that would allow him to see her faster.

Hunter had more fun on this trip than he originally thought he would, but he missed Serenity. Missed the sight of her smile, the warmth of her body in his arms, the softness of her skin against his, the feeling of her lips pressed to his. If there was one thing he knew for absolute certainty on this planet, it was that Serenity was the missing half of his soul.

He'd dated in the past, but never had a woman made him feel

so complete that simply being alone made him ache and mourn the absence of her presence. A lost bet. If it hadn't been for some silly bet, he never would've met the love of his life. The thought of going through life without her was enough to send pain jolting through his chest as if a thousand poisonous darts had just pierced the organ.

The rock music cut off as an incoming call rang through his speakers, pulling him from his mind and back to reality, where he, in fact, not only met Serenity but would soon be marrying her, tethering their souls for eternity. His vision shifted to the screen on his dashboard, and a grin tugged his lips up when he read the caller ID. He quickly rolled up his windows and accepted the call.

"Hey, stranger," he greeted, his tone filled with amusement.

Liam Godrik matched Hunter's tone. "Hey, man."

"To what do I owe the pleasure of hearing your voice?"

"Don't be a creep." Liam chuckled. "I remember you saying that you've got a tech guy working for you. Do you think you can have him investigate something for me?"

"You don't even have to ask, you know that. Is everything alright?" Hunter's voice turned serious at the odd request from his old friend, forcing his brows to furrow as he flicked on his blinker and turned right at the intersection.

They were more like brothers than friends. They served on the same SEAL team for years and had been through thick and thin together. A brotherhood like that isn't something you simply throw away just because you separate from the military. Especially if you're from the same state. They'd kept in contact over the years.

"Yeah." Liam hesitated, unsure of how to phrase his question. "Amarah got a letter in the mail from a dating site, and I need to know if it's a scam or not."

Hunter arched his thick brow that had a vertical scar bisecting it. A scar that was a result of growing up with two younger brothers. To this day, he still couldn't believe he allowed Adam, the middle child, to talk him into jumping off the roof of their house onto the trampoline they'd hauled halfway across the yard. He'd been eleven at the time, but boys will be boys.

They'd suffered through an hour-long lecture from their mother that had them fearing the moment their father came home from work. However, instead of a beating from their dad, he took them aside, acting as if to scold his sons in private, only to laugh and ask how they managed to get onto the roof and who had jumped the highest.

His father cleaned the wound, spread super glue over it, and secured it with a butterfly bandage. Not the best form of treatment, but times were different back then. Simpler. Plus, he got a cool scar out of it. And the ladies always seemed to like it, so he didn't mind too much.

"It wasn't from Desire, was it?" Hunter questioned, forcing his mind out of the past and back onto his present conversation.

Liam hesitated again. "How the fuck did you know that?"

"I'm familiar with the letter. Serenity and I received one as well. Wait a minute... Are you telling me the infamous ladies' man used a dating site to find his wife?" Hunter teased.

Anytime they had returned from a mission, they'd always go out and celebrate, usually to some hole-in-the-wall bar to unwind and toss back a few beers. Since Travis Patterson was married and Bryson Munro was in a serious relationship, Hunter and Liam were the only two single men. Though Hunter was far from ugly and scored his fair share of women, the ladies tended to flock around Liam more, and they were more than willing to accept if he wanted their company that night.

"Fuck off," Liam laughed. "No, Amarah used it last year before we got together and gained herself a stalker."

"Shit, that was her?" Pieces of his conversation with Einstein earlier that week began to fall into place, allowing the puzzle to form a complete picture. Though he and Liam have always been close, they don't share every detail of their lives. So, the fact that his brother kept a story like that to himself didn't surprise him. "Damn, I'm sorry she had to go through that. How's she doing?"

"Time heals all wounds, right?" Liam deadpanned. "Wait a fucking minute… If *you* received a letter, then that means *you* used the site as well. You have no room to give me shit."

The bank had finally come into view, and anticipation filled Hunter's chest. Only a handful of minutes remained until he could pull the love of his life into his arms again.

He huffed out a laugh as he came to a stop at another red light. "Only because I lost a bet with Sweeney."

A while back, Hunter and Sweeney were on an assignment guarding a female celebrity who was filming some scenes for a new movie. Sweeney bet Hunter that she'd make a move on Hunter before the assignment was over and if Hunter lost the bet, he had to create a profile on a dating site and go out on a date with the first woman who messaged him. Hunter had lost and Serenity happened to be the first message nestled in his inbox.

"Sure, I'd say that too," Liam teased.

"Anyway, Einstein said the company owns an island resort and they had sent the same letter to three other couples, plus an apology letter to Amarah. It's real. Serenity said companies do things like this all the time for marketing tactics." Hunter paused before continuing. "Are y'all considering going?"

"Amarah's hesitant, which is understandable given her history with the site. I told her I'd check it out and we'd discuss it later. Are y'all considering it?"

"Serenity was over the moon excited about the offer, and that was before I checked the legitimacy of it. Sometimes I fear that woman is too trusting." Hunter chuckled and shook his head. "I can almost say for certain that when I tell her, she'll want to go."

"Alright, well, I'll talk with Amarah and let you know. Thanks, brother."

"Anytime, you know that," Hunter said, hanging up the phone as he pulled into the bank's parking lot.

The bank was packed as he entered, finding a line of customers waiting to speak with a teller. A handful of people filled chairs in the sitting area to the right, most having their heads buried in their phones, and a kid sat at a small table, playing with an assortment of toys. The security guard peered up from behind his desk and gave him a friendly nod, which Hunter returned as he made his way across the lobby toward Serenity's office.

She'd been a loan officer for years, and after a quick peek into the small space, he was relieved to find she wasn't attending to clients. Instead of greeting her right away, he leaned against the open doorframe, crossed his arms over his chest, and allowed his eyes to drink in the sight of her.

God, she's radiant.

Her raven hair was pulled into a tight bun, a few strands left down to frame her sharp features, her mossy eyes squinting at her monitor, and her bottom lip disappeared between her teeth. Lost in her own little world, she was unaware of his arrival. Unaware of his eyes raking over her slender body, loving the way the forest green dress of hers clung to her curves.

His hands twitched with the need to touch her. Having gone days without it was pure agony. However, various sounds from the lobby filled his ears, reminding him that they weren't alone, but in her place of employment. Unfortunately, he had to remain respectful. For now.

"You look as if you're trying to solve a murder case, Angel." His deep voice filled the small office.

"Oh, God!" Serenity jumped back in her chair, her hand coming up to clutch her heaving chest as she turned to glare at whoever startled her. When her eyes landed on him, recognition sank in, and her features softened, a beaming smile lighting up her face. "Hunter! You scared the crap out of me."

"Sorry," he laughed as he pushed off the doorframe and stopped behind two padded armchairs that faced her desk.

"No, you're not." She laughed as she stood, rounded her desk, and threw her arms around his neck.

Her lips crashed against his a second later with a hunger that matched his own. Apparently, she didn't care about remaining professional at work. Who was he to argue? Their mouths parted, tongues explored, as he brought one hand to cup the back of her neck, the other gripped her hip, pulling her body flush against his. He brought his foot back until it connected with the door and swung it closed.

He groaned against her mouth, wishing they were alone so he could lay her out atop her desk and thoroughly ravish her body. His growing erection was agreeing with that wicked thought, uncaring of the dozens of people mere feet from them who were unaware of the groping happening nearby.

"Hey, Renny. What time were you leaving for—" A female's voice cut off behind him, acting like a bucket of ice water, yanking him out of his lust-filled haze and back to reality. It took much effort to separate his lips from Serenity's. "Am I interrupting something in here?"

Hunter took in the deep blush that tinted his fiancée's olive cheeks before he turned to see Addison Thatcher now leaning against the doorframe, arms crossed over her chest, a mischievous smirk shaping her rounded features.

Addi was Serenity's best friend. Chosen sisters was a more appropriate term. They'd met at the bank years ago and had been inseparable ever since. Addi was now Serenity's boss, after being promoted to bank manager a few months back.

"Oh, don't let me stop you. Please, continue." Addi waved her hand playfully, a sinful gleam sparkling in her chocolate eyes. "I was rather enjoying the show."

"Shut up, you perv." Serenity laughed and shook her head, rolling her eyes at her crazy friend.

Much to Hunter's delight, Serenity didn't step out of his embrace, merely shifted to his side, and wrapped a single arm around his middle. It was as if she simply needed to touch him too.

"I was checking to see if you still had your cake tasting today," Addi inquired, a smile still lingering on her lips.

"Yep, I got back sooner than expected, so I thought I'd surprise Angel at work. We were just about to head out."

Addi arched a dark brow. "Really? Because it appeared as if you were seconds away from ripping her clothes off."

Serenity gasped, her eyes wide with shock. "Not at work! There are dozens of people here. Someone could walk in at any moment."

"Oh, come on. That's what makes it more exhilarating." Addi shrugged, and Hunter couldn't stop the question from falling past his lips.

"And you know this, how?"

Addi smirked. "Sweeney and I christened my new office within the first few weeks of my promotion."

Hunter instantly regretted asking that question. Now, he couldn't unsee the image she'd drawn for them. Addi and her fiancé, Sweeney, a man who was like a brother to him, fooling around in her office. Gross. He could've gone his entire life without that scarring image. Not that either of them was ugly, but they were like family to him, and picturing any of your family having sex is traumatizing for anyone.

"Addison," Serenity gasped in disbelief before curiosity took over. "There are cameras everywhere. How did you manage to avoid them?"

"Eh." She shrugged as if she weren't worried in the slightest. "Sweeney said he had Einstein erase the footage."

Well, it appeared he needed to have another chat with Einstein about boundaries and a chat with Sweeney about using Einstein's abilities for such selfish, childish activities.

"As much as I'd love to continue this conversation," Hunter deadpanned, "we need to get going or we'll be late for the tasting."

Serenity released him and grabbed her purse from the bottom drawer of her desk. He took her hand in his, and Addi stepped aside, allowing them to pass.

"You know, salted caramel is a popular flavor," Addi called after them, her tone filled with mirth. "Just putting that out there!"

Serenity laughed beside him, drawing his attention to her. "Did she suggest that because it's her favorite flavor?"

"Yep," Serenity answered as they finally left the bank.

CHAPTER 7

Amarah Godrik took the window seat, wasting no time before sliding the white plastic cover up, allowing the morning rays of sun to enter the plane. She withdrew her tablet from their carry-on bag before handing it to Liam, who took the aisle seat next to her. She watched as he removed a case of AirPods from the backpack before settling it between his feet. He only removed one though, securing it in his left ear.

She knew he'd want to be able to hear his surroundings in case anything happened, which is also why he always chose to occupy the aisle seat. There's never been a time, even before they got together, when he wasn't constantly vigilant whenever they were in public. She didn't hate that quality about him.

In all honesty, she adored it and found herself grateful for it. Liam was the kind of man who'd run toward the danger without a second thought for his own safety. His single goal would be to stop the threat.

Feeling utterly secure when in the presence of another person, let alone the one you love, was both freeing and empowering. Freeing because his level of alertness allowed her to completely let go and live in the moment without a single worry about her safety.

And for a young woman in today's dangerous world, that's not a luxury to be taken lightly. It was also empowering knowing that a man of that stature had felt that your life was so valuable that he'd give his own life to protect it.

After her husband had gotten the all-clear from his old Navy buddy, Hunter Gatlin, that the offer from Desire was real, they agreed to go, though she was still hesitant. They would've flown privately with the jet Godrik Enterprises owned, but one of their architects was currently using it to fly to Greece to meet up with a client to talk design on a resort.

Instead, they were forced to accept the complimentary plane tickets Desire provided for them. Luckily, the company had splurged on first class, which she was thankful for. They had quite a long flight, around five hours with a layover in Georgia, so the extra room first class provided was a blessing. Especially since her husband was tall, giving his six-foot-two, lean frame plenty of leg room to stretch out and be comfortable.

The lengthy flight allowed her ample time to make quite a dent in her latest romance novel. "Good lord," she muttered breathily as she began to fan herself with her hand.

Liam paused his music and peered over at her. "What is it, Cupcake?"

"Huh?" she said distractedly as she pulled her gaze up from the tablet. "Oh, nothing." She waved her hand dismissively. "Just something I read in my book."

"You're blushing." A knowing grin pulled his lips up.

"Am not!" She tried to defend herself, but it was futile.

She could feel the intense flush heating her cheeks, trying to creep its way down her neck toward her chest.

"Well, come on. Share with the class," he challenged her.

Amarah cleared her throat and began to describe the scene she'd just read, not skimping on the details. "Jesus." Her husband chuckled. "That's at least two felonies if they got caught."

Her tone turned sultry as she peered up at him through her thick, dark lashes. "Then I guess they'd just have to make sure not to be seen."

"Is that your way of telling me that you'd like to act out that scene?" His grin turned wicked as his voice dropped to a low, husky level that sparked fresh heat throughout her body.

"Maybe." She sucked her bottom lip between her teeth, and his eyes dipped, tracking the movement before he brought them back up to her deep blue irises.

He groaned and shook his head. "You dirty girl."

"You made me this way." She shrugged unapologetically.

"And I have no regrets."

Liam's amused voice sent swarms of butterflies soaring through her belly.

"What do you want to do once we reach the island?"

Amarah desperately needed to change the subject, or else she'd be pulling him into the nearest bathroom and renewing their subscription to the mile-high club. They always took his private jet anytime they traveled, whether the trip was for business or pleasure. They'd christened almost every inch of that jet, and the memories had a deep ache pulsing between her legs. An ache that only her husband would ever be able to sate. And thoroughly sate he did. Every time, multiple times.

"I'm good with whatever you want to do. We can explore the island, spend our days lying on the beach like bums, or never leave our room." He shot her a devilish wink.

"I bet it has some beautiful hiking spots." She smiled as she tried to picture what the island might look like.

Over the years, they'd visited numerous bucket list spots and traveled to various countries, exploring the unimaginable beauties of the world. However, this portion of the Bahamas was uncharted territory for them both, and she was excited.

"Most definitely, but it'll pale in comparison to *your* beauty."

He gave her his world-famous smolder that had her groaning inwardly that they weren't somewhere private.

"You're such a sappy romantic," she teased him lovingly.

He used her previous words against her. "You made me that way."

Her gaze peered into his, finding the other half of her soul looking back. She shot back with a quick flex of her brow, "And I have no regrets."

The wheels of the plane connected with the runway as the aircraft slowed and pulled into its designated terminal. Hunter Gatlin and Serenity Jinx gathered up their belongings and stowed them back in a black backpack, which he slung over a broad shoulder. They departed the plane, following the flow of passengers as they walked up the ramp, and entered the bustling airport.

It had been a while since he'd flown commercially. Fuse, however, was on an assignment that required the use of his company's jet. Though he'd always thrived in chaotic environments such as this, he secretly hated them. His eyes never paused their roaming, shifting to locate exits, observing bystanders, and locating possible threats.

He glanced to where Serenity strolled at his side, a look of wonder across her angular features as she lost herself in the shops that filled the airport and all the bright, colorful knick-knacks they had to offer. Sometimes he envied her carelessness, the ease to be able to let go and simply live in the moment. But he didn't have that luxury. It was his job, his duty, to always be aware of potential danger so she could continue to live a blissful, secure, and relaxed life.

He interlaced his fingers through hers as they made their way through dozens of people lost in their own world. He could say he did it so if something happened, he could easily maneuver her to a safe location, but truthfully, he just loved touching her any way he could. Some travelers scurried by as they tried to make it to their flights on time, while others strolled lazily without a care in the world. They followed the signs that would lead them to the luggage claim area and descended a flight of stairs, following a few passengers he recognized from their flight, all in search of their luggage.

They reached a long, open space filled with massive conveyor belts that were empty and stationary. People stood scattered around the carousel, waiting for the workers to finish unloading their belongings so they could claim them and leave.

"I can't believe we're finally here!" Serenity tried hard to contain her excitement, but he could see it bubbling on the surface, seconds away from spilling over. "I can't wait to see the resort."

"Hopefully it's not like those mainstream ones that are always crawling with people everywhere you go." He stifled an unsettled shiver and continued, "If I decide to take you right there on the beach, I'd rather not have an audience."

"Oh my gosh," she gasped and slapped his arm playfully, trying hard to hide the blush now tinting her usual olive cheeks. "I can't take you anywhere." She shook her head and laughed.

"Or in the pool." He tugged her against his front and circled his strong arms around her slender waist, nuzzling his nose in the hollow of her neck, causing Serenity to laugh from where his brown beard tickled her sensitive flesh. "Or maybe against the side of the building. Or in the elevator."

"You're impossible," she said as her arms wrapped around his neck. "Though the thought of getting caught does add a certain level of thrill to it."

Before he could respond, a deep voice came up from behind them, snapping them out of their blissful bubble and back to reality.

"You're an easy target, you know that? I spotted your large ass clear across the airport."

Hunter released his fiancée and turned, the voice sparking recognition in his mind. A grin tugged half his face up when he saw his old friend Liam Godrik standing there, holding the hand of a beautiful woman.

"I may be big, but I've always been quicker than you," Hunter shot back as he shook Liam's hand, and the two embraced in a hug, clapping each other on the back.

When they pulled away, Liam spoke next. "Amarah, this is Hunter Gatlin. We served together in the Navy, and that's his fiancée, Serenity Jinx."

"It's nice to finally meet you." Amarah smiled sheepishly as she clung to Liam's arm. "I've heard so many stories about you over the years."

Hunter had never met Travis Patterson's little sister, another man who was on their SEAL team, but he could see the resemblance. She was Serenity's height with long blonde hair braided back into pigtails that draped over her ample chest. She shared the same deep blue eyes and angular features as her brother.

Hunter laughed. "All good ones, I hope."

"Mostly." Amarah smiled before turning her vision on Serenity. "I do, however, have some not-so-good ones I'm more than happy to share with you. You know, for blackmail purposes."

"Oh, I will definitely take you up on that." Serenity's laughter flowed around the group.

Unease began to sprout in his gut. The Lord only knew what kind of stories his brothers told her. The last thing he needed was Serenity hearing them and using them as ammunition. Though two could play that game. A wicked smile began to slide across his face.

"I can tell you stories about this one too." Hunter motioned toward Liam. "Stories that would definitely land him in the doghouse for a while."

Amarah's eyes widened, her face brightening at the possibility, but her husband's words cut her off.

"Whoa, don't go throwing me under the bus." Liam laughed. "I've kept my mouth shut about certain matters we swore to never voice aloud again. Those stories were all Travis's doing. You know how much of a gossip the man is. I swear he's worse than a group of women at a hair salon."

Hunter's roaring laughter drew the attention of passing strangers, but the group paid them no mind. "I still find it hard to believe Travis let you keep your balls after he learned you got together with his little sister."

Liam waved a hand. "Nah, he got over it."

Hunter found himself thankful that he grew up with brothers. The thought of having a sister who would one day date and eventually marry, knowing that she'd be participating in certain adult activities with said man, would be enough for him to threaten any possible boyfriend with castration if they so much as thought about touching her.

Phoebe Vega, his receptionist, was the closest thing he had to a little sister. In the years she'd been working for him, not once had she ever hinted that she was seeing anyone. She always kept her dating life private. And for good measure. He was sure the last thing she needed was a bunch of testosterone-fueled older brothers scaring off any potential suitor. Shit, he had half a mind to strap a chastity belt around her. There were very few men on this earth who were good enough for a woman like her.

The baggage carousel began moving, gaining everyone's attention as they waited for the bags to start filing out. Both Hunter and Liam grabbed all their suitcases, and they all made their way to the exit, where they saw a man standing with a sign that read *Shuttle Bus for Desire Resort.*

"Welcome! Are you all here for the couples retreat on behalf of Desire?" a gentleman with grey hair and wrinkled, leathery skin asked as the four stopped in front of him. His pressed, cream-colored polo was neatly tucked into a pair of tan khaki pants.

Hunter nodded. "Yes, sir."

"Welcome to the Bahamas." He smiled kindly at the group. "If you go out those doors, there's a white bus waiting for everyone. After the other three couples show up, we'll depart."

"Thank you." Serenity gave him a warm smile as everyone exited the airport.

The luggage compartment beneath the bus was propped open as Hunter and Liam placed their bags inside. Amarah and Serenity climbed the steps and took a few paces down the narrow aisle before plopping into a seat on the left-hand side. Liam and Hunter followed a few seconds later and sat across the aisle from their women.

Hunter grumbled something under his breath, drawing all eyes toward him. He had faced this problem since his growth spurt in middle school. It was a rare occasion when he was provided with proper legroom, and this was not one of those times. It never ceased to amaze him how few vehicle companies kept tall people in mind when designing cabin space.

He heard his fiancée snort. "I think we're going to need a bigger bus."

Both Liam and Hunter had their legs scrunched up and pressed into the back of the seats in front of them, causing both Amarah and Serenity to burst out laughing.

He watched as Liam held his wife's gaze. "Keep laughing, Cupcake, and see what happens when I get you alone in our room later."

"Don't tempt me with a good time," Hunter heard Amarah mutter under her breath.

A few minutes passed before two more men climbed onto the bus, coming to a stop in front of the group of four.

"Hey, I'm Myles King. This is my husband, Colton."

Myles was a slender man who couldn't be taller than five-eight with olive skin, short black hair, and bright brown eyes. His face was free of hair, showing off his angular features. He wore a light blue short-sleeve button-up shirt covered with little palm trees and a pair of cream slacks.

Colton was a dark-skinned man and stood an inch taller than his husband. His head was freshly shaven, and his beard was a little more than a five o'clock shadow. The black shirt and navy-blue slacks he wore clung to him, showing off lean muscles.

"Hey, I'm Serenity. This is Amarah, Hunter, and Liam."

Serenity pointed to each of them as she introduced their group.

"Oh my," Myles gasped as he took in Liam and Hunter and motioned a finger topped with lime green polish between them. "Are you guys… together?"

"No!" Hunter nearly shouted as he quickly reassured the man, avoiding eye contact with Liam and trying hard not to appear awkward.

"You would deny our love in front of others? After all those hours in therapy, I thought we had worked through this."

Hunter's head snapped toward his friend, observing Liam's dark brows pinched together and a feigned look of hurt contorting his angular features, his hand pressed to his chest as if offended.

"I will murder you without a second thought." Hunter's voice was low, but he knew his friend was confident that his words held no true threat. Liam threw his head back and laughed as Hunter narrowed his vision before turning back to Myles and Colton. "I'm engaged to Serenity. Liam's married to Amarah."

"Damn, girls," Myles pulled his dark brows together in shock and nodded approvingly. "Nice job."

"Alright, honey. Stop drooling." Colton laughed lightly. "Leave the nice people alone and let's go find our seats. There will be plenty of time to get to know everyone once we get settled at the resort."

Myles waved a hand toward his husband, quieting him as he shot the girls a wink and a quick smile before passing them down the aisle in search of seating.

A few minutes later, the last two couples boarded the bus but didn't stop to introduce themselves as they quickly found their seats. The old man with the sign who first greeted them climbed the steps and sat in the driver's seat. He took a quick head count, closed the doors, put the bus in drive, and pulled away from the curb.

CHAPTER 8

"How long have you and Hunter been together?" Amarah inquired as she gazed at the woman sitting next to her.

Serenity Jinx was beautiful with her long, straight raven hair, bright eyes the shade of healthy grass, olive skin, and pointed features. The black leggings and dark purple tank top she wore showed off her slender figure.

"Since last summer. What about you and Liam?" Serenity smiled.

"Since last summer as well." Amarah laughed. "Though I've known him since I was eleven."

"Oh wow, that's a long time. What finally brought you two together?" She knew a haunted look filled her blue gaze because Serenity quickly placed a gentle hand on her arm. "You don't have to tell me if you don't want to."

"No, it's ok." Amarah gave her a reassuring smile and told her the story of what transpired between her and Derick Watland.

"Oh my gosh!" Serenity gasped. "What a creep. I'm glad you're alright. I know all too well the damage a stalker can cause."

Two creases formed between Amarah's brows, and Serenity filled her in on the events that happened last August between her,

Addi, and Jack, Addi's ex-husband.

"He sounded like a saint," Amarah snorted, sarcasm dripping from her tone.

"Oh, he's definitely *holey* now."

Amarah knew the morbid joke had slipped out before Serenity could stop it because the woman threw a hand over her mouth, and her vision widened with shock. Serenity had just finished telling her how she'd shot Jack in the chest three times in order to finally stop him. Amarah's gaze rounded briefly before she burst out laughing, and Serenity joined her. That was another thing they had in common. Derick also resided six feet beneath the ground. However, it was Liam who took the man's life, not her.

"What's so funny over there?" Liam called from across the aisle.

The women paused their laughter, glanced at their men, then looked back at each other and started giggling again, tears leaking from their eyes. Their abs hurt by the time they'd finally calmed down. Amarah lost track of time as she fell into easy conversation with Serenity. Topics flowed from one thing to another, and Amarah quickly discovered that she could be very good friends with her.

The slowing of the bus drew the women out of their conversation. The large vehicle pulled into a gravel parking lot before finally coming to a stop. Amarah glanced out the windows and furrowed her brows. There was no resort in sight. Small, colorful shops lined the street with massive palm trees providing ample shade. Numerous people moseyed about, carrying shopping bags or sipping drinks as they chatted with each other.

She peered out the windows on the men's side of the bus and was greeted with crystal blue water as far as the eye could see, and boats varying in size were secured with rope to the numerous wooden docks.

The driver opened the doors and stood, a kind smile softening his aged features. "Please watch your step when exiting the bus and remember to grab your luggage."

"I thought this bus was supposed to take us to the resort?" Amarah asked hesitantly.

Unease tried to creep its way up her spine. After a calming breath and a glance toward her husband and his friend, two men who had spent years of their lives killing for the sake of keeping their country free, the feeling ebbed.

"No, the resort isn't part of the main island. The only way to get there is by boat." The driver's voice remained gentle before he turned and stepped off the bus.

Hunter and Liam stood, exiting first, followed by Serenity, Amarah, and the other three couples. A gentle salty sea breeze assaulted her nose, and the greedy screeching of hungry seagulls filled the air around them. The men grabbed their luggage as they followed the driver toward the marina. The faint smell of fish grew stronger the closer they got. They came to a stop at a large white charter boat, where another man came into view.

The white-haired captain stepped onto the deck, greeting the group with a gap-toothed smile. "Are these all the couples going to the resort?"

"Sure are." The bus driver nodded.

"Welcome aboard," the captain announced as he held out a callused hand, hardened from decades of fishing. "Please, watch your step."

Everyone began boarding, handing their belongings to the captain, who stowed them safely inside the small cabin. Amarah kept close to Liam as she found a spot on the port side and leaned against the railing, peering out over the clear blue, calm waters. Liam wrapped his arms around her waist and rested his chin atop her head as Serenity and Hunter came to stand next to them.

Once everyone was safely on board, the captain untied the boat from the dock. The engine roared to life, and the vessel began to move slowly through the marina. Once they were in open water, they gained speed as they cut through the small waves, the wind causing the women's hair to whip around them.

Amarah had figured they'd be on the boat no longer than half an hour, but several hours had passed before they reached their destination. The group got lost in conversation, only quieting when an island began to rise from the horizon as if God Himself was pulling it from the depths of the ocean. As they drew closer, the resort came into view, finding it surrounded by massive palm trees. A large, forested mountain loomed in the distance. The island appeared relatively small, as if the resort were the only occupant.

They began to slow as they neared a long wooden dock, before the engine cut off and the side of the vessel drifted toward it. The captain stepped off, grabbed the coiled-up ropes, and secured them to the metal hooks on the side of the boat.

Everyone exited, grabbed their luggage, and stopped at the foot of the dock where a man with short fiery hair and pale skin stood, adorned in a floral T-shirt and a pair of tan knee-length shorts. His face and arms were heavily freckled, and his bright green eyes gave the lawn a run for its money.

"Welcome!" he greeted with a bright smile. "My name is Declan McCarthy. As a representative of Desire, I'm pleased to see all your happy faces. I hope your trips were pleasant. If you'll please follow me, I'll show you around the resort and take you to your rooms."

The sound of an engine roaring to life drew Amarah's gaze behind them to see the boat pulling away from the dock and heading back in the direction of the mainland.

She turned back around and inquired, "Are they not staying?"

The fear from earlier tried to return, persistent in trying to ruin her vacation before it had even gotten started, but she quickly shook it off.

"No. They'll be back on Friday when you depart to take everyone back to the mainland." His tone remained gentle as he turned and started toward the resort.

They stepped off the dock onto a bright-well manicured lawn and crossed until smooth concrete covered the ground. Declan led them around a massive rectangular inground pool filled with water as clear as the ocean behind them. Numerous white lounge chairs and a few outdoor sofas that were shielded beneath small canopies were positioned sporadically around the pool.

"The pool is open twenty-four seven. If you're searching for floaties or require extra towels, you can find them in the shed over there." Declan pointed to a small structure that sat nearby.

The more Amarah observed, the more she realized it was less like a resort and more of a massive mansion. The outside was made of tan colored bricks and topped with a white Bermuda roof. Numerous windows line the building, maximizing the oceanic view from every possible angle.

As they entered the open back doors, oversized marble tiles covered the ground floor, multiple sitting areas were positioned all around the space, and a grand staircase protruded off the left wall that resembled one you'd find in an old Victorian mansion. Amarah's jaw dropped as her vision bounced around, trying to take in everything all at once. The chic wallpaper, elegant crown molding, hand-carved woodwork, twenty-foot ceilings, and crystal and wrought iron chandelier made the homes in Beverly Hills appear like a trailer park.

"Through there," Declan pointed to massive wooden doors to the right, "will lead you to the dining room where breakfast, lunch, and dinner will be served daily."

"I thought this was a resort?" Hunter inquired, his deep voice echoing off the bright, open space.

Declan's kind tone and easygoing smile never faltered. "It is."

"Then why are we the only people here? This place is like a ghost town," Liam added.

"This isn't a large commercial resort. This place holds a maximum of ten guest rooms. We've booked the entire week to celebrate you five lovely couples." Declan's eyes shifted around the group before continuing. "You'll be pleased to know that you'll have the entire island to yourselves. The only other people you will see around here will be the staff, myself, and the founder of the company, who you'll meet at dinner."

Declan walked over to a round side table and picked up five key cards resembling hotel room keys, as he motioned for everyone to follow him up the stairs.

Wooden doors to the left and right lined the hallway, five on each wall. Declan efficiently assigned each couple a room, handing them the proper key. He held it in front of the knob, and a soft click sounded, signaling it was unlocked.

"At five this evening, we'll be hosting a welcome dinner. We look forward to seeing you all then." Declan gave everyone a curt nod before turning and disappearing down the stairs.

Each couple departed to their assigned rooms, leaving Amarah,

Liam, Serenity, and Hunter standing in the hallway. Amarah withdrew her phone and checked the time. It was nearly four in the afternoon.

"We have a little over an hour until dinner," she commented as she tucked her phone back into her pocket.

"We should get cleaned up and rest before then," Liam offered, and everyone agreed as they turned and disappeared into their rooms.

"You doing ok, Cupcake?" her husband questioned after closing their door and setting their suitcase atop a low bench that sat at the foot of their bed.

The room was simple but luxurious. The dark-stained furniture consisted of a queen-sized bed, two nightstands topped with reading lamps, a cushioned bench, a dresser, and a small round table with two chairs. A beautiful tan colored the walls, light hardwood planks covered the floor, matching the ones that lined the upstairs hallway, and a plush brown area rug lay in the middle of the space.

Amarah turned to find his green eyes on her as if he was trying to read the answer on her face.

"Yeah." She smiled reassuringly. "I was nervous at first, but the couples we met so far seem lovely and the island is more beautiful than I could've imagined."

She feared that being surrounded by all things Desire would bring back bad memories of her time last year with Derick, but that hadn't happened. If anything, she felt herself relaxing more the longer she was there. Liam's long legs had him in front of her in two strides.

"Good." His grin turned devilish as he scooped her up bridal-style and carried her into the attached bathroom.

She squealed in protest, but excitement quickly overruled all other emotions. He set her atop the counter as he turned and started the shower. The tiled stall was big enough to fit five people with multiple showerheads flowing in various directions.

"We've got an hour to wash up and break in our new bed before we head down for dinner." His wicked promise sent an ache pulsing deep in her core.

"I don't know." She cocked her head to the side as she studied the shower. "I think the shower is the perfect place to kick-start our vacation." Her voice was sensual as she removed her shirt and bra, tossing them carelessly to the floor.

She loved the way her husband's hungry gaze drank in her naked torso as he stepped up between her parted legs and gripped her hips. He acted as if he were seeing her for the first time all over again. It made her feel more radiant than a Miss Universe winner, and she prayed it would never change.

"Mmm, I love the way you think," he growled as he buried his nose in the hollow of her neck and began placing delicate kisses along her smooth, sensitive flesh.

CHAPTER 9

Amarah Godrik pulled the straps of her lavender dress over her shoulders as Liam exited the bathroom. She sucked her bottom lip between her teeth at the sight of him in a dark grey long-sleeve button-up shirt that he had tucked into a pair of black slacks. His head was down as he fiddled with the button on his wrist.

"If you keep looking at me like that, we'll begin round two, and we won't make it to dinner." His voice was low and filled with delicious promises when he finally peered up at her.

"Well then, stop being so hot." She shrugged innocently and turned her back toward him. "Can you zip me up?"

She felt his presence close in behind her as he gently moved her golden strands over her shoulder, his fingers lightly brushing against her bare skin, leaving goosebumps in their wake. He gripped the zipper and began to pull it up her back in agonizing slowness. The action caused her breath to hitch and her heart to skip a beat. When her dress was secured, she felt the warmth of his full lips place a soft kiss against her shoulder. A sensual tingle sparked her nervous system as she turned to face him.

He was so close, mere inches separating their bodies. The spice of his cologne filled her senses, making her want to forget about dinner and spend all night with her head buried in the hollow where his neck met his shoulder, simply inhaling his scent and lying in his strong embrace.

"Have I told you how beautiful you are today?" He caged her in his arms, placed his hands flat against her lower back, and glanced down at her.

"Not that I can recall," she whispered as she looped her arms around his neck.

He brought a hand up and brushed the backs of his fingers across her cheek.

"Allow me to correct that mistake, Cupcake." He bent down and slowly kissed a path from the base of her neck, and stopped as his lips brushed the shell of her ear. "Your radiance steals the very breath from my lungs." He whispered his confession.

"Trying your hand at poetry?" she teased as she closed her eyes and rested her forehead against his. "How did I ever get so lucky?"

"Just by being you." He straightened. "I wouldn't want you any other way."

"Liam." His name was a whisper as she opened her eyes and peered up at him through her thick lashes.

"Cupcake?" He smiled, his tone playful as he pulled her flat against his front, the softness of her curves molding perfectly against his hard frame as if she was made just for him.

"I—" A knock at their door cut off her next words, and she visibly deflated.

Liam groaned and released his hold on her as he walked over to the door and answered it. Hunter stood there, his massive frame nearly filling the entirety of the doorway. He was dressed in a red long-sleeve button-up shirt that played well with his sun-kissed skin and was tucked into a pair of black slacks that were tailored exquisitely to hug his thick legs. He wore half of his brown hair tied back in a knot behind his head, and the rest hung down to his shoulders.

Amarah's eyes widened in shock. She would admit that Hunter was attractive, but the sight of such a dangerous man—scratch that, two very dangerous men dressed in fine dining attire, was erotic in the best way possible. Looking at them, you'd never know they were both capable of dealing a swift and merciless death without getting so much as a drop of blood on their expensive clothing.

Someone would make a killing, no pun intended, if they made that into a calendar. Women would be lined up around the block to purchase them.

"Are y'all ready?" Hunter asked.

"Unfortunately," Liam groaned.

Hunter smirked and stepped away from the doorframe. Liam held their door open for her as she exited. She heard him groan and smiled, knowing he caught a whiff of her perfume. She peered over her shoulder to watch as Hunter chuckled and shook his head.

Liam arched a brow at his friend. "What?"

"You've got it bad, brother." Hunter laughed as he ran a hand over the brown scruff of his beard.

Liam shifted his gaze to Serenity, who had looped her arm through Amarah's. "You're one to talk."

Amarah peered forward again as she and Serenity led the way and descended the stairs. "You look stunning," she said when they reached the ground floor.

Serenity wore a strapless black dress that hugged her torso tightly and stopped mid-thigh. Her straight raven strands were left to hang down her back, and her bright green eyes sparkled with delight.

"Thank you!" Serenity beamed. "So do you. That color looks sinful on you."

"Yeah, it does!" Liam called out from behind them, and the girls peered back over their shoulders.

"Eavesdropping, are we?" Amarah teased and gave her husband a quick wink before turning forward and entering the open doors of the dining room.

She gasped in awe. Truthfully, it was more of a dining hall. Like one you'd find in a castle. The long, rectangular room held a massive wooden table with twenty tall, backed chairs surrounding it. Elegant floral arrangements and shiny silver candleholders lined the middle of the table. The entire back wall was lined with floor-to-ceiling bookshelves, and the three remaining walls were painted dark green and lined with elegant wrought iron sconces, adding a luxurious glow to the space.

A server dressed in a white long-sleeve shirt tucked into a pair of black pants walked around the space, carrying a tray filled with long-stemmed glasses. A bubbly, almost beige-colored liquid filled the glasses. If Amarah had to guess, it was champagne. Liam grabbed two glasses as well as Hunter, handing one to each woman. Serenity released her arm and went to stand next to her fiancé.

"Thank you." Amarah smiled as she accepted the glass from her husband, but didn't bring it to her lips just yet.

Her vision was busy skimming over the other company that filled the room. Myles and Colton were over in a corner talking to a couple she had yet to meet, and the last couple finally waltzed into the dining hall.

A tall woman with brunette hair cut short to her jawline stopped in front of them. "Hi, I'm Cami Evans. This is my husband, Parker."

Her sweet Southern accent was strong, and if Amarah had to place it, she'd have to guess Georgia. Cami's golden eyes sparkled as they landed on Liam. Amarah arched a brow in amusement as she watched Cami's gaze drop to Liam's feet and slowly rise back up.

After a quick examination, Amarah knew that the woman's coral silk blouse, black slacks, and heeled black boots had to cost at least a few grand. Her lips were lined with a shimmery gloss that popped against her tanned skin and sparkled with every movement.

Parker stood next to her as he casually sipped from his champagne. His blond hair was cut short to his head, and his slate eyes trailed slowly up Amarah's form. She forced herself to contain the repulsed chill she felt.

"I'm Amarah. This is my husband, Liam."

"This place is just... lovely, isn't it?" Detest contorted Cami's flawless face, and even a deaf person would be able to hear the judgment lacing her tone.

Liam's eyes roamed around the room as he took a casual sip from his glass. "I find the décor quite elegant for the space."

Cami's laugh was high-pitched and as fake as her tan as she batted her lashes toward Liam. "Oh, most definitely."

Amarah had to resist an eyeroll. "How long have y'all been married?" she inquired, trying to keep a civil conversation.

"Almost two years now. We got married in Greece. Though that resort was more... upscale than this... *cozy* place." Cami may have had a kind smile plastered to her face, but her condescending tone was like nails on a chalkboard.

"I bet it was lovely," Amarah said, maybe a bit too sweetly. As if in confirmation, she heard her husband snort quietly beside her. She swatted nonchalantly at his arm, a silent plea to play nice or she'd lose what little hold she had over her composure. "What do y'all do for work?"

Cami's eyes sparkled proudly at her husband. "Oh, Parker's a neurosurgeon."

Was Cami truly proud of her husband's work, or did she love the income it provided? Whatever it was, Amarah couldn't help but chide herself for judging a relationship she knew nothing about. For all she knew, they truly cared for one another and were deeply in love. Even if they both had wandering eyes.

"What about you guys?" Cami's question was addressed solely to Liam, acting as if Amarah didn't exist. "How long have you been married?"

"Six months." Liam wrapped an arm around Amarah's waist and pulled her tightly against his side. The motion sent warmth spreading through her chest. She swore he was a mind reader, making her feel seen when so much as a flicker of doubt tried to creep in. "Although we've known each other for over a decade."

"Oh?" Cami's honey gaze rounded in surprise. "What did you do to snag him after all those years?"

Amarah opened her mouth to respond, but was cut off as Declan McCarthy strode into the room dressed in a formal black suit and clapped his hands together, gaining everyone's attention.

"Welcome, everyone! My, don't you all look lovely this evening? Please, please, take a seat and we'll get started." Declan smiled warmly as he motioned with his hands toward the table and moved to stand at the head of it.

Liam snagged the last chair on the right end of the table, and Amarah sat to his left. Hunter and Serenity mirrored their positions on the opposite side of the table. Everyone shifted to the remaining seats as they waited for Declan to continue. Once all the guests were seated, he resumed his speech.

"Take a look around the room, at the people sitting next to you or across from you. You all have something in common." He paused, allowing everyone time to gaze at the new faces now positioned around the table. "A dating site has blessed you with the love of your life."

"Or a stalker," Amarah scoffed and muttered under her breath, but quickly covered it by bringing her drink to her lips.

She felt Liam's hand rest atop her thigh. He gave it a reassuring squeeze, and she loved the comfort his touch always brought her. When she sat her glass down, she met Hunter's unique ice blue and hazel gaze. His face was masked as his vision dropped to her glass before shifting back toward Declan. She quietly released an unsteady breath and turned back to their speaker.

"A dating site that wouldn't have happened without the creativity and ingenuity of one brilliant, hardworking woman—the creator. So please, join me in welcoming the founder of Desire, Jade Munro." Declan finished with a beaming smile as everyone began clapping.

A short, petite Asian woman glided gracefully into the room, her smile shining brighter than the sun. She was wrapped in a one-shoulder, olive-green evening gown that hugged her slender body and brushed the floor with each step. Her raven hair was pulled into a tight bun, and her lips were lined with red, popping against her porcelain skin.

Amarah felt Liam's grip on her thigh tighten, unknowingly gaining her attention. His face was schooled into a carefree expression, acting as if he were merely bored. But she saw past it, picking up on the hints of discomfort. The stiffness of his body, his rigid shoulders, the way his green eyes were glued to their host.

She watched as numerous emotions flowed through her husband's vision, each trying to fight for dominance. He acted as if he knew her. She watched as Liam and Hunter shared a silent glance and observed that Hunter mirrored Liam's surprise, from his rigid muscles to the emotions swirling through his irises.

How do they know this woman?

"Thank you, Declan, for the wonderful introduction." Jade smiled at the redheaded man.

Amarah didn't miss the way Declan looked at Jade as if she hung the moon. He returned a smile just as bright as he stepped to the side, giving Jade plenty of room so he wasn't intruding on her spotlight.

"I am so happy to see all your beautiful smiling faces." Jade's chocolate eyes drifted around the room, pausing briefly on Hunter and Liam.

Amarah watched as they widened briefly, an unknown emotion flashing through them as her petite body tensed. But with the blink of an eye, she recovered and continued her speech.

Oh yeah, they definitely know each other.

Amarah just wished she knew the terms on which they were acquainted. She opened her mouth to ask her husband if he was alright, to ask if he somehow knew Jade because he was being uncharacteristically quiet. He and Hunter both.

Was she an old client of Godrik Enterprises, and something happened? If Hunter also knew Jade, maybe they knew her from their military days. However, Jade didn't strike Amarah as the military type. Was she one of their former lovers?

That thought alone had her lunch halfway up her throat. She knew Liam had a past, and she couldn't fault him for it, but running into a spouse's ex-lover would be hard for anyone, not to mention *extremely* uncomfortable. Maybe asking him in a room full of people wasn't the right place. Maybe she'd just wait until they were alone in their room. Whatever their connection, it was definitely a sensitive subject.

"Where do I begin?" Jade clapped her delicate hands together and brought them close to her chest. "This was a project that was near and dear to my heart. I was inspired based on my own experience with love, and because of that connection, Desire was born. I guess the perfect place to start is at the beginning, the day I met a man who changed my world forever. I was in my last semester at Virginia State University, three months away from graduating with my bachelor's degree in computer programming. I worked part-time at a bar located right outside of a military base. This is going to sound like the start of a bad joke," she laughed lightly, "but once upon a time, four Navy SEALs walked into a bar…"

CHAPTER 10

FEBRUARY 2010

"Can I get another Miller Light?" one of Jade's usuals asked in a gruff voice, a retired gentleman who usually spent his Friday nights on the same wooden barstool with cheap beer and the sports channel that played on the numerous flat screens mounted along the walls of the dive bar.

"Of course." She gave the bald man a bright smile as she reached her delicate hand into the cooler filled with ice, grabbed the slim bottleneck, popped the top, and set it in front of him.

"Thanks, hun," he said as he gave her a wrinkled wink and a grin.

She playfully rolled her dark eyes and laughed. The music from an old neon jukebox began to get drowned out by the growing crowd as a steady stream of people filed in and out of the place. Some conversed around the dimly lit space, others spun their partners around the small makeshift dance floor by the jukebox, and every pool table was occupied and in various stages of the game.

Jade left her spot behind the bar, knowing her coworker could handle the customers for a few minutes as she went around to wipe down tables and collect empty glasses and bottles onto a tray that were left scattered around by departing customers. As she weaved her way through the crowd, the thick, black wooden front door opened, drawing her attention toward the entrance.

Four men strode in with their heads thrown back in laughter as if one of them had just told the funniest joke. She could tell right away that they were all military. Spending her entire life just outside of a base, she learned to identify them just from how they walked, talked, carried themselves, or even the looks they plastered across their faces.

Three of the men were taller and very handsome, but her dark vision instantly zoned in on the shorter one, causing her breath to hitch. Her eyes raked over his tawny skin, observing his well-defined body accentuated by the simple jeans and burnt orange sweater that clung to him. His black hair was cut short, and his face was clean-shaven, exposing a strong square jawline.

The stranger had calmed down on his laughter, although his full and plump lips were still parted in a breathtaking smile, showing off bright white teeth as his eyes scanned his surroundings. His gaze halted instantly when he spotted her staring at him.

Her body directly responded to the sight before her. Heat began to spread deep in her belly, her pulse skyrocketed, and she sucked her bottom lip between her teeth. The intense and immediate reaction shocked her. Sure, she'd dated a fair share of hunks before, but no man had ever had this strong and instantaneous effect on her body before.

Jade found herself physically unable to look away as if she were a helpless animal who had stepped into a hunter's vicious trap. He gave her a wink and a grin as he turned and followed his friends toward the bar, causing a swarm of butterflies to explode in her stomach.

Finally, with his back to her, she shook off the trance he'd unknowingly put her in as she continued to weave through the bar, her tray gradually growing heavier with dirty glasses. Periodically, her gaze darted back toward the bar, and each time she did, she was met with piercing golden irises. She couldn't help the smile that played across her lips at the thought of the mystery man being just as infatuated with her as she found herself with him.

She approached a dirty table littered with empty bottles, and she couldn't stop her eyes from rolling. She set the black tray atop the scuffed wooden surface as she began to collect slim bottles between her delicate fingers and tossed them into the large trash can that was not even five feet away. *The laziness of people will never cease to amaze me.* She shook her head in disappointment as the sound of clinking glass filled her ears with each toss.

"Hey, beautiful, what time does your shift end?" a male voice sounded from behind her, drawing her out of her inner monologue.

She turned around to find a man old enough to be her father sitting at a table with two other men around the same age. He smiled, not shy about the numerous gaps where his teeth should've been.

"Why?" Jade remained calm but asked hesitantly, trying hard to hold off the grimace that tried to contort her face.

Working in that type of environment, she was no stranger to pervy or creepy men.

"So I know what time we'll both be getting off."

The old creep wiggled his eyebrows suggestively and didn't try to stop his eyes from roaming down her front. *Eww.* She steeled her spine, not allowing the chill that crept down it to show.

"Yeah, I'm not interested," she dismissed the man as she turned back around to finish clearing the table.

A large hand grabbed her left ass cheek, giving it a firm squeeze through the denim of her jeans.

"Oh, don't be coy, sweetheart. I promise I'll—"

Before the pervert could finish his sentence, Jade grasped the wrist of his wandering hand and spun around, twisting his arm at an unnatural angle behind his back like a chicken wing. Her free hand gripped the back of his neck and forced his cheek to become one with the scuffed wooden table. He tried to wiggle out of her grasp as he cried out in pain, but she had him firmly held in place.

"We have a no-touching policy here." She kept her tone calm but firm as her chocolate vision shifted between his two friends, each wearing mirrored, horrified expressions across their aged faces. "If that's what you're after, there's a strip club down the street."

"I'm... I'm sorry..." The handsy man mumbled his apology as best he could, given his face was smooshed into a hard surface.

"This is your one and only warning. If this happens again, I'll remove your balls from your body, grind them up in the blender, and force them down your throat. Do you understand?" she asked as she cocked her head to the side and glanced back down at the creep.

"Y-Yes," he stuttered, true fear lacing every letter.

Jade released him and stepped back. He quickly jumped up from his chair and clutched his arm across his chest, trying his best to massage the pain away.

"Come on... let's go," he called to his friends as he kept his eyes on her and started to back away toward the exit.

His friends quickly got up and followed him.

She hiked a brow in amusement as she crossed her arms over her small chest and watched them leave. Only when they were gone did she feel other pairs of eyes on her. Though she only felt it a handful of times, their unmistakable weight and intensity meant she knew *exactly* who they belonged to.

She spun to find four men standing close by, each with a beer clasped in their hands and amused expressions across their rugged faces. Jade's vision, however, was solely focused on the bronze-skinned hunk.

"Nice moves." He grinned approvingly, his voice as smooth as silk, causing a wave of desire to wash over her like a tidal wave.

"Thank you," she said a bit breathlessly as she tilted her chin.

He was average height for a man, standing a few inches shy of six feet, but with her topping out at five-foot-three on a good day, most people were tall to her.

"I'm Bryson," he introduced himself before turning toward his friends. "This is Travis, Liam, and Hunter."

"Nice to meet you all." She nodded her head toward them and smiled. "I'm Jade." She let her dark chocolate eyes scan his company, but her attention was back on Bryson a few seconds later.

"A beautiful name for a beautiful woman," Bryson said with a delicious grin. A rosy blush heated her creamy cheeks as she tucked a few raven strands behind her ear. "Are you good?"

He nodded his head toward the door, indicating to the three men who had just left.

"Oh, that was nothing." She shrugged her slim shoulders and smiled. "You should see it when we announce last call."

"They don't pay y'all enough for what y'all have to put up with." Liam drawled from Bryson's left before taking a swig of his beer.

Liam had broad shoulders and stood a few inches over six feet with short black hair, bright green eyes, a neatly trimmed black beard, and a body packed tightly with lean muscles. She took in the dark ink that snaked up his left arm and disappeared beneath the sleeves of the sweater he had pulled halfway up his forearms.

"No, they don't," Jade agreed with a snort.

"Are you going to ask for her number or not?" Travis grinned cheesily as he nudged his elbow into Bryson's arm.

Travis nearly matched Liam in height and had the same muscular build. His eyes were as blue as the sky on a cloudless day, and his long sunny hair brushed his shoulders. A light brown scruff was trimmed closely to his sun-kissed face.

"I'm not sure," Bryson half-laughed as he turned to look at Travis. "It didn't end so well for the last guy who flirted with her." He turned and met Jade's gaze again, causing more wings to flutter erratically within her.

"She's five-foot-nothing," Hunter, Bryson's other friend, said sarcastically. "You're scared of a child-sized woman?"

Jade met Hunter's piercing gaze with a color combination she'd never seen before. They had a warm hazel center with ice blue surrounding them. He gave her a quick wink, silently communicating that he was merely teasing. She couldn't stop the smirk that spread across her red-painted lips.

Hunter was the tallest of the group, standing an inch or two taller than Liam. His long brown hair was tied in a knot behind his head, and she noticed a small scar that ran vertically through his left eyebrow. He was large, packed with thick muscles, and intimidating. He wore a pair of blue jeans and a red flannel, reminding her of a scary lumberjack.

"Hell yeah!" Bryson laughed, the sound more beautiful and melodic than any of Mozart's compositions. "If I ask for your number, will you promise not to turn my balls into a smoothie? I'm pretty attached to them."

Once she stopped laughing, she cocked her head and studied him for a long moment, weighing her options. Should she? She'd only just met the guy. She couldn't chalk up her body's reaction to him as pure attraction. There was something else there, something not yet discovered that had the potential to be something she'd never experienced before and might never experience again.

Deep down, she knew she was going to oblige, but not just yet. She thoroughly enjoyed making him sweat. Bryson shifted his weight to his other foot as he took a swig of his beer. Then she pulled out the notepad and pen from her apron and scribbled her number down. She tore the paper off and passed it to him.

Bryson's smile touched his golden eyes, which began to sparkle with joy, and the sight nearly stole her breath away. Upon examining the paper, his face contorted in confusion.

"What's this?" he questioned with full amusement dancing through his tone.

Mischief swam within her dark gaze. "It's my number."

"But it's in… uhh… I don't recognize the language," he said with a hesitant grin and shook his head.

She turned and picked up the tray of dirty dishes again before turning back to the group of men. "Well, if you're truly interested, you'll figure out how to translate it."

She gave him a wink before walking off back toward the bar, letting her hips sway a little more than usual, feeling the weight of Bryson's vision on her. Her smile grew more satisfactory when she heard all of his friends roar with laughter.

The sound of Jade's phone ringing pulled her from a wonderful dream about a certain hunk she'd just met the night before. She cracked open her eyes and squinted at the blinding screen, seeing that it was a little after one in the afternoon. Since she didn't get home till the early hours of the morning, sleeping in that late on a weekend was normal for her.

"Hello?" she answered in a groggy and frustrated voice.

"Good afternoon, beautiful." A smooth voice drifted through the line, instantly waking her up quicker than any coffee could.

"Bryson?" She gasped as butterflies tickled her stomach.

"You sound surprised." His tone expressed his amusement. "Did you think I wasn't serious?"

"No." She laughed. "I just figured it would've taken you longer to figure out my number."

"I live on a military base, my little kunoichi. Did you think I wouldn't be able to find someone who not only recognized Japanese but could read it?" He chuckled and she beamed at his nickname for her, knowing it was a title given to female shinobis—those who were covert agents, or mercenaries in feudal Japan.

"I respect a man who doesn't like to waste time."

"Tomorrow is never guaranteed, and I've waited twenty-seven years to meet you. I don't plan to waste another minute if I don't have to." His confession made her heart leap with joy. "So, can I take you out for a late lunch?"

Jade's smile could be heard through the phone. "I'd love that."

"Text me your address. I'll pick you up in twenty minutes." She could hear his smile too, and she swooned. Hard.

She pulled her brows together in suspicion as she sat up in bed and stretched. "How do I know you're not a creep who won't show up at my house and try to murder me?"

"Because you'd kick my ass and probably win." He laughed fully at that, and her heart skipped a beat.

"You better not be even a minute late, mister," she teased.

"I wouldn't dream of it." Bryson chuckled before hanging up.

Jade quickly jumped out of bed, smoothed her covers back into place, and practically ran to the bathroom attached to her bedroom. After flying through her morning routine, she applied a light layer of makeup, finishing with her signature red lipstick she always wore like battle armor. She walked to her closet and pulled on a pair of black skinny jeans and an oversized cream sweater. Temperatures in Virginia in the middle of February got rather chilly.

She left her raven hair spilling down her back as she tucked her phone into the back pocket of her jeans and walked into the living room. Her parents were out running errands, so the quiet house didn't surprise her. A knock sounded on her front door, pulling her lips into a grin.

"You made it with two minutes to spare." Jade threw open the door, and her breath hitched.

Bryson stood just a few feet away, a hand tucked into his jeans to keep it warm while the other ran over his smooth chin nervously. She couldn't stop her eyes from raking down his front, taking in the dark grey sweater and denim that hugged his thick, muscular legs. Her mouth watered at the sight of him, and her body heated despite the frigid temperature outside. Yet again, the sight of this man alone had her body reacting on pure instinct in a way it'd never done before.

He remained quiet, taking her appearance in as well. She could feel his vision like a lover's caress as it ran from her head, down her torso to her feet, and back up just as thoroughly.

"You can't look at me like that." His voice was low and sent a delicious shiver down her back.

"Like what?" She cursed herself for allowing that to come out breathlessly.

"Like you want me to tear the clothes from your body with nothing but my teeth." His jaw ticked, and he clenched his fists at his side as if trying to fight the urge to do just that.

Jade took a step toward him without thinking, her body reacting on instinct. "Would that be so bad?"

The little distance that separated them was too far. She needed to be closer to him. Her chest rose and fell at a quickened pace due to her accelerated heart rate.

"You only met me last night." His eyes darkened to a shade of rich honey as he caught a whiff of her perfume.

"You said it yourself that tomorrow is never guaranteed," Jade quoted his words back to him as she took another small step. She was close enough to feel the heat radiating off his body as she craned her head up to peer into his hungry eyes. "Tell me I'm imagining this," she whispered as she rested her hand gently atop his strong chest. "This... pull... between us like a magnetic field."

"That would make me a liar." He spoke low. "The moment I saw you last night, I felt a need I've never felt for any woman before. It's as if you're gravity itself, drawing me straight to you."

His confession knocked the very breath from her lungs.

"I... I feel it too," she agreed in a whisper.

Jade felt his hands press flat against her back as she found herself caged in his strong arms. Surprise quickly shot through her that she didn't feel scared or overpowered in his embrace. If anything, she felt that was exactly where she belonged, as if her home was in his arms. Another delicious shiver raced down her spine, straight to her sex. She snaked her arms around his neck and met his intense gaze with one of her own.

"We aren't going to make it to lunch, are we?" she asked, unable to stop the grin that pulled at one side of her lips.

Bryson flashed her a smile that promised wicked, sinful acts that had her clenching her thighs together. "The sun would have long since set by the time I finished exploring every inch of your creamy skin."

Her tone was playful but sensual. "You only have a few hours before my parents will be home."

A heartbeat later, his lips were claiming hers in a hot and passionate kiss that ignited a five-alarm fire not just in her core but throughout her entire body. She matched his needy energy as she kissed him back. His hands cupped the back of her thighs as he hoisted her up and crossed over the threshold of her house.

CHAPTER 11

Amarah Godrik glanced around the long table in the spacious dining hall, observing the looks of complete awe across the guests' features. Well, minus Liam and Hunter, who thankfully masked their shocked expressions and now sported looks of calm civility. She had to give Jade Munro props, the woman knows how to tell one hell of a story. She found herself captivated by Jade's tale of how love unexpectedly found her.

"I started working on the Desire project shortly after graduating from college, and after months of hard work, it was finally ready to launch. Over the years, it grew larger than I ever dreamed possible, and today, thousands of couples all over the world have credited their happy relationships to Desire." Jade smiled, her dark gaze scanning over all the guests in the dining hall before continuing. "Please, spend this week in the sun, in the water, in bed with your significant other." She laughed, and everyone joined in. "This week is all about you. Relax, have fun, and thank you."

The room erupted into applause as Declan pulled out the chair at the head of the table. She nodded her thanks and sat. He took the chair to her right as a handful of servers entered the room carrying plates covered in a silver dome. The dishes were set in front of each guest, and the lids were removed.

Juicy thick steak, cubed seasoned potatoes, and steamed green beans filled the dishes. The food looked wonderful, even if the smell did cause Amarah to gag, but she clamped her jaw shut. She coached herself through a slow, deep breath before she picked up her steak knife and fork and cut into the meat.

She was thankful that one of her questions was answered after listening to Jade's tale, even if it left her with a dozen more. It was hard for her not to sigh in relief when it was confirmed that Jade was not one of her husband's ex-lovers. However, if she was involved with Bryson, the last member of her brother Travis's, Hunter's, and Liam's SEAL team, wouldn't they be happy to see her?

Yet the moment she entered the room, it was as if the men's shock was replaced by agony. What happened? Did the men have a falling out of some kind? Did Jade and Bryson get divorced? Amarah had observed the beautiful piece of jewelry that adorned Jade's ring finger on her left hand. Were they merely separated?

From what little bit Amarah observed about Declan, he was fawning all over Jade. She doubted a married woman, even one who might be currently separated from her husband, would allow a man like that close to her side. Besides, after listening to her story and hearing how she spoke so highly about Bryson, that option was highly unlikely.

Then, a more sickening feeling began to settle deep in her gut. Did something terrible happen to Bryson? Amarah was certain that if the man had died somehow, she would've heard about it from her brother or Liam over the years. Unless the topic was too sensitive a subject for even them to share.

Conversations flowed around the table as everyone ate their dinner. However, her group remained silent. Hunter and Liam refused to utter a sound, and after a worried glance from Serenity, Amarah knew she wasn't the only one concerned about them. But like Amarah's previous thought, that was a conversation meant to be had later on, in private.

When dinner was over, the servers cleared away the plates, and everyone stood, conversing around the room as Jade visited with each couple. Finally, whatever shock Hunter and Liam were in had worn off. They didn't talk much but made comments here and there when needed.

No matter how hard she tried to resist, Amarah found her eyes periodically drifting back to Jade. Her head was often thrown back as her melodic laugh filtered through the room. After a while, Amarah observed her take a deep breath before walking over to their group.

"Hello, Hunter. Liam." Jade's voice was soft, and a hint of uncertainty could be heard.

Hunter gave her a cautious nod. "Jade."

A small smile tugged at the corners of her mouth. "I'm surprised to see you guys here. It's been… a while."

"It has," Liam agreed.

To the untrained eye, no one would've noticed. However, Amarah knew her husband like the back of her hand, so she caught the pained look that radiated from his eyes. Not to mention, you could cut the tension around them with a knife.

Hunter questioned next. "What are you doing here?"

Jade's brows furrowed as she cocked her head. "This is my event."

Though it was a simple statement, it came out as more of a question, as if she were uneasy. Yeah, there was definitely some murky water between the three of them, and the unknown was killing Amarah.

"Did you bring us here?" Liam asked, his mask firmly in place, and his tone, even and calm.

"No, I'm just as shocked at seeing you guys as you were at seeing me. For such a large world we live in, it can be quite small sometimes. My assistant, Declan McCarthy, handled everything and chose all the couples for this trip. I was just told when and where to show up." She paused, allowing herself a steady breath. "I am glad he chose you, though. Who are these beautiful ladies?"

"This is my wife, Amarah." Liam motioned toward her with his hand. "And that's Hunter's fiancée, Serenity."

"So, the Hunter and Liam from your story," Serenity addressed Jade hesitantly before shifting her gaze to the men, "were the two of you?"

Amarah remained quiet as she watched intently and noted the unusual facial expressions and body language that passed between Jade, Liam, and Hunter.

"Yes," Hunter paused briefly before continuing. "Back in the Navy, our team consisted of myself, Liam, Bryson, and Travis, Amarah's older brother."

Amarah didn't miss the slight strain in his voice as he spoke Bryson's name. She also saw the emotion that shot through Jade's chocolate eyes at the mention of her husband, but it was gone just as quickly. That sickening feeling deep in her gut only worsened.

"Did he come with you?" Serenity questioned innocently before looping her arm around Hunter's bicep, giving it a soft, supporting squeeze, and peering up at him. "I'm sure it would be great to reconnect after so many years."

"He... passed away." Liam's words were clipped as if it was difficult or even painful to talk about it.

Amarah's heart broke wide open, and by the shock and mortification marring Serenity's angular features, she knew the woman was most likely wishing the floor would open up and swallow her whole.

Amarah caught the slight flare of Jade's eyes at Liam's choice of words. Another sickening feeling told her there was more to that story, but she remained quiet. God only knew the hurt that Jade had gone through. The hurt she was *still* going through. If she had lost Liam, the mention of his name alone would be enough to stop her beating heart, no matter how many years had passed.

A subtle movement caught her attention, and her eyes fell on Jade's left hand. She was nervously twirling a beautiful ring with a shiny jade stone surrounded by diamonds. The thought of her still wearing her wedding ring after all these years made tears sting the backs of Amarah's eyes.

Jade quietly cleared her throat before donning as strong a smile as she could muster. "If you'll excuse me, I have more rounds to make. Ladies, it was a pleasure to meet you."

After Jade left, the air around the group seemed to lighten as both men visibly relaxed further. Amarah knew that interaction must've been hard for all of them, not to mention awkward. She didn't know the amount of history with the group, but even she could feel the strain choking everyone in the circle.

"Are you ok?" Amarah asked her husband in a tone so low, only he'd be able to hear.

She laced her fingers through his and leaned against his left arm.

"Yeah." Liam smiled, though she could tell it was forced. "It's been nearly a decade since the incident, but seeing her brought it all back as if it happened only yesterday."

Incident. Why did that single word constrict her throat, making it nearly impossible to speak? What happened?

Amarah hugged him tightly around the waist. "I'm so sorry."

"Though it was hard witnessing his death, Travis took the loss of Bryson the hardest. He'd been shot on a previous mission and wasn't medically cleared to go back into the field. So he sat that mission out. Travis beat himself up for a long time, feeling responsible, thinking he could've saved him if he went."

That cracked her heart even further. She remembered receiving the news. It was the summer before her freshman year of high school. She was out to dinner with her parents, celebrating her birthday, when her mother received a phone call from a number she didn't recognize. It was the American Red Cross, calling to inform her that their son had been injured in the line of duty. Literally, worst birthday ever.

They'd immediately left the restaurant and called Sandra, Travis's wife. Only, it was Liam who answered the phone, saying that Sandra was in the hospital room, speaking with the doctors. He'd filled them in with a bit more detail but still left a lot out. He assured them that the bullet missed anything vital and that Travis would make a full recovery.

Amarah knew her older brother better than anyone, aside from his wife. She knew the kind of man he was. Though there was physically nothing Travis could've done, she knew a part of him would always blame himself for the loss, even fifty years from now. A lonely tear cascaded down her cheek for the pain all three of those men went through, are currently going through, and will always experience for their lost brother. She quickly swiped it away before anyone noticed.

"I'm sure if there was a chance he could've been saved, you or

Hunter would've done *everything* you could." She peered up at her husband, hoping her words would help.

"We tried everything..." He trailed off, his voice cracking as if his mind had taken him back in time, and her heart shattered further for him.

She knew those men grew as close as brothers, and she tried to put herself in their shoes. If she'd lost Travis the way they'd lost Bryson, she would've died right next to him. She simply held onto Liam, knowing just her being there and listening was what he needed at that moment.

He cleared his throat as he bent down and placed a kiss on the top of her head. "I'm ok, I promise."

She tilted her head up, peering into his beautiful, bright green eyes. He gave her another smile, this one genuine, and the sight warmed her heart. She glanced over to see Hunter and Serenity embraced similarly. Hunter appeared to be doing better as well, and Amarah felt an invisible weight lift off her shoulders.

"Well, that was freaken awkward." Serenity blew out a heavy breath as she and Hunter returned to their room for the night. "I can't believe I said that!" she groaned.

She'd never been so mortified in her life, and she was almost a hundred percent certain that her cheeks were still red from embarrassment.

"You had no way of knowing, Angel. Don't beat yourself up about it." Hunter closed their door.

She watched as he waited until he heard the soft click, signaling it was locked, before turning to her.

"Y'all had no idea she created a dating site?" she inquired as she bent at the waist, her heels dropping to the floor with a soft thud.

"No. Bryson told us she was working on something big but wasn't at liberty to say until Jade gave him the ok." He released a heavy breath. "I'm guessing the website was that secret project."

"Poor thing. I couldn't even imagine…" Her voice cracked.

Serenity's heart broke for Jade. She couldn't fathom losing Hunter in such a way… or any other way. That line of thought always had her throat constricting with emotions. She knew Hunter's private security job could be risky at times, but she trusted him and his men to look out for each other and make sure everyone came back in one piece. But that didn't stop the bad thoughts that liked to creep in, their sole mission to torment her.

Hunter's long legs closed the distance between them as he gently cupped her face in his large hands and tilted her eyes up to meet his.

"You won't ever have to wonder what that's like, Angel. I'm not going anywhere."

I wonder if Bryson said the same thing to Jade? She couldn't help but snort at him. He's always been freakishly observant. Like, on an inhuman, unnatural level. Him reading her mind right then, saying the words she needed to hear, didn't surprise her.

"You better not," she warned in a shaky voice.

He arched a brow in challenge as amusement filled his tone. "Or what?"

"Or…" She trailed off as she thought hard for a good threat. "Or I'll resurrect you from the dead just so I can kill you myself for leaving me. Then I'll trap your spirit in a doll and put you on my shelf, so you'll never be able to leave me again." She held his gaze.

"Mmm, I like the thought of being able to watch you for eternity. I'd get to watch you undress and sleep." He placed a kiss against the sensitive skin of her neck, drawing a shiver from her. "But my favorite would be watching you play with yourself." His voice was a low growl that sent goosebumps sprouting along her arms.

"You're such a creep," she whispered as she tilted her neck to the side, giving him better access.

"You know you love it."

Hunter guided her backward until her legs hit the edge of their bed. He kept pressing her back until she lay flat atop the covers and his large torso loomed over hers. Her breathing had shifted, coming in shorter, quicker spurts as her heart rate spiked with need.

He dropped to his knees before her, snaked his hands under her dress, and slid her panties down her legs in one fluid motion, tossing them behind him. She craned her head up to see his heated gaze lock with hers as he lifted the hem of her black dress and disappeared beneath the fabric.

She held her breath in anticipation and gasped when she felt his hot breath against her slick entrance. The next thing she knew, he was devouring her with such hunger, you'd think he had been starving for a week. His tongue, teeth, and fingers assaulted her in every delicious way possible.

She craved more friction against her swollen and sensitive clit as she gripped his head in her hands, over the fabric of her dress, and began rocking her hips. A growl of approval vibrated against her heated core as if he got off on her using him for her own pleasure.

"That's it, Angel. Ride my face until you come."

She heard his lust-filled words, and the vibration they caused against her center had her toes curling with pleasure.

She was so close, the tightening in her stomach growing with each pass of his beard scraping against her sensitive flesh. Her finish detonated within her, sending every nerve ending into overdrive as wave after wave of toe-curling ecstasy coursed through her. She moaned his name as he thoroughly lapped up every bit of her finish. When he was done, he reappeared from beneath her black dress, stood, and ran the back of his hand across his mouth and beard. A move she found more erotic than it had any right to be.

Serenity panted as Hunter began to slowly undo his belt, unbutton his slacks, and free his throbbing and veiny erection from his trousers. Her eyes were glued to his hand as he tugged on himself once, twice, following every movement with anticipation as her bottom lip disappeared between her teeth.

"Kneel." The command was calm but firm, and she nearly moaned from that alone.

She did as she was told and knelt before him. He gripped a handful of her raven locks as he rubbed the swollen head of his cock against her lips, smearing a line of pre-cum across them. Her tongue darted out as she licked him off her lips, and his eyes darkened as he watched her intently.

He cocked his head to the side. "Do you like the taste of me, Angel?"

"Yes," she moaned as she peered up at him through her lashes.

"Do you want more?"

"Yes, please," she begged.

"Open that pretty little mouth of yours then."

His smile turned devilish as she obliged, and he filled her, slowly pushing in, inch by inch, until he hit the back of her throat.

His groan of satisfaction sent a fresh wave of arousal coursing through her. Her eyes began to water, but she pushed through as she coached herself through slow breaths and began moving her tongue along his veiny shaft. His other hand sank into her hair as he pulled out to the tip, giving her a minute to catch her breath before he began to roughly fuck her mouth.

Serenity moaned around his cock as he hit the back of her throat with each thrust, causing tears to fall down her cheek and saliva to drip from her mouth. She didn't tap out though. She loved it when he went rough with her. The dirtier the better, and she found herself clenching her thighs together to alleviate the fresh ache between her legs.

"You look so fucking good when you're choking on my cock, Angel." He spoke through gritted teeth as his grip on her hair tightened and his thrusts became more erratic.

All too soon, he groaned in pleasure as he spilled down her throat. He only pulled out once he was sure she took every drop he had to offer. Serenity swallowed before licking her lips and running her fingers under her eyes, clearing up her smudged makeup.

CHAPTER 12

Jade Munro closed the door to her bedroom, leaning back against the cool, solid wood as fat tears cascaded down her round cheeks. A soft sob escaped, filling the quiet space around her. She clamped her hand over her mouth, not wanting to risk any of the guests, or Declan, potentially hearing her breakdown.

Though it had been almost a decade, seeing Liam Godrik and Hunter Gatlin was almost too much for her. The four men were nearly inseparable back in the day. So much so that Bryson had mentioned he wanted Hunter to be the godfather of any children they may've had, and she had found herself easily agreeing.

She knew there might come a time in life when she'd run into them again, but she was blindsided at dinner, nearly losing it when she saw them sitting at the end of the dining table, mere feet from her. She wasn't prepared for the raw emotions that surfaced, practically drowning her.

Was this the universe screwing with her? Hadn't it already caused her enough agony by taking the love of her life away from her? She quickly wiped her cheeks clean, straightened, and entered her bathroom, stripping out of her dress. The warm spray of the shower caused a small moan to escape, the warm water immediately helping to relieve the tension rapidly building across her shoulders.

It took her weeks to prepare her welcome speech in the mirror, practicing over and over until she was able to recite the story of how she met Bryson without shedding a single tear or her voice cracking once. She thought she'd finally mastered her emotions enough to at least get through dinner. That was until she saw them. Two men who were like brothers to her husband.

She closed her eyes and focused on the hot water. Her mind began to drift back to the story she told at dinner, and to the parts she left out. Parts that she kept private and close to her heart. The part where she and Bryson finally left her bedroom after numerous rounds of lovemaking in search of food.

FEBRUARY 2010

Jade and Bryson strolled down the street, fingers intertwined with each other as they passed numerous shops. Some with trinkets displayed in the large glass windows, others with mannequins dressed in the latest fashion. The smell of home-cooked food filled their nose as they approached a small diner tucked between a thrift store and a bookstore.

"Thank you," she said sheepishly as he held the glass door open for her.

The chiming of a bell signaled the arrival of new customers. She didn't understand why she was shy around him after the hours of orgasms they just coaxed out of each other.

"Welcome in! Take a seat anywhere you'd like," an older woman called from behind the counter as she filled drinks and placed them atop a circular tray.

"Do you prefer a booth or a table?" Jade questioned as her eyes scanned the restaurant, decorated to look like it belonged back in the fifties.

Blue and white vinyl booths lined both walls, and white and black checkered squares were placed in a diamond pattern across the floor. A few tables and booths were occupied by other customers, but thankfully, it wasn't too busy.

"Booth, preferably in the back," Bryson answered.

He recaptured her hand in his as if he couldn't stand the thought of not touching her, as if she might disappear if he didn't hold on to her. Her heart swelled at the thought. He weaved them through the tables placed sporadically around the middle of the diner and stopped when they came to the last booth.

He reluctantly let her hand go as they took their seats, his back to the wall and Jade sitting across from him, her back to the restaurant. She couldn't help but laugh as she grabbed a menu and started skimming its options.

"What's so funny?" he asked her, peering up from his menu.

A slight blush crept across her creamy cheeks, warming them. "I just let you do... very intimate things to me, and I don't even know your last name. God, that makes me sound like a whore." She laughed and gently shook her head.

"Munro." He chuckled as a wicked grin spread across his handsome features as if he were reminiscing over the last few hours. "And for the record, I don't think you're a whore."

Her blush deepened at his compliment, but their server approached with a warm smile spread across her face, forcing Jade's response to die in her throat.

"Hey, I'm Sabrina, and I'll be taking care of you today. What can I get you guys to drink?"

Bryson glanced toward Jade, signaling her to order first. "I'll take a water, please."

"And for you, hun?" Sabrina asked in a motherly tone.

"Coffee, please. Black."

"Coming right up!" Sabrina smiled at the two and walked off.

"How long have you been bartending for?" Bryson questioned.

"A year. It's helped me build quite a nest egg so I can buy a house after I graduate college." She laughed lightly as her vision skimmed her lunch choices. She felt a piercing gaze weighing down on her and knew the culprit. When she glanced up, she was met with shimmering gold. Her brows furrowed when she took in the stunned look on his face. "What?"

"You've been this close to me for so long, and I've only just now met you?"

She didn't know how to respond as her heart somersaulted with joy. He slowly shook his head as if disappointed with himself.

"What are you going to college for?"

Jade took a deep breath and mentally prepared herself. Her previous experience with telling men her career interests had them groaning in disappointment. Most men wanted nothing to do with an intelligent, independent woman, preferring one more docile and ditsy.

"Computer programming." She gave him a timid smile and held her breath in anticipation of his response.

"Sexy *and* smart, the perfect combination." He winked at her, and heat flared to life within her.

Yep, I'm doomed, she groaned inwardly.

"You're the first man I've met who thought that way." She sighed as relief washed through her. "What about you? What branch are you in?"

"Navy," he answered as Sabrina dropped off their drinks and took their food orders. He cautiously sipped his coffee, testing its temperature before continuing. "I'm a SEAL."

Jade nodded approvingly. "Are your three friends from last night SEALs as well? Liam, Hunter, and…" She tilted her chin toward the ceiling and narrowed her vision as she tried to recall the last one's name.

"Travis," Bryson answered for her. "Yeah, we're all in the same unit. Anytime we go out on missions, we're generally always together. We're all pretty tight, like brothers."

"I'd imagine so. It'd be hard not to be with everything you guys encounter together and have to do to ensure you all make it back home in one piece."

His rich eyes roamed over her face admiringly. "Speaking of which," he took a deep breath, "we're heading out of the country tomorrow for a week."

She frowned. "Am I allowed to know where you're going?"

"No," he said gently. Pain flashed through his whisky irises as if he wanted nothing more than to tell her. As if keeping secrets from her was a physical pain to him. "I just wanted to let you know so you didn't fear I ghosted you after sleeping with you."

She paused for a moment as she allowed her vision to roam over his handsome features. "I know you wouldn't do that. You're not that kind of guy," she said confidently.

Bryson arched a brow in challenge as he leaned back and crossed his arms over his chest. "You just met me. I could be a total piece of shit."

"Ahh, but I remember you saying last night that you were pretty attached to your balls."

He cocked his head to the side as if unsure of what that had to do with anything.

"I am." His words were slow and hesitant.

"So, had you slept with me and then vanished, I would've tracked you down and forced a nasty ball smoothie down your throat."

He burst out laughing, causing other customers to glance their way in wonder.

"And that's exactly why I will always inform you before I leave town."

"Do you go out on missions often?" Worry laced her words.

She pegged him for the military kind last night when she saw him, but knowing exactly which branch he belonged to was finally sinking in. She knew the military could be a dangerous job, especially for anyone deployed, but knowing he goes out on missions quite frequently had a foreign feeling constricting around her heart.

His saying of "tomorrow is never guaranteed" brought an entirely new meaning to the phrase, and she wasn't quite sure how to handle it. She'd only just met him yesterday, but their unusual connection, their strong attraction had her feeling like she'd known the man for years. And the thought of losing him, especially so shortly after meeting him, had fear and panic prickling her skin and unease churning her stomach.

As if reading her mind, Bryson reached across the table and gathered her delicate hands in his large, calloused grasp.

"I'll be alright. This isn't my first rodeo." He kept his tone gentle as he chuckled lightly. "Now that I know you'll be here waiting for me, it's given me a newfound motivation to make damn sure I come back safely."

Jade kept quiet, allowing his words time to sink in. "You

better." She cleared her throat of any emotion that tried to surface. "So, where are you from originally?"

The necessity of the subject change was like a fish needing water to live. He released her hands when Sabrina delivered their food.

After she departed again, he spoke. "North Carolina."

"You're a long way from home." She peered at him before taking a bite of her burger. "Is it hard being that far from your family?"

"Not really. I've never been that close to them. My mom ran out on us when I was three, so it was just me and my dad for a while. He got remarried when I was thirteen. The woman had two kids, a boy and a girl, from a previous marriage. After they moved in, it felt as if I were the outcast of the family. They always went out of their way to make me feel unimportant, and my dad never defended me or stopped them. I signed up for the Navy the day of my eighteenth birthday, and the moment I had my high school diploma in hand, I was gone. Never looked back."

His story had her heart hurting for the poor boy who was neglected by the only family he had. Then anger tried to take over at his father for allowing his new family to bully his biological son.

"Your father sounds charming." Sarcasm dripped from Jade's voice as she rolled her eyes, dipped her fry in ketchup, and plopped it into her mouth.

"Father of the year." He snorted. "What about you? Any siblings?"

"Nope. I'm an only child. I don't know if that was a blessing or a curse. My parents have always been around and supported me and my interests, but they aren't exactly the kind to express their love openly."

"Just gives me more space to shower you with enough love to

satisfy you for life."

Jade met his gaze and saw the honesty of his words in them. Tears stung the back of her eyes. Sure, she'd dated before, but she was never serious about finding a husband. She only dated casually to have that physical connection with someone. In all honesty, she didn't plan to begin looking for a husband, if at all, until many years after she had settled into her dream career.

That was until she met Bryson. The unexplainable connection between them, the promise of his words, and the promise of a future filled with love and happiness had her changing her mind and quickly reevaluating her desires in life.

Now, she found herself wanting that life with him so desperately. Like a man on the brink of dehydration as he used what little strength he had left to crawl toward a stream of water that would be his salvation. Suddenly, that life with him was all she wanted, and she'd grasp it and hold on to it for dear life.

The shock of cold water brought Jade back to the present. Her shower had turned fridged, causing her to wonder just how long she lost herself in memories of the past. She quickly went through the motions of soaping up and rinsing off before wrapping a towel around her and stepping out of the shower.

Her eyes were red and puffy. She hadn't even realized she'd been crying. A tired sigh escaped her parted lips as she stood in front of the mirror. After shaking her head clear, she numbly dried off, got dressed, and climbed into bed feeling cold, hollow, and alone, just as she had every night for the past nine years.

CHAPTER 13

Amarah Godrik had lost count of all the hidden images she'd been able to find in the patterned texture of the ceiling. After everyone had retired to their room for the evening, she and Liam had gotten cleaned up and crawled into bed. That was nearly two hours ago, and she was wide awake.

She'd tried counting, getting as high as eight hundred and sixty before growing bored. She tried meditating while lying in bed, slowing her breathing to a nice steady rhythm, but her mind kept wandering, so that tactic got thrown out the window. She even planned on climbing on top of Liam to expel some energy, orgasm, and tire herself out, but by the sounds of his steady breaths, he was sound asleep.

So here she was, lying on her back, trying to make images of the textured ceiling. She'd found a bunny, a rabid dog, what could've passed as a Greek statue posed suggestively, and a handful of flowers. A frustrated breath slipped past her lips, and she turned her head toward her husband again. Maybe she should wake him up.

He'd never been opposed in the past to being roused by her using his body for her pleasure. In fact, he rather encouraged it. But after the shock at dinner this evening, she knew he was emotionally drained. He'd barely spoken when they returned to their room. He wasn't mean or snappy with her, but she could tell he was lost in his own mind. Lost in memories of the past.

It killed her that she couldn't take those from him. He was her husband, her best friend, the love of her life, and the father to her unborn children. She should be able to help him conquer the demons of his past. But she knew some battles needed to be fought alone. Instead, she'd made sure to simply be near him. To shower him with love, to let him know that he wasn't alone, and to offer an ear if he needed to vent or talk through things.

No, she'd let him rest. As gently as possible, she removed the covers and slid out of bed, trying not to jostle the mattress for fear of accidentally rousing him. She grabbed her bathing suit and slipped into the small, attached bathroom. After changing and pulling her sunny hair up into a messy bun, she slipped the sheer swimsuit cover over her body, grabbed a towel, and slipped out of the bathroom.

She was halfway toward the door before she paused and listened. Liam's breathing was still a steady melody in the quiet room. Reaching for the door, she was halfway through twisting the knob when a deep voice sounded behind her.

"Going somewhere, Cupcake?"

Amarah's scream got caught in her throat as she whirled around and clutched her hand to her chest. It felt as if her heart was trying to burst from its boned cage beneath her flesh. Her husband stood directly behind her in nothing but a pair of boxers, his short black hair tousled from sleep.

"Holy shit!" She panted as she worked hard to steady her breathing. "You scared the crap out of me. I didn't even hear you get out of bed."

"You didn't answer my question." He arched a thick brow in challenge as he peered down at her. His gaze dropped from hers, took in her attire, and then met her sapphire eyes again before he drawled, "Going somewhere?"

"I... I couldn't sleep." She bit her lip, knowing she was in for a scolding. Her next words came out in a rush. "I left you a note in case you woke, and I wasn't back yet."

"You know how I feel about you going places without me, especially in an unfamiliar environment." His tone was unnervingly calm, though she saw the sternness in his eyes.

Amarah knew he was right. Especially after she'd been kidnapped last year by Derick in such a public place. She knew Liam didn't keep her on a leash, and she was free to go where she pleased, but within reason. Sneaking down to a pool in the middle of the night on a remote island filled with strangers was asking for trouble. Looking back on it, this probably wouldn't win her any prizes in the best decision contest.

His grin turned wicked as his green gaze dropped down her front again, the sheer dress did little to cover the crimson bikini she wore beneath. "Why didn't you wake me? I would've been happy to tire you out."

The moonlight streaking through the window shone across his heavily tattooed, very naked torso. Sleep still lined his sharp features, and his short hair was tousled in a delicious way that had her hand begging to run through the dark, silky strands. She gave a sensual smile as she stepped closer to him and placed a hand against his bare, warm chest, feeling a steady rhythm beating beneath.

"You could come down to the pool with me."

Without fail, she knew he'd picked up on the shift in her body, causing his tone to drop and begin to fill with desire. "Feeling adventurous, are we?"

"Maybe?" She gave her shoulder an innocent shrug. "Or maybe I just really want to swim."

"You always were a terrible liar, Cupcake."

She was. Though she didn't necessarily see that as a fault, exactly. More of an inconvenience for times such as this.

He chuckled as he turned, grabbed a pair of black swim trunks, and changed into them before grabbing another towel.

The hallway was dark, aside from small wall-mounted sconces that provided enough light to allow low visibility. No lights illuminated beneath any doors, signaling that all the guests were asleep. They walked hand in hand in silence as they descended the stairs and exited through the glass doors that led to the back patio.

The night sky was free of clouds, providing an unobstructed view of millions of stars and the constellations they formed. The three-quarter moon rose high above them, supplying ample light to the area. Colorful lights illuminated the large rectangular pool in hues of reds, purples, blues, and greens.

"It's so beautiful here." Amarah sighed as she set her towel down on a lounge chair, slipped off her flip-flops, and shimmied out of her sheer coverup.

"It's even better when there's no one else here." Liam's sly comment gained him a light slap on his arm from his wife.

She laughed as she started toward the pool stairs. "You're the most introverted extrovert I've ever known."

"I don't know what that means, but I'll take it as a compliment."

He flashed her a smile as he followed behind her. She swayed her hips a bit, knowing his stare was glued to her ass. She could feel it as if it were a phantom caress.

"It means, for someone who is forced to be a people person for work, you sure do like your solitude."

She tested the temperature of the water with her toes and sighed when she found it just right.

"I expend my daily quota for people at work, so when I leave, I like to enjoy my quiet time." He shrugged his broad shoulders as he descended the stairs, not even bothering to test the temperature first.

Amarah stepped off the last stair, the water hitting her knees as she watched her husband wade further into the pool before eventually beginning to swim toward the deep end. She chewed on her bottom lip, mesmerized by each stroke of his arms, loving the way his muscles moved beneath his tanned, inked flesh.

He cut through the water like a knife through butter. Every stroke was precise, like he'd performed it in the Olympics and placed first. When he reached the edge, he flipped beneath the water, pushed off the wall, and began to swim back. For something that was not sexy in the slightest, she found the sight before her very erotic.

When he was able to touch again, he strode toward the spot she'd rooted herself to. Her blue gaze dropped as inch by agonizing inch of his torso was exposed, following the trail of dozens of droplets of water as they rolled down his lean and defined muscles. Her breathing became unsteady as a fire ignited deep within her core. A fire that, no matter how many times her husband sought and thoroughly sated her, kept coming back hungrier than the last.

"I fucking love it when you look at me like that," Liam growled, stopping mere inches from her.

She braved a peek and nearly moaned when she saw his soaked

swim trunks clinging to him, leaving nothing to the imagination and accentuating the very hard erection that lay just beneath the fabric. Her mouth went dry as she snapped her gaze to meet his.

She observed the hunger burning in his vision. A hunger that matched hers. "Like what?"

He slowly trailed the tips of his fingers up her arms, causing her to shiver with anticipation. "Like you want to run that talented tongue of yours all over my body."

"Talented, huh?" Her voice was a whisper as his fingers neared her elbows.

"Very much so. What that tongue of yours can do should be illegal. Especially when it's wrapped around my cock." His fingers neared her shoulders as he dropped his head and placed a kiss along her collarbone. "God, the thought alone is enough to bring me to my knees and ready to do your bidding."

She tipped her head to the side to give him better access as her eyes fluttered closed, focusing solely on his lips and his touch. "You're pretty talented yourself. That tongue of yours knows just how to please me."

Liam's fingers continued up and over her slim shoulders and began their descent, down the sides of her full, perky breasts. A moan slipped from her mouth, and her hardened nipples poked against the thin fabric of her top. He continued down the curves of her sides, over the slope of her hips, before grabbing handfuls of her round ass and hoisting her up.

Amarah wrapped her legs around his waist and held on to his shoulders as he turned and started toward the deep end. When the water reached right below his strong pecs, he turned and placed her back against the side of the pool. She could feel his erection pressing into her aching center, and the feeling sent her hips grinding against it of their own accord.

"Shall we have a little contest, Cupcake? To see who's better with their tongue?" His voice was thick with lust as he placed soft kisses up her neck and bit the lobe of her ear. "To see who can make the other come the fastest?"

"You know how competitive I am. Are you sure you want to do this? I'd hate to see you lose."

Her nails dug lightly into his shoulders as she dragged them across his skin, causing him to groan in pleasure and rock his hips further against hers.

"Oh, Cupcake, even if I lose, I still win." His laugh was wicked. "Grip the edge of the pool."

His demand had a thrill shooting through her body that had her toes curling and desire flowing through her veins like heroin. She outstretched her arms to the side and gripped the concrete.

"When I get down there, throw those sexy legs over my shoulders and squeeze them around my head." Liam placed one hand on the edge of the pool, next to her head, and began to sink further into the water.

"Wait!" Amarah choked out. "What are you doing?"

"Going first." Desire danced through his eyes.

"What if it takes a little bit? You could drown."

Fear started to creep in. She was already worked up, not to mention being out in the open like this added a forbidden thrill that only turned her on further, but the average person could hold their breath for maybe a minute if they were lucky. Could he get her to finish that quickly?

She knew how to do CPR, but the last thing she wanted was her husband drowning while they were supposed to be on vacation. Her cheeks started to heat just thinking about how she'd begin to explain that situation to the paramedics.

"Did you forget what I used to do for a living?" His laugh was low, causing wings to explode within her. "I can hold my breath for three minutes. Give or take a few seconds."

He paused, allowing his eyes to rake over her soaked breasts. He placed his mouth over one mound and bit down on her nipple through the fabric. She gasped and then sighed as he repeated his actions against her other hardened nipple.

When he pulled back, he spoke again. "But I'll only need two."

He gave her a wink before he took a deep breath and slowly disappeared beneath the surface.

Cocky asshole, she laughed to herself.

When he was in position, she quickly placed her legs over his shoulders and squeezed, not hard enough to harm him, but enough to hold herself in place. She felt his free hand move her bikini bottoms to the side, and he wasted no time before his tongue started its assault. He licked up and down her center with vigor and determination to win.

"Oh, shit," she gasped as his mouth closed around her swollen clit and sucked hard against it.

Amarah had been right. The foreplay of his words and the sight of him, soaking wet, had her halfway to her orgasm. The tightening in the pit of her stomach constricted at an alarming rate, and she knew it wouldn't be long.

She felt two fingers sink deep inside her warmth as his mouth focused on her sensitive bundle. Her moans of pleasure filled the night air around the patio as her head fell back against the edge of the pool and her eyes fluttered closed. When he hooked his fingers up and worked her G-spot, she came undone.

Her finish shot through her as she cried his name and ground herself against his fingers and face, loving the way his rough beard felt against her smooth flesh. She wasn't sure how long he'd been down there, but his fingers were still working inside of her, so it couldn't have been three minutes yet. When she came down from her high, she felt Liam's fingers withdraw and readjust her bottoms back into place.

He surfaced slowly with a satisfied grin on his handsome face. "I believe that was only a minute and a half." Pure cockiness filled his tone.

"Bullshit!" She panted. "There's no way you held your breath, got me off, and kept count all at the same time."

"Shall I do it again?" he asked and slowly began to sink.

"No!" she protested.

Her clit was so sensitive, it would be too much and hurt if he went again.

Liam chuckled and grabbed her legs, wrapping them around his waist so his hips met hers again. He cupped her ass and turned, starting toward the shallow end.

"Stop!" Amarah demanded. "Where are you going?"

"To the shallow end where my hips are above the water."

"Absolutely not!" she protested. "Go back to the side of the pool."

"Absolutely not," he shot back. "You can't hold your breath that long, and I won't risk drowning you for my own pleasure."

"I'm not backing down from this challenge." Her grin was wicked as she held his gaze. "I'm going to win, and I won't even need to use my hands."

His eyes darkened, but he did as she said, moving back to the edge of the pool. The water resting at his ribcage would put it at her nose if she stood flat-footed. She could see the hesitation that flashed through his face, but she knew he trusted her, which filled her with pride and confidence. When his back was against the pool wall, he released his hold on her as she gripped the side with one hand.

"Pull down your trunks," she commanded him, a thrill shooting through her at his obedience.

Though the water distorted the image, when she glanced down, she knew he was exposed and ready for her. She held his gaze for a moment, heat sparkling through her irises that mirrored the pool before she took a few slow deep inhales, then three quick breaths, and disappeared beneath the water.

With one hand braced on the edge of the pool, she wrapped her legs around his and held onto his ass with her other hand. When Amarah was in place without fear of floating back up, she opened her mouth as he guided himself inside. She felt Liam's body jerk as the heat of her mouth closed around his thickness.

She wasted no time, bobbing her head up and down while her tongue ran long passes down the sides of his veiny shaft. She felt his hand grip her messy bun as she forced herself to take him deeper until he hit the back of her throat. This was the sweet spot. She knew if she deep-throated him over and over, she would have him finishing in no time.

And she was right. When she felt her lungs begin to scream, she felt his cock flexing against the roof of her mouth as he came, spilling his hot release down her throat. When she knew he had emptied himself, she withdrew him from her mouth and swallowed before surfacing and taking a deep breath of sweet air.

"Fuck, Cupcake." He tucked himself back into his trunks and pulled her against him, her legs wrapping around his waist.

"How long was that?" she asked with a satisfied smile as he swiped her wet hair out of her face.

"I don't care. You win." He panted and kissed her passionately.

CHAPTER 14

A soft click roused Cami Evans from sleep. She'd always been a light sleeper, unlike her husband Parker, who could sleep through a tornado blowing through a nuclear power plant. Her groggy eyes fluttered open as she recalled her foreign surroundings through a hazy fog.

Their room at the resort was simple but elegant. A calming tan painted the walls, light hardwood planks lined the floor, and the dark-stained wooden furnishings were kept minimal. A plush queen-sized bed, two nightstands, each topped with a small lamp, and a six-drawer dresser topped with a mirror.

She lazily blinked the blurriness away as she squinted toward the red numbers illuminating the alarm clock that topped the dresser across the room. It was just after two in the morning. Their room was nearly as dark as the Mariana Trench, making it difficult to make out details. All she could detect through the shadows were solid, unmoving patches of more darkness where each piece of furniture resided.

She turned her head to the right, reached over, and placed a hand gently on her husband's arm, making sure he wasn't the cause of the noise that woke her. His soft, steady breathing was the only sound to be heard around them.

An uneasy feeling began to settle deep within her chest, but because she couldn't see or hear anything out of place, she pushed it aside, chalking it up to their foreign surroundings. She rolled flat on her back as she rested her head back down on the fluffy pillow and adjusted the plush covers around her chest. It didn't take long before her eyes fluttered closed as she began to slowly drift back to sleep.

A gloved hand cupped her mouth, forcing her to remain quiet, causing her honey gaze to shoot open wide in pure terror. A second later, she felt something akin to cold metal slide effortlessly across her neck. The unknown object emitted searing pain like she'd never known before, erupting through her entire body. She tried to scream, but the hand over her mouth held her firmly in place, preventing her from calling for help.

Everything happened so fast that Cami didn't stand a chance at fending off her attacker. The darkness concealed them, as if they had made a bargain with the shadows to become one with them while they carried out this nefarious act. Was it Parker? Was it someone else? Was she asleep, and all of this was just some horrible nightmare?

That's it. A nightmare. She'd had vivid dreams before. One of the side effects of the prescription medication she took for her chronic headaches was such vivid dreams that half the time she had to discuss them with her husband the next morning to figure out if they were real or purely a figment of her imagination. This was nothing different. She simply needed to wake herself up as she learned to do each time before.

Before she could attempt to rouse herself, she felt something warm running down the side of her neck as it began to pool beneath her body. Her mind worked frantically to identify the substance. Was it water? Was there a leak in the roof? Was she sweating from the nightmare? Fear widened her irises even further as reality quickly sank in. This was no nightmare, and it was her blood that was now soaking into the mattress beneath her at an alarming rate. The agonizing pain across her throat only served to solidify that fact.

Her fight or flight instincts kicked in, sending her hand up to grip the wrist that covered her mouth in an attempt to remove it, but with each passing second, her vision began to fade, and she grew weak as a cold numbness began to creep through her body like fog through a graveyard. She screamed inside her mind like she'd never done before, praying Parker, anyone, would sense her distress and come to her aid.

However, deep down, in the pit of her soul, she knew this was it. She was dying… She couldn't die. She'd just celebrated her thirty-second birthday three weeks ago. She and her husband planned to start trying for kids over the next year. They had their whole lives ahead of them. In less than two minutes, her entire future had been stolen from her. All her hopes and dreams, gone.

With each passing second, she felt her subconscious begin to slip, the pool of blood gathering beneath her grew, and in a matter of seconds, her body lay motionless beneath the covers. Her golden eyes, once so bright and full of life, dimmed and glazed over as they stared lifelessly at the ceiling.

Hunter Gatlin's gaze shot open to the sound of someone screaming for help. He felt Serenity jerk awake beside him, but his mind was focused elsewhere. In a matter of seconds, he was out of bed, threw on a pair of black basketball shorts that lay nearby, and rushed out their door. Liam met him in the hallway, shirtless with a pair of blue plaid pajama pants slung low on his hips. Their masked expressions mirrored each other's, though concern swam in their vision.

The sound of a door opening a few feet down the hall sent both their heads jerking in that direction. Parker Evans stumbled backward out of his room, causing Hunter's blood to run ice-cold through his veins. Parker wore only a pair of sweats, but his bare torso had smeared crimson all over it. A sight Hunter was all too familiar with. Blood...

Was it his? Did he hurt himself? Did Cami hurt him? Did he hurt Cami? *What in the fuck is going on?* It took all of half a second for numerous theories to fly through his skilled mind as he took in the scene unfolding before him. Then, his vision narrowed on the large, bloodied knife Parker clutched in a trembling hand. His stomach pitched, fearing the worst.

Did this man hurt his wife? How badly was Cami injured? His natural instinct to protect urged him to subdue the threat so he could get to Cami and try to help her before it was too late. If it wasn't already too late.

If there was one thing Hunter knew for certain in life, it was that he was put on this earth to protect those who couldn't protect themselves. He'd known it from a young age. He'd always been the one standing up to bullies in school, getting his brothers out of any trouble they found themselves in, being the designated driver for any friends who drank too much at parties in high school.

That's why he didn't second-guess himself when he stepped into the recruiters' office the day he graduated high school, diploma in hand, and signed over his soul to the government for the next few years. It's also why he founded Red Sky Security after separating from the Navy. Protecting people was in his blood.

"Parker," Hunter called to the man. His voice was calm but radiated power.

Parker didn't seem to hear him. The man took another unsteady step backward as he kept his gaze fixed on something inside his room.

"Parker," Hunter called again, his tone a bit more assertive. The man's head slowly turned toward Hunter, and the look of fear and panic in his slate eyes gave Hunter a very bad feeling. "Drop the knife." He instructed calmly now that he had the man's attention.

Parker's brows pinched together as he slightly cocked his head as if in confusion. Then, his eyes slowly fell to the tainted blade gripped in his bleached grasp. He quickly tossed it aside as if the metal burned his palm.

The moment the knife hit the floor, Hunter crossed the hallway toward him in a flash, gripped his shoulders, and swept the man's feet out from beneath him. Parker crashed to the floor as Hunter flipped him over, secured his wrists behind him, and pressed his knee into his back, holding Parker firmly in place.

Parker groaned as his arms were wrenched behind his back, but he didn't try to resist. Liam knelt next to Hunter a few seconds later as he began to bind Parker's wrists with a long white shoelace he'd taken off a white sneaker that lay just inside Parker's room. When the man was no longer a threat, both Liam and Hunter stood, observing that a crowd had now gathered in the hallway. All the couples in their pajamas with disheveled hair and sleep still lacing their features stood with looks of confusion, fear, and horror as they tried to understand what was happening.

Liam disappeared into Parker's room and came back a minute

later, slightly shaking his head toward Hunter.

"Fuck," he cursed beneath his breath.

He didn't need Liam to say it aloud. He knew that Cami was dead. He took a step in the doorway as his expert eyes traveled around the room. He observed no signs of a struggle, no signs of forced entry, and the deep, nasty canyon that now separated the flesh of Cami's neck. When he turned back toward the hallway, Jade Munro and Declan McCarthy began pushing their way through the crowd of guests.

"What's going on? I heard shouting," Jade asked frantically as she secured a black silk robe around her slender frame.

"Call 911. Cami's dead," Hunter instructed, his voice void of emotion.

Unfortunately, this wasn't the first dead body he'd seen. As a SEAL, he'd been trained to control his emotions and keep a level head in situations like these. Though he'd been out of the Navy for years now, he reverted to those days as if no time had passed. The rigorous training he'd been forced to go through didn't simply vanish overnight.

Numerous gasps sounded through the hallway when other guests heard the devastating news.

"Holy shit!" Jade brought up a shaking hand to clutch her chest. Then her chocolate gaze fell to Parker, who lay motionless, face down in the hallway as if he'd already accepted his fate. "Did he…" She trailed off as if it was physically painful to finish her question.

Hunter watched as Declan peered around his large shoulder, and his eyes bulged with shock. The gruesome scene behind him caused Declan's pasty complexion to pale further.

"I'm not sure," Hunter answered honestly.

Did Parker do it? *Could* he do it? He'd only met them last

night at dinner. From what little he observed, they seemed happy. They both had wandering eyes, but he doubted that was cause for murder. For all he knew, they could've had an open relationship. No one truly knows what transpires in a relationship behind closed doors.

From what he gathered as he scanned the room, Parker was the best suspect. Unless... *Unless the murderer had a key.* That thought sent his vision scanning the small crowd of guests as if observing everyone in a new light. Could one of them be a killer?

Jade nodded her head apprehensively, turned, and disappeared down the hallway in search of her phone, with Declan following close behind. Amarah and Serenity had stood in front of their doors, clutched in each other's arms as they watched with concern and worry. They finally left their spots as they moved forward.

"Are you ok?" Serenity asked as she wrapped her arms around Hunter's bare chest.

"I'm a lot better than him right now," Hunter joked, pointing toward where Parker lay prone in the hallway, but his voice was solemn.

Serenity slowly rose to her tippy toes and peered around his broad shoulder. Her movements were hesitant as if she knew she wouldn't like what she was about to see, but he knew her curiosity was getting the better of her. If she wanted to look, he wouldn't stop her. This wouldn't be the first dead body she'd seen. Not after what transpired last year when she'd been kidnapped by Jack Maddlen. Though he wished it were he who stopped Jack, he knew Serenity had to be the one to put an end to her stalker.

He felt her body lock up as she took in the horrid scene behind him. She averted her gaze and buried her head in his chest. As he began rubbing soothing circles across her back, he spared a glance toward Liam and Amarah.

Amarah, much like Serenity, braved a look but turned away hurriedly, hesitated for a minute, threw her hand over her mouth, and sprinted back to their room. Liam hesitated, his green irises shifting between his room and Parker.

"Go. I'll watch him," Hunter said, understanding the inner battle his friend fought.

Liam gave him an appreciative nod before disappearing into his room and closing the door behind him.

It took the authorities numerous hours to arrive by boat. Everyone had returned to their rooms, and Hunter never once let Parker out of his sight. He sat in the hallway, his darkly inked forearms resting atop his bent knees, and his head tilted back against the wall. Parker never once tried to make a break for it or even fight against his restraints.

All the man did was lie flat on the ground, his head turned toward the wall as he muttered his wife's name along with things like "I didn't do it" and "I'm so sorry." Hunter recognized the signs of shock, which made him further question whether the man was truly innocent. He could very well just be a good actor.

It took the police another couple of hours to bag up Cami's body, process the crime scene, thoroughly question every guest, and take Parker into custody. By the time the authorities finally left the island, Hunter had been mentally drained. He entered his room, where Serenity waited, and fell back on the bed, blowing out a long breath.

She came to lie beside him as he wrapped her in a strong embrace. "How are you holding up?"

"I should be asking you that, Angel. I'm no stranger to situations like these."

"I just can't..." She trailed off and inhaled an unsteady breath. "Cami was so full of life at dinner. I can't get my mind to recognize what I saw in that room with the woman I met last night."

"I know." He pulled her tighter against himself and placed a soft kiss atop her raven hair, allowing her scent to center him.

"Do you really think her husband did it?"

"Honestly?" He exhaled harshly. "I have no clue."

CHAPTER 15

With the eventful start to everyone's morning, no one made it to breakfast. Amarah Godrik felt exhausted come lunchtime. She had been roused suddenly by Parker screaming for help and Liam jumping out of bed and rushing out the door without a word or concern for his own safety.

Pride had bloomed inside of her at knowing her husband was the kind of man who'd risk his life to help a complete stranger. When she emerged from their room, she and Serenity stood clutched in each other's embrace as they stared in confusion at why Liam and Hunter had Parker restrained and lying in the hallway.

But when her eyes took in the bloodied knife that lay on the floor a few feet from Parker and the red smears that covered his exposed torso like an abstract painting, a dreadful feeling took root in the pit of her stomach. That feeling was confirmed when she braved a peek into Parker and Cami's room. She wasn't someone who grew squeamish at the sight of blood, but what she witnessed had her heaving up what little she had left in her stomach from the night before.

No matter how hard she tried, she couldn't get the image out of her mind as if it had been seared into her brain with a branding iron. Liam had rushed into their bathroom a few seconds later and held her hair as she dry heaved a few more times, rubbing soothing circles across her back. Once her body had calmed down and they'd been questioned by the police, her husband had lain with her in bed and held her all morning.

As everyone filed into the dining room for lunch, there was a heaviness in the air, and hardly anyone spoke. Most likely still in shock from the earlier events of the day. She knew she was. Once everyone was seated around the table, Jade Munro pushed her chair back, the wood scraping against the floor, and stood.

"Well." She released a heavy breath. "I don't think any of us expected this vacation to kick off with a start like this morning. It is with a heavy heart that I can confirm Cami Evans has passed away. The details are still unknown as the police continue their investigation. My thoughts and prayers go out to Cami's family."

Jade paused for a moment as she cleared her throat of the emotion that seemed to have gotten lodged within. "Though our week started with a grave loss, please don't let that deter you from having a relaxing vacation. This time is about celebrating you and the love you've all found."

Jade sat back in her chair as servers brought out lunch for everyone. Amarah didn't miss the way Declan's eyes followed every movement Jade made and the way he clung to every word she spoke. She wondered if there was anything going on between the two. If so, Amarah was happy for her. She knew Jade had been dealt a rough hand, and if Declan made her happy, Jade deserved every bit of it. Everyone deserves a second chance at love.

The servers removed the silver domed lids that covered the plates that were set in front of each guest. Deli sandwiches, crispy french fries, and a small bowl of mixed fruit were revealed.

Amarah's stomach was still a bit queasy, but she forced herself to eat. She needed to replenish her energy after emptying her stomach all morning.

Now that she was eating for two, it was pertinent to take care of herself. The reminder of the baby now growing inside of her had her hand cupping her lower stomach beneath the table, away from any wandering eyes that might notice. It was confirmed at a doctor's appointment she had last week that she was around eight weeks pregnant. She'd thought this vacation would be the perfect place to tell Liam the news.

She'd tried to tell him last night, but they were interrupted by Hunter and had to go down for dinner. She'd played through the motions of pretending to sip her champagne and nearly blew it when the smell of dinner made her gag. But she calmed herself with slow breaths, and thankfully, the nausea passed.

The way Hunter had looked at her during dinner as if he suspected, made her nervous. She wanted to be the one to tell her husband. It would kill him if he found out from anyone else. Thankfully, Hunter never mentioned it. Though he didn't strike her as the kind to voice secrets like that. He seemed more of the kind to keep his theories to himself and watch them play out. Maybe he didn't suspect a thing, and she was merely being paranoid.

"I've been pondering it all morning," Serenity spoke in a hushed voice to the group after the servers left the room. "Parker's a doctor. He took a vow to help make people better, not hurt them. I don't think he did it."

"There was no sign of forced entry or a struggle when I examined the space. Plus, he was clutching the murder weapon when we found him. If he didn't do it, he better have one hell of a defense attorney," Liam said, his tone neutral and free of suspicion.

"If he didn't do it, I couldn't imagine being in his shoes right now. Waking up to that, the sight of your loved one's body in such a horrific manner…" Amarah trailed off, unable to finish and banishing that line of thought from her mind.

She felt Liam's hand rest atop her thigh, and she instantly relaxed. She turned her head to the right and gave him a thankful smile as she started picking at her food.

"He was a neurosurgeon, right?" Serenity inquired after popping a crispy fry drenched in ketchup into her mouth.

"That's right," Amarah confirmed, recalling the way Cami had bragged about it last night. "Why do you ask?"

"Well, I'm no expert by any means." She laughed lightly to herself and shook her head. "But, that was a…" She paused, trying to find the right words not to offend the dead. "That was a nasty gash. Shouldn't it be more… I don't know… cleaner, if a surgeon had done it?"

Amarah didn't miss the surprise that showed within Hunter's blue and hazel eyes as he gazed at his fiancée. Approval pulled his lips into a grin that she'd picked up on such a little detail most would've missed.

"Maybe he did it that way on purpose so the authorities wouldn't suspect him, just like you," Hunter suggested, causing Serenity's face to scrunch as she pondered her theory further.

"Maybe it was a crime of passion?" Amarah's tone rose towards the end, signaling her uncertainty.

"Crimes of passion don't generally happen in the middle of the night after one's been sleeping," Hunter added as he took a large bite of his sandwich.

"How do you know when it happened?" Serenity inquired, her dark brows furrowing.

"We've seen enough dead bodies in our time to be able to roughly predict how long they've been lying there," Liam added.

Hunter nodded his agreement, his mouth full of food.

"Oh, right…" both Amarah and Serenity said in unison as their gazes dropped to their plates in front of them.

Most of the table was quiet as everyone finished eating. The sound of a chair scooting back across the room drew everyone's attention to Declan, whose skin appeared less pale than it did after seeing Cami's body.

"Once everyone is finished eating, we ask that you change into your swimsuits and meet us out at the pool for music, drinks, and great conversation." Declan's attempt at a bright smile caused the freckles that dotted his face to pop.

Though spirits were low at the beginning of lunch, the energy in the room began to lift, and by the end, everyone seemed almost back to normal. Almost.

"I feel… guilty… if we have fun given what happened this morning," Amarah admitted as she tied the skirt cover that matched her swimsuit into a knot on her hip.

Her pink polka-dot bikini played well with her sun-kissed skin. She was thankful she was in the early stages of her pregnancy and not showing in the slightest yet. How she'd cover a baby bump without anyone knowing would have proven rather difficult.

"Why?"

Liam stepped out of the bathroom wearing only a pair of dark green swim trunks that stopped at his lower thigh.

A happy sigh fell from her lips at the sight of all those lean muscles on his tall frame put on full display. His torso was free of hair, leaving nothing to obstruct the view of his gorgeously tanned and heavily tattooed flesh.

"I don't know. Because Cami died."

She forced her gaze to her husband's beautiful irises. She had to, or else she'd push him down on the bed and run her tongue all over his exposed skin, and they'd miss the pool party. Maybe it was the pregnancy messing with her hormones, or maybe it was the simple fact that her husband was a very attractive man, but these last few weeks, she couldn't get enough of him.

Morning, afternoon, night, it didn't matter. All she seemed to think about was getting her husband alone so she could use his body. She felt the heat of a blush sting her cheeks as she forced away the very inappropriate images her brain conjured up as if it lived to torment her.

"People die every day, Cupcake, but the world keeps moving forward. It has to. Don't feel guilty about continuing to live your life while you still have one. Tomorrow is never guaranteed."

His words were gentle, but there was intense emotion swirling through his eyes upon finishing that last sentence. As if it held some deeper, hidden meaning. She wanted to prod further, to ask what was bothering him, but she figured it had to do with Jade. Being close to a reminder of a brother you've lost must dredge up old, nasty wounds that never fully healed. Instead, she let it go.

"Plus, we don't know the truth about their relationship. Yeah, they played the happy couple in public, but they could be entirely different people behind closed doors."

Her husband crossed the room as he ran the tips of his fingers down the outside of her arms. Goosebumps rose along the path he trailed, and her breath hitched. As if sensing the shift within her, he reached a hand around the back of her head, rolled up the single French braid her golden strands were tied into around his knuckles, and gave it a gentle pull, forcing her chin up.

"Now, let's go downstairs before I push you against the wall, pull those tiny bottoms of yours aside, and fuck you until you scream so loud, they'll hear you over the music," he growled against the shell of her ear in a low and hungry tone.

Amarah let out a soft moan at the threat, completely ready to skip the party and stay locked in their room with her husband. The grip on her braid tightened as she felt Liam pull her flat against his hard front as if he had come to the same conclusion. Right before his lips connected with hers, a knock sounded at their door.

"Someone better be dying!" he shouted, but then cursed under his breath as he felt his wife's body tense beneath him and knew that, given this morning's events, the joke was ill-timed.

"Someone will be if you force me to socialize alone." She heard Hunter's deep voice sound through the door. "Ouch, what was that for?" he muttered.

She wondered if Serenity had hit him for that little comment. Amarah chuckled lightly. She was starting to like those two very much. Serenity seemed like a genuinely good person, and Amarah could use more of those in her life. Plus, she was happy that Liam and Hunter were still so close, even after being separated from the Navy for years now.

CHAPTER 16

Music playing from speakers mounted on the back of the mansion filled the air around her as Jade Munro stepped out the back door and onto the concrete patio that surrounded the massive inground pool. A bar had been constructed and was serving alcoholic beverages of all kinds.

Before she greeted anyone and began mingling, her bare feet carried her straight toward the bar, knowing she was going to need one hell of a stiff drink after this morning's fiasco. After a minute, the bartender handed her a chilled glass of vodka soda, heavy on the vodka. She gave the bartender an appreciative smile and turned, allowing her eyes to skim over the few guests who had already shown up.

After a long gulp of her drink, she took a deep breath, cleared her mind, and walked up to Colton and Myles King, who stood to the side of the pool. Each man had a glass of amber liquid clutched in their grasp.

"Damn girl, that swimsuit was made for you!" Myles gushed as his brown gaze took in the dark crimson one-piece bathing suit she paired with a black sash tied at her slender waist. The sides were cut out, showing off the creamy skin that covered her ribs.

She beamed. "Oh, thanks." The compliment slightly lifted her spirit. "Where do you guys call home?"

"We're from Washington," Colton answered. "The state, not D.C. I know, not as cool, but we love it there."

She'd never been to Washington. The constant cloud cover and rainy weather scared her. She'd fallen into a nasty depression after the loss of her husband and figured that type of weather would only make it worse. That was the last thing she needed.

"What about you?" Myles inquired.

She took a sip of her drink before answering. "Virginia."

Colton's face lit up, and his smile was nearly blinding. "I've always wanted to visit Virginia. So much culture and history everywhere you look."

"He's a high school history teacher," Myles explained. "Anything old world *really* gets him excited."

It was easy for Jade to spot the love he held for his husband purely in the way he peered at Colton. A jolt of jealousy and hurt spread through her chest. She used to have someone she looked at the same way these two gaze at each other.

Before she could linger further on that loss, a woman's laughter drew her attention to the right in time to see Aaron Davis step behind his wife, Quinn, wrap his strong arms around her middle, and bury his face in her neck. The sight before her triggered a memory, sending her back to another time and place.

MAY 2010

Jade exited the car and popped open the trunk so she could gather her black cap and gown that was neatly folded to the side. Strong arms came up from behind her, and she was pulled against a hard and warm chest. A scream got caught in her throat as the stranger buried his face in the hollow of her slender neck.

"I'm so damn proud of you," Bryson Munro whispered against her sensitive skin, causing goosebumps to rise and a delicious shiver to roll over her as her body began to awaken.

Her fear quickly turned into excitement at knowing the love of her life was there to celebrate with her. The day she'd worked so hard for had finally arrived. She was graduating from college today. After four years of hard work, stressful midterms, numerous papers, and a few all-nighters, it was finally over.

The two-hour drive to Virginia State University with her parents had been quiet. Not a strained or awkward one, but rather a comfortable silence. Though she knew her mother and father loved her completely, they were never a chatty bunch.

She turned around in his hold and threw her arms around his neck.

"You came!" She beamed.

"Are you kidding me? I wouldn't miss this for the world." He gave her an award-winning smile that nearly brought her to her knees. His whisky vision trailed down her front, taking in her little black dress with straps that connected behind her neck and hugged her chest and curves tightly before flowing down and stopping mid-thigh, making her creamy skin pop against the soft material. "You look incredible," he whispered, almost in disbelief.

The last three months since they'd met had been nothing short of magical. She wasn't sure how it was possible, but with each passing day, she found herself growing more in love with him. Although she was still discovering new things about him, and would still for years to come, there were already countless things she admired and adored. His strength, his kindness, his loyalty, and his ability to push her to be the best version of herself she could be were just a few among the many.

She claimed his lips in a lover's embrace as warmth ignited low in her core. His hold on her tightened possessively as he deepened the kiss, and their tongues entangled in a familiar dance.

The sound of a throat being cleared pulled them back to reality as they broke their kiss. She peered over Bryson's shoulder to find three tall and intimidating men standing a few feet away. Liam Godrik, Travis Patterson, and Hunter Gatlin were dressed in fine clothes, just like Bryson, that were at complete odds with their rugged demeanors.

Then her chocolate eyes scanned over the fourth person. A beautiful redhead who had her arm looped through Travis's. Her genuine and kind smile was a breath of fresh air in a world full of fake people.

Bryson released his hold on her, and she quickly hid the disappointment that blossomed at the loss of contact. "Jade, this is Sandra, Travis's wife."

Sandra released her husband's arm, walked over to Jade, and pulled her into a tight hug. "It's so good to finally meet you. I've heard so many wonderful things about you. You're just as beautiful as Bryson described. Congratulations, by the way." She pulled away, and her deep blue eyes sparked with joy, causing the freckles that dotted beneath her gaze to pop against her creamy complexion.

"Thank you." Jade couldn't help but laugh as she tried not to blush.

Hunter, Travis, and Liam took turns congratulating her, and she smiled and nodded at each one. She adorned her cap and gown and began to pose for photos with her parents, Bryson, and even a group photo with everyone.

"Now, let's get you inside so I can cheer as you walk across that stage." Bryson interlaced his fingers with hers and escorted her toward the large gym, following the crowd of people.

He gave her a quick kiss on the lips before he reluctantly released her hand and went to find seats in the family section. She found her spot in the student section and waited anxiously as everyone filed in and got settled.

The ceremony dragged on, like someone trying to walk through a pool of molasses, and she couldn't stop her eyes from drifting to the family section and landing on a familiar pair of golden irises. Each time she glanced at Bryson, he'd make a funny face or would make a silly motion that would cause her to giggle to herself. Sometimes he'd wink or blow her a kiss that had her shifting in her seat as she clenched her thighs together to relieve the annoying ache between them.

The announcer began calling names, and it was finally her turn. She climbed the few stairs onto the platform, whispered her name to the announcer, and waited.

"Jade Hayashi," the announcer spoke into the microphone, and she began to walk toward the center of the stage.

A group of loud cheers rang out through the gym, echoing off the walls as she glanced to see her parents, Bryson, and his friends all standing, clapping, screaming, and whooping obnoxiously. She felt her cheeks begin to color and her eyes sting with emotion.

How did she ever get so lucky to meet a man like him? She was thankful for the blessing, and she reminded herself to never take it for granted. She focused her attention back on stage as she shook a few hands and received her diploma. After she departed the stage and sat back in her chair, the rest of the ceremony passed in a blur. Before she knew it, the crowd was tossing their caps into the air and scattering like cockroaches in search of their friends and families.

One of the curses of being short was that she'd always get lost in a busy crowd. It was always challenging to find her way or locate someone. Thankfully, it didn't take long for Bryson to find her as he pulled her into a tight hug and placed a few kisses on her neck. The rest of her entourage came trailing behind as she hugged everyone, and they all congratulated her again.

"Time to celebrate!" Travis sported a devious smile, his ocean gaze sparkling with mischief.

"Your ability to turn anything into a celebration is alarming." Liam chuckled and shook his head.

"There's nothing wrong with that," Travis defended himself.

"There is if the woman doesn't want to celebrate," Hunter drawled as he motioned with his hand toward Jade. "Why not ask her instead of assuming?"

Travis sighed dramatically before turning his attention to Jade, who'd stood there quietly as she watched the chosen brothers tease each other. He pleaded with his blue eyes. "Would you like to go out to celebrate this incredible kick-ass achievement?"

"I don't know." She grimaced. "It's been a long day. I think I'd rather just go home and curl up on the couch with some popcorn and a movie." She watched as Travis's shoulders deflated and sadness lined his angular features. She couldn't help but laugh. "I'm only teasing. What did you have in mind?"

The wicked expression that crossed his face had her already regretting her decision. "I know of a place."

"I doubt she wants to go to a strip club," Hunter teased as he ran a large hand over the scruff of his brown beard.

"Why would I ever waste an ungodly amount of money in a place where you can't even touch the girls? You always end up leaving broke with a bad case of blue balls. I've got my own stripper who'll gladly let me touch and happily fuck her."

Travis pulled Sandra to his side and gave her a passionate kiss on the lips. When Sandra pulled back, her face was almost as red as her hair as she tried to bury her face in her hands. Jade couldn't help but admire their connection and hoped she and Bryson would work out like those two.

Bryson turned to Jade's father and spoke. "Don't worry, Mr. Hayashi. I'll bring her home safely."

"Of that, I have no doubt," her father said, giving his daughter's boyfriend a curt nod.

With that, Jade bid her parents farewell, intertwined her fingers with Bryson's, and stayed close to his side as he led them through the packed parking lot back to his truck.

"Jade?" A voice that sounded miles away yanked her from a pleasant memory, filled with unending love and happiness, back to the dark and dreary present, filled only with pain.

Jade shook her head clear to see mirroring expressions of concern marring Myles and Colton's faces. That's right... She wasn't in Virginia. She was on a tiny island in the Bahamas. It had been almost a decade since the events of that memory transpired, and if she focused hard enough, she could still feel the warmth of Bryson's hand against hers, the strength of his fingers intertwined with hers.

She subconsciously rubbed her fingers together, as if allowing herself one more second to reminisce before she cleared any emotions from her voice and addressed the two confused men standing before her. Men she was in the middle of a conversation with before she was teleported to a much happier time.

"Please forgive me." She placed her hand against her heart and gave them as bright a smile as she could manage. "Something snagged my attention, and I missed the last thing you said."

She motioned with her hand for the men, whichever one had been talking, to continue. Tears threatened to sting her vision as emotions lodged in her throat, but she dug deep, gathering every ounce of strength she could muster to control her emotions before they ran amok.

CHAPTER 17

With fingers interlocked with her husband's, Amarah Godrik stepped out the back door and onto the concrete patio that surrounded the massive inground pool, followed closely by Hunter and Serenity. People dressed in various styles of swimwear were gathered in small clusters here and there, lost in the pleasures of conversation.

Her vision quickly found a short raven-haired woman with creamy skin standing across the pool, talking to the couple she hadn't had the chance to meet yet. It was no surprise to find Declan McCarthy next to her. *They do make a cute couple.* The thought had a small smile tugging one corner of her mouth up.

"Do you want something to drink?" Liam inquired as he led them toward the bar.

"A water, please," Amarah answered.

She felt a gaze on her that didn't belong to her husband, and her eyes shifted to Hunter, finding his unique vision studying her.

"Since my stomach was upset this morning, I don't think putting alcohol on it is a good idea," she added quickly, hoping that Hunter would buy the excuse and not suspect anything else.

He seemed to, since his gaze shifted to Serenity as he asked what she wanted to drink. After everyone had a glass in their hand, they made their way to an empty spot off to the side. The last couple they'd yet to meet made their way over to them.

The woman was dressed in a one-shouldered one-piece swimsuit with a matching sash tied around her waist. It was dark blue with the sides cut out to show off her golden skin beneath. Her long brunette hair fell in luscious waves down her back, and her eyes were the shade of rich honey.

"I'm Quinn Davis. This is my husband, Aaron." She motioned with a well-manicured hand to the dark-skinned man next to her.

Her Eastern New English accent was thick and beautiful. Amarah wondered exactly where she was from. Massachusetts, Rhode Island, or Connecticut, maybe?

Aaron's black hair was cut short, his squared jawline was free of hair, and his body was tall and slender like a runner. A patch of dark curls dusted his muscular chest, and his red swim trunks stopped just above his knees.

"Nice to meet both of you," Liam greeted them with a smile. "I'm Liam Godrik. This is my wife, Amarah. That's Hunter Gatlin and his fiancée, Serenity Jinx."

"It's a pleasure to meet you," Aaron said, giving Amarah and Serenity each a dazzling smile as his gaze discreetly observed their slender forms.

Though not discreetly enough, since Amarah was able to catch it. She didn't miss how Quinn's vision drank in both Hunter and Liam as well. Much like how Cami and Parker did last night at dinner.

"I have to give you ladies props. You snagged yourselves a couple of very handsome gentlemen," she practically purred.

"Thanks." Serenity arched a brow at the woman for her

boldness.

Good to know I'm not the only one who noticed her lustful stares.

"Would either of you lovely couples be interested in trading for a night?" Quinn sucked her bottom lip between her teeth as she continued to shift her gaze between Liam and Hunter. "Or both? I don't mind. The more the merrier."

Hunter and Liam both nearly choked on their drinks at her boldness, which only made Quinn's smile grow wider and her honey eyes sparkle with mischief.

"I'm sorry, what do you mean exactly? Trade what?" Amarah asked hesitantly, but a feeling in the pit of her stomach told her the answer before Quinn voiced it.

Her laugh was melodic as she answered. "Partners, of course."

"Oh, are y'all swingers?" Serenity questioned, her tone filled with nothing but genuine curiosity.

"Yes, ma'am," Aaron drawled, shooting Serenity a wink that had a slight blush creeping across her cheeks at his boldness.

"Thanks for the offer," Hunter said after recovering from being taken by surprise. "But I can assure you, neither myself nor Liam likes to share."

Quinn let out a breathy sigh. "That's a shame." She stuck her full bottom lip out in a pout before speaking again. "Well, if any of you change your mind, you know where to find us. Come on, baby. I'm in need of a refill."

Quinn shot them a quick wink before turning and swaying her hips as she walked away. Aaron gave the group one last smile before following his wife toward the bar.

"I wouldn't have minded sharing." Serenity looked toward Amarah. "Don't you agree?"

She gave Amarah a look that said play along and a wicked

smile tried to tug at her lips. *Oh, yeah. I like her a lot.* Amarah loved messing with her husband any chance she got, so she was more than happy to tease back.

"Definitely! You shouldn't have answered for me." Amarah let out a disappointed sigh. "I think it might've been fun."

Both men's heads snapped to their women.

"You've got three seconds, Cupcake, to tell me you're joking before I throw you over my shoulder and haul you upstairs," Liam threatened.

"Three seconds? How generous, brother." Hunter's voice was low and dangerous. "I'm only giving you one, Angel."

Serenity and Amarah shared a look before doubling over in laughter.

"We're only teasing," Serenity forced the words out as she tried to catch her breath.

They were clutching their stomach by the time they composed themselves again. Both men let out a frustrated breath as Liam shook his head and Hunter pinched the bridge of his nose.

"Maybe introducing them was a bad idea," Hunter grumbled.

"I'm starting to think you're right." Liam took a long swig of his drink but couldn't stop the grin that pulled at one side of his lips.

Amarah and Serenity finally calmed down as they wiped the tears from their eyes and straightened. She caught movement out of the side of her eye and saw Colton and Myles King approaching with warm and welcoming smiles, both holding a fresh glass of amber liquid.

"You ladies look stunning!" Myles said by way of greeting. "Gentlemen." His tone dropped as his eyes drank in Hunter and Liam. He let out a small sigh before shaking his head clear. "I need to borrow your beautiful ladies for a moment. Girl talk." He shot a wink to Hunter and Liam, grabbed Serenity's free hand, and began walking off to the other end of the patio.

Amarah laughed and followed closely behind as Colton stayed back to chat with Hunter and Liam.

Myles stopped and turned toward them. He took a sip of his drink and winced at the burn. He opened his mouth to speak, but his eyes snagged on Amarah's glass, and his brows furrowed.

"Honey, are you drinking water?" Myles sounded almost appalled. "Don't you dare tell me you're trying to watch your figure?"

He dropped his brown vision down her front and back up.

"No," Amarah reassured him. "Just... after this morning, I'm not really in a drinking mood right now."

"This morning is exactly *why* you should be drinking." He laughed and shook his scotch at her playfully, causing the cubed ice to clink against the glass.

"What are your thoughts about it?" Serenity inquired.

Amarah's curiosity was piqued too, wondering what conclusion everyone else had come up with.

"Well, Colton thinks the husband did it. Typical." Myles rolled his eyes playfully. "But from what I gathered last night, Parker wouldn't hurt a fly. And Cami may have had a bold personality, but she didn't strike me as the kind to slit her own throat. Which means..." he paused dramatically, then dropped his voice to a hushed whisper, "that someone else killed her."

Serenity arched a thick brow as her vision darted around the crowd nervously. "You think there's a murderer among us?"

"Girl, the thought nearly has me ready to be on the next flight out of here. Unfortunately, the boat won't be back until the end of the week, which means we're stuck on this island, and I'm half tempted to barricade Colton and myself in our room until Friday." He held up his hand and shook his head as if he wanted no part in whatever sick game a potential murderer might be playing.

"I think that's a bit of a stretch." Amarah's voice was filled with apprehension.

Myles arched a thin brow at her in challenge. "Is it though?"

She didn't respond. What would she say? His theory was plausible, if a little farfetched. Her eyes landed on Liam across the way. And just like in the past, even before they were together, Liam felt the weight of her stare, and his green gaze shifted to meet hers. He gave her a grin and a wink before looking away and focusing back on his conversation.

Amarah, Serenity, and Myles lost track of time as they gossiped about anything and everything under the sun. She wasn't sure how much time had passed, but she found herself thankful for the distraction, so she didn't spend all day thinking about Cami and all the what-ifs that came with it.

"Excuse me, ladies, but I need to steal my husband back." Colton's rich voice gained their attention. His smile was kind and filled with admiration as he held out a hand toward his husband.

"Oh, all right." Myles gave a shy smile and placed his hand in Colton's. "We'll talk more later." He smiled as the two walked back toward the mansion.

Hunter and Liam joined them right as Serenity began to speak. "If you'll excuse me, I have to use the restroom."

"Same. I'll walk with you," Liam said, sparing a glance toward Hunter.

The two spoke with only their eyes as if they'd done that dozens of times in the past. Hunter gave her husband a nod, and Liam and

Serenity departed toward the house.

Amarah never once doubted Liam's faithfulness toward her. He'd cut his own hand off before he ever cheated on her, and she knew that with every fiber of her being. He most likely did need to use the restroom, but she knew he wanted to go with Serenity to make sure she was safe. The fact that Liam also thought there could be a murderer among them only made the uneasy feeling in the pit of her stomach worsen.

"So." Hunter's deep voice drew her from her thoughts. "How far along are you?"

His question caught her off guard, nearly causing her to choke on her water. She coughed several times as she wiped the spilled liquid off her chin.

"I'm sorry. What?"

"Don't play dumb with me." He chuckled, flashing her an amused look. "I'm a very observant man."

She let out a long breath, and her shoulders dropped. "Eight weeks. Give or take a few days. How did you know?" Her eyes widened in fear as her gaze dropped to her stomach before shooting back up to his. "I can't be showing yet. Am I?" Panic laced her words.

"You're not, I promise." He gave her a reassuring smile, and she blew out a breath.

Her relief turned into a grimace. "What gave it away then?"

"Maybe it was the fact that you were apprehensive about accepting the champagne last night. Or maybe it was how you only pretended to drink it. Then again, it could've been how you nearly threw up at the smell of dinner last night. Or maybe it was how you actually threw up this morning. No, hold on. I think it was the fact that you chose to drink water."

His eyes dropped to the glass she clutched in her hand.

"Alright, alright, jeez." She shook her head but grinned. "I feel bad for Serenity. She isn't able to sneak around or surprise you with anything, is she?"

"Nope." He grinned back. "Congratulations, by the way."

"Thank you," Amarah said sheepishly. "Please don't tell Liam. He needs to hear it from me."

"I won't say a word." His eyes told her he meant his promise, and relief washed through her. "Why haven't you told him yet? You're not afraid he'll be upset, are you?"

"No, nothing like that," she reassured him. "I found out right before we left and thought this vacation would be the perfect place to surprise him. I was about to tell him last night, but we got pulled away to dinner. Then everything that happened this morning and... I don't know." She sighed heavily. "Maybe I should wait until we get back to the privacy of our own home."

"Was it planned?"

"Definitely not!" A laugh of hysteria slipped out. "But shit happens when you party naked. We've talked a lot about having kids, but agreed to wait a bit so we could enjoy it being just the two of us for a little while. I'm not at all upset, just surprised."

Hunter laughed fully at that, causing his large shoulders to move. "Whenever you do tell him, I know he'll be happy."

His words warmed her heart, and her mind ran wild with thoughts of the future. Thoughts of Liam holding their tiny newborn baby in his strong arms. Him chasing the kid around the yard or tossing them in the air. Images of him tucking the child into bed and reading them a story each night. It was enough to make her eyes sting with emotion and her heart feel full and happy.

CHAPTER 18

Serenity and Hunter walked hand in hand down the beach, the warm sand slipping between their toes. The music of the pool party grew fainter the further from the resort they got. Her raven hair blew gently around her shoulders from the soft sea breeze, and the sound of waves crashing against the shore filled her with peace.

"Do you think something is going on between Jade and Declan?"

He was quiet for a moment as if fully analyzing everything he'd seen before he answered.

"It appears that way." He kept his gaze ahead of them as if focusing on the horizon where the sea kissed the sky.

She didn't know much about Jade Munro, but what little she'd gathered from their awkward conversation at dinner yesterday and what he'd told her in private, Jade had gone through a lot in her life. Losing a loved one is never easy. Especially if said loved one was your spouse.

A part of her did like the fact that Jade was possibly getting a second chance at love with Declan. If the connection she saw between them was correct. No matter what trials people may face, everyone deserves a chance at a happy, blissful life. Or in Jade's case, a second chance. Or even a third. We only get one life, after all. It's up to us to make the most of the time we're provided with.

Concern thickened the air around them as she tried to tread lightly on the topic of their host. The last thing she wanted was to bring back painful memories for Hunter, but she couldn't squash the curiosity sprouting in the back of her mind.

"Is it hard for you to see her?"

He finally broke his vision from the horizon to peer down at her. Serenity loved gazing into his eyes, unlike any she'd ever seen before. Just as beautiful as the first time she saw them, peering out of the visor of his full-faced helmet as he lay on the pavement after a car had rear-ended him on his motorcycle. An arctic blue with a warm hazel center, something that was at complete odds with each other.

It was a reflection of the ice-cold, hard exterior he displayed in public and the warm, caring, thoughtful nature that resided inside his beautiful soul. She watched as those eyes roamed her face as if the answer to her question was written in her features.

The day of his motorcycle accident, the day they first met, was where his nickname for her originated. Angel. *Because when I was lying on that pavement, the moment I first saw you leaning over me, I thought I had died and went to heaven.* The memory pulled a small smile across her mouth, despite the heaviness of their current topic of discussion.

"A little," he finally answered. "Bryson was a brother to me. To us," he corrected himself. "We were stationed in Virginia at the time. The night he met her, we'd gone to a bar where she was working. He *instantly* became infatuated with her and wouldn't shut up about how beautiful she was."

His laugh warmed her heart, even though his words cracked

it, hurting for the man who'd lost someone so close to him. She didn't speak. She waited patiently for him to tell his story, wanting to hear it so desperately.

"When she gave him her number, she wrote it down in Japanese, telling him that if he was serious about wanting to take her out on a date, he'd find a way to decipher it. The man went door to door in our barracks that night, asking everyone if they could read it, not caring that it was well after midnight. After getting cursed out in every colorful way under the sun, he'd finally struck gold and went to bed like a smiling idiot. Screw the three-day rule. He had called her the very next morning, and they'd been together ever since. He'd always been pretty flirty with the ladies, but I knew this was different simply by the way he talked about her. We were more than happy to accept her into our circle."

Hunter went quiet for a moment as if trying to swallow down the emotion trying to clog his throat. Serenity gave his hand a reassuring squeeze, silently communicating that it was ok and urging him to continue. He took a deep breath and did just that.

"Jade used to be so full of life. Cocky and confident, and pretty feisty when pissed off. But after Bryson died, she became a shell of her former self. Even now, she's still reserved, as if her soul only shines half as bright. I stayed by her side the day we put him to rest. I wish I could've done more for her, but what she truly needed, I couldn't give her. No one could. Bryson back in her arms where he belonged, not buried six feet beneath the cold ground." His voice cracked on the last few words.

"Hey." She softened her voice, releasing his hand to cup his bearded cheeks, forcing his gaze to hers. "I don't know what happened, but I can damn sure say that it was *not* your fault. If there was any way you could've saved him, I know without a shadow of a doubt that you would have, even if it meant trading your life for his." She paused as her mossy eyes darted between his. "You cannot put that on your shoulders. When God says it's your time, *no one* can cheat death."

Hunter gripped her hips and pulled her against his hard front, claiming her lips in a passionate and desperate embrace. It was as if after such a heavy and sensitive conversation, he needed to be reminded that the woman he loved was alive and well and right where she belonged. In his arms.

She felt the desperation as well. The need to feel his heart beating healthily beneath his tanned flesh. To feel the warmth of his strong hands touching any part of her. The need to breathe in his cologne to remind herself that he wasn't just a figment of her imagination. He was real and solid like the ground beneath their feet.

His tongue sought entrance immediately, and she opened. Her body melted against his as a fire ignited within her core. She felt him begin to grow hard through the thin fabric of his swim trunks, and she moaned against his mouth as she ground her hips against his erection, gaining a groan of approval from him. He broke their kiss, and their lust-filled eyes clashed with each other like swords on the battlefield.

"Careful, Angel. I'm not afraid to throw you down on this beach and claim you for all to see."

His delicious threat only acted as fuel to the fire that brought every nerve ending to life, making her body hypersensitive.

"I wouldn't be opposed to that." She smiled sensually. "However, we didn't bring a blanket and I'm not ok with getting sand all up in my... lady parts."

She tried hard to stifle the cringe that tried to shake her

shoulders at the uncomfortable image she accidentally conjured.

Hunter expertly scanned their surroundings before he took her hand in his and began walking up the beach to the tree line that led into the woods, his strides long and purposeful, causing her to jog just to keep up.

She laughed but followed willingly. "Where are we going?"

"To find a tree I can fuck you against."

She nearly tripped in the sand at his honest and so matter-of-fact confession. Her head swiveled around, making sure they were indeed alone as they finally entered the cover of the woods. He paused as his eyes bounced from tree to tree as if carefully examining each one. She knew the moment he'd found the winner because his long strides had them there in a matter of seconds.

He gripped her hips, spun her around, and pushed her back flush against the trunk. She gasped, but his lips were claiming hers again before she could take another breath. Her eyes fluttered closed as he pressed himself firmly against her soft curves and their tongues explored each other's mouths. Hunter took both of her wrists in one of his large hands and raised them above her head, pinning them to the trunk of the tree.

She moaned at the complete domination he had over her. She felt his free hand loosen the knot of the sheer skirt that covered her bikini bottoms. The fabric fell from her hips as he broke the kiss and pulled back. He brought it up and tied a knot around one wrist. Her eyes widened in surprise, but she trusted him completely. He circled the trunk, gripped her other wrist, and tied another knot around it.

With her wrists bound to the tree above her head, she was at his complete mercy. He came back to stand in front of her, his eyes darkened with pure lust, and the sight had her thighs clenching together. Serenity let her eyes roam the features she'd memorized over the last year.

"Let your hair down." Her words were a breathy request as her chest rose and fell at a quickened rate.

He didn't have to. He was in complete control, but with a wicked smile on his bearded face, he removed the elastic tie, allowing the long brown strands to fall to his shoulders. She loved seeing his hair like that. Her eyes dropped to the scar that bisected his left eyebrow, down to his exposed torso, so large and packed with thick muscles. Over to his strong arms that were painted in dark, beautiful ink and the light dusting of brown hair that covered his chest, circled his navel, and disappeared beneath his trunks. Her fingers itched to run through it, but they were secured elsewhere.

Then her vision sank even further to the large bulge straining against his trunks. She sighed contentedly, knowing the immense pleasure that weapon of his granted her body. When her eyes clashed with his, she saw a wicked smile across his features as he waited patiently, allowing her time to drink in the sight of him, hungry and hard before her.

"Look at you, Angel. So beautiful and helpless, tied to a tree." He stepped closer to her as he ran the tip of his nose up the collar of her neck, stopping to whisper in her ear. "I can use you for my pleasure alone. I can do whatever I want to this tight little body of yours, and there's nothing you can do to stop me. I don't even have to allow you to come."

"Please," she begged in a whisper of her own.

His mouth sucked on the lobe of her ear, causing a breathy whimper to escape from her parted lips. He brought his hands up to cup her full breasts, giving them both a firm squeeze, causing a moan to slip free.

"I could pull those bottoms of yours to the side, fuck you until I fill you up and leave." He gave her breasts another squeeze. "Leave you here all alone and unsatisfied, with my come coating your walls and dripping down your legs."

"Hunter, please," Serenity begged again as she ground her hips against his hardened cock.

He groaned, allowing her to use his body for her own pleasure.

"Please, what, Angel?"

He nipped and sucked against the sensitive skin of her neck. Not enough to leave a hickey, but enough to draw more agonizing pleasure from her.

She couldn't get her words to form properly. Her mind was too lost in lust. When she didn't answer, he slapped her left breast, gaining a gasp from her as her mossy eyes shot open.

"Use your words, Angel." He gave her right breast a slap, and his vision tracked the movement. "Please, what?"

"Please—Come—Make me—Fuck me." Her words were jumbled, and he chuckled devilishly.

"Mmhmm," he hummed against her neck, causing a delicious shiver to curl her toes. "Do you mean please fuck you and make you come?"

His voice was low and sensual as he slipped his hand beneath the front of her bikini bottoms and ran his fingers up and down her soaked entrance.

"God, yes!" she moaned as she tried to push her hips further into his hand, needing more than what he was allowing her at the moment.

He sank one finger deep into her. Then two, drawing a surprised gasp from her that turned into a sigh of relief.

"Good girl," he cooed. "See what happens when you use your words?" His fingers pumped inside of her, causing her back to arch off the tree. "You get rewarded."

His free hand pulled the fabric covering her left breast to the side, exposing her perky nipple to the warm summer air. His mouth closed around it as his teeth bit down, and he swirled his tongue in tight circles.

"Hunter," she panted as she peered down, loving the sight of his mouth on her.

His fingers left her center but stayed under the fabric of her bottoms. He popped his mouth off her breast and locked eyes with her, arching a thick brow at her in challenge.

His smile turned devilish. "Find your words, Angel."

She groaned in frustration, which only drew a deep chuckle vibrating through his strong chest.

"I need more." She took a few breaths before adding, "I need you to fuck me."

"As you wish." He straightened and pulled his trunks down far enough to free himself.

His erection sprang free, a string of pre-cum stretching from his lower stomach to the swollen head of his cock. More wetness beaded at the tip, and she nearly whimpered with anticipation. He moved the fabric of her bottoms to the side and slid the head of his sensitive erection across her center. He gripped the back of her legs, raised them up, and finally sank deep inside of her core.

They both groaned at the first moments of being connected. He began thrusting into her, hard, not giving her body time to stretch around him, but she didn't protest. She greedily welcomed each harsh movement. His mouth dipped down, gripped the fabric of her swimsuit top, and pulled it to the side, freeing her other breast.

"I fucking love the way your tits bounce as I pump into you," he growled, his eyes trained on her full breasts that jiggled with every connection of their hips.

The trunk of the tree bit into her back, but she didn't pay any mind. Serenity was too lost in desire. The tightening in her stomach grew at an alarming rate.

"Fuck," she panted. "Don't stop!"

He grinned as he kept moving inside of her. "I wouldn't dream of it."

All too soon, her body bowed off the tree as she constricted around him. She screamed his name as wave after wave of ecstasy coursed through her. He quickened his pace and came with her, spilling deep inside of her. They were both panting for breath by the time they came down from their finish, and he withdrew, adjusting her bottoms back into place to catch his release as it leaked out.

"Do you think anyone heard?" she asked as Hunter untied her hands and freed her from the tree.

"I hope so." He shot her a wink.

She shook her head and interlaced her fingers with his as they slowly made their way back to the resort.

CHAPTER 19

Amarah Godrik was thankful to wake up the following day to find everyone very much healthy and alive as each couple languidly filed into the dining hall for breakfast. She sat in her usual spot at the table with her husband to her right and Serenity and Hunter sitting opposite them. Though she tried hard not to, her vision drifted to the two empty chairs that used to house Cami and Parker Evans. Now, it only served as a horrible reminder of the gruesome scene she witnessed in their room yesterday morning.

Jade Munro strode into the room wearing a pair of jean shorts that showed off a large amount of her creamy legs and a yellow tank top. A warm expression shaped her rounded features.

"Good morning, everyone," she sang as her assistant pulled out her chair for her. She gave him a shy smile in return. "Thank you, Declan."

A few people greeted her back before she spoke again. "I hope you all brought some hiking shoes. I know this beautiful waterfall about a mile or so inland that I'd love to show everyone. Make sure to wear your swimsuit underneath your clothes. The water is so inviting and clear that you can see all the way to the bottom."

Excited murmurs broke out around the table as Jade finally

sat down, and servers entered, arms laden with breakfast trays. The delicious smell of fresh eggs, crispy bacon, and fluffy pancakes filled the air, sending Amarah's stomach growling in response.

Breakfast foods are acceptable to you, little one? Noted. She laughed internally at her growing baby.

Once everyone had their fill, each couple departed back to their rooms to get ready for the hike. Amarah had on a simple black bikini underneath a pair of jean shorts and a black tank top. She slipped her feet into her sneakers and braided her blonde hair into pigtails.

"Are you ready, Cupcake?"

Liam was dressed in a simple dark grey T-shirt, a pair of black swim trunks, and sneakers.

"Yes." She smiled brightly at him as he laced his fingers through hers and they made their way downstairs.

Serenity and Hunter were already down there waiting for them, dressed in similar clothes.

Once everyone had filed into the living room area, Jade addressed the group. "Let's not waste any more daylight." She smiled as she made her way out the back door, leading the group with Declan at her side, chatting away about something Amarah couldn't hear.

"Do you think they're together?" She spoke in a tone only Liam would be able to hear.

His brows furrowed together as he peered down at her. "Who?"

"Jade and Declan. Anytime I see her, he's never far from her side."

His height allowed his gaze to easily travel over the crowd of people toward Jade and Declan, who led the way.

"I'm not sure. They do seem pretty friendly with each other."

"Friendly?" she asked incredulously. "Declan looks like a lovestruck puppy every time he looks at her."

"If they are, I'm happy for her." Nothing but pure sympathy could be heard in his hushed tone. "Jade deserves something good in her life after everything she went through."

She couldn't stop herself from asking the question. "If something ever happened to me, would you try to find love again?"

She felt her husband's grip on her hand tighten, causing her vision to shift up to his. The severity that burned deep within his irises nearly sent her stumbling over her feet, and her breath caught in her throat.

"No, Cupcake. If something ever happened to you, I'll be buried in that casket right beside you."

Her heart skipped a beat, and she knew, without a shadow of a doubt, that every word he spoke was true. *Ditto.* She kept the thought to herself, love constricting her vocal cords, making it impossible to speak.

They rounded the side of the mansion and crossed the manicured lawn as they neared the tree line of the woods. The full canopy provided a much-welcomed shade from the summer sun as they hiked down a dirt path, twisting and turning through the dense foliage. Occasionally, they had to step over a fallen log or two, but for the most part, the walk was rather relaxing.

The sounds of nature always calmed Amarah, and she found herself smiling more than once as her eyes periodically spotted furry forest animals scurrying by in search of food. Soon, the therapeutic sound of rushing water reached her ears, and before she knew it, they broke through the tree line. A gasp fell from her lips as the stunning scenery was revealed to her.

A massive waterfall cascaded down over numerous rocks

that jutted out of the forty-foot-high cliff wall. The massive pool beneath was indeed crystal clear and flowed into the river that ran down the tree line and disappeared around a bend.

"This place is absolutely stunning!" Quinn Davis gasped as she shed her clothing and dove straight into the pool.

Aaron followed quickly behind his wife. They both surfaced and began to tread the water.

"Last one in comes last tonight," Amarah heard Myles say to Colton in a sultry voice, gaining a chuckle from his husband as they both quickly tossed their shirts aside, kicked off their shoes, and jumped in feet first.

Jade removed her tank top, revealing a pastel green bikini top as she sat on the flat, rocky ground, leaned back on her hands, closed her eyes, and raised her face toward the sky. Amarah smiled when she saw Declan sit next to her. Though he kept his shirt on. Most likely from not wanting to expose his pasty torso to the sun and risk a burn.

"Come on in, guys. The water is wonderful!" Aaron shouted as he began to float on his back and slowly swim laps around the pool.

Amarah and Serenity undressed and piled their clothes on a rock. They neared the edge, held hands, and jumped in together. When Amarah surfaced, she saw Hunter and Liam sitting on the edge of the pool, their shirts off and legs submerged in the water.

"That's one hell of a view, isn't it?" Serenity sighed dreamily as her bright green eyes drank in her fiancé.

Hunter's long brown hair was tied in a knot behind his head, allowing an unobstructed view of his rugged face. Amarah took in the small scar that bisected his left eyebrow and the handful of scars that marred parts of his torso and disturbed the dark ink on his arms. If she had to bet money on what caused them, she'd have to guess those were knife wounds. Most likely from his military days.

"It most definitely is. One I'll never tire of seeing," Amarah wholeheartedly agreed, though her vision was transfixed on her husband.

Liam's short black hair was brushed to the side, his black beard was trimmed close to his face, and his eyes were as green as healthy grass. Beautiful black ink snaked up one arm, crossed over his chest, and ran down his other arm. His torso was packed with muscles, much like Hunter's, but his was leaner and free of any hair.

"Amen." Serenity laughed, and both women swam up to their men. "What? Too scared to get in?" she teased them.

"No, just not a fan of swimming. I've been in enough water to last me a lifetime." Hunter smirked, gaining an agreeable laugh from Liam.

Amarah and Serenity swam a few feet away and began to tread water as they chatted amongst themselves, joined by Colton and Myles a few minutes later.

CHAPTER 20

Jade Munro watched as Quinn and Aaron Davis swam out of the pool, entering the mouth of the river as they got lost in each other's company. Longing clenched her lungs like a vise, making it almost unbearable to breathe. When she purchased the small island for her business, wanting to open an adults-only resort, she hadn't known just how painful it would be to see so many couples blissfully in love.

That's why she tried to keep herself distracted as much as possible, exploring all the island's hidden gems. She never knew a spot as magical as this existed. Not until Declan had shown it to her on a visit to touch base with the contractors and get a glimpse of the progress of construction.

He sat next to her atop the rocks, his freckled cheeks and the tip of his nose tinted pink due to his time in the sun. If he didn't want to risk a burn, he'd need to find some shade, or they'd have to leave soon.

"One of the camp counselors was leading me and about fifteen other boys down a worn path through the woods for our evening hike," Declan rambled on, a carefree smile across his face as he reminisced about the summer he spent at camp as a kid. "I was towards the back with a boy I became quick friends with. Since almost the entire group of people walked ahead of me, I didn't think I had to watch too closely where I was stepping."

"Oh, no." Jade bit down on her lips, trying to contain a smile. "Did you trip and fall? Step in a hole?"

"Ugh, I wish," he groaned. "No, my dumb ass had to step on a snake."

Her vision nearly doubled in shock. "What? Like a real live snake?"

"Well, by how much it was wiggling beneath my boot, I'm ninety-nine percent positive it was alive."

She threw her hand over her mouth and peered intently at him. "Did it bite you? Was it venomous?"

"I haven't the slightest clue. I didn't get close enough to examine its color. Thankfully, I stepped on its neck, so when I noticed it, I jumped back about five feet and screamed like a girl."

She threw her head back, unable to contain her laughter. "You did not!"

"I swear on my mother's life." He matched her laughter. "I think I scared it more than pissed it off because it slithered off the path back into the woods faster than I could blink."

"I'm glad you didn't get hurt. However, a morbid part of me kind of wishes I witnessed the scream."

He shook his head but never once stopped smiling. "Let me paint you a picture. My soul momentarily left my body."

Every muscle on Jade's petite frame instantly locked up, her heart jumped into her throat, and her stomach churned. Instantly, she was teleported back through time. No longer sunbathing on those rocks by the waterfall. Instead, she was back in the small one-bedroom apartment she shared with Bryson.

SEPTEMBER 2010

Bryson Munro collapsed on the bed next to Jade, their bodies slick with sweat as they gasped to catch their breath. He pulled her to his side as she rested her head against his chest, loving the melody his erratic heartbeat drummed for her.

"I think my soul momentarily left my body." He chuckled.

She ran the tips of her fingers over the defined muscles of his chest and abs, loving the way his body tensed beneath her touch.

"That wasn't the first time you brought me to another plane of existence."

He laughed fully and kissed the top of her rumpled jet-black hair. The last seven months had been the best of her existence. Her love for this man only grew deeper with each passing day. He was her home.

That was the main reason she hadn't stuck with her original plan of buying herself a house after graduating from college. She was unsure if he'd get new orders and would be forced to relocate. If that were the case, she'd leave with him without hesitation.

Jade had wanted to move out of her parents' home, craving the privacy her own space would provide for herself and Bryson. Until things got more permanent between them, she had settled for a small one-bedroom apartment close to the military base. She had also been busy working on a secret project that was dear to her heart.

She told no living soul. Not yet. She'd been inspired by her incredible connection and love that never seemed to stop growing for Bryson and wanted to help others find a similar connection.

She spent long hours planning, designing, and coding but after months of hard work, her dating website was almost ready to launch. Their connection was also her inspiration for its name. Desire.

"I stumbled across a listing for a house I think would be perfect for us," he said, pulling her from her thoughts.

Her voice was heavy with sarcasm as she smiled brightly. "Oh, you just happened to stumble upon it, huh?"

"I did. It's crazy how the universe just seems to drop things in front of you sometimes."

Her eyes fluttered closed as she continued to trail her fingers over his smooth, rich skin. "Tell me about it."

"It's recently built, two-story, four bedrooms, two baths. It has a kick-ass office you can use to work from home. There's plenty of room to start a family. Beautiful fenced-in backyard with lush grass. I can picture a dog or two running around while we chase our kids around the yard."

Jade could feel needles stabbing into her throat at his description. Not because it scared her or because she didn't want that too. Rather, how easily she could picture it and how badly she found herself wanting to turn that into a reality.

A tear escaped her closed lids, and she quickly wiped it away, not wanting him to see her like that. It didn't work. Bryson caught the movement and cupped her chin, craning her neck so she was forced to look at him.

"I didn't mean to upset you." His tone was gentle and sympathetic.

"You didn't," she quickly reassured him. "Quite the opposite, actually. Your vision for our future sounds perfect."

Another tear rolled down her cheek, and he slowly swiped

his thumb across the path. He gently rolled her to her back as he nestled himself between her creamy thighs. The backs of his fingers brushed her cheek as his loving gaze roamed over her face.

"It *will* become our reality." His words were a promise that sent love further constricting her chest.

"How many kids do you want?" she inquired.

"I don't know." A devious grin shaped his sharp features. "Two or three, maybe? What about you?"

"You could give me five and I'd be ok with that." She choked out a laugh as his eyes widened.

"Five, huh?" He placed a few soft kisses against her collarbone, and his vision darkened. "That would mean we'd have to try quite a bit to make sure you got pregnant that many times."

Her toes curled into the covers atop their bed at his sinful threat.

"I think we need to get married first before we buy a house and start trying for kids." She chuckled.

Since they weren't married, Bryson was still required to live on base in the barracks room he shared with Hunter Gatlin, but that didn't stop him from moving most of his belongings into her apartment anyway. He slept there most nights with her in the bed they shared. Hunter didn't mind. He quite enjoyed having the barracks room all to himself, and he was happy that his buddy was in a wonderful relationship.

"I think you're right." He hummed in a low voice that sent fresh heat to her core. "But that can be quickly arranged."

She cocked her head to the side and peered up at him questioningly. "How so?"

"Marry me." His words were more of a command than a question.

Her chocolate eyes widened, half from shock, half from surprise, pulling a nervous laugh from her. "What?"

"I want that future for us so desperately, like the body needs a heart. *You* are my heart. Without you, I couldn't live. Do me the honor of becoming my wife, the mother to my unborn children, my best friend, a partner that will be by my side as we wrinkle and grey, and watch our grandchildren play. I totally didn't mean for that to rhyme." He laughed.

Jade's eyes quickly shifted between Bryson's and tears blurred her vision as every word he spoke caressed her soul. A soul she knew without a shadow of a doubt mirrored his, and when put together, would make a perfect match.

"Yes," she whispered as joyful tears cascaded freely down her cheeks.

She was thankful her voice worked at all, given how much his confession touched her. Their lips collided in a passionate and needy embrace as their tongues explored each other's taste.

When he pulled back, pure happiness could be seen across every angle of his face. "How does next weekend work for you?"

The question caught her off guard and she cocked her head to the side. "Work for what?"

"To get married." His simple words stole the very breath from her lungs.

"Bryson!" She laughed at his eagerness. "I'd marry you within the hour if we could. I'm not sure how much you know about planning a wedding, but it's nearly impossible to do so in such a short time frame."

He was quiet as he thought, his face scrunched up in concentration. "Then let's scrap the wedding altogether and elope."

"Elope? Where? In Vegas?" she joked and rolled her dark eyes.

"Yes." He nodded as a grin shaped his full lips.

She opened her mouth to protest, but couldn't find the right words. What would she say? His idea sounded more intriguing by the minute.

"Think about it. The only family you have is your parents, and you aren't that close with them. They wouldn't be upset about missing a wedding as long as they knew that you were happy. I've all but disowned my family, so why waste money on a lavish wedding when we could put that toward our dream house?"

Again, all his points were hitting the nail on their head. Jade was finding it hard to rebuke. The longer she thought about it, the more she knew deep down that he was right. Why waste money when only a handful of people would even show up?

When she had her mind made up, she peered up at him, a wonderful feeling warming her from the inside out. A feeling that made her feel as if she were floating carefree through the sky. A feeling she never wanted to vanish. Love and pure happiness.

"Ok. Next weekend, then. It's a date."

Bryson mirrored her smile. Without warning, he aligned the tip of his freshly hardened cock against her center that was slickened from both of their finishes from mere moments ago and buried himself deep within her.

"To this day, I still have a phobia of snakes." Declan McCarthy's voice sucked her out of a blissful memory and back to the waterfall they rested beside as the guests of the resort swam and mingled in the clear water.

She gave him the brightest smile she could muster, though it was a shadow of what once was before she turned her head away and pretended to skim her vision over the clusters of happy couples. An agonizing jolt of pain, one she'd grown too familiar with over the years, ripped through her chest, causing a lone tear to betray her by rolling down her rounded cheek. She quickly wiped it away, allowed herself a few deep, calming breaths, and focused all her attention back on the man beside her and the conversation he had no clue she'd mentally checked out of.

CHAPTER 21

"What is that?" Quinn Davis's question drew the company's attention toward her.

The conversation Amarah was having with Serenity, Myles, and Colton ceased as they all glanced in the direction Quinn's vision was trained in, trying to figure out what it was exactly she saw.

"Shark!" Her drawn-out, high-pitched scream echoed off the rocks, sending dozens of birds scattering into the sky as they fled the sanctuary of the treetops, as if the danger could possibly reach them up there.

She began to swim for the river's edge and quickly climbed out. She turned just in time to see her husband get yanked beneath the water. "Aaron!" Quinn's desperate scream echoed around them further.

Amarah's body was frozen in shock as she watched, her brain unable to properly process what her vision was relaying. Hell, she was positive everyone around her ceased to even breathe. Seconds of deafening silence flowed through the small pool, sending a high-pitched ringing deep into her eardrums.

It felt as if minutes had ticked by before Aaron surfaced and let out a guttural scream that sent a mixture of fear and adrenaline coursing through Amarah's bloodstream. Red started to cloud beneath the water's surface as a dark grey dorsal fin became visible. The predator thrashed around violently, shaking Aaron like a rag doll.

"Fucking swim to me, Cupcake!" Liam called to Amarah from his spot on the edge of the pool. His voice snapped her out of the threatening trance the shark attack had put her in to see that her husband and Hunter had jumped to their feet.

"Angel, for fuck's sake, swim!" Hunter roared at Serenity.

His booming voice seemed to snap Serenity out of the same fear-induced paralyzing shock Amarah had experienced, and both girls wasted no time in swinging their arms and kicking their feet frantically behind them.

Luckily, they were only a short distance away, and their men hauled them effortlessly out of the water, caging them both in strong protective arms. Amarah turned her head to see Colton climbing out of the water and helping Myles to safety. Jade and Declan rushed over to Quinn's side. A bit of relief washed through her at knowing everyone else was safely out of the water. However, that relief was short-lived when Quinn screamed again.

"No! Aaron!" Her bloodcurdling cry broke Amarah's heart. "Someone help him! Please!" she begged, fat tears streaming in rivers down her face.

Amarah watched in horror as the dangerous animal forcefully thrashed Aaron around the water as if he were nothing but a child, his cries of agony filling the air around them and echoing off the nearby trees. So much blood poured out of Aaron, clouding the water around him and only acting as fuel for the shark's frenzied state. Declan moved to jump in, but Jade's grip on his arm halted him.

"No! You can't go in there. It will only get you too," Jade pleaded with her assistant as her grip on his arm tightened protectively.

Declan looked torn between staying with her and helping Aaron, but there was no use. Once a shark had its jaws on you, there was typically no getting it off. With each passing second, the amount of blood that turned the river crimson grew to a life-threatening amount. Even if the shark did let go, Aaron had lost too much to be able to survive until help arrived.

Then in the next second, he was pulled under again, and the area grew as quiet as a graveyard. The eerie silence made the hair on the back of Amarah's neck stand on end, and the ringing sounded in her ears again.

"No!" Quinn fell to her knees. She took in a ragged breath before she let out a guttural cry that shattered everyone's heart into millions of raw jagged pieces.

Aaron never resurfaced, and the shark turned and began swimming back down the river toward the ocean. Declan knelt beside Quinn as he pulled her into his arms, and she sobbed against his shoulder. Nobody so much as moved a muscle or uttered a sound. Collectively, they all stood in mourning at the realization that another guest had just lost their life.

After what felt like a lifetime, Declan managed to get Quinn to her feet as he began slowly following the path back to the resort. Everyone quickly dressed and followed suit. Still, no one said a word. Tension was thick among the solemn group as they finally made it back to the resort. Declan climbed the stairs with Quinn still sobbing and clinging to him for support. Violent tremors rocked her slender frame as Jade followed closely behind.

"Sharks live in the ocean, not rivers. How..." Myles King trailed off, his voice unsteady.

"Bull sharks can." Hunter spoke in a tone void of emotion. "They've been known to swim miles upriver in search of food."

"I think it's best if we all head back to our rooms and rest," Liam offered.

Liam never once let go of his wife after pulling her out of the water, as if he feared the shark would come on land and get her if he did. She appreciated it. Her husband's nearness had always calmed her. Her mind and body felt numb after witnessing such a horrific and violent attack. She'd watched enough *Shark Week's* over the years and heard plenty of shark attack stories, but to witness it firsthand? It was like nothing she could ever put into words.

"I agree." Colton nodded his head as he wrapped an arm around his husband's shoulders and began guiding him up the stairs.

As the group topped the stairs, they ran into Declan.

"How's Quinn holding up?" Serenity asked in a weak voice.

"I think she's in shock." His words were uneven as he looked over his shoulder toward Quinn's room and then back toward the group. "Jade said she'd stay with her for a while."

"That's good," Liam commented. "She shouldn't be left alone right now."

Declan nodded numbly before he walked past, pushed open his room, and disappeared inside. Liam stopped in front of their door and turned to face Hunter and Serenity. Now that they were the only ones left in the hallway, he spoke freely.

"Something's not adding up." He kept his voice low as he spoke directly to Hunter. "Call it a gut feeling, but I don't think that attack was random."

"Son of a bitch," Hunter cursed under his breath. "I was praying you wouldn't say anything. You just confirmed my suspicions."

"I want to go back to the area tonight." Liam's jaw ticked before he continued. "See if I can find anything out of place."

"What?" Amarah gasped. "No! Are you crazy? I'm not letting you go back there. What if the shark is still there?"

She tried to keep her voice low, but fear dripped from every syllable. How could he even suggest something like that? Pure terror settled deep within her belly, only serving to tighten the knot of nerves growing within.

"Shh." Liam spoke gently to her as he cupped her chin and forced her to meet his gaze. "I'm not going to get into the water, Cupcake. I just want to have a look around the area."

Her deep blue eyes blurred with unshed tears. "And what if there actually is a killer out there?"

She couldn't lose him. She *refused* to lose him. She'd fight death himself if he tried to take the love of her life, the father of her unborn child, away from her.

A wicked gleam shone in Liam's vision, one she hadn't seen since that night at the cabin last year with Derick Watland. "Then I guess we'll see who's more skilled."

The uneasy feeling in the pit of her stomach dug its roots deep and sprouted leaves. God, she felt as if she were about to throw up. And it had nothing to do with the little baby growing inside her belly.

"Bring Amarah to our room when you leave." Hunter held Liam's gaze as if to show the honesty he meant behind each word. "I'll keep her safe until you get back."

Liam nodded curtly, and they each entered their rooms without another word.

CHAPTER 22

Liam Godrik had spent the rest of the day with Amarah. He knew she was uneasy about him going out that night to investigate, so he stayed close to her, knowing his presence always helped to calm her. He loved it so much that he was her peace because the Lord knew she was his. He'd made love to her. Twice.

Partly to help her relax, but also because he was selfish. He could have her every day for the rest of his life, and it wouldn't be enough. He'd cared for her as an older brother during her childhood and would eliminate anything that threatened her safety or happiness, but the moment he saw her all grown up in her cap and gown at her graduation, something shifted within him.

Gone were the days of the skinny, nerdy, and innocent teenager. That girl had been replaced by a confident, intelligent, and beautiful woman whose body had filled out in all the right places. He didn't know what changed, but in that moment, she ruined him for any other woman.

Over the next two years, Liam had tried hard to get Amarah out of his head, out of his heart, but she had unknowingly sunk her claws deep within his soul. He tried to lose himself in women while stationed in Virginia, anything to get Travis's little sister off his mind, but he could never get himself to take them home. Even kissing a woman who wasn't Amarah, all of a sudden felt dirty and wrong.

After separating from the military and settling back in Oklahoma, the next two years proved more torturous. He thought being celibate for the years he was away was bad, but the next two years he was home were pure agony. Being forced to be in her company every two weeks at Travis and Sandra's family cookouts nearly killed him. He wanted to be the reason she smiled, the reason for her happiness, to touch her, to kiss every part of her body, to claim her and ruin her for any man as she did him for every other woman.

Liam hated Derick Watland for what he did to Amarah last year and everything he put her through, but in a way, he was thankful. Her stalker gave them both the push they needed to admit their feelings for one another, and when Liam had finally tasted her, he sank his teeth deep within her soul, selfishly claiming it for himself. He was addicted from the very first kiss.

He never grew tired of touching her, of tasting her, of hearing her scream his name until her voice went out. Amarah was the very air that filled his lungs with life, the food that nourished his body, and the rest that provided him with the strength to conquer each day.

If there was a possible threat to the woman who brought him unending happiness, to the woman who'd carry his children one day, he'd eliminate it without question or remorse. His soul had already been tainted by the acts he was forced to carry out for the sake of his country's freedom. Adding more deaths to his body count wasn't anything new to him.

He waited until he had the cover of nightfall working in his favor. When the resort fell quiet, he eased open their door and peered into the hallway. There wasn't a soul in sight and no lights illuminated beneath any doors. Not even Hunter's, though Liam knew he was still awake.

He took Amarah's hand in his, loving the feel of her warmth against his skin, and led her across the hall. He knocked once, paused, knocked rapidly three times, paused, and then knocked quickly two more times. A secret knock they established years ago in the Navy. Hunter opened the door a second later without hesitation.

Amarah hesitated as if letting go of his hand would cause him to vanish. He grinned inwardly, knowing it would take a lot more than the devil himself to take him away from her.

He shot her a quick wink. "I'll be right back, Cupcake."

"Don't say that!" she whispered the shout, but he didn't miss the fear lacing each word. Hearing how frightened she was tore apart his heart. But that sound right there, the terror that was infecting his wife and causing her smile to falter, was the reason why he needed to do this. "It's bad luck. Haven't you ever seen a horror movie?"

"Those rules don't apply to me because, in this movie," he placed a gentle kiss against her forehead before continuing, "I'm the monster. Besides, I'm probably making something out of nothing. Everything will be alright, I promise."

"I love you." Her voice cracked on the last word, nearly ripping his beating heart right out of his chest cavity.

"I love you too. So fucking much, Cupcake."

She released his hand and stepped into Hunter and Serenity's room. Serenity wrapped an arm around her and walked her to the edge of the bed, where they sat together. The sight warmed him, knowing that Amarah had a friend like her at her side.

His gaze snapped to his brother's as unspoken threats and promises were made. Hunter promised to protect Amarah with his life, and Liam threatened to take that life if he failed to keep that promise. With a curt nod, Liam turned and strode down the hallway, not making a single sound. He descended the stairs as his eyes scanned the bottom floor, making sure he was truly alone.

When he hit the tile, he kept his steps light as he crossed the space and entered through a door he knew led to the kitchen. The room was massive, like one you'd find in a restaurant. It was spotless and updated with stainless steel appliances and high-end furnishings. His vision scanned the countertops until he found what he was looking for.

He crossed the space and removed a large butcher knife from the knife stand. His gaze snagged on an empty slot, and he'd bet a thousand dollars that the knife that killed Cami Evans belonged there. Now that he was armed, he made his way back through the main floor and exited the mansion, becoming one with the shadows as if no time had passed since his days in the military.

He found the trail easily, and thanks to the light from the moon above, the woods weren't pitch-black. He followed the trail, never once breaking a twig or making a single sound. Liam knew he was close when the sounds of the waterfall filled the quiet air around him. He paused at the tree line, where he was still cloaked in darkness as his expert vision scanned his surroundings and his trained ears listened for any indication that he might not be alone.

When he was certain he was the only one out there, he removed a small flashlight from the pocket of his black cargo pants and flicked it on. A narrow beam of light illuminated a small area in front of him, but it was enough to get the job done. He kept his eyes trained on the ground, finding the signs and prints of everyone from their hike earlier that day.

He'd always been a natural at tracking. He spent his childhood with his father and grandfather outdoors, hunting and fishing, and they taught him everything he knew. He could tell what animal left what print, how long ago it was left, and how fast the animal was traveling when it left the mark.

It wasn't just impressions left in the dirt, either. He could follow a trail through thick foliage, across a gravel road, through an open field. A broken twig, an impression in the ground, a snapped leaf, a shifted rock, his expert eyes picked up on the slightest hint of disturbances made by passing creatures that went unnoticed by most. If a mission required any kind of tracking, he was the one they turned to for the job. He made a pass down and back up the river, not seeing anything that stood out to him.

He walked a bit downriver until he came to a narrow part, took a running start, and leaped over the gap, landing stealthily on the other side, like a feline. He walked up and down a few times, checking that side for any unusual signs. When he found none, he let out a frustrated breath. The bad feeling in the pit of his stomach was telling him he was missing something. But what?

The sound of the waterfall drew his attention as he pondered where to search next. Then his eyes followed the water to the top of the cliff. A feeling he couldn't ignore had him gripping the small light between his teeth as he began to scale the forty-foot cliff wall. After a few minutes, he hauled himself up and over the top.

He gripped the light and trained it on the ground as he took slow and sure steps, making sure to scour every inch of available ground. A small rope ahead caught his attention, causing his thick brows to pinch with curiosity. The rope was tied to the base of a nearby tree, and the end disappeared into the river at the top of the waterfall.

He gripped the light between his teeth again as he knelt and began to slowly remove the rope from the water. Something heavy was tied to the end of it, and when it breached the surface, Liam's blood ran cold.

Motherfucker, he cursed mentally. Secured to the end of the rope was a small metal cage. But it's what was in the cage that had fury building within him.

Numerous fish had been cut into chunks and stuffed inside. After examining the cuts, Liam was certain they were made with a knife. Someone had caught these fish, cut them up, stuffed them in this cage, and tied them upstream so that their blood would run down the river and out into the ocean, in hopes of attracting a shark.

The cage must've been placed sometime last night or early that morning because he never saw a hint of red coming down the waterfall or lingering in the pool where everyone was swimming. Who knows just how long that shark was lingering in that river?

He released a heavy sigh. His gut feeling was right. Parker Evans was innocent. There was a murderer among them. The questions now were who was it, why were they killing people, and who was next? Was there some kind of order to whom they planned on eliminating? He gently placed the cage back into the water, making sure to leave everything exactly how he found it.

He stood, and something else caught his attention. There were boot prints in the ground, faint but recent. Judging by the size and shape, they were hiking boots that belonged to a man or a woman with an above-average foot size. He followed the trail and wasn't surprised when it led him all the way back to the resort. He turned off his light, slipped it back into his pocket, and made his way back upstairs.

He repeated the unique knock, and Hunter didn't hesitate to open the door. Liam quickly stepped inside, and Amarah leaped into his arms a heartbeat later. He caught her effortlessly and buried his face in the curve of her neck.

"I'm so glad you're safe," she whispered against the sensitive flesh of his neck, sending a shiver that went straight to his groin.

He took a few slow, deep breaths of her scent, allowing it to relax him before he set her down and faced Hunter, who waited patiently next to a very anxious Serenity.

"Good news or bad news?" he offered as he sat his wife down on her feet and met his brother's gaze.

"Ah, shit." Hunter cursed, ran a hand over his beard, and shook his head. "I knew it."

"What?" Serenity questioned as her gaze shifted frantically between the men. "What is it?"

"Good news. We're not all crazy. Our suspicions were right." Liam kept his voice low, even though they were the only ones in the room. "Bad news is that our suspicions were right."

"Someone here is a murderer?" Amarah's eyes widened in horror and then darted around the room as if they were suddenly not alone.

Liam nodded as he clenched his jaw a few times.

"What did you find?" Hunter questioned.

"Someone chummed the fucking water. Baited the shark upriver, right to our little swimming hole."

"Who would do such a thing? And why?" Serenity couldn't hide the terror in her voice.

Hunter pulled her to his side and rubbed soothing circles

across her back. It seemed to help a little as Liam watched her shoulders visibly drop.

"I'm not sure. The prints I found near the cage filled with fish guts were male hiking boots."

"The only ones who didn't get into that water, besides you and I, were Jade and Declan." Hunter spoke as if thinking out loud rather than addressing the group. "Jade's feet are too tiny, but Declan could be a good match."

"Or Myles or Colton. Or any of the staff," Serenity offered. "Declan almost jumped into the water after Aaron, but Jade stopped him. That doesn't sound like the actions of a killer to me."

"Plus, I saw his reaction to finding Cami's body," Amarah added. "If the guy got any paler, he could've passed for a corpse himself."

"He could also be a really good actor," Liam rebuked in a flat tone. "But we can't speculate. We have to stick with facts. For right now, every man here, minus you and I, is a suspect. We just need to find out why someone would want all of us dead. What do they plan to gain from it?"

"I think we should bring in backup. At this rate, we'll all be dead come Friday when the boat comes to take us back to the mainland," Hunter offered as he removed his phone from the pocket of his pants.

Liam watched as Hunter dropped a pin on their location, pulled up Einstein's contact, typed a single word, and pressed send.

"What the—Motherfucker…" Hunter trailed off. "I have no signal."

His gaze shot up, his face schooled, but Liam could read everything he was feeling from his eyes alone. He was afraid, worried, and pissed the fuck off. Liam felt the exact same way.

Everyone quickly removed their phones and checked. No one had a signal.

"We're on a small, remote island. Maybe they just don't have any cell towers here." Serenity tried to keep her voice hopeful, but failed. "I haven't been on my phone since we got here."

The men exchanged a look, another silent conversation occurring between them.

"What is it?" Amarah inquired as her eyes darted between them.

Hunter held her gaze. "I saw a tower up on the mountain as we docked the first day."

"Meaning?" Amarah asked hesitantly and grimaced as if she already knew she wouldn't like the answer.

"Meaning our signals are being jammed on purpose." Liam's voice was laced with warning. "When was the last time anyone used their phone?"

"This morning to check work emails," Hunter answered.

"That means the murderer could've jammed the signal at any point today. Shit," Liam whispered the curse as he tried not to crush his phone in his grip. "Did your text go through?"

"No," Hunter gritted out as his jaw ticked with fury.

Liam pinched his brows tightly. "What does 'nuggets' mean, by the way?"

That was the single word Hunter tried to send to Einstein along with their location.

"It's a code word I created with my team. If anyone sends it, it means they need backup ASAP with the firepower of an entire military."

"That would've been nice," Liam deadpanned. "Out of all the words you could've used, nuggets? Really, man?"

Hunter shrugged his shoulders. "What? It's a word not often brought up in conversation and never used by itself."

Liam released a long and frustrated breath. "Well, it looks like we're on our own. We have to find a way to survive until Friday."

CHAPTER 23

Jade Munro jerked awake from the feeling of something brushing against her leg. She hadn't slept next to someone since before Bryson died. Who the hell was in her bed? She blinked her chocolate eyes clear to find that she wasn't in her room. Her gaze dropped to the form sleeping beside her. Long, wavy brunette strands lay strewn across the pillow.

Quinn Davis… It all came back to her. The horrific events that transpired yesterday: the shark attack, Aaron dying, and spending the evening with Quinn to make sure she'd be alright. The woman practically begged her to stay the night. Jade's heart ached at seeing Quinn so broken, a shell of her former self. A feeling she knew all too well.

She released a quiet sigh, slipped from beneath the covers, and quickly used the bathroom, splashing cold water across her face and pulling her straight raven hair into a high ponytail. Upon reentering Quinn's bedroom, she found the woman still asleep.

Wanting to stay with her until she woke, Jade plopped down in a padded armchair beside the bed and began to fidget with her wedding ring. She glanced down at the stunning piece of jewelry and smiled, as if remembering a time when life was absolutely perfect.

SEPTEMBER 2010

"Do you think I'm crazy?" Jade asked as she tried to sit as still as a statue in a wooden vanity chair so Sandra Patterson could finish applying her makeup.

The bridal dressing room at the Blissful Beginnings Wedding Chapel in Las Vegas was small but elegantly designed with plush dark grey carpets and cream-colored walls. Only a handful of furniture pieces filled the space. Two dark-stained wooden vanities with oversized mirrors, numerous small navy blue velvet stools, and a massive full-body mirror. Metal hooks lined the front walls, allowing ample space to suspend garment bags.

When they'd arrived, the men departed to the groom's dressing room, leaving Jade and Sandra alone to get ready. Her stomach felt as if she were riding the world's most intense roller coaster on repeat. She didn't understand why she was so nervous. She loved Bryson more than life itself. But a small, annoying voice in the depths of her mind had her fearing that maybe they were rushing things.

They'd only been dating for seven months. Marriage was no small matter and one not to be taken lightly. Seven months isn't nearly enough time to fully get to know someone you plan on tying yourself to for the rest of your lives. Though if Jade had to tie herself to someone, mentally, physically, and spiritually, she'd pick Bryson every time.

She'd known he was different from the moment he stepped foot into the bar she worked at, his head thrown back in laughter, his golden eyes sparkling with life and joy. She knew the connection she felt with him was not normal. It wasn't puppy love or a fling. No. What they had was rare and cataclysmic. It was the kind of love that would move mountains, that would rattle the heavens and the earth, the kind of true love that would inspire Shakespeare to write about.

Sandra paused the mascara application and cocked her head to the side. "Crazy in what way?"

Jade wrung her hands together in her lap as Sandra resumed carefully applying another layer of mascara to Jade's thick lashes. "For getting married so soon. Let alone eloping here in Vegas?"

"Of course not." Her voice was soft and sympathetic. "Love is different for everyone. What works for some may not work for others. What you two share is unique and beautiful. Only you and Bryson will ever truly understand the connection between y'all. Don't ever stop to worry about what others might think. This is your life, and if you're happy with it, love it and live it."

She knew Sandra was right. She knew that voice in her mind was only trying to plant seeds of fear and doubt within her soul. But she refused to nurture it and allow it to grow. If she only had half her soul, it might have been able to blossom but hers was complete. The other half of it was forty feet from her, in another room, getting ready to marry her, to choose her as his life partner.

Jade shook herself free of doubt as Sandra capped the mascara and placed it on top of the vanity next to the rest of the makeup. She shifted in her seat and gasped at her reflection.

"Oh my gosh…" She was at a loss for words.

Sandra kept her makeup light, but it was still elegant and more beautiful than she could've ever done herself. A small braid on each side of her head was brought around and tied together in the back, serving as an elegant raven crown. The rest of her dark hair fell in luscious waterfall curls down her back.

"I know, I'm scary good," Sandra boasted with a beaming smile. Her bright red hair was pulled back into a tight bun, leaving a few pieces down to frame her creamy face. "Now, let's get you into your dress."

Both women quickly unzipped their garment bags, revealing heaps of elegant lace. Sandra slipped into her dress, and Jade zipped up the back. Her friend was glowing as she stood in front of the mirror in a beautiful pastel pink strapless sundress that flowed gracefully to her knees. The fabric bubbled outward around her baby bump in the most beautiful way. She was about five months along with their first baby, a girl, and Travis nearly fainted when he found out.

Jade then slipped into her own dress right as someone knocked on the door. Sandra cracked it open, using her body as a shield in case it was Bryson. It was bad luck for the groom to see the bride before the wedding, and Sandra was big on superstitions. Jade strained to hear what was being said, but only heard the muffled sounds of a male voice.

Was it Bryson? Did he change his mind? Is it one of his buddies informing her that he left? Her dinner was nearly in her throat, but she clamped her mouth shut, almost at risk of cracking a tooth as she tried to calm herself with slow, deep breaths. She squared her shoulders, lifted her chin, and forced those horrible thoughts to go away. Sandra gave a curt nod and closed the door.

"It's time," she practically squealed with excitement.

Jade stood behind the closed double doors, the bouquet of white roses and lilies shook from her trembling hands. Muffled music sounded from the other side of the door, and she knew if she ever did anything right in her life, it was this: to marry Bryson. With a nod showing she was ready, two staff members pulled the doors open, and she gasped.

The chapel was small but clean and modern with grey slate tile placed in a diamond pattern across the floor, and the walls were painted a soft cream. A handful of white wooden pews lined both sides of the aisle with beautiful white roses and lilies mounted on the ends, matching her bouquet.

A bald older gentleman in a grey suit that did nothing to hide his round belly stood behind a small white wooden podium at the end of the aisle. Sandra was beaming as she stood in the bridesmaid spot to the left. Liam Godrik, Hunter Gatlin, and Travis Patterson stood to the right, all dressed in form-fitting, black as night, three-piece suits with their hands clasped in front of them, looking devilishly wicked.

However, Jade only had eyes for one man. Her soul mate was standing at the end of the aisle, his shimmery whisky gaze trained solely on her. She started to walk as the rest of the room, of the world, quickly faded away as if she and Bryson were the only two people on the planet. Her black heels clicked against the tile floor and echoed off the walls with each step.

Her dress was just the way she liked it. Simple. The luscious white silk was clasped behind her neck and hugged her body, trailing on the ground behind her. It was free of beads, lace, buttons, or designs that would normally overpower a dress they were supposed to accentuate.

When she saw the tears running down Bryson's schooled features, her heart cracked like the Grand Canyon. There stood a man who had taken countless lives and sacrificed so much.

Someone who had been hardened due to the acts he had to carry out and secrets he was forced to keep for the safety of his country, and simply the sight of her walking down an aisle shattered his shield.

She could see the love he held for her in his eyes alone and it was all she could ever ask for. Jade felt her own tears roll down her cheeks as she reached the end of the aisle and turned to face the love of her life.

"You are the most exquisite woman I've ever had the pleasure of looking upon," he whispered in her ear, sending a wonderful shiver down her spine.

He straightened and cleared his throat as the music faded and the officiant began to speak.

"Dearly beloved, we are gathered here in the sight of God and in the face of this company to join this man and this woman in holy matrimony. If anyone has just cause why these two should not be joined together, speak now or forever hold your peace."

None of their friends uttered a sound, so the officiant continued, and before she knew it, it was time to say their I Do's.

"Jade Hayashi, do you take this man to be your husband, to live together in holy matrimony, to love him, to comfort him, to cherish him, and to keep him in sickness and in health, forsaking all others, for as long as you both shall live?"

"I do." She spoke without hesitation, her tone filled with admiration as she slipped a black wedding band onto his ring finger.

The officiant turned and recited the vows to Bryson.

"Bryson Munro, do you take this woman to be your wife, to live together in holy matrimony, to love her, to honor her, to comfort her, to cherish her, and to keep her in sickness and in health, forsaking all others, for as long as you both shall live?"

"I've waited my entire life to find a woman like you. Now that I have, I'll do everything in my power to never lose you. I do." He ended with a wicked smile as he slipped a silver wedding band around her ring finger.

Her eyes widened as she took in the ring. It was a simple, thick band with a pear-shaped jade stone set in the center, surrounded by small glistening diamonds. Light bounced off the gems, causing them to sparkle magically.

"It's beautiful," she whispered as emotion stung her eyes.

"Not as beautiful as you, my little kunoichi." He shot her a wink when her gaze clashed with his.

Without waiting for the officiant, she threw her arms around his neck and claimed his mouth. He wrapped his arms around her waist and lifted her into the air while their friends began to whistle, cheer, and clap.

"By the power vested in me under the laws of the State of Nevada, I now pronounce you husband and wife." The officiant chuckled as the ceremony concluded.

Their tongues fought for dominance as they deepened their kiss, and their bodies began to wake up and flood with desire. They were panting when they finally parted. Bryson gently set her back down as he interlocked his fingers with hers and started walking down the aisle toward the double doors.

Jade reluctantly released his hand as they went back to their separate changing rooms. Sandra closed the door behind her as Jade fanned her hand toward her face. Her body felt like it was on fire, and she would give anything to have her husband between her legs just then. Her *husband...* That thought sent butterflies doing somersaults in her belly.

"Hold on, I forgot something. I'll be right back," Sandra said, and she nodded in understanding.

Jade paced the room until her body and hormones had calmed down. She reached her hands around her, grasped the zipper of her dress, and was about to unzip it when the door to their changing room opened.

Her eyes widened when Bryson entered and quickly shut the door behind him. "What are you doing in here?"

He didn't speak. He took a few long strides and closed the distance between them as he gripped her face and claimed her lips in a hungry and desperate embrace. Fresh heat ignited within her core as she ran her hands down the front of his torso, loving the feeling of his muscles tensing beneath her touch.

"Sandra's buying us five minutes alone," he growled, lust dripped from his tone and danced through his gaze as he locked eyes with her, waiting for her consent before he proceeded.

A wicked smile lifted her rounded features, and her tone turned sensual. "I don't know about you, but I only need two."

Approval flashed through his golden irises as he wasted no time in hiking up her dress around her thighs, cupping her ass, and hoisting her up. Her creamy legs wrapped instantly around his waist as he took three strides and pinned her against a wall. She began licking and sucking on his earlobe as he made quick work of unbuttoning his pants and freeing himself.

He didn't test her readiness. She was always quick to get wet for him. A trait she knew that he loved so much.

"I can't wait to be buried deep inside of my wife for the first time." His voice was strained as if he was using every ounce of strength to contain his urges.

With a single thrust, he pushed himself deep inside her heated core. He groaned in pure ecstasy, and Jade moaned at the fullness he provided her.

"You better stay quiet, unless you want the entire chapel to hear you scream your husband's name as you come all over my cock." Bryson removed the handkerchief from his suit pocket. "Open," he demanded.

She happily submitted as he stuffed the fabric in her mouth, muffling her sounds of pleasure. When she was gagged, he began thrusting violently into her. She was thankful for it, or else the entire chapel would've indeed heard her. Hell, people half a block away would've been able to hear.

The wedding, the kiss, the sight of him alone in that suit already had her body worked up, so the moment he entered her, she already felt a tightening in the pit of her stomach and knew it wouldn't be long before she was sent over the edge.

By his movements, she wasn't the only one who'd be coming quickly. He grunted with each slam of his hips, over and over until they both came together in an explosion of passion. Her cries were muffled by the handkerchief, and she dug her nails into the fabric that covered his shoulders as wave after wave of her finish crashed through her. He didn't stop moving as he came, making sure his wife accepted all he had to offer.

He rested his forehead against hers as he fought to catch his breath. "God, I fucking love you."

Jade removed the gag and chuckled as she gave him a quick kiss. "I love you too."

"Now that we're married, we can officially start trying for kids." He wiggled his brows suggestively.

"Maybe we should buy that house first." She laughed and shook her head at her husband's eagerness. "Our apartment is too small to add a baby to it."

He withdrew from her center and set her back down gently. They both adjusted their clothing before he left to change, and Sandra entered the room again.

She grinned as she wiggled her fiery brows mischievously. "It smells like sex in here."

"You can smell it?" Jade's cheeks started to color with embarrassment.

"It's not that bad. Pregnancy nose, remember?" She pointed to her slim and straight nose and laughed. "I'm worse than a K-9."

They quickly changed, put their dresses back in the garment bags, and met the guys out front as they filed into their vehicles and spent the night celebrating and exploring the Vegas strip.

A knock at Quinn's door brought Jade back to reality. Something wet against her cheeks caught her attention as she slowly brought her hand up and swiped across her rounded features. Her fingers were soaked when she pulled them back to examine them.

She hadn't realized she'd been crying. Quickly, she dried her cheeks with the backs of her hands and glanced over at Quinn, who was still asleep, buried beneath her covers. Jade stood from the small armchair, crossed the room, and opened the door to find Liam, Amarah, Hunter, and Serenity standing in the hallway.

CHAPTER 24

Amarah Godrik woke the next morning to find Hunter Gatlin slowly pacing the room. They'd stayed in Hunter and Serenity's room last night so Amarah and Serenity could sleep while Hunter and Liam took shifts guarding the door. As if sensing her, Hunter stopped and met her sapphire gaze.

"Good morning," she greeted quietly, not wanting to rouse her husband or Serenity.

"Good morning," Hunter greeted back.

Despite their attempts, Liam's eyes opened as he sat up in the chair he'd passed out in, and Serenity began to stir in the bed next to Amarah. Her bright green eyes blinked a few times before they shifted around the room. Serenity sat up and rubbed the sleep from her eyes.

"I see we made it through the night." Serenity's smile was small as she tried to lighten the mood amongst them.

Hunter snorted and crossed the room as he placed a kiss atop her disheveled raven hair. "Good morning, Angel."

"Good morning." She smiled at him. "Please tell me you got some sleep?"

"A little, yeah," he reassured her.

"We should go back to our room and freshen up before breakfast." Liam offered as he stood, stretched out the kinks in his muscles, and held an outstretched hand toward Amarah. She took it and slipped out of the bed.

"We'll regroup before heading down to breakfast," Hunter said, and Liam nodded in agreement.

Neither Amarah nor Liam talked as they hurried to get cleaned up and put on fresh clothes. They went simple, jeans and a T-shirt, and Amarah twisted her golden strands back into a single braid down her back, not wanting to fight with it today. Ten minutes later, they met Serenity and Hunter in the hallway. They had the same idea, going casual in jeans and a T-shirt, unsure of what the day might throw at them.

They passed by Cami and Parker Evans's room. The door was closed, and yellow caution tape barred the doorframe until the cops finished their investigation. They made a quick stop at Quinn's room. Liam rapped his knuckles lightly against the door. Everyone was surprised when Jade opened the door, her raven hair pulled into a high ponytail.

Jade gave them a small and tired smile. "Good morning, everyone."

"How's Quinn holding up?" Liam kept his voice low.

Amarah saw his gaze lift as if looking past Jade and at Quinn, who lay in the bed.

Jade's eyes were filled with sorrow. "As good as she can, given her circumstances."

Amarah's heart broke for both Quinn and Jade. For Jade, because she knows the pain of losing a spouse, and Quinn, because she had to witness her husband's death. And it was a violent one at that, which made it all that much worse.

"We just wanted to check on her. We'll see you at breakfast."

Jade gave Liam a slight nod of her head before stepping back and closing the door. They all made their way downstairs and into the dining hall. They sat in their usual seats as what was left of the guests began to slowly file into the room.

Two empty chairs surrounded the table yesterday. Today, there were four. The number kept growing and Amarah felt bile try to creep its way up her throat. She clamped her jaw tightly and focused on her breathing, willing the nausea to go away.

Myles King smiled at Amarah and Serenity as he entered. He gave them a small hug and chose to sit next to Amarah. Colton sat across the table next to Serenity. After everyone was in attendance, minus Quinn, the servers filed in and placed a plate and glass in front of each person. They quickly exited as a familiar weight of grief and dread descended upon the room. Jade conversed with Declan, and their small group remained quiet until Amarah caught a whiff of something odd and followed the smell.

"What did you order to drink?" she asked in a half-laugh as she arched a brow at Myles to her left.

"Uh, orange juice?" Myles answered hesitantly as he looked at her like she had just grown a second head.

She placed her hand under her nose, her face scrunched up in disgust. "What did you spike it with?"

"Nothing!" He defensively placed his hand against his chest. Then he arched a brow and dropped his tone. "Why? Do you have anything good?"

Amarah chuckled and shook her head as she took a sip of her water. "I think that juice has expired."

She could now feel Serenity's, Hunter's, and Liam's gaze on her. Colton paused halfway through cutting his pancakes as he peered up from across the table to watch the interaction.

Myles brought it up to his nose, swirled the yellow liquid around in the glass, and took a whiff.

Two creases formed between his brows. "I don't smell anything."

"Really?" she questioned in shock.

The smell was so potent to her, it was almost overpowering. Then a thought hit her. Maybe only she could detect it from a heightened sense of smell due to her pregnancy. Her gaze quickly traveled around the table nervously before returning to Myles, hoping she didn't just out herself to her husband, whom she had still yet to inform of the big news. How could she with all the death happening around them?

No, she'd wait until they got off this God forsaken island. *If* they made it out of there. She quickly forced that line of thought from her head before she threw up all over the table, ruining everyone's meal. She couldn't think like that. She had to remain positive. She had to, for their baby's sake.

Myles pulled back from the drink and eyed it like it was a snake about to strike. "What does it smell like?"

"Like…" Amarah paused as she took another sniff of the air around her before covering her nose again. "Like almonds but… wrong."

"Babe, did you hit your head or something?" Worry filled Myles's tone as his dark eyes searched over her face and down what he could see of her body. "Are you stroking out on me?"

"She would be smelling burnt toast if that were the case, dear." Colton shook his head and chuckled.

"Oh, right." Myles waved a hand dismissively toward his husband before shrugging his shoulders. "I'm sure it's fine." He tried to reassure Amarah as he brought the glass to his mouth.

"Wait!" Hunter shouted, causing everyone around to jump at the sudden boom of his voice.

"Oh, God! What?" Myles shrieked and nearly dropped his glass. "What is it?"

All eyes were on Hunter as he outstretched his long arm. "Give me your drink."

Myles passed the glass with a look across his face that said Hunter had lost his mind too. Hunter brought the drink to his nose, closed his eyes, and took a deep breath. He moved the glass away, took a few small sniffs as if clearing his airways before bringing the glass back and taking another slow breath.

"It's faint, but there's a hint of it. Bitter almonds."

Hunter's unique vision shot to Liam as they had yet another of their silent conversations.

"Cyanide." Liam gritted out through clenched teeth, and Amarah saw his jaw tick with anger.

"Cyanide," Myles repeated the word quietly as if it sounded familiar, but he couldn't place it. Then his brown eyes widened in horror. "Like the poison?"

That caused everyone to eye their own drinks with suspicion and unease.

Jade's head snapped up from her conversation with Declan. "What about poison?"

Worry etched itself into her rounded features.

"Someone tried to poison me!" Myles's voice rose in disbelief. "What in the actual fuck!"

"Hunter?" Jade asked hesitantly as she slowly rose from her chair. "What is he talking about?"

Hunter kept his voice flat, but his face was hard as he raised the glass of orange juice for her to see. "There's hints of cyanide in his drink."

"Are you certain?" Declan asked in complete shock.

"Please, by all means, take a sip and prove me wrong." Hunter challenged him with a look that would make most grown men cower.

It worked. Declan shrank back as if trying to become one with his chair.

"Why would someone do that?" Jade's gaze frantically dropped to her own glass as if it might be poisoned as well. "How?"

"We have reason to believe someone here is picking us off one at a time." Liam's words were laced with warning as if challenging the murderer to react and expose themselves.

Numerous gasps echoed off the walls of the dining hall. Everyone began to peer frantically around at each other as if fearing the person sitting next to them might be a killer.

"What reasons have made you draw that conclusion?" Colton asked hesitantly.

Hunter gave a sly grin that sent goosebumps rising along Amarah's arms. "Cyanide doesn't just fall into someone's drink accidentally."

"I also discovered that someone chummed the river we swam in yesterday, purposefully trying to lure in a shark… or multiple," Liam added as his trained eyes examined each guest.

If Amarah had to guess, both Hunter and Liam were analyzing every guest sitting around the table. Picking apart every move they made, every twitch of their muscles, dissecting every word they spoke, cross-examining every reaction they expressed to each new bit of information. If a killer was among them, she had full confidence that those two would be their best bet at identifying the culprit.

"And what about Cami?" Jade challenged hesitantly as if she might regret asking.

Hunter held Jade's chocolate gaze. "I've been around enough killers in my day to say with confidence that Parker Evans did not kill his wife."

Terror flashed through Jade's vision as her gaze shifted around the table as if inspecting each guest as well. Her next words were shaky. "What do we do?"

"How long have you sat on this information instead of informing the group if all our lives are at risk?" Declan appeared as if rage was trying to surface at being left in the dark about such a serious threat.

"Because it was just a hunch." Hunter motioned to the poisoned orange juice resting atop the table. "Until this morning."

"We should call the cops," Myles offered as his gaze shifted around, looking for someone to agree with his thought.

"I tried to send a text last night." Hunter shook his head. "Someone's purposefully jammed the signal to the island."

"Wait. How do we know *you're* not the killer?" Myles inquired.

"I wouldn't have stopped you from drinking the juice," Hunter deadpanned.

"Oh, yeah." Myles's face showed half disappointment and half relief. "Good point."

"Then what do we do?" Declan asked frantically.

"Please tell me we aren't stuck on this island with an unknown killer until Friday?" Colton tried to hide the panic in his voice but failed.

"There's an old boat dock on the other side of the island," Jade offered. "It was run down when I bought the place and hasn't been touched. I don't know if any of the boats there work or not. Is anyone here a mechanic?"

Amarah peered hopefully over toward her husband. "You fix up old muscle cars."

"Car and boat engines are a bit different, Cupcake. Plus, it depends on the type of motor the vessels have, whether they're inboard or outboard motors. Then you throw in the advancement in technology, and newer boats are at a whole 'nother level. I wouldn't feel confident enough to try and attempt to get one running." He gave her a kind smile.

No one else spoke, and Amarah's stomach sank.

"Do we lock ourselves in our rooms until Friday?" Declan offered.

"There was no sign of forced entry into Parker and Cami's room." Everyone eyed Liam with confusion, causing him to sigh before continuing. "Meaning the killer has keys to our rooms."

More gasps sounded around the table. Amarah and Serenity kept quiet. They knew all the information and had nothing to offer that wasn't talked about previously in private.

"What if we have a group sleepover?" Myles offered next. "That way, if the killer makes a move, they'll be revealed."

"That's not a bad idea," Colton said, giving his husband an approving smile.

"Alright, let's vote. All those in favor of locking yourself in your own rooms until Friday, raise your hand." Hunter waited patiently as everyone's gaze shifted around the table, looking apprehensive, but not a single person raised their hand. "All those in favor of a group sleepover?"

One by one, everyone slowly raised a hand, some trembling with unease.

"It's settled then," Liam addressed the room. "Return to your rooms, pack your things, and bring them down to the lobby. We'll have the men start bringing down mattresses to the living room. We'll push all the furniture to the side and set up makeshift beds. If anyone has to use the bathroom or go anywhere for any reason, we travel in pairs. There will be two people on watch at all times that way everyone has someone who can vouch for them. Any questions?" Deafening silence surrounded them. "Alright, meet down in the living room in half an hour."

With that, they all stood from their chairs and climbed the stairs, disappearing into their rooms. Amarah and Liam stopped at Quinn's door and briefly filled her in on what was going on so she could gather her things and meet downstairs with the rest of the group.

CHAPTER 25

As agreed, half an hour later, all guests were standing in the living room. All the furniture had been shoved to the side, and mattresses from each room had been brought down and now lay in two neat rows across the tiled floor. Everyone's luggage lay next to their bed, and the help had been sent away and told to barricade themselves in the servants' quarters, where they had access to food, bathrooms, and beds until Friday, when the boat came to collect everyone.

All the guests sat at the foot of their beds, facing each other, all with a mix of nervous and scared expressions marring their features. And for good reason. They were all now forced to share a room with the murderer. Eyes shifted from person to person, all trust was lost, and paranoia was high as everyone had their own speculations as to who the killer might be.

Hunter finally broke the agonizing silence that dominated the room. "We need to set up a watch schedule."

Numerous nods were exchanged amongst the group.

"No disrespect but I feel couples should not be on watch together," Jade offered.

Liam nodded reluctantly. "You're right."

The thought of his wife standing watch with anyone but himself had him on edge. What if the partner she was on watch with was the killer? He may not be able to be with her during that time but he damn sure would be awake and have his eyes trained on her every second until she came back to bed and was by his side again.

"Why not?" Myles rebuked.

"Because if Serenity was the killer, I'd lie my ass off and vouch for her to protect her," Hunter answered honestly. "And each of you would do the exact same for the one you love."

"Oh, right, good point," Myles muttered as Colton wrapped an arm around him and pulled him against his side.

"How about this?" Amarah spoke up, gaining the attention of eight pairs of eyes. "We'll switch off every two hours. Declan and Colton will take the first watch, followed by Jade and Myles. Then Hunter, myself, and Quinn. Followed by Liam and Serenity?"

Liam peered to his left where his wife sat next to him at the foot of their mattress. Pride danced within his green eyes as he gently squeezed her hand, silently communicating that her idea was smart and incredible, just like her.

When no one objected, Colton spoke next. "I think a few of us should at least go and check out the boat dock. Maybe we'll get lucky?"

"But no one here's a boat mechanic," Declan added. "We discussed that at breakfast, remember?"

"I know my way around a boat." Quinn's soft voice broke the silence, and all heads snapped in her direction.

Her docile tone was at odds with the confident, bold woman everyone knew her to be. However, seeing your spouse brutally murdered in front of your eyes would knock anyone's spirits down. Liam absorbed the new piece of information, his skilled mind already calculating numerous possibilities on how they could use it to their advantage. Quinn wasn't at breakfast, so everyone believed that fixing up a boat was a lost cause. If she could look over them and restore one enough to charter everyone back to the mainland, maybe they could depart the island today.

Myles's manicured brows pinched tightly. "You do?"

Quinn nodded slightly. "I grew up in Rhode Island. My father owns a marina there. I used to help him fix up rundown boats to sell for extra money."

Liam watched as newfound hope sparked in everyone's eyes.

"Would you be willing to hike a few miles to the boat docks and have a look?" Hunter questioned.

"If it gets me the hell off this island, yes," she agreed.

"Alright, Quinn, myself, and Colton will go. See if we can get a boat started. Jade, do you have a map of the island?" Hunter asked, turning his attention toward her.

"Wait," Declan spoke up. "How do we know you won't just leave us here if you get one working?"

Liam sighed to himself, resisting the urge to pinch the bridge of his nose. A few deep breaths had his patience refocused. He knew this was to be expected. Most civilians don't handle situations like this well, with calm and clear heads the way he and Hunter do. Suspicions were high, all trust was lost, and everyone was on edge.

"Neither Colton nor I would leave the island without our partners," Hunter said matter-of-factly.

When no one argued the point further, Jade and Hunter left the room to retrieve a map she had in a small office on the main floor. Once they returned, Hunter plotted the best course, and the three left the resort.

The boat dock was three miles up the shoreline. Hunter Gatlin made sure everyone stayed close to the tree line, following it north around a bend on the island. The group remained quiet. Hunter knew that both Quinn and Colton were weary. He could tell by the stiffness of their shoulders, the way their vision kept shifting frantically over their surroundings, how Quinn kept her arms wrapped around her middle as if that would shield her from harm.

An hour had passed before the boat dock finally came into view. Two long wooden piers stretched out over the water, each with two old-looking vessels secured to them with rope. A rundown wooden shack with a metal roof that looked like it was one good gust of wind away from falling over stood nearby, shaded by trees.

"There are four of them. That's a good sign, right?"

Hunter could hear the hopeful and desperate tone of Colton's voice.

"Maybe." Hunter wished he could be as hopeful as Colton, but he'd always been more of a realist than a dreamer.

Though he was a realist, Hunter couldn't get himself to crush the man's spirit, so he kept his mouth shut. Not to mention, an unsettling feeling took root in the pit of his stomach. If there was a murderer among them, and there was sufficient evidence to back that theory, surely they'd make sure there was no way off the island. Ensuring to trap their victims here until *they* were ready to leave. Because that's exactly what he'd do if he were the killer.

"Colton, go and check the shed. See if there are any tools we might be able to use. Quinn, take the pier on the left. I'll take the one on the right."

"Wait, I thought we weren't allowed to go anywhere by

ourselves?" Colton asked hesitantly.

"We're in the middle of nowhere." Hunter spread his arms to their surroundings. "If any of us disappears, the identity of the killer will be revealed."

"Good point." Colton gave a curt nod before turning on his heel and striding toward the decrepit shed.

The rickety pier creaked under Hunter's weight as he walked over the clear blue water toward the first boat. The vessel rocked gently as the current moved past. The floor of the boat was dry, which was a good sign. At least he knew that there were no holes. He pressed a foot down on the side, testing its sturdiness. When he was confident it would hold him, he stepped aboard and glanced around.

The white paint was chipped, rust coated the metal of the railings, and the upholstery was faded and sported numerous tears. Though it may be rundown and ugly, it was still afloat, and as long as the engine was in good condition, it would serve its purpose. He moved toward the stern, pausing to poke his head inside the small cabin that housed the helm.

There was no exposed wiring where animals may have gotten into and chewed up, and no broken glass over the gauges. He kept moving toward the back, only to halt. Where the motor should be, mounted to the back of the vessel, was a barren space.

"Of course," Hunter sighed before muttering a string of colorful curses under his breath.

He peered to his left, where the other boat was rocking gently in the ocean. The condition of the boat didn't matter if there was no engine. Another curse slipped past his lips when he saw no motor mounted on the back of that vessel as well.

His suspicions were right. Someone made damn sure there was

no way off the island. He turned and stepped off the boat, back onto the dock, and returned to shore, where Quinn met him.

"Please tell me your boats had engines?" he asked.

"No." Her shoulders dropped in disappointment, and her tired honey eyes filled with defeat. "Since you asked, I'm guessing yours didn't, either?"

"No, but maybe there's one in the shack we can use?"

Though Quinn tried her best to stay positive, he could see the doubt written across her angular features as clear as day. They walked up the beach, toward the rundown shack, and entered through the small wooden door that Colton had left open. The man was busy scouring an old workbench filled with a variety of tools.

"Any luck?" Colton questioned.

"None of the boats have engines." Hunter's eyes scanned around the small, decrepit building. "Did you find one in here?"

Besides the workbench and tools, not much else filled the space except for a few rusted fifty-gallon drums and a variety of trash littering the ground.

"Not that I could see," Colton's tone quickly deflated.

"We could always makeshift some paddles and row ourselves back to the mainland?" Quinn suggested.

"No. The ride here took hours," Hunter shook his head. "It would take days to row by hand. Plus, we'd risk getting lost and stranded at sea. I'd rather be trapped on this island with the killer than on a tiny boat in the middle of the ocean."

With their shoulders in a slump, they left the shed, only for him to halt when something shiny caught his eye. He turned toward the back of the small building, where various pieces of metal lay across the dirt-covered ground, the rays of the sun reflecting off the smooth surfaces. He approached the pile with Quinn and Colton following close behind. They all stopped in their tracks when they observed the mound of broken plastic, bent metal, and loose wires that were piled high behind the shed.

"Well, we found the engines." Exhaustion was evident in Quinn's voice.

All four boat engines appeared as if someone had smashed them into pieces. Parts littered the ground, and it was hard to tell where one ended and another began.

At least now we have concrete proof that someone is forcing us to stay on this island.

"Any way one can be salvaged?" Again, Colton tried to remain hopeful.

Quinn gave him a sympathetic look and shook her head. "Not unless you're Magneto and can re-bend the destroyed metal to its original form."

When it was confirmed that they wouldn't be getting off the island via boat, they made the hour-long trek back, their spirits more broken than before.

CHAPTER 26

An hour and a half had passed since Hunter, Quinn, and Colton left to check out the boat docks. Jade Munro was perched crisscross atop her mattress, her forearms resting atop her knees as she fiddled with a loose string dangling from a seam at the bottom of her pants. Liam was pacing back and forth through the room, and Amarah and Serenity were perched on Myles's bed alongside him, trying their best to console him.

"Don't worry." Serenity placed her hand on his shoulder. "Colton will be back before you know it."

"I know." Myles released a heavy exhale. "At least he didn't go alone. I feel more comfortable knowing he's with that hunky fiancé of yours." Both Serenity and Amarah couldn't contain their laughter. "So big, and burly, and…" he sighed contentedly, "manly."

"I'm glad Hunter can help to put your mind at ease," Serenity laughed.

Myles gave her a small smile before saying, "I pray Quinn can work some magic and get us off this damn island."

Amarah released a hopeful sigh. "She said she grew up around boats. If anyone has a chance of getting one up and running, it's her."

"I still can't believe Aaron's gone." Myles ran a hand over his smooth chin. "And for Quinn to have witnessed it the way she did... No amount of therapy or prescription medication will make it easier for her to forget or move on from that."

"She seems like a strong woman." Amarah gave him a reassuring smile. "I'm sure that given some time, she'll be alright."

"Did you know they just bought a house?" Myles inquired.

"Really?" both Serenity and Amarah asked in unison.

"Yeah, back in Rhode Island. She told me the other day that they had just closed on it two weeks before coming here and that they couldn't wait to move in once they got back home."

Jade's vision snapped toward the group, her brows pinching as a jolt of pain shot through her chest like a bullet wound.

OCTOBER 2010

Bryson Munro pulled his truck into the driveway of a beautiful two-story family home that was painted a medium grey with bright white accents and topped with a black shingled roof. Numerous large windows lined the front of the house, all framed with crisp white wooden shutters. A massive wraparound covered porch made the home stand out among the others that lined the cozy street of the quiet neighborhood.

Jade couldn't contain her excitement as she jumped out of the truck, tilting her head up as she took in their new home. So much was going to happen there. She'd launch her business here. This is where they'd bring each of their children home from the hospital. This is where she and her husband would grow old and retire. This would be their first and their forever home.

Without warning, she was swept into a pair of strong arms as her husband carried her up the walkway lined with a variety of colorful plants and full shrubs. He ascended the three wooden steps and set her down gently in front of the door.

"Over there," he pointed to a wooden porch swing off to the side, "is where we'll watch all the thunderstorms as they roll through."

It was suspended by chains from the ceiling of the porch. A thick cushion lined the seat, and fluffy, bright pillows were placed in the corners.

Jade pointed back toward the road. "The school bus will pick up and drop off our kids right over there."

She had to admit, the house he swore he had "stumbled upon" had been perfect in every way. They had set up a showing after they got back from their wedding in Vegas, and the moment they pulled into the driveway, a feeling deep in her gut told her this was the one. The same feeling that told her Bryson was the one, and it hadn't steered her wrong yet. So she continued to listen.

As they toured the home with the agent, she found numerous reasons why this was the perfect house for them and zero reasons why it wouldn't work. It had plenty of bedrooms. The home was newly built and spacious enough to accommodate their future family. The backyard was large and fenced in. It had a home office that would suit her needs perfectly, and it was located in a fantastic neighborhood close to the military base Bryson worked on. They'd submitted an offer that night, and two days later, they'd received a phone call saying the sellers had accepted.

After the lengthy closing process, it was all theirs, and she was on cloud nine. To top it all off, Bryson's contract with the Navy was up in seven months. He could either renew for another few years or he could leave the military. After hours of discussing every option, looking at every angle, and weighing the pros and cons, they agreed that he wouldn't reenlist.

He wasn't a bachelor anymore. He had her to think about and the family they planned to start in the very near future. Though the military would provide them with a comfortable life with great benefits, they both agreed he couldn't risk his life anymore. And every mission he went on could be his last. It's that way with every SEAL. The possibility of leaving his family alone in this world was his biggest motivator.

He'd devoted nearly ten years of his life to his country, seen the world a time or two, and was ready to settle down into civilian life. Jade tried to picture what that would look like for him. For them. Though they'd only been together for eight months, he'd left on operations quite frequently. Bryson told her that he never wanted to miss a birthday, holiday, birth of a child, sports game, talent show, or any important occasion because he had to leave for work. He promised he'd be there for it all, and she didn't protest. She wanted him by her side until they died together, hand in hand, of old age.

Bryson dug a brass key from his front pocket and peered over at her, love swirling through his whisky eyes. "Ready to go inside?"

She clasped her hands together and beamed with excitement. "Yes!"

He made swift work of unlocking and opening the front door. Before she could take a step, she was again scooped up into his strong embrace as he carried her over the threshold. He set her down in the foyer and shut the door behind them.

"This will house the many tiny shoes of our children." He motioned to the large wooden bench resting against the wall that had cubby storage built beneath it. "And that closet will house their coats, gloves, and scarves for those bitterly cold winter days." He pointed to the small closet off to the side.

She laced her fingers through her husband's as she began to walk down the hallway. "Right here," she pointed to a spot on the wall by the staircase, "will be marked with measurements, tracking their height as our kids celebrate each birthday."

They entered the kitchen and paused, looking around the open space updated with ample cabinets, granite countertops, and stainless steel appliances.

"Here is where we'll teach them to cook, and over there is where we'll have dinner as a family every night." He pointed to the dining room that would house a massive table with numerous chairs.

They entered the living room and paused. "We can roast marshmallows over there." She motioned to the massive fireplace that was framed with large windows that showed a clear view of the backyard.

"And there is your office." Bryson pulled her through the open French doors off the living room. "I can't wait to see what that brilliant brain of yours cooks up in here. Speaking of..." He gave her a gentle kiss atop her head. "Will you finally tell me what you've been working on?"

She had to focus hard to contain her smile. Her dating website, Desire, had come a long way and in a matter of weeks, would be ready to launch. She planned on telling him. Just not yet.

"Nope." She gave him a wink. "Soon though. I promise."

They left and began to climb the stairs.

"This will make a perfect nursery," she sighed dreamily.

"And so will that one, and that one over there." He pointed to the other spare bedrooms down the hall.

Jade laughed, the melodic sound echoing off the empty walls that would soon be filled with pictures and artwork. "We might end up having to pair them up if we have too many kids. I've always wanted a bunk bed, but being an only child, I never got one."

"I'll get you the biggest bunk bed I can find. Maybe one with a castle playhouse on top?"

"Most definitely!"

They walked down the hallway, hand in hand, passing a full bathroom before entering their bedroom at the end of the hall. The massive space was filled with natural light from the numerous windows along the back two walls.

"And in here," Bryson stepped behind her and wrapped his arms around her middle, "is where all our babies will be conceived."

"I don't know," she laughed. "That kitchen island looked like a pretty good spot. And so did the laundry room, and my office…"

He spun her around and captured her lips with his. She looped her arms around his neck as she deepened the kiss, their bodies melting to fit perfectly together like a beautiful puzzle. He pulled back and peered down at her.

"We've got nothing but time to break in *every* inch of this house." His smile sent butterflies soaring through her stomach.

The doorbell rang, pulling them out of their happy little dream and back to reality.

"That would be the movers. Are you ready to start making this house feel like a home?" He arched a brow at her.

"You're here with me." Tears lined her eyes as she tried hard not to let them fall. "It's already a home."

"You're damn right it is." He placed one last kiss against her forehead before they walked back downstairs, hands clasped tightly together.

A large hand rested gently against Jade's shoulder, sending a surprised jolt through her body and a scream to get caught in her throat.

"Whoa." Liam spoke calmly. "I didn't mean to scare you. I just wanted to make sure you were ok."

She took multiple deep breaths, trying to steady out her racing heart as her vision skimmed across the room. Hunter, Quinn, and Colton weren't back yet. Amarah, Serenity, and Myles still sat on his mattress. While they were lost in conversation, she got lost in a blast from her past. A wonderful memory that left water lining her chocolate eyes.

"Jade?" Liam's tone was almost a whisper.

She quickly swiped at her eyes and shook off his hand from her shoulder. "I'm fine." She cleared her throat and peered up at him. His usual masked expression had dropped, revealing just how worried he was for her. "I promise I'm alright."

She must've sounded more confident that time because Liam gave her a reluctant nod and walked away, resuming his casual pacing of the living room.

CHAPTER 27

Upon returning, Hunter Gatlin filled the group in on their finds, or lack, at the boat dock. Everyone had split off into their own groups and relaxed in the living room. Or tried to as much as possible. That was a hard concept for most, given that someone among them had killed two people already and most likely had more names on their target list before they were through.

Some read books, some played cards or board games, while others sat in silence or strolled about the room to stretch their legs. When it came time for lunch, Liam, Colton, Declan, and Serenity entered the kitchen together as the remainder of the group stayed in the living room. They made quick work of throwing together sandwiches and grabbing handfuls of snacks and bottled water.

They distributed the food upon returning, everyone choosing to eat in silence. Afterward, everyone was left to their own devices to pass the time. They had set up designated bathroom breaks where the women would go as a group, and when they returned, the men would go. They did the same for dinner as they did with lunch, gathering armloads of food and water and carrying it back to the living room.

The tension in the room grew more taut the further the sun

sank toward the horizon. Even though everyone knew people would be watching over them, they were still uneasy about being so vulnerable and exposed at a time like this.

The day had gone by without a hitch. No one acted or said anything mistrustful or even tried to go off by themselves. Everyone was very cooperative, even if their guards were built stronger than Fort Knox. As the women departed to the bathrooms to get ready for bed, Liam watched as Hunter made his way over and perched next to him on the edge of the mattress.

"We may have two people watching over us at all times," Hunter kept his voice low so no one would be able to eavesdrop, "but I trust everyone here about as far as I can throw them."

"I'm right there with you." Liam nodded in agreement. "What are you thinking?"

"We'll switch off, just you and I, like we did last night. That way, someone we know and trust with the lives of our women is always on the lookout until everyone wakes in the morning."

A sly grin pulled at Liam's angular features. "You took the thoughts right out of my head."

Without another word, both men held out a closed fist, shook it three times, and threw out their sign. A game they used to play back in the military, anytime a decision had to be made amongst the group. Liam threw out scissors while Hunter chose rock.

Hunter furrowed his thick brows. "Who the hell chooses scissors?"

"I don't know." Liam shrugged innocently. "I was hoping you'd choose paper."

Since he lost, Liam would take the first watch. It was fitting, anyhow, seeing as Hunter had the third shift with Amarah and Quinn. Liam would stay awake for half the night before rousing

Hunter to keep watch for the second half.

When the women returned from the bathroom, no one was shocked to find they'd changed but were still dressed in normal clothes. No one wanted to be in flimsy nightgowns or skimpy pajamas if something went down in the middle of the night and the killer attempted to strike again. The men then departed for the bathrooms and returned in fresh everyday clothes as well.

As the remainder of the guests settled beneath their covers for the night, Declan McCarthy and Colton King began pacing the room quietly as one by one the space began to fill with only the sounds of steady breathing. Liam Godrik stayed awake as he snagged his wife's tablet and pulled up her Kindle library. He couldn't help but chuckle to himself when he found it filled with romance books of all kinds. Fantasy, thriller, dark, even monster romances. Whatever the hell that was.

A cover with a big, blue-horned alien piqued his curiosity. He clicked it and began reading as his wife lay asleep, snuggled safely against his side. The first two hours had passed without a hitch. Declan roused Jade, and Colton woke Myles for the second shift. Liam watched quietly as Jade and Myles began to pace about the room, and Declan and Colton crawled into their own beds and quickly fell asleep.

Liam returned half of his focus to his book, keeping the other half on the two people wandering aimlessly about the living room. He was soon questioning himself when he realized just how much he liked the book. He was nearly halfway through it, speed reading to get to the next page as fast as possible, but he'd take that secret to the grave.

He'd never give his wife a hard time for reading such books again. It was better research than Google or porn. Liam was mentally taking notes from scenes that aroused him so he could reenact them with Amarah once they made it back home. Because they *would* make it back home. He'd give his last breath to ensure his wife survived this fucking sham of a vacation.

An hour into the second watch, hushed voices drew his attention from his tablet. Because it was quieter than a courtroom right before the jury reads their verdict, he could hear the conversation perfectly.

"But I have to pee," Jade practically whined as she kept her voice no louder than a whisper.

"Are you serious, woman?" Myles scolded her in a hushed tone. "We aren't supposed to go off by ourselves."

Jade motioned an arm around the room filled with slumbering guests.

"Then come with me. Everyone's asleep anyway."

"And give the killer a chance to claim their next victim? I don't think so."

"What if I'm the killer?" Jade teased lightheartedly.

"Yeah, that definitely won't get me to go to the bathroom with you." Myles' tone was filled with sass as he placed his hands on his hips and pinned her with a stern look.

"Ugh," Jade groaned quietly. "Well then, help me find an empty bottle."

"Why?" Myles questioned hesitantly and furrowed his groomed brows. Then his eyes widened in horror. "Eww! You will not pee in a bottle in a room full of people!" he whisper-shouted.

"Why not?" She threw her hands up in frustration. "Everyone's asleep, and I'm not worried about you seeing my lady bits. You're gay."

"Hello, Mr. Hottie Pants is awake over there." He pointed a

polished finger in Liam's direction. "I'm sure he wouldn't take too kindly to watching a woman, who isn't his wife, pee in a bottle."

Liam snorted to himself, rather enjoying the exchange between the two and grinning at Myles's little nickname for him.

"For the love of all things holy, just go to the bathroom, Jade. Myles, go with her. I'll cover until y'all get back," Liam whispered to the arguing couple.

Their heads snapped toward him in unison. Liam didn't need a light to know they were both probably blushing from knowing that he had heard their entire conversation.

"No one is supposed to be alone." Myles crossed his arms over his chest and popped out a hip. "What if you're the killer?"

"If I were the killer, I would never have brought the matter to everyone's attention at breakfast this morning," Liam drawled in a bored tone.

Myles hesitated for a moment as if lost in consideration of Liam's words.

"Fair point." He nodded his head. "But that doesn't eliminate Jade over here as a suspect. What if she's the killer and tries to off me in the bathroom?"

Liam didn't miss the utter disgust that filled Myles's hushed tone, pulling a grin across Liam's bearded face.

"Then scream really loud and Mr. Hottie Pants will come to your rescue," Liam said.

"Alright, but you better be shirtless, Mister," Myles submitted.

"Deal." Liam chuckled.

"God, I swear if I die on the floor of a public bathroom I'm going to be extremely pissed off."

A visible shiver rolled down Myles's spine as he pivoted on his heel and followed Jade down the hall toward the bathrooms.

Liam glanced over to where Amarah lay curled into his side, loving how close she was. He reached over and lightly brushed a few blonde strands out of her face, tucking them behind her ear so nothing obstructed the view of her gorgeous features. Then he leaned down and placed a soft kiss against her forehead, causing her to sigh sleepily and snuggle further into his warmth.

It was crazy, the level of love he held for that woman. An amount he never thought was capable of a single human. An amount that was probably borderline unhealthy or even psychotic and stalkerish. But he didn't care. Though some of his life choices may have been questionable, he wouldn't change a thing because everything he did in life, every path he took, led him straight to the love of his life, the other half of his soul.

Sometimes, he loved to simply watch her sleep. The peaceful and contented look that lined her angular features held him captive. He wondered more times than once what she dreamed about, wishing he could join her. A few minutes had passed, and Liam heard no scream yet, meaning Jade and Myles must be alright and would be returning from the bathroom shortly. After another minute, the smell of rotten eggs hit him, causing him to shield his nose and glance about the room.

What was that smell coming from? Had someone farted in their sleep? Natural gas had its own distinct smell, which wasn't rotten eggs, so he knew there wasn't a hazardous leak somewhere. He peered around the room, looking up toward the ceiling, and saw no smoke filling the space, so he knew it wasn't a possible fire.

When his vision faltered and he became light-headed, his eyes widened in horror. His years of training and the numerous operations he was a part of had filled his head with so much knowledge over the years that he could be a walking encyclopedia.

Knowledge about a wide range of topics that were drilled into his brain and are there to stay.

He knew the cause of the smell: hydrogen sulfide. Also known as knockdown gas. A dangerous and non-visible gas that, when inhaled, would knock someone out, and the room was now filling with it. With his hand still covering his nose, he threw the covers off himself and rolled out of bed.

His body was sluggish, and it felt as if someone had upped the gravity of the Earth, making it nearly impossible for him to stand. Instead, he began to crawl on all fours toward Hunter. He opened his mouth to call out, but no words left his throat. Finally, he reached Hunter and shook his arm forcefully.

Hunter's eyes fluttered open lazily, and Liam's heart dropped to his stomach. He knew it was too late. Though he was able to cover his nose and extend his chances by another minute or so, Hunter wasn't so lucky. Liam's body grew heavier with each passing second, and all too soon, darkness stole his vision, and he collapsed to the floor.

CHAPTER 28

Liam Godrik's eyes felt like lead as he tried and failed to shake off the grogginess. Why was he so tired? Why was his brain all fuzzy? He tried hard to recall his last memory. What had they been doing? He felt his head fall forward as he tried again to open his eyes.

Slowly, they cracked, allowing dim light to sting his sensitive irises. He blinked rapidly, trying to clear his blurred vision. Did he fall asleep when he was supposed to be on watch? Where was he? He didn't remember there being so much grey in the living room. Finally, his vision began to focus, and the sight before him sent all the color draining from his face.

Amarah sat about ten feet across from him. Thick steel chains were wrapped around her arms, torso, and legs, anchoring her to a cold metal chair. He went to reach for her but was halted in place, unable to move even an inch. He too was secured tightly to a metal chair with a thick padlock securing the chains around his body.

His wife's head hung forward as if still asleep. His gaze studied her chest closely, and a sigh of relief passed his lips when it was rising and falling in a slow but steady movement. She was alive. His gaze shifted to the left, to find Serenity's head rolled back and secured to a chair of her own.

Movement to Liam's left drew his head in the direction to see Hunter starting to wake. The room they found themselves in was cold and damp. Grey stones covered the walls, and the concrete floor contained a small drain. *That's never a good sign.* A basement of some kind was his best guess. A long metal table was set up nearby that had various tools lining it, as if in preparation for torture.

Well, this should be fun.

"What the fuck?" he heard Hunter groggily curse under his breath.

Hunter tried to strain against the chains, the veins in his arms and neck popping to the surface of his tanned skin with the effort, but it was futile.

"About time you woke up." Liam's mouth felt drier than the Sahara, but he kept his voice quiet, unsure if anyone was watching them.

Hunter's head snapped up. His vision narrowed on Liam, then shifted toward the table lined with shiny mental instruments. "Shit…" He trailed off and peered back at Liam to see the man motioning with his head forward. Hunter's gaze followed. "Motherfucker," he cursed further when he saw Serenity and Amarah in front of them.

Liam tried to keep the mood light. "You've always had such a colorful vocabulary."

It was all he could do not to slip into madness at being utterly helpless. He'd failed. Failed to rescue his wife. Failed to rescue his brother and his fiancée. Failed to get the remaining guests off this island of hell. Pure rage began to bubble beneath the surface of his skin.

"Yeah, well, I feel the occasion calls for it," Hunter grumbled. "What happened to keeping watch?"

"Hydrogen sulfide," Liam groaned, pissed at himself for falling victim to it.

Hunter shook his head. Liam knew his friend wasn't frustrated with him but rather with their situation. About that time, both Amarah and Serenity began to move as they slowly drifted back toward consciousness. Both men remained quiet until the women were fully aware of their senses.

"Liam?" Amarah's question was laced with fear. "Where are we?"

"I don't know, Cupcake." He gritted his teeth, hating that they tried so hard to keep a level head and stay safe, only to end up in this unfortunate situation.

"Hunter?" Serenity's tone matched Amarah's.

"It's alright, Angel. Just stay calm," Hunter tried to soothe his fiancée. "We'll get through this."

A male voice called from the top of the stairs. "Oh, good. I was wondering when you guys would wake up."

Amarah and Serenity tried to turn their heads toward the voice, but they couldn't. Liam's eyes narrowed as he descended the stairs, the wood creaking beneath the man's weight. His blood ran cold when a freckled face and fiery hair came into view.

"Declan fucking McCarthy," Hunter growled low in warning.

"What?" both women gasped as their eyes widened in disbelief and shock.

"Should've known it was the ginger." Disgust dripped from Liam's words.

Declan crossed the space and sent a right fist into the left side of Liam's face. Both women gasped as Declan gripped Liam's black hair and yanked his head back, their green eyes clashing.

"That was very rude." Declan smiled in satisfaction.

"Yeah, well, I never said I was a nice person." Liam sent spit flying into Declan's freckled face.

Declan released Liam's hair and wiped his face clean before backhanding him, sending his head snapping in the other direction. Liam flexed his jaw before chuckling lightly.

Declan walked around the back of the girls, grabbed handfuls of their hair, and yanked their heads backward. They hissed at the sting but kept quiet.

A wicked thrill glistened in his eyes as he peered toward Hunter and Liam. "Maybe I'll start with you two."

"What do you want, Declan?" Hunter growled as he flexed against the chains again, sending a clinking noise echoing off the stone walls.

"Do I have your attention now?" Declan arched a fiery brow toward the men before releasing the women's hair. "You see, someone very dear to me has been hurt by you both, and it's time to collect."

"We've never met you before this trip." Liam scrunched his brows together. "Who could we've possibly hurt that's close to you?"

"Me," a female voice sounded from the top of the stairs, and Liam's body went completely still.

No... It can't be.

Liam's gaze met a familiar pair of chocolate eyes as Jade descended the stairs and strode toward the table in full view of everyone. Her black hair was pulled into a high ponytail, and she was dressed in a pair of blue skinny jeans and a T-shirt.

"Jade?" Both Serenity and Amarah gasped.

"Hello, boys." Jade gave them a wicked smile and looked upon each of them as if savoring the moment. "God, I've waited for this day for nearly a decade."

"I told you I'd make your vision a reality, baby." Declan puffed out his chest and stood a bit taller, as if proud of himself for helping with her wicked plan.

Baby? The word wormed under Liam's skin like a nasty parasite. He'd observed them the entire weekend and knew they were close from the looks of things, but hearing it just sounded... wrong.

"You did." Jade gave him a bright smile. "I should've never doubted your love for me."

"I don't hold it against you, my love. When I first met them, I questioned my own abilities." Declan laughed as he glanced between Hunter and Liam before turning back to Jade. "But the thought of how happy this revenge would make you drove me to new limits."

He closed the space between them, pulled Jade into his arms, and claimed her lips. She melted into him as she kissed him back with such passion. Declan dropped his arm and grabbed a handful of her ass, giving it a firm squeeze. She moaned against his mouth where their tongues intertwined in a familiar dance.

Liam wanted to look away, but his gaze, like his body, was held captive. He wasn't the only one, either. Amarah, Serenity, and Hunter all stared, unblinking, at the unexpected encounter. Hunter's horrified expression matched Liam's as if witnessing it was somehow a betrayal to their dead brother.

They were breathless when they finally parted, and Declan turned toward the group.

"Where would you like to start, baby?"

"I'm not sure. The possibilities are endless." Jade picked up an ice pick and twirled it around in her palm as if testing its weight. "What do you have in mind?"

"We could start with removing small pieces of flesh? Or pulling out teeth. One at a time." His head cocked to the side as he studied each of his victims. "We could also remove fingernails. I hear those hurt like a son of a bitch."

"All good ideas, my dear." Jade set the ice pick down and picked up a large butcher knife, flicking her thumb along the edge. A sadistic gleam sparkled in her eyes. "But I have a better idea."

"Tell me." He smiled wickedly, never once taking his eyes off Liam and Hunter.

"I think we should start right..." Jade spoke in a sweet voice as she gripped the knife, rocked up onto her toes behind Declan, and slid the blade across his creamy neck, "here."

Blood shot out from the wound, sending droplets to land atop Liam and Amarah's jeans. Declan's green eyes widened in shock as he clutched his neck in a failed attempt to quench the bleeding. A thick river of crimson seeped through his fingers as gurgling sounds escaped his mouth and reverberated off the stoned walls.

He stumbled forward before dropping to his knees and slowly bled out before collapsing to the ground, face down in a bloody pool. His body twitched violently, but after another minute, no more sounds escaped his mouth, and his eyes gaped lifelessly toward the wall. Jade ran the back of her hand across her mouth and spit on Declan's lifeless body.

None of them dared to breathe, let alone speak, as they sat there in complete shock and watched the scene unfold before their eyes. What the fuck was even going on? Liam feared this must be some kind of vivid nightmare, but after several attempts to force himself awake, dread settled deep within his bones.

Jade gently set the knife back atop the table, not even bothering to clean the blade. She stepped over Declan's body, not minding that the soles of her shoes were now stained red with his blood. She gripped one of his arms and began to drag his body toward the far wall. It took a bit of effort for her, but she managed it. A thick line of crimson smeared the concrete flooring in a path from the pool of blood to where his body now lay beside the far wall.

Jade straightened, dusted off her hands, and smiled. "Now that he's out of the picture, let's begin."

CHAPTER 29

Amarah Godrik had been thrown completely off guard, leaving her at a loss for words. Her vision zeroed in on the little droplets of blood that now stained her blue jeans as if snared in their brutal trap. She'd just watched a woman whom she pitied and suspected to be a good person murder a man in cold blood with a literal smile on her face.

Jade Munro was not at all who Amarah thought she was. Amarah had to give Jade props. The woman had everyone fooled, even Liam and Hunter. Two people who knew her closely once upon a time. But time changes people, and so does tragedy. It appeared that both had altered Jade for the worse.

Hunter was the first to break the silence. "So you two aren't a thing?"

"Declan and I? Hell no." Jade visibly shuddered with disgust.

This woman should've pursued a career in Hollywood with acting skills like that. Jade had the entire house eating out of the palm of her hands, and Amarah felt like a fool, scolding her kind heart for buying into Jade's sob story.

"Then why bother with him?" Liam questioned.

Amarah had wondered the same thing. Why risk sharing her

plans and involving someone who might report you to the police? Someone who might not see things the way Jade did, or whose moral compass didn't point in the exact direction as hers. Hell, why risk involving someone if she just planned to kill them in the end?

Jade shrugged her slender shoulder. "He was a means to an end."

Her chocolate gaze shifted around the room, taking in everyone's confused and horrified looks.

"What happened to everyone else? Myles, Colton, Quinn?" Serenity asked hesitantly. "Is one or all of them dead now?"

Jade's chest rose as she took in a deep inhale before releasing it and rolling her shoulders.

"I warned Declan not to try anything bold," she sighed. "But he grew cocky. With you two men now convinced there was a murderer, I was forced to rework my plan and speed up my timeline. Once I'm finished here, I'll do what Declan failed to."

She let out another long sigh before leaning back against the table and crossing her arms over her chest.

"Where shall I start?" She tipped her chin toward the ceiling as if lost in deep thought.

"From the beginning would be fucking nice," Liam muttered dryly.

"I suppose I can give you a reason for the atrocities I'm about to commit." Jade's smile was wicked and sent Amarah's dinner to the back of her throat.

No, she would not throw up. She would not show weakness. She clamped her jaw tight as she took slow, steady breaths and pushed the nausea away. She had to survive. It wasn't just her life she had to think about now. She had a baby relying on her for nourishment and growth, and she'd be damned if she went down without one hell of a fight.

VIRGINIA - ONE YEAR AGO

Jade Munro sat behind a large mahogany desk at Desire headquarters, light spilling into her corner office. Her eyes were trained on her dual monitors as she reviewed last month's numbers. A gentle knock sounded at her office door, pulling her attention away from her work.

"Come in," she called out, and watched as Declan McCarthy opened her door, clutching a tablet in his pasty hand.

She'd had to hire a new assistant after her previous one decided not to return when her maternity leave was over. Jade was beyond relieved when the woman finally went into labor. Watching her assistant's belly swell and grow with life was an agonizing daily reminder of a joy that was once stolen from her after the death of her husband.

The hiring pool was vast for her new assistant position, and Declan had seemed like a great fit during his interview. However, after being hired, he quickly became infatuated with her. Not in a bad or creepy way, but rather in a sweet and caring way. Which was so much worse in her opinion.

He'd reminded her of a golden retriever. Gentle-natured, always smiling, happy, and wholly loyal. But none of that mattered. Her heart had been given to another man many years ago, and he took it with him to his grave.

"Have you seen the news today?"

The worry lacing his voice sent a terrible feeling forming in the pit of her stomach. Her brows pinched tightly as Declan rounded her desk, placing his tablet down in front of her. A national news webpage was pulled up, and as Jade read the bold article title, her stomach soured.

Oklahoma Woman Gained A Stalker After Using A Popular Dating Website.

She devoured the article, her vision skimmed frantically across the lines as her assistant stood quietly beside her. She felt bad for everything Amarah Patterson went through and cursed Derick Watland for giving her website a bad reputation.

She read on to discover the woman had recruited the help of a close friend. When she read Liam Godrik's name, recognition sparked old, painful memories. Memories she'd spent years burying in the dark depths of her mind. She ground her teeth together as white-hot rage seared through her.

For the last eight years, she'd thought long and hard about different ways she could exact her revenge on Bryson's former team and make them pay for his death. A death she was convinced had been their fault. They were brothers. They were supposed to keep each other safe. Their ultimate failure left her to pay an unimaginable price.

The course of the next week had been a PR nightmare. Jade had stayed out of the public eye and had her team handle everything. They were great at what they did, and by the following week, the news had moved on to bigger stories, and everyone seemed to forget. Her site didn't take that big of a hit, thank goodness. People knew that Desire wasn't responsible for the stalker or his actions. It was just an unfortunate event that could happen to anyone while online dating.

Two weeks had passed, and Jade was scrolling through her emails when a notification popped up on her monitor. Her rounded features contorted with curiosity. When she clicked on it, it took her to a newly created profile on her website. When she saw the man's picture, it was as if time stood still, and her body forgot how to breathe.

He was older now, his features more mature than the last time she saw him, but there was no mistaking those unique eyes, the long brown hair, and the scar that bisected his left eyebrow. She read Hunter Gatlin's name at least ten times to make sure there was no mistake.

Years ago, she integrated a facial recognition software so that if anyone from Bryson's old team made a profile on her website, she'd be alerted. She knew the odds were slim but not impossible. And there it was, staring mockingly at her. Over the years, she'd kept tabs on the men through social media and other... less ethical ways so that when her plan was ready, she was up to date on what had been going on in their lives.

After years of silence, she'd finally gained a connection with the two men she held responsible for her husband's death. It was as if Fate was speaking directly to her, telling her it was finally time.

After she left work that day, she drove in complete silence to a mid-sized graveyard that was close to her house. The house she and Bryson bought just after they got married. A house they'd planned to fill with their growing family only housed her. A lonely, broken shell of what once was. It wasn't a home. It wasn't even a house anymore. It had become a tomb. Her tomb.

Jade had tried to move several times, but she couldn't get herself to leave so many memories behind. Though they were painful, they helped keep her husband alive and fresh in her mind.

She pulled down a narrow-paved road that wound through the well-manicured lawn lined with headstones of all shapes and sizes. She parked, crossed the grass, careful not to step on other graves, and stopped in front of a black granite upright headstone.

The edges were rounded with the name *Munro* carved in large, elegant font across the top. The words *Bryson Munro, April 10th, 1982 – November 20th, 2010* were engraved on the left-hand side. Two overlapping hearts filled the middle, and the right held the words *Jade Munro, January 3rd, 1988*.

She'd bought the plot next to him and had a double headstone erected so that when it was her time, she could be buried where she belonged, right next to her husband, until the end of time.

"Hey, baby." Jade knelt and brushed a few blades of grass off the base of the headstone left there by the gardener who tended the property. "I miss you."

She sat down on her side of the grave, legs extended in front of her and crossed at the ankle, her back leaning against the cold granite. She visited often, usually a few times a week, and talked like they did at dinner every night when he was alive. She'd tell him about her day, what was new in her life, things she was struggling with, and wished more than anything he would respond.

A few times, she swore she heard his melodic laugh when she told him something funny or felt a hand caress her shoulder when she was struggling, but she knew it was all just figments of her imagination. She closed her eyes and pictured Bryson sitting next to her, enjoying the sun soaking into his beautiful tawny skin.

"You won't believe the week I've had."

A hysterical bubble of laughter slipped out as she filled her husband in on the story with Amarah, Amarah's stalker, and

Liam, and the profile Hunter had created on her website.

"It might take some time, but I *will* get my revenge. I know what you're going to say. That it wasn't their fault, and I should forgive them, let go, and move on, but I can't." Her voice broke, and she felt a hot tear roll down her cheek. "They were supposed to bring you back home to me, and they failed. I will make them pay. I swear it. They don't deserve to live their lives, full of love and adventure, to get married, have children, and grow old, when your life was cut short and you were forced to reside here until the end of time."

Rage began to pool deep within her cold heart, and slowly, a plan started to take shape in her mind. A plan that only grew darker and more devious as she tweaked and refined it more times than she cared to admit. She knew this would take time, but she was a patient woman, and the gratification would be well worth the wait.

CHAPTER 30

Amarah Godrik was dumbfounded. Jade had orchestrated a revenge so in-depth, and they fell right into her trap. She cursed herself for being so stupid and naive. She should've listened to her gut and not accepted the apology offer. The funny thing was that there was never an apology. Jade didn't care that a stalker used her site to torture and traumatize a woman. All Jade cared about was her revenge.

"How did you get Declan to go along with your scheme?" Hunter inquired.

"When someone wants your love so desperately, you'd be surprised at the lengths they'd be willing to push themselves to." Jade paused for a moment as she looked toward Declan's body. Not even a single ounce of remorse entered her chocolate eyes. "Manipulation isn't easy by any means, but over time, I was able to make him see that after helping me with this," she motioned to the four of them before her with her hands, "we could finally be together. That was all the motivation he needed."

"Hydrogen sulfide isn't just something people have lying around. How did you set it up to capture us?" Liam interrogated.

"Oh, come on. Do you guys take me for a fool? I knew the kind of men you both were when I met you guys. I knew I had to be careful in my planning." Jade picked at a loose cuticle on her finger as if she were bored with the conversation already. "I spent months prepping this island for *every* possible contingency plan I could think of. Honestly, this entire place is one big death trap."

"You're an evil woman," Serenity spat.

Jade chuckled as she straightened and turned toward the table. "It's crazy what trauma and grief can do to a person."

Her head swiveled from side to side as if deeply considering her next move. She picked up a pair of brass knuckles, slid her fingers through the holes, and made a tight fist with her left hand.

"You've always been the most observant." Jade came to a stop in front of Hunter, and Amarah didn't miss how Serenity's body tensed. "Have you figured out the pattern to my victims yet?"

Before Hunter could answer, she sent her fist into the side of his face, forcing his head to snap to the side. Amarah heard Serenity inhale sharply beside her. Hunter grunted, and Amarah saw rage burning in his eyes as he glared up at Jade. A small stream of crimson ran through his beard from the slits the brass knuckles cut open on his skin.

"You're killing off one person from each couple." Hunter spoke in a deep and even voice, void of emotion. "I just don't know why."

Without warning, Jade sent another fist into his face. Her small body seemed to tremble with rage.

"Because," another punch, "I want to make them hurt." Her tone rose with every word. "I want everyone to feel the pain I feel every day when I wake up and am forced to live yet another day without the love of my life."

Her voice cracked, and it broke Amarah's heart.

It all made sense. It wasn't right, by any means, but she

sympathized with Jade. She couldn't imagine the unspeakable loss Jade had been forced to live with.

There was no aggression or malice in Amarah's next words. "Then why continue to live?"

Liam's gaze shot to hers, and numerous emotions swirled in his bright greens. Amarah spared him a glance before returning her attention to their capture. Jade whirled around and crossed the space, bending at the waist and stopping inches from her face. Amarah didn't pull back, didn't flinch. She merely clenched her jaw and held Jade's gaze.

"You don't think I tried?" A hysterical sound escaped. "I did. I stood on the edge of a high-rise building. I pressed a knife against my wrist, held a gun to my temple, gripped a bottle of pills, but each time I was about to commit, I heard his sweet voice. Bryson was next to me each time, talking me down."

Amarah saw the true pain in Jade's dark eyes, saw the agony in her features, and heard the devastation in every word. Tears threatened to spill, but Jade held them back.

"I'm so sorry," Amarah whispered in complete honesty.

Jade straightened and backhanded Amarah. She sucked in a sharp breath as pain erupted across her face from the brass knuckles, and warm liquid began to drip slowly down her cheek.

Venom dripped from Jade's voice. "Save your pity for someone who wants it."

"Stop!" Hunter and Liam shouted in unison.

Jade laughed, but two deep creases formed between her brows in challenge. "Why?"

"Because she's..." Hunter stopped himself before he could finish his sentence.

Jade cocked her head to the side, newfound interest filling her rounded features. "She's what?"

Liam snapped his head toward his friend. "She's what?" His voice was no louder than a whisper, but the small space and stone walls amplified it.

Amarah met Hunter's vision. He remained quiet, and she knew that he intended to keep his promise. She would be eternally grateful, but now was as good a time as any. They might not live through this, and Liam deserved to know. Even if the day never came to meet their baby.

"I'm pregnant," Amarah admitted, no louder than Liam's question.

She met her husband's eyes, and the sight before her ripped her heart in two. He dropped his gaze to her stomach and paused before he brought them back up.

"You're pregnant?" Liam's voice broke, and all she could do was nod slowly, fighting against the tears that so desperately wanted to fall.

"Oh, this just keeps getting better!" Jade clapped her hands together and laughed melodically, smiling wickedly at Liam. "To know you'll suffer *exactly* as I have makes me happier than you could ever have imagined."

"What do you mean by that?" Hunter inquired.

"Did your thorough observation skills not pick up on it back then? Huh... It did for Sandra."

Hunter's face scrunched before his vision widened. "You were pregnant?" He asked cautiously.

"Once upon a time, yes..."

CHAPTER 31

NOVEMBER 2010

Jade Munro placed a strainer in the sink and dumped the boiling pot of noodles into it. She set the pan aside and shook the strainer from side to side, shifting the noodles around, making sure to drain as much of the water as possible. She then placed the cooked noodles in a large bowl, added some sweet tomato and basil sauce and homemade meatballs, before mixing them all together.

The timer chimed as she grabbed a hot pad and removed the pan of garlic bread from the oven. She began to plate their spaghetti and garlic bread when Bryson entered the kitchen, came up behind her, and wrapped his arms around her waist. He gave her a gentle squeeze as he kissed her creamy neck, sending goosebumps sprouting.

Droplets of water fell from his hair onto her shoulder, and she gasped at the cold sensation.

"Let me get that for you." He chuckled as he ran his tongue along her smooth skin and licked up the water. She moaned and let her head fall back against his chest. "Dinner smells amazing, by the way." He released her and stepped back.

"Thank you." She smiled. "Before we eat, I've got a present for you."

She grinned satisfactorily at the shocked expression on his face. It took about a week for them to unpack and settle into their new home. Since they came from a one-bedroom apartment, there wasn't much furniture to move around, so they spent a few days shopping and fully furnishing the house. Now, it looked and felt as if they'd spent years in the place. It was warm and inviting and everything she could've ever dreamed of.

They even got to experience their first Halloween in the neighborhood. They had run out of candy a few hours in from all the kids that stopped by, giving them yet another thing to look forward to when they finally had kids of their own.

"What's the occasion?" He leaned back against the counter and crossed his arms over his bare chest.

She shrugged casually. "Does a wife need a reason to get her husband a gift?"

Bryson wore nothing but a pair of black and grey plaid pajama pants that hung low around his slim waist. Her gaze dropped, following the path of his abs that led to a trail of dark hair and a muscled V that disappeared beneath the waistband of his pants. The sight had her body heating up and arousal coursing through her.

She reluctantly tore her eyes away and disappeared down the hall. She returned a few seconds later holding a small blue gift bag. She set it on the counter next to him and stepped back, trying hard to contain her bubbling excitement.

He smiled as he grabbed the bag and removed the white tissue paper. Pulling out a small white stick with a pink cap on the end, she watched as his face contorted into confusion as he turned the object over in his hand a few times before peering back up at her.

"What is this?" He laughed in confusion.

"Remember our wedding day?"

"My little kunoichi, I could live to be a hundred, and I'd never forget that day."

"Do you remember the little tryst we had in the changing room?" Jade's tone was sensual at the reminder, and it did nothing to calm her raging hormones.

A wicked grin split his full lips. "That was my favorite part."

"What can happen when two adults have sex with no protection?"

She may have been enjoying this a little too much.

He arched a brow. "STDs?"

"Oh my gosh!" She snorted and shook her head. "No! Besides that."

Bryson was quiet for a moment, lost in thought. She subconsciously brought her hand to rest on her lower stomach, and his eyes tracked the movement like a hawk watching its prey.

His words came out in a whisper. "Are we pregnant?"

All Jade could do was nod her head as a large smile exploded across her face.

Bryson placed the stick on the counter, closed the distance between them, and dropped to his knees. He lifted her shirt as he placed his hands gently against her flat, creamy stomach.

"There's a baby in there?" He looked up at her, his voice thick with emotion. "I'm going to be a father?"

"Yes!" Her voice cracked as happy tears fell freely down her cheeks.

He placed two soft kisses against her stomach before he whispered, "I can't wait to meet you, little one. I already love you so damn much."

He stood and claimed his wife's lips with his own.

When he pulled back, Jade spoke. "I want to keep this between us." Bryson's brows knitted together, so she elaborated. "Just until we make it through the first trimester. That's when women are most at risk for a miscarriage."

"You don't have to explain anything to me." He kept his voice gentle as he placed a soft kiss on her forehead. "If you wanted to keep it a secret until the delivery, I'd be ok with it."

"Thank you." She smiled. He never ceased to amaze her. "Now, let's eat. I'm starving."

"The spaghetti will have to wait. Right now, I'm in the mood for something else," he growled as he picked her up and placed her on the counter.

"Bryson!" Jade squealed in protest, but she didn't argue when he motioned for her to arch her hips so he could remove her shorts and underwear.

He tossed them somewhere behind him as he scooted her ass to the edge of the counter, dropped to his knees, and devoured her heated center with such hunger that she nearly saw stars. After he made her come twice, he stood, pulled the waistband of his pajamas down enough to free himself, and fucked his wife right there on the counter.

Two blissful weeks had passed since Jade surprised Bryson with the fact that she was pregnant, and each night before he went to sleep, he'd kiss her belly and tell the baby he loved them. Each night, she counted her blessings and woke up feeling like the luckiest woman in the world.

"How long will you be gone?" she questioned as he stuffed the last of his clothes into a duffle bag.

"A week or two at the most."

She didn't push any further. She'd love to know where he was going and what he had to do, but knew he wasn't allowed to discuss any details of the missions he went on. Not knowing was always the worst for her, but she'd do what she did every time he left. She'd fill her days, keeping herself so busy that time passed quickly, and pray each night that he'd come home safely to her.

It had been a week since she'd officially launched her dating site. It was another thing she asked him to keep quiet about. At least until it grew more successful. It already had a promising start. Each day, hundreds of new accounts were created, and the site was gaining a lot of traffic and attention across all social media platforms.

"Just be careful, ok?" Jade caressed her stomach. "It's not just me you have to come home to now."

"I'm always careful, my little kunoichi. You can't get rid of me that easily." He chuckled lightly as he dropped to his knees and placed soft kisses on her stomach. "I can't wait to watch your belly swell, knowing our baby is growing deep inside."

"The doctor said we should be able to know the gender in about a month. Do you want to know, or do you want to be surprised?"

She craved the subject change, so she didn't worry about him leaving.

"Of course I'll want to know." Bryson laughed and stood. "I never understood how people wait till the baby is born before finding out. There are clothes and furniture that need to be bought, not to mention a name would need to be picked out and the nursery decorated. How can you do all that if you don't know the gender?"

She shrugged. "They do a lot of neutral colors, I guess."

"You mean boring colors? No, thank you." His full laugh made her heart flutter with love.

Jade shook her head and joined him as he pulled her flush against his hard frame and kissed her passionately.

When he pulled back, his eyes darted to the alarm clock in their room, and he groaned. "I have to go. Start thinking of names as well, and we'll compare notes when I get back."

He kissed her again, one last quick peck before finally pulling away and saying, "I love you."

"I love you too."

Jade forced a smile to hide her nerves. She'd wait until she was alone to cry and fret. She had to be strong for him. He already had enough to worry about.

The following week drug by slowly for Jade. She was thankful that she had her website to keep her busy. Creating a company from scratch took a lot of elbow grease and long hours. The website only grew with each passing day. She'd put out advertisements across all social media platforms, and the number of created accounts was nearing ten thousand across the country. She had a good feeling that this would be a success.

The chime of the doorbell rang through the home, pulling her attention away from her laptop. Who could that be? Bryson wasn't due back for a few more days, and Liam Godrik and Hunter Gatlin were with him. Travis Patterson had been shot and injured on a previous mission, so Sandra was taking care of him at their home. Other than them, they never got any visitors. Jade's parents weren't the kind to drop by unannounced.

She rose from the desk, exited her office, and padded down the hallway. When she pulled open the front door, she observed two men dressed in the Navy's Full Dress Blue uniforms standing with stoic expressions across their clean-shaven faces. Her body instantly went numb, and her hand began to tremble against the doorknob.

"No… please don't," Jade whispered, begging the strangers not to speak the words she knew deep down were coming.

Tears stung her eyes, and terror clogged her throat, nearly choking her. It felt like all the air had been sucked from her lungs, and the weight of an elephant was sitting on her chest, refusing to allow her to take a breath. Her grip on the doorknob tightened as she fought hard not to let her tears fall.

"The commandant of the Navy has entrusted me to express his deep regret that your husband, Bryson Munro, was shot and killed in action late last night. The commandant extends his deepest sympathy to you and your family in your loss." The shorter gentleman spoke in a solemn tone as if he truly wished he didn't have to deliver the news.

"Oh God…" Jade's voice cracked as she lost the battle with her tears.

They began to rush down her cheeks, like a dam that had burst wide open. Her legs gave out as she fell to the floor, but no harsh impact came. The taller gentleman must've planned for her reaction because he'd caught her as she went down. He eased her to the floor and crouched so he could hold her in his arms while she broke.

A steady flow of people filed into the small church, all dressed in mourning and wearing somber expressions. Some dabbed at their eyes with a tissue, some embraced one another in comforting hugs, others sat in silence on the wooden pews. Jade was aware people spoke to her, but she couldn't tell you what they said. Probably something along the lines of "I'm sorry" or "I'm here for you if you need anything."

As if any of it mattered. It was all just empty words. She could count the number of people she knew on her fingers. The rest, their connections to her husband, were a mystery. She hated being the center of attention. Always one who preferred to blend into the crowd. With what little energy she had, she pulled herself together, put on a brave face, and sat in the front of the church.

She wanted nothing more than to crawl into their bed, hug Bryson's pillow, drift off to sleep, and wake up from this horrible nightmare in her husband's arms. But this wasn't a dream. It was a harsh reality that would have to become her new normal. A life without the love of her life. A life with half of her soul stolen from her.

What she wouldn't give to feel his warmth around her again. To feel his warm lips against her skin. To feel the caress of his words. Eventually, she wouldn't even remember the sound of his voice, and the thought alone killed her. When she'd been told the devastating news, a very large part of her died right alongside her husband.

Hunter Gatlin never once left her side that day, but Jade hardly sensed his presence, too lost as the claws of depression dragged her down to their lonely, shadowy pits. The ceremony went by in a blur. She couldn't recall who spoke, what was said, what stories were told about her husband, or even what songs were played.

She stared blankly at the dark mahogany coffin that was half-open and displayed at the front of the church with an American flag draped over it. A coffin that had become her husband's new resting place until the earth's death. Periodically, her eyes would drift to the left where enlarged pictures of her husband were displayed.

One was his official Navy photo. Another was of him, Hunter, Liam, and Travis standing on a beach, shirtless and flexing with smiles that brightened the picture more than the sun brightens the earth. The last was of Bryson and herself on their wedding day, him dressed in his black tux and her in her white dress. He'd dipped her as if they were dancing and their lips were connected.

If she focused hard enough, she could still feel the ghost of that kiss. Still feel the warmth of his mouth, taste the mintiness of his breath, feel the security she always felt in his arms. But all too soon, those feelings and memories would fade, and she'd be left hollow, with nothing to remember him but pictures. She feared that day more than she feared death.

Strong but gentle hands guided her out of the church when it was time to move to the cemetery. Hunter helped her into the limo that would take them, Liam, Travis, and Sandra, to the gravesite. The rest of the procession would follow behind.

She wanted to scream at Hunter, to curse him, to hit him, to plead with him to tell her it was all a sick joke, to beg for the truth of exactly what happened, but she couldn't gather the strength. All she could manage was to simply go through the motions.

Jade sat in the front row of white folding chairs that faced an eight-foot by two-and-a-half-foot rectangular hole in the ground that would house the love of her life for all eternity. Immediate family and friends filled the other chairs while the rest of the crowd gathered behind them. More than once, she thought about crawling in there with him. Unafraid of tight spaces or suffocation, she would welcome death with open arms if it would reunite her with Bryson. The words of the preacher's speech were muffled as she trained her gaze on the casket suspended over the whole.

The next thing she knew, a man in a pristine Navy uniform knelt before her as he gently placed the folded American flag in the shape of a triangle in her lap and spoke his condolences. The sounds of the twenty-one gun salute firing jarred her each time they rang out across the quiet cemetery, echoing off the trees. She felt hot tears streaming down her face. After all the crying she did in the days preceding the funeral, she was unsure how she could still produce more.

The funeral wrapped up after they lowered the casket into the ground, and the next thing she remembered was Hunter walking her through the front door of her house. A home she shared with her husband. A home that was once filled with laughter, love, and wonderful memories was now quiet, empty, and cold.

Hunter helped Jade out of her shoes as he escorted her up the stairs and into her bedroom. He pulled the covers down, helped her into bed, and tucked her in. She was unaware he had disappeared until he returned a few minutes later with a glass of water, a box of crackers, and a box of tissues. He set them all down on the bedside table before he leaned down toward her.

"I'm so sorry." His voice cracked as he placed a gentle kiss against her forehead and left.

A week had passed since Jade had laid Bryson to rest. It was the worst seven days of her life. She'd hardly gotten out of bed, she didn't shower, she barely ate, and she finally expelled all the tears she had to give. People tried to call or visit her, but those texts, calls, and knocks on her door went unanswered. She refused to see or talk to anyone until she was ready. Whenever that day would be, she didn't know.

How could she entertain company at a time like this? What would she say? What would they say? That they were sorry? That they were there for her if she needed anything? She was so tired of that word.

Sorry.

Sorry wouldn't bring Bryson back. Sorry wouldn't heal her shattered heart. Sorry wouldn't give their child a chance to know their father. What she needed the most, no one on earth was able to give her: her husband, alive and well, lying beside her, his arms wrapped protectively around her.

She merely lay there in bed, day and night, caressing her stomach that held their growing baby, the last piece of her husband she had left on this planet. Her mind was unnervingly quiet as she stared numbly at his pillow. A pillow she'd smelled too many times than she cared to admit. A pillow that grew cold and stale with each passing day, and a part of her died even further as his scent slowly began to fade from the fabric.

She pulled all the strength she had left to get herself out of bed as she padded slowly across the carpet toward the bathroom. As she went through the motions of peeing and wiping, a glimpse of red caught her eye. She brought the toilet paper up and examined a spot of bright crimson staining the tissue.

"No, no, no. Please, God, no!" Her hand trembled as she wiped again, only to see more fresh blood. "NO!"

CHAPTER 32

Amarah Godrik felt something hot leaking down her face. It wasn't blood from Jade's backhand. It was tears. Though she, her husband, and her new friends were the ones chained to chairs in that godforsaken basement, most likely about to die, it was she who felt shattered for Jade.

"But because of you both," Jade shifted her eyes between both Hunter and Liam, "I not only lost my husband, but the pain and grief I endured caused me to lose our child too."

She walked over to the table and picked up a small pocketknife that lay open, revealing the sharp three-inch blade. She turned on her heel and stopped in front of Liam as she sent a powerful armored fist into his face, then jabbed the blade into his right shoulder blade. He hissed at the sting as she removed the knife, blood coating the silver blade. Jade stepped in front of Hunter and repeated the punch and jab into his shoulder, not bothering to wipe the blade beforehand.

"Because of you both, I lost the only connection I had left to my husband!" she shouted with fury as a tear unwillingly rolled down her cheek.

She returned to the table and slammed the blade down before

stepping in front of Liam again. Amarah's breath caught in fear of what Jade would do next to her husband. Jade began striking as she spoke.

"Because of you both, I'll never know what it sounds like to be called mom!" Punch. "To hear my child say I love you!" Punch. "To read it a bedtime story and kiss it goodnight!" Punch. Jade then turned on her heel and stopped in front of Hunter. Punch. "To watch it walk across the stage at graduation!" Punch. "To watch them fall in love and have kids of their own!" Punch.

"Stop!" Serenity begged.

Jade was breathing heavily by the time she stopped hitting the men, hot, angry tears streaking from her vision. She removed the brass knuckles and flexed her hand, hissing in pain. Though they were armored, her knuckles were scraped up and bloody, a mixture of her own, Liam's, and Hunter's blood discolored her skin. But she seemed to revel in the pain as if knowing that each hit, each wound would bring her one step closer to her satisfying revenge.

Both Hunter and Liam's faces were a bloody mess as they both leaned to the side and spat toward the floor, blood mixing with saliva. Amarah grimaced as she took in her husband's appearance, and her own rage started to surface.

"Bryson never mentioned it," Liam whispered.

There was no anger in his words, no fear, no pain, only what Amarah knew was sorrow and regret that he wasn't able to save his brother.

Jade walked over to the table, slammed the brass knuckles down, picked up a hammer, walked back to Liam, and brought it down on his left hand. He clamped his jaw tight and groaned loudly as pain exploded through his hand and shot up his arm.

"Don't you ever speak his name in my presence again!" Jade

screamed in fury.

"Stop, please!" Amarah pleaded.

There was no definitive sound of crunching bones, so she was hopeful that Liam's hand wasn't broken. Just very badly bruised.

"Oh, don't worry. I don't plan on killing the men." She smiled wickedly. "I just want to hear them hurt first."

Dread pooled deep in Amarah's gut as Jade's words fully sank in. Jade's whole purpose was to kill one person from every couple there, so they were forced to feel the pain she'd lived with for the last decade. It somehow made her feel better knowing she wasn't the only one suffering from tremendous grief. Though she wasn't. People lose loved ones every day. Parents, grandparents, siblings, spouses, and even children. This world was full of pain and suffering.

Amarah knew that didn't matter to Jade though. She wanted people close to her to suffer as she had. It made sense for Jade to kill her and Serenity, so Hunter and Liam were forced to live every day with the pain they caused Jade. In all honesty, it was the perfect form of revenge, no matter how barbaric it was.

Amarah watched as Hunter tried to strain against his chains again, but only his fingers were free to move around. The wound in his shoulder slowly leaked blood, further soaking into his shirt.

"If this was about revenge on the team, then why isn't Travis here too?" Amarah asked hesitantly.

She tried to refrain from asking the question and drawing unwanted attention to Travis and his family, but he was her older brother. Deep down, she needed to know if they were in danger, even if she wouldn't be alive to warn or help them.

Jade trained her gaze on Amarah. "He didn't go with them on the mission. Something about being previously injured. Had he," she motioned with her hand toward the men, "he'd be chained right there next to them."

"What happened to…" Hunter stopped himself before he spoke Bryson's name, most likely not wanting to enrage Jade further and gain himself a hit with the hammer still clutched tightly in her fist. "It wasn't our fault."

His voice lost all its strength as his gaze shifted to the bloodsoaked floor.

NOVEMBER 2010

Hunter Gatlin rounded the corner of a compound on the outskirts of a city in Kuwait, near the southern border of Saudi Arabia. Liam Godrik and Bryson Munro followed close behind. Though they were cloaked by the shadows of the night, their night vision goggles illuminated the area in hues of green. With the barrels of their M4A1 Carbines raised and ready to fire at a moment's notice, they slowed as they neared a gap in the adobe wall that served as a privacy fence around the property.

With a simple gesture of his hand, Hunter halted the group while he peered around the barren grounds in search of the safest route across. The compound was a two-story adobe building with square cutouts that acted as windows. Last week, they'd received correspondence that the leader of an up-and-coming terrorist organization would leave the safety of his home and the small army that protected him. He'd be staying in an undisclosed location for a few days while he met with arms dealers.

Unsure of when they'd get another chance to eliminate a dangerous criminal who had the potential to grow to an unstoppable size, they didn't sleep on the information. With only a handful of his most trusted men to protect him, minus Travis Patterson, Hunter observed a path that would get them inside without making any noise. With another motion of his hand, he rounded the opening, hugged the wall, and kept his steps quiet.

He eased his weapon down, so it hung on the sling strapped across his body, removed his knife from the sheath on his leg, and gripped the blade tightly in his gloved fist. Staying in a crouched position, he came up to the back of a guard, covered his mouth with his free hand, and slid his blade across the guard's throat. A quiet gurgling sound filled the night air as he eased the man's body to the ground.

He slid his blade across the guard's clothing, wiping it free of blood, and sheathed it before grabbing his rifle again. When he turned, he noticed both Liam and Bryson had taken out two other guards nearby with similar techniques. With this side of the ground clear, they made their way to a side door.

Once in place, Hunter nodded to his brothers, silently asking if they were ready to enter. With their weapons raised, they both nodded back, and Hunter quietly opened the door and stepped aside. Liam and Bryson entered and split, one going right, the other going left, clearing corners of the room as Hunter entered behind them.

The white walls of the house were barren and free of any decorations or pictures. Dingy yellow square tiles lined the floors in a diamond pattern, and the mismatched furniture was sparse, only filled with the bare minimum.

The living room was empty, so they made their way through a doorway that led into a dining room. Liam and Bryson fired their rifles, disposing of a group of three unsuspecting men sitting at a table playing cards. Everything happened so quickly that the terrorists had no time to grab their own rifles that were propped against the table within arm's reach. With the suppressors attached to their weapons, the shots were muffled, so their presence wasn't announced to the entire house.

When that room was cleared, they moved on, not wanting to linger. They passed down a hallway and a few more rooms, all empty except the last. Two men were in the middle of a heated argument when the door to their bedroom swung open, and Hunter and Liam fired their weapons. The terrorists didn't know what hit them before their lifeless bodies fell back against the mattress, rolled off, and lay motionless on the dirty floor.

Hunter watched as Liam crouched to examine the faces of the men, seeing if either of them was the intended target.

"Ground floor is clear. Ready to move upstairs?" Liam asked as he stood.

"Ready." Bryson gave a curt nod.

"Whoever kills the least buys the first round of drinks when we get back home." Hunter smiled.

Bryson chuckled. "Better get ready to pay up."

They left the room as Liam peered up the stairwell that would take them to the second floor. With a nod from both Hunter and Bryson, Liam started up first. All three men kept their steps light, like a cat stalking its prey. They checked every corner as they went and entered a narrow hallway lined with doors.

Starting with the first room, Liam opened the door as Hunter and Bryson entered. After clearing it, they repeated the same action with the second room. Hunter observed someone occupying the bed and with his barrel raised, he crept near but refrained from firing because what he saw had unease settling in. He turned and signaled to Liam and Bryson that something was up.

Both men stepped beside him, their eyes widening as they took in a boy no older than twelve who lay sound asleep, unaware of their presence. With a quick nod of their heads, they knew what to do. Liam threw back the covers and placed a hand over the kid's mouth to keep him quiet. The boy's dark eyes shot open as his arms and legs began to flail around, trying to get free. Hunter captured both of his wrists as Bryson slipped a zip tie around them. When his wrists were secure, they repeated the action with his ankles.

The boy tried hard to move, to cry out for help, but with his arms and legs bound and Liam's hand over his mouth, his efforts were futile. Hunter quickly ripped a small strip of cloth from the sheet. When Liam removed his hand from the kid's mouth, Hunter didn't spare a second before gagging him and circling his head a few times with a long piece of tape Bryson had at the ready, holding the gag in place so he was unable to remove it.

"Why the fuck is there a kid here?" Liam's voice was hushed, but Hunter didn't miss the annoyance lacing his words.

"I don't know. They said the compound would be free of women and children." Bryson responded as if recalling the information given to them during their briefing.

"What do we do?" Hunter asked. "We can't kill him."

"We keep him with us until the mission is complete, then we leave him here. He's resourceful, he'll free himself." Liam said the plan, and both Hunter and Bryson nodded in agreement.

Hunter gripped the boy's bound wrists and threw him over his broad shoulder, leaving the kid's legs to dangle down the front of his torso. He tried to kick and pound against Hunter's body in the hope of hurting him, but the efforts were in vain. Hunter was no small man.

Bryson took the lead, followed by Liam, then Hunter as they reentered the hallway. With only one more door, they knew their target had to be behind it. Bryson opened it without lingering and entered with Liam and Hunter hot on his heels.

Four men were standing around the massive primary bedroom. Two had rifles in hand and didn't hesitate to raise them toward the SEALs. But Bryson and Liam were ready. They took the armed terrorists out first as Hunter tossed the kid into a corner out of the way, and took out the last two men. After clearing the attached bathroom, they looked over the faces of the men.

"Is that him?" Bryson asked as he cocked his head to the side.

Liam squatted next to the body and pulled the collar of his clothing aside, revealing a tattoo that snaked up the side of his neck.

"Yeah, what's left of him." Liam snorted.

Hunter gathered the evidence needed to confirm the target had indeed been eliminated. A sound came from behind them, and as Bryson, Liam, and Hunter turned to look, they found the boy kneeling with a rifle aimed right at them.

His feet were still bound, and he was still gagged, but the restraints that held his wrists were gone. He'd grabbed one of the rifles that belonged to the terrorists and didn't hesitate to fire. The boy only got off three rounds before Liam fired back, killing him.

The boy, along with the rifle, fell to the ground next to a small knife and the snapped zip tie that was used to bind the kid's wrists.

Liam blew out a breath and lowered his weapon as he asked, "Everyone alright?"

"All good," Hunter answered. When Bryson didn't answer, Hunter turned toward him. "Bryson, you good?"

Hunter could only see his back, where his brother stood, and his blood ran cold.

"Bryson!" Liam shouted as he took a few steps and faced him. "Oh fuck!"

Liam's eyes widened in horror, causing Hunter to move without thinking. What he saw had his stomach churning. Bryson stood still with terror paralyzing his movements, his gloved hand clutched at his neck. Bright red seeped through his fingers, dying his once black gloves crimson. A heartbeat later, Bryson dropped to his knees as Liam followed.

Liam quickly ripped a clean scrap of fabric from one of the bodies nearby and pulled Bryson's hand away from his neck. "Goddammit." His voice broke when he took in the hole now marring Bryson's neck.

Liam quickly wrapped the fabric around his neck and tied it. Not tight enough to cut off his airway, but tight enough to try and stop the bleeding.

"Bryson, can you hear me?" Hunter knelt next to his brother. His voice was laced with worry. Bryson's golden eyes, which were once filled with so much life, now looked vacant as he met Hunter's ice-blue and hazel gaze. "You're going to be ok. We're going to get you out of here." He couldn't stop his voice from cracking.

"Damnit! I can't stop the bleeding without choking him." Liam's words were no louder than a pained whisper.

His eyes looked toward Hunter in a plea, sending a cold sensation throughout his body, numbing it from the inside out. Hunter had never felt so helpless before. He'd been around so much death, taken so many lives himself, that it wasn't anything new to him. But this... This was different.

To watch someone he loved dying in front of his eyes and knowing there wasn't a damn thing he could do to save him. If

God, Lucifer, hell, he'd make a deal with Death himself if they'd allow him to trade his soul for Bryson's. He'd sign that contract in a heartbeat without an ounce of regret. But this was reality. An ugly, fucked up reality where they both knew that nothing could be done.

As if coming to the realization and accepting his fate, Bryson brought his hands up. Both Hunter and Liam looked toward their brother's open palms. Liam gripped the right as Hunter gripped the left, both holding tight in a way that expressed their love and let him know that they wouldn't leave him to die alone.

Bryson's eyes shifted to Liam, then moved to Hunter, before peering directly toward the ceiling. A single tear fell out of his golden irises before life finally faded from them. That's when Hunter and Liam finally broke. A time they relived only in their nightmares and would never speak about to anyone. Not even amongst themselves. It was a moment that was shared between brothers and would stay between them, left there in that room.

After composing themselves, Hunter spoke, but his voice was hollow. "He deserves a proper burial."

They'd have to carry Bryson's body back, all the way to the extraction point that was a few miles away. But he knew Liam wouldn't argue. They would both rather die before leaving a brother behind to rot away from home. Liam nodded his understanding as he gripped Bryson's arm and rolled him up onto his shoulders in a fireman's carry.

"Let's go." Liam's voice was void of emotion as he started for the door.

Though Bryson was heavy, especially with all the gear he wore, Liam never once put him down or accepted Hunter's offer to carry their brother's body the rest of the way. Hunter knew that it was because a part of Liam felt responsible for not being able to stop the bleeding. It was as if this was Liam's way to atone for that sin by making damn sure that he brought his brother back home. They didn't utter another sound as they mourned and finally arrived at the extraction point two hours later.

CHAPTER 33

Jade Munro paced the length of the table that sat off to the side between Liam and Amarah as Hunter finished his story. Amarah could feel more tears pouring down her cheeks at finally hearing the truth behind Bryson's death. She couldn't begin to fathom what Hunter and Liam had gone through, not only witnessing his death but having to carry his body back with them.

Jade stopped pacing, grabbed a pair of pliers, and stormed over to Hunter. "I don't believe you!" she shouted as she gripped his right hand and removed the fingernails of his index and middle fingers.

"You sick, sadistic bitch!" Serenity shouted as Hunter groaned at the intense pain.

Jade spun around, gripped a handful of Serenity's raven hair, and yanked her head back.

"Unless you want to bleed too, I suggest you watch how you talk to me." She seethed as she gripped one of Serenity's nostrils with the tip of the pliers.

She tugged against the sensitive skin in preparation to slice it.

"Enough!" Hunter shouted, causing Jade to glance back toward him.

"I think you're right." Jade released Serenity and stood. Everyone let out a shaky breath before she spoke again. "Though I would love to draw this out longer, I have other things to do before I disappear for good."

She placed the pliers back atop the table as she picked up what appeared to be a letter opener. The handle was stainless steel and made to look like the hilt of a sword, while the five-inch double-edged blade narrowed into a fine point. Amarah's eyes widened as Jade twisted toward her and gave her an enthusiastic smile.

"Jade," Liam warned in a voice so low and dangerous that it sent a chill down Amarah's spine. A tone she'd never heard before and never wanted to hear again.

Jade paused and eyed him with an arched brow as if curious as to what he would say next.

"If you kill my wife and my unborn child, I will hunt you down. And when I find you," his gaze shifted to Amarah's before snapping back to Jade's, "I'll make what you did here today look like child's play. I can keep a victim alive and conscious for days, and the things I'll do to you will be so agonizingly gruesome, it'll have the fucking Devil taking notes."

Amarah watched as what appeared to be fear and hesitation briefly flashed through Jade's vision at Liam's threat, but was gone just as quickly.

"It's a date." She shot him a wink before walking up behind Amarah's chair.

"Jade!" Liam shouted more forcefully, but she ignored him.

She grabbed Amarah's braid and pulled, forcing Amarah's chin toward the ceiling and fully exposing her neck. Jade leaned in close to her ear as she whispered so low that only Amarah would be able to hear, "This is nothing personal against you. In all honesty,

I envy you. You'll get to be with your baby for eternity. I know I'll never meet mine. Not where I'm going."

Amarah's stomach plummeted, but she held no malice toward the woman. She knew deep down that Jade was never truly this evil. That grief from losing two people she loved more than life itself had warped her brain, twisting it and causing darkness to spread like a disease, infesting and poisoning her heart.

Hell, she sympathized with Jade because if Amarah were ever in Jade's shoes, she'd want revenge too. Which is why the next words that fell from her mouth weren't screams of anger, desperate pleas for her life, or even damning the woman's soul to hell for an eternity of torment.

"I forgive you." The honest whisper fell from Amarah's lips.

She felt Jade stiffen behind her as if hesitating. As if Jade hadn't expected to ever be forgiven. A breath later, Amarah felt cold metal against her throat.

"Jade, please don't!" Serenity cried out.

"I'm begging you, please stop." Hunter's voice was low and guttural. A desperate tone Amarah had never heard from the man before.

Amarah locked eyes with Liam as he strained hard against his chains.

"Don't do this, Jade!" Veins popped in Liam's arms and neck as he fought with every ounce of strength he had, trying his best to rip through solid metal.

She watched as fear, grief, and fury burned within her husband's irises. She gave him a reassuring smile, silently communicating that everything would be ok.

"I love you," Amarah confessed, wanting those to be the last words to leave her lips.

"No!" Liam's roar boomed off the stone walls, and three seconds later, complete darkness consumed her.

There was no pain, no chill that numbed her body, no feeling of blood leaking down her skin. Was that it? Was she dead? That wasn't what she'd expected. There was no light, no glowing gates to heaven, just darkness. What was going on?

A breath later, she felt the cold metal against her throat vanish as Jade released her hair. She felt Jade's presence retreat from around her as an explosion sounded at the top of the stairs. Without her eyes, Amarah's other senses kicked into overdrive as she heard the stairs creaking beneath someone's weight.

Three gunshots rang out in quick succession, the sound pinging off the walls and causing Amarah's ears to ring. She heard a thud as if someone had fallen, then everything fell quiet. Only the sounds of breathing, both steady and uneven, could be heard.

"Clear." A male voice spoke from directly behind her, causing her to flinch. "Hit the lights, Einstein."

A second later, a dim yellow light flooded the basement room, causing everyone to blink a few times as their eyes readjusted.

A man Amarah had never seen before took in the horror of the room and whistled before he spoke. "Damn, Boss. You got yourself in quite a pickle."

He was tall and packed with lean muscles that were covered in beautiful, bronzed skin. His black hair was cut short on top and faded on the sides. The black T-shirt he wore showed off one arm covered in dark ink, and the other sported an old scar that ran in a thin, single line down the length of his forearm, stopping at his wrist.

"Doc!" Serenity screamed with relief.

Doc gave Serenity a pearly white smile. "Hey, Renny."

The man had a pair of night vision goggles resting atop his head, and she watched as he lowered his rifle, allowing it to hang from a black strap across his torso. A small piece of metal caught Amarah's vision as she observed a small silver cross earring that hung from his left ear.

Two more men stepped off the stairs and observed the room fully before one lowered his own rifle, and the other twirled black knives around his fingers before slipping them into the pockets of his bulletproof vest.

"Jesus, Big Daddy, you look like shit." The one with the knives laughed as he stopped to observe the table full of various torture instruments, some bloodied. A whistle escaped his lips. "I'm upset I wasn't invited to the party."

Hunter sighed, but there was a smile of relief on his face. "Shut the hell up, Sweeney, and get us out of these fucking chains."

Sweeney was just as tall and broad as Hunter, but his brown hair was cut short. His golden eyes popped against his tanned skin, and he kept himself clean-shaven, making his square jawline more prominent. One arm was sleeved out in bright, colorful ink that peered out beneath his T-shirt.

Amarah allowed herself to relax fully now that it was confirmed Hunter knew these men and they were, in fact, good guys. The last man she didn't know the name of yet came around her chair and squatted in front of her. He removed what looked like lockpicking tools from a pocket of his bulletproof vest.

"Hey, I'm Fuse." He gave her a kind smile as he got to work and had the padlock open in seconds.

"Amarah." She returned his smile, though hers wasn't so bright due to exhaustion and the adrenaline rush her body was coming down from.

Fuse reminded Amarah of a Viking straight from Norway. He was about six feet tall, packed with bulky muscles. His blond hair was shaven on the sides with the top pulled into a tight braid that hung to his shoulders. His eyes were as blue as the Arctic, and his pointed features were covered in a brownish-reddish beard that he kept trimmed to a light stubble.

As Fuse began unwinding the chains from her body, she let her gaze survey the room. Doc had freed Serenity and moved to begin working on freeing Liam. Sweeney was busy untying Hunter. When Amarah was free, Fuse stepped back and dropped the chains into a pile on the floor. Amarah stood and turned, only to freeze.

Jade lay motionless on the floor a few feet behind her chair. Blood oozed from the small hole in her chest, soaking her shirt. Another stream of blood ran down the side of her creamy face from the bullet hole between her eyes. Her chocolate irises were glossy as they stared toward the ceiling.

Amarah's brows knitted. She heard three gunshots, but there were only two holes that she could see. Either one of the bullets missed, which she highly doubted given the accuracy of the shot between Jade's eyes, or two bullets entered the same hole. Whoever Doc was, Amarah knew he was not someone to mess with. She took a tentative step toward Jade and knelt beside her body.

"I hope you're reunited with your husband and your baby." She sent up the whispered prayer as she reached out with a shaky hand and closed Jade's eyes, putting her soul to rest.

Liam was finally free and at her side a second later. She felt his arms around her as he pulled her flat against his chest, grunting from the stab wound in his shoulder. Her husband squeezed her tightly, making sure not to use his left hand, which was now turning slightly purple with a nasty bruise. Amarah threw her arms around him and buried her head into his chest, allowing the beat of his heart and the smell of his faded body wash to relax her.

His words were filled with worry. "Cupcake, look at me. I need to hear you say you're alright."

She pulled back and peered up at him.

"I will be. For right now, just hold me."

She pressed her head against his chest as she felt him slightly relax and rest his chin atop her head.

CHAPTER 34

Once Hunter Gatlin was freed, his long legs had him across the space in two strides as he pulled Serenity against himself. He buried his nose in the crook of her neck and took deep breaths. His fiancée threw her arms around him and held on for dear life.

"You were right!" Her words were muffled against his shirt but still clear enough to be heard. "We're never vacationing on a tropical island again. It's our kryptonite."

Hunter laughed at her words. With what happened after Addi's wedding last summer in Hawaii and then this, tropical islands were proving to be *very* bad luck for them. And he had no intention of testing their luck a third time.

"How about we stick to cabins in the woods?" Though his voice was weak, he knew she could hear his smile, and it caused her to laugh against him.

"Deal!"

"Trust me, I'll forever be thankful that y'all are here." Hunter looked toward his men but didn't release his hold on his fiancée. "But how in the hell *are* y'all here right now?"

"Einstein." Sweeney grinned and pulled out his cell phone from a pocket in his black cargo pants.

Hunter was even more confused. He knew that boy was a certified genius, but no one outside of this island could've known what was going on. Sweeney put the call on speaker, and everyone turned their attention toward the phone.

"Is everyone alright?" Einstein picked up after the first ring. His words were rushed and filled with concern.

"Yeah, it appears we got here just in the nick of time," Sweeney answered.

"Start talkin', Einstein," Hunter said, needing answers.

Einstein hesitated before saying, "Ok, but you have to promise you won't get mad."

"Einstein," Hunter growled his warning.

"I used a program that cloned everyone's phone. I can see anything and everything you do, who you talk to, what's being said. I promise I don't spy on y'all. I only use it for emergencies. When I got a notification that you tried to send a text that failed, I checked it and saw you tried to send me your location with the word 'nuggets.' So, I called everyone in and sent them to the pin with the force of a small military. You're welcome."

Though he started hesitantly, by the end, Einstein's voice was filled with pure cockiness. Hunter shook his head but couldn't stop the grin that pulled at his sore face.

"We're going to have a serious chat about privacy when I get home, but as for right now, I could kiss you." Hunter blew out a breath. He clenched his jaw at the ache that throbbed across his face and pulsed within his two nailless fingers.

"Please don't, Bossman. I mean, you're hot and all, but you're not really my type. You know... a woman." Einstein laughed and ended the call.

"The authorities have been notified and are on their way," Fuse addressed the room, and Hunter nodded.

"What did you do to piss off the Asian?" Sweeney chuckled as he crouched near Jade's body, examining her closely.

"That's Jade Munro. She blamed Liam and I for the death of her husband. He was on our SEAL team back in the day," Hunter answered, his voice solemn.

"Shit…" Sweeney stood, and his demeanor turned serious. "Sorry, man."

"It's in the past now."

"What about the ginger?" Sweeney turned toward Declan McCarthy. "Evil minion or a poor victim?"

"Evil minion," Hunter answered around a soft chuckle that hurt his aching body with each movement.

He knew Sweeney meant no disrespect. That's just how he was, no filter, and charismatic, especially in intense situations. But Sweeney had a good heart and was one of the most loyal men Hunter had known. He watched in curiosity as Sweeney pulled out his phone again.

"Hey, sweetheart." Sweeney smiled like a lovestruck teen in high school.

Hunter didn't need to ask who he'd called. He knew it was Addi, Serenity's best friend and the love of his friend's life.

"No, everyone's alright." Sweeney paused as his eyes quickly ran over Hunter. "Well, Big Daddy looks like he went twelve rounds with Mike Tyson and lost, but he'll be fine. Renny appears in perfect health." There was a pause before he closed his eyes and pinched the bridge of his nose. He held the phone toward Serenity and chuckled. "Addi wants proof of life."

Serenity took the phone, and Hunter reluctantly released his hold on her as she walked aside to speak. He crossed the space and stopped next to Liam and Amarah.

"Are you alright?" he asked Amarah, but the question was meant for them both.

Amarah pulled back from Liam's chest and glanced toward him. "Physically, yeah."

She gave him a small smile, and Hunter's eyes dipped to her stomach before coming back up to meet Liam's gaze. Liam gave him a nod, signaling that he too was alright.

"Let's get y'all patched up," Doc said, returning down the stairs with a white medical box in his hands. A red circle with a white cross was printed in the middle of the lid.

"Is that how you got your name?" Amarah inquired as she stepped out of Liam's hold so he could get looked at.

"No," Doc chuckled as he set the box on the table and opened it. He began rummaging through the various medical supplies. "I was named after the infamous gunslinger, Doc Holliday."

Amarah's face scrunched in confusion. Hunter watched her gaze shift to where Jade's body lay, and saw the exact moment Doc's words clicked into place. Doc was one of a handful of people on the planet who could take out a target with a sniper rifle over a mile and a half away.

"Oh." Amarah's voice was quiet.

After a few minutes, Liam and Hunter were patched up enough to stop the bleeding until professional medical care arrived. Doc had also cleaned up the cut on Amarah's cheek from where Jade had backhanded her with the brass knuckles. Serenity had finally wrapped up her phone call and rejoined them.

"What about Quinn, Colton, and Myles? Are they ok?" Serenity's gaze shifted to the top of the stairs where the wooden door used to be.

What remained of it now lay in shambles along the stairs and in a pile at their base. Hunter had wondered the same thing upon waking, but he had other pressing matters to worry about at the time.

Fuse answered, gaining everyone's attention. "We found them breathing but unconscious, locked in a closet on the ground floor. We couldn't find y'all anywhere till we heard voices coming from a hidden door in the dining room."

"We found the door to the basement locked," Sweeney added. "I was about to pick the lock when Fuse decided to blow the whole fucking thing to pieces." He laughed, motioning a large explosion with his hands.

"When I heard the scream, I feared we were too late." Fuse shrugged his broad shoulders. "I got a little carried away. You're welcome."

"Ah, that explains your name," Amarah muttered, but the stoned walls amplified her voice. Fuse flashed her a cocky grin and winked.

Everyone climbed the stairs, leaving the tortured hell of the basement and all the death behind them. Everyone gathered among the mattresses lining the floor in the living room as they waited for the authorities to arrive. Myles, Colton, and Quinn nearly had a heart attack upon witnessing the physical state of Hunter and Liam, and after learning the ugly truth about their host, Jade Munro.

CHAPTER 35

It had taken the authorities hours to process the scene and question all the guests. Well, what remained of them, that is. Hunter and Liam had their wounds cleaned, stitched, and bandaged. After the authorities bagged up the bodies, the guests were told to pack up their belongings and board the police vessels, where they'd be taken back to the mainland. They spent a few more hours at the police station answering more in-depth questions before they were finally released.

With numerous witness statements all stating the same line of events and specific details, along with all the substantial evidence gathered back at the resort, the authorities sided with the guests, holding both Declan McCarthy and Jade Munro responsible for all the deaths. While gathering evidence, the authorities found a set of fake IDs and passports among Jade's belongings with new names on them, helping to further prove Hunter and Liam's comment about how she planned to disappear after she was done killing.

Thanks to everyone's testimonies, Parker Evans had also been released and freed of all charges for the death of his wife, Cami. The guy looked rough, having been locked in a cell for the last few days, but given enough time, he'd recover and be alright.

It had been two weeks since everyone returned to their homes across the country. Colton and Myles King returned to Washington, Quinn Davis to Rhode Island, and Parker Evans to Georgia. Liam, Amarah, Hunter, and Serenity took Hunter's company jet back to Oklahoma along with Hunter's team. However, they did make a quick stop in Virginia, where they laid Jade's body to rest in the grave right next to her husband.

Amarah was more than thrilled to be back stateside and in the comfort and security of her own home. Liam had made her schedule a doctor's appointment as soon as they were unpacked to get her and the baby checked out. She didn't protest. She knew deep down that their baby was alive and well, but confirmation would be nice that the knockdown gas she had inhaled didn't hurt the growing baby.

After expressing their concerns to her doctor, he agreed to a full examination and, after an ultrasound and blood work, found everything to be in perfect condition. Their baby was alive and well, measuring ten weeks, with a strong heartbeat. Amarah had looked toward Liam, who was by her side but had his eyes trained on the black-and-white image of their child. The look of pure joy and complete happiness on his face brought tears to her eyes, and she knew the sound of that little heartbeat was a joyful melody he'd play on repeat until the end of time.

Now, she and her husband lie in their king-size bed that looks like a twin in their massive bedroom. The room was decorated in sage greens, browns, and creams. Liam lay on his side with his head resting atop her chest. He'd lifted the hem of her nightgown above her navel so his fingers could trace lazy circles over the flat planes of her stomach. A stomach that now housed their child and would swell with life in the months to come.

She ran her fingers through his raven hair, massaging his scalp in a manner that always seemed to relax him. This had become their nightly routine since he found out she was expecting. She hated the way he found out, cursing herself for not telling him the day she learned the news. The look on his face had broken her heart.

Pure joy had momentarily sparked in his eyes, but it was quickly extinguished by pain and fear. Pain that he was chained to a chair and unable to keep his wife and child from harm, and fear of losing them both. But that was now behind them in the past. Everything worked out, and everyone was alright. That's all that mattered.

"I think it'll be a boy." His deep voice wrapped around her like a security blanket, the only sound to be heard in their room.

"Oh, yeah? What makes you think that?" she asked, not stopping the massage of his scalp.

"Father's intuition," he teased. "My grandfather had three boys, and my father had me. Testosterone rules our family."

She shook her head and chuckled. "I feel bad for your mother and grandmother."

"What about you, Cupcake?" he inquired, still running lazy circles across her bare stomach. "What do you think it is?"

"I don't care what it is. As long as it's healthy, that's all that matters."

"If it's a boy, we can name him Anakin, after Darth Vader. Or Logan, after Wolverine." Liam propped himself on his elbow and looked toward her, his voice and expression growing more animated with each new name that came to his mind. "Or Draven from *The Crow*, or—"

"Whoa! You're getting way too excited about this." She fully laughed, loving how enthusiastic he became anytime he talked about their baby. "What are you, ten years old?"

His grin turned wicked. "You know, if this were a few hundred years ago, I'd be solely responsible for naming *all* our children."

"Thank God this is the twenty-first century, and the mother gets a say." She shook her head at her husband, but love and admiration filled her eyes. "And besides, he could be a she."

His eyes widened briefly at the realization. "Lord help me if we have a daughter. If she's anything like you, I'd better start saving up for bail money."

Amarah chuckled but furrowed her brows. "For you or for her?"

Liam paused for a moment as if thoroughly considering her question.

"Both," he said confidently.

She laughed, cupped his bearded cheeks, and pulled his face towards her. She claimed his lips in an embrace that conveyed every emotion she felt toward her husband. He responded by sliding his tongue into her mouth as they tasted each other, and he settled between her parted thighs.

With his arm resting beside her head, he elevated his hips so he could push his boxers down enough to free himself. She felt the tips of his fingers graze over her heated center, over the fabric of her underwear, causing her to moan into his mouth. A deep sound vibrated in her husband's chest as if he were pleased to find her already wet and desperate for him.

Without breaking their kiss, he pulled her underwear to the side and with a single thrust of his hips, pushed deep inside of her. There were no words exchanged between them. No rough or hurried movements. Her husband took his time with her, making each thrust slow and deliberate, conveying the full depths of his love, causing that wonderful coil in her stomach to tighten further with each connection.

Her hands gripped his toned ass, over the fabric of his boxers, trying to pull him closer as if she could take him deeper. Their tongues chased and tasted each other as he continued to move his hips until they came together, their cries of passion and the love they shared filling the quiet room around them.

Hunter Gatlin slowed the speed of his blacked-out Harley Sportster motorcycle as he approached the entrance to a lavish neighborhood. Serenity extended her right arm, signaling to the vehicle behind them that they were turning in that direction.

"Are you nervous?" she asked as she wrapped her arms back around his middle and leaned with him into the turn.

The Bluetooth in their full-face helmets allowed them to speak to each other.

He hesitated before answering. "A little. It's been over four years since I've seen them."

"I'm sure it'll be as if no time has passed." She reassured him by rubbing her hand up and down his back, on the outside of his black leather riding jacket.

She's probably right, he thought.

He didn't understand why he was so nervous. Though it'd been years, he and Travis still kept in touch. He always sent best wishes on birthdays and holidays, even Travis's kids' birthdays. After Liam had informed him of Travis and Sandra's little tradition of family cookouts every two weeks, Liam had extended him and Serenity an invitation, knowing Travis and Sandra would love a chance to see him again and reconnect.

He let out a long breath. Send him alone behind enemy lines

with nothing but a knife, and he wouldn't bat an eye, but this, he was never good at social functions. Instead of talking and meeting new people, you'd most likely find him in the back of the room, trying to become one with the shadows until the event ended, and it was socially acceptable to leave.

However, these weren't random people. This was a family he'd made over a decade ago that accepted him with open arms. Serenity was right. He just needed to stop thinking too much about it. As they neared the massive single-story home that was surrounded by lush green grass with a beautiful flower garden surrounding it, he saw numerous vehicles filling the driveway.

He turned his bike into the driveway and parked, kicking out the stand and leaning the bike against it. He climbed off and straightened before turning and helping Serenity off the back. They took off their helmets, and she quickly smoothed her long raven hair back into place before approaching the front door.

Hunter was about to knock when the door opened, and Liam stood there with a beer in his hand and a grin on his face.

"I thought that was your bike I heard. Come on in. Glad y'all could make it."

They entered the beautiful, updated home and followed Liam through the open-concept main floor. They set their helmets down atop the counter in the kitchen before following Liam out the back door that led to a large, covered patio.

"Look who I found," Liam addressed the small crowd of people.

Travis was manning the grill with what looked like his father standing next to him, each holding a beer in their hands. Amarah, Sandra, and what had to be Travis's mother sat on an oversized sectional sofa by a brick fireplace. Three small children, two redheaded girls and a blond-haired boy, jumped energetically on a trampoline in the yard. When Liam spoke, all conversations ceased, and every head turned toward them.

Travis stood there stunned, with his mouth half open and his brows furrowed together as if he couldn't believe the sight before him. He'd grown out his hair since the last time they'd met. His blond locks were down and brushing past his shoulders, and his light brown beard was full and neatly groomed.

"Hunter!" Sandra squealed as she jumped up from the sofa, crossed the patio, and threw her arms around his middle. "Oh my gosh, it's so good to see you!"

Her fiery hair was French braided down her back, and her beaming smile made her blue eyes and the freckles that dotted beneath pop. She pulled back, and he leaned down and kissed her creamy cheek.

"It's good to see you too, Sandra. You look fantastic." He straightened and grinned as she took a step back and did a quick twirl.

"Thank you." She beamed. "Who's this?"

Her gaze landed on the woman who clung to Hunter's arm, a nervous smile across her olive face.

"This is my fiancée, Serenity Jinx."

"Fiancée! Why the hell is this the first time I'm hearing about this?" Sandra slapped Hunter's arm, drawing a deep laugh from him that echoed around them. "Welcome to the family!" She pulled Serenity into an embrace before stepping back. "What's your poison? Beer? Wine? Mixed drinks? Straight liquor? No judgment."

"A beer would be great, thank you." Serenity laughed as Sandra took her hand and led her to the outdoor sofa that was positioned in front of a large fireplace.

Hunter watched as Amarah greeted his fiancée with a loving smile and a hug. Warmth, pride, and love swelled within him at the sight. Travis finally worked over his shock and walked over, clasped hands with Hunter, and pulled him into an embrace.

"It's been a while, brother." Travis stepped back and offered him a beer.

"The kids have gotten big," Hunter commented as his gaze followed them jumping and wrestling with each other, unaware of what was happening around them.

"Too big, too fast." Travis sighed. "You know you've fucked up now, right?"

Hunter arched a brow and took a swig of his beer. "How so?"

"By introducing your fiancée to my wife and sister." Travis shrugged his shoulders as he peered over to see his wife making Serenity feel at home. "She'll be requesting y'all's presence at every cookout now."

Hunter shook his head and chuckled. "I'll clear my schedule."

"Well, shit, man. Tell me what the hell you've been up to. You started your own security company, right?" Travis asked as he returned to the grill, flipped the burgers, and rotated the hot dogs. And just like that, it was as if no time had passed. Hunter, Liam, Travis, and Oscar, Travis's father, fell into conversation as if they'd done this a hundred times before.

EPILOGUE

PART 1 – SEVEN MONTHS LATER
LIAM & AMARAH

It was Saturday, which meant the family's biweekly cookout at Travis and Sandra's house. Amarah loved watching Travis, Liam, and Hunter interact with each other. It gave her a glimpse of the past when they were around each other daily, and the sight made her heart happy. The men had their heads thrown back laughing at something her brother had said, and she couldn't help but smile.

"It's good to see them so happy, huh?" Serenity nudged her lightly in the side with her elbow.

"It truly is." Amarah nodded with teary eyes.

"I can't tell you how much I've missed seeing that. It brings back old memories." Sandra sighed from Amarah's left as they sat on the outdoor sectional couch under the covered patio.

After the horror on that island in the Bahamas blew over, Hunter and Serenity began attending the cookouts every other weekend. Travis was shocked to hear Hunter had been living so close for so long and jumped at the chance to reconnect with someone who was as close as a brother to him. A cramp shot through her stomach that had her inhaling sharply and wincing.

"Amarah, what is it?" Sandra gripped her bicep lightly as her voice filled with worry. "Are you alright?"

"I'm good," Amarah said, taking a deep breath. "Just Braxton Hicks contractions." She laughed lightly. "It's passed now."

She felt as huge as an elephant with only days left until her due date. She hated having to rely on anyone for anything, but since her belly started expanding like a balloon on steroids, she hadn't even been able to put on her shoes for the last two months. Thankfully, the weather was warm enough for her to wear slides and flip-flops. Although Liam was always willing to help put her shoes on with a smile on his face.

She couldn't believe how blessed she was with him as her husband. He'd been so attentive and loving, always making sure she took care of herself, ate properly, and was there to help with anything she needed. He never missed an appointment and always rubbed her feet and back anytime she hinted that they may have been hurting. He'd gone out in the middle of the night more times than she'd care to admit, getting her whatever food she was craving at the time. And not once did he utter a single complaint.

"Those were a bitch." Sandra shook her head. She'd know since having done this process three times.

"Yeah, they are." Amarah laughed as the men walked over to them.

Travis plopped down next to Sandra, and Hunter sat next to Serenity as Liam stood in front of Amarah and smiled a boyish grin that never failed to send warmth blossoming through her. She tried and failed to get up. Even went as far as rocking a few times to gain momentum, but it was futile. She let out a frustrated breath, and her brother started laughing.

"Let me strap a bowling ball to your stomach and watch you try to stand or get out of bed." Amarah glared at Travis. Sandra sent a swift elbow to his ribs, causing him to grunt in pain. "Thank you, Sandra." Amarah shook her head before looking toward Liam. "Can you help me up? I have to pee."

"Of course, Cupcake." Liam gave her a wide grin as he held out large, strong hands toward her.

She gripped them, and he pulled her effortlessly and gently to her feet.

"Thank you," she said, a bit winded.

Being so far along in her pregnancy, it was hard for her to take full breaths, and she got exhausted after merely crossing a small room. Forget about sleeping on her back or sleeping in general. Rest was a thing of the past, and apparently, so was filling her lungs. She was exhausted. She took a few steps only to stop as another cramp shot through her stomach. She gripped her swollen belly and winced. Her husband was at her side in an instant.

"What is it?" Fear laced his words.

"I'm alright, just another Braxton Hicks contraction," Amarah reassured him, then straightened. "It's gone now."

She let out a long breath as she took two more steps and halted. A gush of liquid fell onto the patio beneath her dress, and her head whipped around toward her husband. Complete disbelief marred her sharp features.

"Oh, gross. Did you just pee?" Travis asked, half laughing as two creases formed between his brows.

"No, you idiot. Her water just broke," Hunter answered with a grin, shaking his head at Travis.

"Time to go," Liam said as he gripped his wife by the shoulders and began steering her through the house.

Amarah couldn't move very fast, and she felt as if she was waddling like a penguin. She was ready to get this baby out of her. They made it halfway through the living room before she was forced to stop again. She reached for her husband's wrist, gripping it as a stronger contraction ripped through her. She was gasping for air after it passed a few seconds later.

Without warning, he scooped her up in his arms as he made a beeline for his truck. He set her on her feet, opened the door for her, and helped her into the passenger's seat. He quickly buckled her in before shutting her door and climbing into the driver's seat.

Amarah watched as everyone exited the home and gathered in the driveway with expressions ranging from shock to happiness to worry. Her husband flew out of the driveway and sped down the road, uncaring of the numerous traffic laws he was breaking.

"Honey, I'd like to make it to the hospital alive." She panted with a strained smile.

He kept his focus on the road as he flew by honking vehicles. "And I'd like to make it to the hospital before the baby arrives."

"Worst case scenario," she paused to take a few breaths, "can you deliver a baby?"

He cut his eyes at her before shifting them down to her swollen belly and back to the road. "Yes, but I'd rather not."

Her hand gripped the door handle as the other shot to the dash as another contraction hit. She tried to take deep breaths through the pain, but groaned towards the end. She knew they'd only get worse and more frequent the closer it was to the baby coming.

Her eyes shot over to see Liam's foot pushing further on the gas pedal. It never ceased to amaze her just how serene he was in intense situations. Aside from his white-knuckled grasp around the steering wheel, he was the picture of calm, cool, and collected.

"We're almost there, Cupcake. Just take deep breaths."

Amarah laughed hysterically. "Let me kick you in the balls and see how easy it is for you to take deep breaths."

Liam's roar of laughter helped to momentarily ease her pain, but another contraction hit, causing a guttural groan to slip free.

Before she knew it, he whipped into the emergency room parking lot and brought the truck to a halt beneath the covered entrance. He threw it in park and was at her door in record time. A nurse met them with a wheelchair as he helped her out and sat her down gently.

"I'll grab the bag and meet you inside." He gave her a quick kiss on her sweat-slicked forehead as the nurse turned and wheeled her through the entrance.

Another contraction tore through her, and she was forced to clamp her mouth shut so she didn't scream in the waiting room full of people. The last thing she needed was to traumatize the child dressed in a baseball uniform. He appeared to have broken his wrist as he sat next to his mom, clutching his hand against his chest. *The poor kid has already been through enough.*

Her grip on the armrests of the wheelchair was tight as she held her breath until it passed, copper filling her mouth as she fought to remain quiet. Liam met them at the elevator doors with the hospital bag filled with everything they'd need for their stay. They exited the elevator on the fifth floor as the nurse wheeled her into a private room where more nurses met them.

"How far along are her contractions?" a nurse with brunette hair tied into a tight bun asked as she helped Amarah stand.

"Roughly three or four minutes," Liam answered in a calm tone.

"You're handling this pretty well," the nurse commented and began to help Amarah out of her clothes and into a hospital gown.

He snorted as he helped the nurse get his wife situated on the bed. "I'm not a stranger to intense or stressful situations."

"Are you looking for a job? We're always hiring, and we could use more people like you," she joked, and Liam matched her laughter.

Another contraction hit, forcing Amarah to reach for her husband's hand in a grip that defied the physical strength of such a small woman. He let out a soft groan, and when it finally passed, she released him.

"I'm so sorry." She panted frantically as her eyes darted toward her husband's hand, where red crescent moon marks now marred his tanned skin.

"Don't be. Break my hand if you need to, Cupcake. Don't worry about me." He gave her a reassuring smile as the nurses helped her legs into the stirrups.

"Has her water broken?" a raven-haired nurse asked as she slipped her hands into rubber gloves.

"Yes," he answered for his wife, who was panting breathlessly beside him.

"Alright, dear, I'm going to check and see how dilated you are," the woman instructed before placing her hands beneath Amarah's gown.

"Okay." Amarah dropped her head back against the pillow, thankful that her hair was braided back and out of her face.

"Can you go get the doctor?" the raven-haired nurse instructed in a calm voice to another nurse with chin-length blonde hair. She nodded and quickly left the room.

"Is something wrong?" Amarah heard a hint of unease trying

to creep into Liam's tone.

That caused her heart rate to spike to nearly triple its usual pace. If his mask was beginning to slip, things must be worse than she thought. Is something wrong with her? *Oh God, is the baby ok?* A hundred horrible scenarios flashed through her mind in the blink of an eye.

"No," the nurse reassured him with a smile. "The baby is almost crowning. It appears you'll get to meet your bundle of joy faster than you thought."

Amarah blew out a heavy exhale and felt her shoulders slacken with relief. Until another contraction hit, and a guttural scream echoed off the walls.

The doctor entered a few minutes later, a tall man in his late fifties, as he quickly washed his hands and slipped on a pair of gloves. A group of nurses rushed to prepare everything for him as he examined Amarah before speaking.

"Alright, on the next contraction, I want you to push with everything you've got," the doctor said, and she nodded.

"You've got this, Cupcake." Liam held her hand and smiled.

"Stop smiling at me like that," she groaned. "That smile is what got us into this situation."

Laughter filled the room as the doctor and nurses worked. When the next contraction started, Amarah bore down, gritted her teeth, and pushed. Pain like she'd never experienced before erupted through her, and she wanted to stop but forced herself to work through it. Her husband never once left her side as she continued to push through each contraction for what felt like hours. Before she knew it, a cry erupted through the room, and she burst into tears as the doctor held up their baby.

Liam was all too eager to cut the umbilical cord, and the nurse brought the baby over and laid it against her chest. The moment their son was in her arms, her world was complete. Happy tears began to flow freely as she peered down at her child. Time ceased to exist, and everything she'd just gone through seemed to be momentarily forgotten. She'd go through that pain a million times over if it ended like this, with her baby, healthy and crying, squirming against her bare chest.

Everything that followed passed by in a blur. The nurses took their son to get weighed, measured, and cleaned up as the doctor and nurses worked to clean her up. Before long, she was moved to a recovery room, where she spent the next day being monitored. The following afternoon, they got the all-clear that momma and baby were healthy and free to go home.

Numerous cars filled their driveway, and Amarah recognized who each belonged to. She smiled when she entered the home and found her family and friends waiting for them in the living room. Liam held the carrier in his hand before gently setting it down on the floor.

Travis, Sandra, her parents, Serenity, and Hunter all had bright and welcoming smiles shaping their faces. Even her nieces and nephews were trying hard to contain their excitement over the new baby. They all took turns hugging and congratulating the new parents. Liam knelt down, unlatched the straps that held their tiny baby in place, and gently picked him up. She couldn't help but smile as she watched him handle their son as if he were a bomb that would detonate with any slight movement. He cradled their child in his strong arms, the baby appearing like a small toy.

"Everyone." Amarah turned to address the room. They'd agreed on a first name months ago, but she'd asked if she could pick the middle name. Liam obliged, and she told him that she wanted to keep it a secret until after he was born. She had to be sneaky when filling out the papers in the hospital so Liam couldn't read what name she picked. "I'd love for you to meet our son, Malik Bryson Godrik."

Liam, Hunter, and Travis's eyes all widened at hearing the middle name. She had thought long and hard about it since everything happened on the island and knew that if their baby was a boy, she wanted to honor their fallen brother. Each man expressed so much emotion in their eyes and across their face, no matter how good they were at masking their features.

Liam's eyes filled with love and admiration for her that her heart swelled so much, she feared it would burst. He leaned over, placed a kiss on her forehead, and whispered, "I love you."

EPILOGUE

PART 2 – SIX MONTHS LATER
HUNTER & SERENITY

"Are you ready for this?" Addi questioned Serenity, who stood next to her behind closed doors made of thick, dark wood.

"Yes and no," Serenity admitted nervously with a small laugh. The butterflies inside her stomach were on overdrive with anticipation and excitement.

"Last chance to run, sweetheart," Jeremy, Serenity's father, said as he came to stand beside his daughter, sporting a playful smile.

He had on a full grey suit with a maroon dress shirt and a matching handkerchief in the jacket pocket. His black hair was cut short, his mustache was neatly trimmed, and his green eyes were framed by laugh lines.

"I can buy you some time. Big Daddy may look tough, but I know his weak spot." Sweeney smiled mischievously at Serenity.

"No, let's do this," she said, shaking the nervousness off as she looped her arm through her father's as the music started to play from the other side of the doors.

The wooden doors parted, revealing a beautiful church with large stained-glass windows and a tall, domed ceiling. The wooden pews were decorated with bright flowers and white lace. Addi gave her friend a wink before she looped her arm through Sweeney's as they started down the aisle that was littered with pink and white rose petals.

The music faded, and a brief silence fell over the church. Once the music started up again, everyone rose and turned toward the back as the double doors opened again and Serenity walked out with her father. Her vision snapped to Hunter the moment she saw him, and her heart ached with joy.

She watched as his eyes traveled down her body, taking in the simple white silk strapless dress that clung to her curves and flowed elegantly to the floor. His gaze made its way back up and halted on hers. So much emotion swirled in his ice-blue and hazel eyes as she witnessed a tear cascade down his bearded cheek. He quickly wiped it away and smiled brightly at her.

Serenity caught sight of Amarah and Liam standing in the second row with baby Malik cradled in Liam's arms. Travis, Sandra, and their three small children stood next to them. Her smile widened further when she saw Colton and Myles King standing beside the group.

Though they had to fly in from Washington, she was beyond glad to see their smiling faces again. In better circumstances than what transpired back on that island in the Bahamas all those months ago. She gave them all a bright smile before coming to a stop at the foot of the arbor as the music faded and everyone took their seats.

She heard Sweeney whisper to Hunter, "I've got tissues in case you cry."

"Fuck off," Hunter mumbled and laughed at his best man.

Fuse, Doc, and Einstein stood behind the two. Each man was veiled in black as night tuxes, making them look devilishly horrifying.

"Who gives this woman away to be married to this man?" the pastor asked, dressed in a dark blue suit.

"Her mother and I do," Jeremy said as he shook hands with Hunter before placing Serenity's hand in his.

He gave his daughter a quick kiss on the cheek, wiped a tear from his eye, and turned to take his seat next to his crying wife in the front row.

"Dearly Beloved, we are gathered here in the sight of God and in the face of this company to join this couple in holy matrimony. If anyone has just cause why they should not be joined together, speak now or forever hold your peace."

The crowd didn't object, and the pastor continued. Before she knew it, it was time for the vow exchange.

"Serenity Jinx, do you take this man to be your husband, to live together in holy matrimony, to love him, to comfort him, to cherish him, and to keep him in sickness and in health, forsaking all others, for as long as you both shall live?"

"I do," Serenity said with a smile on her face as she slipped a silver band on Hunter's ring finger, her green eyes beaming bright with love.

"Hunter Gatlin, do you take this woman to be your wife, to live together in holy matrimony, to love her, to honor her, to comfort her, to cherish her, and to keep her in sickness and in health, forsaking all others, for as long as you both shall live?"

"You're damn right I do," Hunter said as he slipped a silver wedding band surrounded with diamonds and emeralds around

Serenity's delicate ring finger.

"Then by the power vested in me under the laws of the State of Oklahoma, I pronounce you husband and wife. You may kiss your bride." The pastor wrapped up the ceremony as the crowd erupted in cheers and applause.

Hunter spun and dipped Serenity down as if dancing and kissed her passionately. "Ladies and gentlemen, I would like to introduce you to Mr. & Mrs. Hunter Gatlin!" the pastor announced to the church, and they erupted with more cheers.

Hunter laced his fingers through his wife's as he escorted her down the aisle and to the large reception area in another room of the church.

Tables lined with elegant white lace filled the space and framed a large wooden dance floor. Food and beverages were lined down one wall, and a DJ booth was erected by the dance floor. As everyone filed into the space, Hunter and Serenity walked to the middle of the dance floor. She draped her arms around his neck as he placed his large hands on the small of her back.

The music started playing, and he began moving her around the space.

"When I thought you couldn't get more beautiful, you prove me wrong, yet again." He smiled down at her.

She blushed as she met his heated gaze. "You clean up pretty nicely yourself."

She paused and sucked her bottom lip between her teeth. His vision narrowed on the movement and darkened.

"What's going through that beautiful mind of yours?"

She spoke in a sensual tone as she peered up at him through her lashes. "That I want you to fuck me while wearing that tux."

"Great minds think alike," he growled in agreement before

whispering in the shell of her ear, "I know that dress will look wicked hiked up around your hips."

"Even though we had an unexpected guest, this day was absolutely perfect." She tried hard to hide the smile that wanted so desperately to show.

His brows pinched as his vision scanned the crowd of people watching them have their first dance. "Really? Who?"

"One that will become the newest addition to our family."

He stopped mid-step and his gaze snapped to hers, his face contorted in deep thought. Serenity swore she could read his entire thought process through his eyes alone.

"Are you..." He trailed off, and he zoned in on her flat belly, his usual masked expression stripped bare, allowing her to see every emotion he felt.

"Pregnant?" she finished the question for him. "Yes." She let her smile fully show as he lifted her into his arms and spun her around.

"Are you sure?" he asked as he gently set her back down.

"I had a doctor's appointment last week and they confirmed it."

He was beaming at this point, and he let it all show, the excitement, the love, the joy, all of it. He placed a delicate touch against her stomach, and another tear fell from his eye.

"I'm going to be a dad," he whispered to himself as if in disbelief. She swiped the lonely tear away with her thumb. "This truly is the best day of my life, and it will be up until the day this baby is born. I can't wait to hold it. I love you so much. Both of you."

He captured her lips with his, and the world melted away around them.

THE END... FOR REAL

DON'T MISS OUT!

Here's a sneak peek at Doc's story in book 2 of
Brothers of the Red Sky –

An Unexpected Love

CHAPTER 1
BRIELLA

I drown out the noise in the crowded waiting room, a place that's become like a second home to me as I reside in one of the familiar but rather uncomfortable armchairs that fill the space. My thin silver laptop rests atop my denim-clad thighs, a Word document open, displaying a client's manuscript that I desperately need to be focusing on.

For the last six years, I've chauffeured my mother to and from her physical therapy appointments. As the years passed and she progressed in her recovery, the number of appointments had dwindled from multiple sessions a day to twice a week. In that time, not much has changed about the clinic.

The oversized windows still flood the space with natural light, and the same pristine white tiles cover the floor. The mounted TVs with the volume turned low broadcast the same telenovelas on a never-ending loop. I've memorized and learned quite a bit of the language to confidently navigate my way around Mexico if I ever found myself lost in the country. The air still reeks of a combination of cleaning products mixed with determination and hopeful thinking from the clinic's patients.

A large mahogany reception desk sits in its place by the front door, and the same middle-aged woman, her inky black hair forever pulled up into a tight bun, resides behind it, answering the phone and greeting patients with a gentle smile. The kind of smile that gives complete strangers the courage to face any trial.

"You did great today, Joanna." A male voice catches my attention, and I glance up from my computer, pausing my work.

A well-built, middle-aged man with short salt and peppered hair and a matching beard holds the door open for my mother, beaming brightly at her.

"Thank you, Patrick. I feel like I'm almost back to my old self."

Though my mother is forty-two, she doesn't look a day over thirty-five. We share the same straight chocolate hair, pale grey eyes, angular features, and slim figures.

"Stick with me, and I'll have you better than your old self."

Patrick gives her a quick blue-eyed wink, causing a light blush to paint my mother's features as she turns and walks toward me. I close my laptop and stand, not stopping the knowing smile that pulls my lips toward the ceiling.

My mother's face scrunches in question. "What?"

"Don't 'what' me." I wiggle my brows, mischief dancing through my vision. "What was all that about?"

"Nothing, he's just helping me get back to full health." My mother shrugs innocently. "Were you able to get any work done?"

"Oh no, you aren't changing the subject." I laugh as I stow my computer away in its case and hold the door open for her. "Is there something going on between you two?"

Hope blossoms deep within my chest, like a flower's first bloom in spring. Since birth, it's been just the two of us, and in that time, she's *never* dated, let alone so much as mentioned a guy to me. She might as well be a non-practicing nun for all I know. To say the sight of her blushing over a man makes my heart ecstatic would be a drastic understatement.

"We're just friends, honey. He's my physical therapist. He doesn't mix business with pleasure, and I respect that."

Ah, a motto I hold myself to, *especially* with my second job. Once you cross that fine line, things could get chaotic, and no one likes a mess.

"Well, maybe when you're all done, y'all can begin *mixing* left and right." I shoot her a wink as we cross the crowded parking lot and climb into my black Chevy Equinox.

"Briella!" My mother's cheeks are now a healthy apple red.

I'd be lying if I said I didn't get a kick out of getting her all flustered.

"Joanna!" I mock playfully, then add, "He is pretty cute though."

If I'm not mistaken, that was a dreamy sigh that just left my mother's lips. A sound I've never heard from her before, and that blossomed newfound hope spreads throughout every vein in my body, making me feel as if I could fly. "That he is, my little butterfly. That he is."

Deciding to give her a reprieve from my teasing, I turn up the radio, and we lose ourselves in a 1980s Spotify playlist, belting out every word and dancing not-so-gracefully, despite the weird glances we get from strangers in passing cars. After I drop her off at her apartment, I drive myself home.

I have a ton more editing to do on my client's manuscript before I can set it aside and get ready for my second job. I'm attending an art exhibition with a wealthy lawyer who's a major donor to the gallery, so I'll need to make sure I allow myself plenty of time to get ready.

I need to appear as if I grew up in that world. A world with two parental figures, a lavish private education, access to my parents' credit cards where I'm free to spend ungodly amounts of money without repercussions, a closet so grand it could be a bedroom that overflows with name-brand clothing I only wear once, and meals prepared by a family chef. That, however, couldn't be further from my reality.

I paint my lips with a rosy pink matte lipstick before checking over my reflection one last time. My vision shifts to my phone, and I count it a win that I'm ready right on time. After slipping my phone, ID, and money into a small silver clutch, I grab my keys and leave.

This wasn't exactly how I saw my life after graduating from high school. I'd planned on taking a year off to travel the world, exploring its beauties and wonders, tasting the cuisine, both food and men, and maybe even falling in love a time or two. As a teen, I'd saved up every one of my paychecks, so I'd have enough to sustain myself until I got back home and was ready to start college.

However, a few days after graduation, my entire world flipped inside out. I was lying on my bed, my laptop open in front of me, knees bent and feet swaying lazily in the air, debating if I wanted to book a flight to Ireland or Greece for my first of many stops. An entire world of possibilities was within my reach when I got a phone call that I relive too often in my nightmares. A call informing me that my mother had been in a terrible car accident.

She'd been T-boned by a drunk driver who'd run a red light. The impact had severely broken numerous bones, punctured a lung, and given her internal bleeding, putting her on the verge of death. I've never felt fear like that before. The thought of possibly losing the only family I've ever known—my mother, my best friend—had me praying to God each and every day just to heal her.

Instead of Paris, Scotland, or England, I spent my entire summer in a tiny, sterile hospital room next to her bed, refusing to leave her side until she was discharged. Though it's been years, the incessant beeping of monitors still haunts my dreams, like a demon that's attached itself to me with the sole intention of terrorizing me until I depart from this earth.

Instead of moving out and starting my own path in life, I stayed at home to care for her. I drove her to and from numerous medical appointments and ran all of her errands, all while putting myself through college—online, of course, because that gave me the flexibility and freedom she needed from me back then.

I thought we had finally made it through the worst of it, but boy, was I terribly wrong. The hospital bill had come in, and my heart plummeted as if I were standing in a pool of quicksand that was determined to keep me trapped in its dark depths forever. My mother had a good job that provided her with medical insurance, but it didn't cover everything. For a place whose sole intention is to heal the sick and injured, they aren't shy about demanding tremendous amounts of money from their patients. Simply put, it's extortion.

I'd never seen a bill with so many numbers before in my life. I couldn't let my mother see it. She had enough stress to deal with as she was forced to relearn how to do everything: walk, write, and even feed herself.

As her only family, it was my responsibility to figure out how to pay just over two hundred thousand dollars we were now indebted to. I'd called and set up a monthly payment plan, but after you factored in interest, my children would've still been paying on it long after my death. That didn't sit right with me. I had to come up with a way to bring in a large amount of money, and fast. An idea had struck me that had me cringing, but what choice did I have?

I became… an escort of sorts. Minus the sex. Men could hire me when they needed a date for a work function, political event, sports gala, etc. A hired plus-one, if you will. I'd always been complimented on my beauty, so why not use it to my advantage?

I could never sell my body, but I could sell my time and company. I could swallow my pride enough to be eye candy on a rich man's arm for a night. I've been doing that for a few years now and have built up a good clientele. Because of this, I've been able to pay those medical bills down to around forty thousand dollars. Give or take a few bucks.

At this rate, I'll be able to pay them off within the next year, and I can finally quit my little side gig and just focus on my day job as an editor. Maybe I'll even travel the world as I planned before. I wonder if my mother would accompany me. On top of never seeing her with a man, she's never taken a vacation. But with a kid at home and no family offering to babysit, how could she?

I never allow clients to pick me up from my home for numerous reasons. One, they could be a psychopath, and I have no interest in being murdered and left in the woods somewhere to rot. I couldn't leave my mother to deal with this ugly world alone. Two, I'm a *very* private person. Though I attend these functions and have to smile and play nice all evening, we never engage in personal conversations. My clients know the bare minimum about me and vice versa. Three, I live in a small apartment. It's nice, and I'm not embarrassed or ashamed of my home, but my clients are all millionaires.

The types of wealth that reside in mansions or penthouses with multiple vacation homes scattered around the globe. It goes back to keeping my personal life private. I don't want them to know how much or how little money I come from. Instead, I have them pick me up at a local five-star hotel. I make adjustments accordingly if we go out of town for the event, but thankfully, those situations are rare.

I park my car in the attached parking garage of the hotel, my reasonable vehicle sticking out like a sore thumb surrounded by pristine cars. Cars that cost ungodly amounts of money with a wax coat so shiny it's near blinding. I enter the grand lobby, take a seat, and pretend to act as if I belong there instead of the Motel 6 down the street. As if my checking account holds thousands of dollars at any given time, instead of a mere hundred bucks, if I'm lucky.

Ten minutes later, my clutch vibrates against my lap. Reaching in, I remove my phone and see a text waiting for me.

Jared Grayshaw: We just pulled in, parked under the awning at the entrance.

After a deep breath, I stand, run my hand down the front of my gown, and make my way outside with my clutch gripped in the other.

"Good evening, Ms. Dawson. You're looking as stunning as ever," Tommy, a middle-aged personal driver, greets me with a kind smile.

He holds open the back door of a black SUV as I gracefully slide in.

"Thank you, Tommy." I beam at the kind soul who never fails to give me some sort of compliment.

As Tommy shuts the door and rounds the vehicle, I take in my date for the evening. Jared Grayshaw. He's become a regular over the past year. Though I said I never open up to clients and always keep them at arm's distance, he was a surprising exception I didn't see coming. He's become more like an older brother I never knew I needed. Handsome, late twenties, with blond hair and bright green eyes, wearing an expensive tuxedo that's always impossibly lint and wrinkle-free.

"Good evening, Mr. Grayshaw," I tease as I adjust my full-length silk gown around my legs.

"Mr. Grayshaw is my father, Bri." He laughs as he finishes sending what I'm assuming is either a text or an email before slipping his phone into his trouser pocket. His vision slides down my front, a cocky grin playing on his full lips. "Tommy was right. You do look stunning."

I've been doing this long enough to confidently read the kind of men these guys are within the first few minutes of speaking with them. Some are all business and never say or do anything inappropriate. Those are my favorites. Some are playboys who like to push the boundaries I set, but after firmly reminding them of said boundaries, they behave. Most of the time. Then you have guys like Jared. The ones who know *exactly* what their money and good looks can get them. The cocky ones who like to flirt but never push the boundaries.

Thankfully, Jared has never tried to flirt with me. He gives me compliments, sure, but there's no hidden agenda for trying to get into my pants. And instead, I met a wonderful person whom I can call a friend.

In a world that has revolved around my mother for the last six years, I don't have many friends of my own. I don't have the time for leisure activities like day shopping with the girls, dinner dates, nights at the club getting lost in drinks and good music, or even a few hours to simply go see a movie. If I'm not taking my mother to doctors' or physical therapy appointments or running errands for her, I'm at home working so I can afford things like food, rent, electricity, and running water, which are unfortunate necessities, because as much as I love the woman who birthed me, I need my own space.

After a comfortable, silent fifteen-minute car ride, we come to a stop in front of the gallery. Tommy opens my door, and I accept his hand as I slide out, followed by Jared. He extends his elbow toward me, and I loop my arm around it. This is the extent of the contact I allow between myself and any of my clients.

The sounds of people conversing fill my ears as we enter the gallery. Jared grabs a long-stemmed glass from the tray of a nearby server and hands the bubbly yellow liquid to me before grabbing one for himself.

"I hate these things," he leans in to whisper in my ear, making it appear to any onlookers that we're lovers and he's whispering sweet promises about how the night will end.

I grin as I take a sip of champagne and peer up at him through my long, dark lashes. "Then why come to them?"

"To show face and network." He releases a small, deflated sigh. "It's all a game to these people."

My gaze drops to the glass clutched in my hand. "Sounds miserable and lonely."

I know all too well what it's like to feel lonely. What it's like to have to pretend to be someone you're not. What it's like to sacrifice your true wishes and desires in life for the sake of others. My entire adult life has revolved around someone else. Not that I regret it, not one bit. But sometimes I wonder what my life would look like if she'd never been in that accident. If I ended up living out my original plan of traveling the world.

Would I have chosen to come back and settle in Oklahoma, only minutes from my mother? Or would I have made the breathtaking cities of Paris or Rome my new home? Perhaps I would've picked Greece, where I could sprawl out on a beach, soaking up the rays of the sun while I edited manuscripts with the crashing waves as peaceful background noise. Would I be married to a man with a dreamy accent surrounded by our mixed heritage children?

Maybe that's what drew Jared and I together. Our souls noticed something familiar in the other, or something missing, and reached out toward the lifeline, like a person who fell overboard, clinging to the life preserver for all their worth.

"At least I've got you at my side. We can be lonely together." He shoots me a playful wink, and I shake my head but can't stop the grin that tugs the corners of my mouth up. "Ready?"

I snort at the irony. "I should be asking you that."

The next hour passes in a bit of a blur. Jared speaks with various people, putting on a show and appearing as if he lives for social outings like these. Some guests have women on their arms, others came alone, but all are dressed in their best for the evening. I have to give him props. He could go far in Hollywood with acting skills like those. If he hadn't told me the truth of his feelings beforehand, I would have never known that his evening was filled with silent suffering.

Finally, he escorts me, arm still looped through his, around the gallery. I allow my vision to drink in all the breathtaking pieces.

Some are sculptures, ranging in size, shape, and materials from wood, plastic, clay, stone, and more. Others are hanging canvases. The paintings vary from oil, acrylic, abstract, and realism. Others are enlarged photographs of people, buildings, flora and fauna, and stunning landscapes. I'm not a big art person, but even I have to admit the collection is magnificent.

We observe a large painting, both of our heads cocked to the side as we try to decipher the art.

Jared squints as if that will help him to better see the piece. "I... I think it's a cat?"

My brows pinch as I tilt my head to the other side, hoping the new perspective might help clear the image. "Where do you see a cat?"

"Just there." he motions with his hand. "See how it's kind of slanting to the side?"

"Huh," I huff out more to myself than anything. "I thought it was a puddle reflecting the lights of a city."

I give up trying to play Where's Waldo with the cat that he swears he sees, and drink down the last of my champagne. That was my second glass, and I'm officially cutting myself off. Not that I'm drunk, but my body does have a welcomed warmth spreading through it, giving me enough energy and courage to smile and make it through the rest of the evening.

He hums quietly in consideration as if trying to see things from my eyes. "I guess that's the good thing about abstract. There's no right or wrong. It's all about the viewer's interpretation."

Just as I'm about to respond, an unknown voice sounds from behind us, leaving my words clogged in my throat.

"I didn't expect to see you here tonight." The rich, amused voice rolls over me, causing my breath to hitch when I finally turn and observe the beautiful man it belongs to.

CHAPTER 2
DOC

"Are y'all up to grab drinks tonight?" Boss asks after we finish our morning workout. His long brown hair is secured in a knot atop his head, and sweat has his clothes clinging to his tall, bulky frame. "Serenity said that she found a place tucked away in the heart of downtown that has pretty great reviews."

"Uh, did you forget the last time Renny found a new place for us to try?" Fuse hikes a thick brow in caution. "I've never been hit on by so many men in my life. Don't get me wrong, it was a great confidence booster, and I had a hell of a time, but those places aren't really my scene." He chuckles before tipping his head back to drain the remainder of his water bottle, sending his long blond Viking-style braid swaying between his shoulders.

We join him in laughter as a memory from a few months back flashes through my mind. Renny, Boss's fiancée, swore on her life that she had no idea that Hearts On Tap was the hottest gay bar in town. Of course, that didn't stop her and Addi from nearly peeing on themselves from laughter at our awkwardness when men kept approaching us, asking to buy us drinks, to dance, or flat out inquiring whether we wanted "company" that night. Because gossip spreads faster than germs in a kindergarten classroom in places like those, once word got around that we were all straight, everyone pretty much left us alone. That didn't stop some from gazing hungrily at us from across the bar.

"I promise," Boss holds up a large hand as if taking an oath, "there will be no repeats of last time."

"Right." Fuse slowly elongates the word as if not convinced in the slightest. After another few seconds, he shrugs and says, "Ah, what the hell? I'm in."

"Sure, I'm game," Einstein chimes in as he wipes his face free of sweat with his shirt, revealing a creamy torso with lean muscles and dark hair that circles his navel and disappears beneath his shorts.

"Even if it was another gay bar, Addi and I are in." Sweeney's grin is full of mischief as he adds, "Say what you want, but that place played a killer soundtrack all night long."

Addi is Sweeney's fiancé. They've been together for nearly a year, and after meeting her, there's no more perfect woman for him. She's spunky, sarcastic, has no filter, and is not afraid to speak her mind. Honestly, those two together are the life of any party. Even in a room full of complete strangers.

"Sorry, Boss. I can't tonight." I wipe my brows free of sweat with a towel I wetted with my water bottle. The icy cold against my heated skin acts as a shock to my nervous system, but it feels too good to stop. "I've got a side gig, working security for an art exhibition."

For the past two years, I've worked for Boss at Red Sky Security. It's a company he founded after separating from the Navy that provides affluent clients with short-term bodyguards for various occasions. With his background as a SEAL, that type of business couldn't be run by more capable hands. And though it's located in Oklahoma, we get clients from all over the world. Sometimes the assignments take us out of town for a few days, other times it's merely a few hours of work locally.

On the days we're not on guard duty, we meet at Red Sky Security and work out in the full gym Boss had built in the back. We finish by sparring and rolling with each other. It helps us stay in shape and keeps our fighting skills fine-tuned in case they're needed while we're on protection duties.

I love the men I work with like brothers. Boss is the best man I've ever worked for. He's fair and laid back and doesn't get upset if we take odd security jobs on the days we don't have assignments with him. Which most of us do. Not because we're hurting for money. He pays us all very well. But mostly because we're all single, minus Boss and Sweeney, and we like to keep busy instead of going home to a quiet and empty house all the time.

Einstein is our little evil genius tech wizard and skilled hacker. He was given the call sign due to how scary smart he is. He's our eyes and ears when we're out on assignments. Fuse is an explosives expert. Anything that goes boom, he's your guy. Sweeney, the charismatic psycho, prefers knives over any other weapon. We gave him the name after the fictional serial killer from the mid-1800s, Sweeney Todd, who was a barber who killed people with a straight razor. I was given the name Doc after the infamous gunslinger Doc Holliday. I'm a skilled sniper and the best shot in the group. As for Boss, well, that one's pretty self-explanatory.

Sweeney shifts his golden gaze to me, his wicked grin promising trouble. "A hundred bucks says you get five numbers slipped into your pocket from unsatisfied wealthy housewives."

"Count me in, but I say three numbers." Boss's deep laugh

echoes off the gym walls.

Fuse counters next with a large, cocky smile. "Nah, seven for me. Those women are like vultures around young men. It's creepy."

"I'm with Fuse. I say anywhere from seven to ten numbers." Amusement sparkles in Einstein's deep sapphire eyes.

"Y'all are on!" I laugh and shift my gaze among them. "But I say I walk out of there with one number."

They all burst out laughing because it would be a cold day in hell before that ever happened, and we all know it. We enter the locker room to shower and change.

After making it home, I change into a black button-up dress shirt and tuck it into a pair of form-fitting black slacks. I'm about to leave when my phone rings. Removing it from the pocket of my slacks, I groan when I see my mother's face pop up on the caller ID.

"Hey, Mom." I pinch the phone between my ear and shoulder as I perch on a wooden bench by my front door and slip on my spotless black leather dress shoes.

"Colt, honey, you were supposed to call me yesterday." Her melodic voice filters down the line. "What happened?"

"I'm sorry. I got busy at work and it slipped my mind."

That's a lie. Well, a half-lie. I *was* busy at work yesterday, but it didn't slip my mind to call her. I was trying to put off this conversation for as long as possible.

"Don't you dare lie to your mother. I raised you better than that."

I inwardly groan and release a long breath. "Sorry."

"So? Will you be bringing someone with you to the resort? I

need to know for the seating chart." I hear papers rustling in the background. "Where did I put that thing?" My mother mutters. "Oh, there it is."

I assume she's retrieved said seating chart.

"Why do I need to bring anyone?" I keep my tone light as I finish with my laces and rest my forearms atop my knees. "Isn't my wonderful company enough?"

"Of course it is, honey." Her sweet voice turns sympathetic. "I'm just saying that it would be nice to see you with someone. To see you happy."

"I am happy." I can't help but cringe when I hear how flat my voice sounds.

"I'm sure you are, honey," she says, not convinced in the slightest.

I sigh heavily and run my hand over my smooth face. "Mom, we've talked about this numerous times before. My answer isn't changing. I don't have time to date right now. My job keeps me very busy."

That's another lie. Well, half-lie. Again. My primary job at Red Sky Security allows me plenty of time for a personal life, but I choose to keep myself busy with odd jobs here and there. I have to, because when I don't, when I'm alone, the quiet grows too loud, and I find myself stuck in memories of the past. Memories that thrive on sinking their hooks deep into my psyche. Memories that luxuriate in my agonizing pain of a time in my life that I'd prefer never to relive. So I make sure to minimize the solitude any chance I get.

"What did I say about lying?" I swear I can hear the deep arch of her brow from her tone, and another groan slips past my lips. Elijah and I could never sneak anything by our mother growing up.

I swear that woman had eyes and ears everywhere. And since then, her superpower has only grown stronger. It's quite frustrating, actually. "Honey, it's been five years. You can't keep letting the past scare you out of dating."

The betrayal I've worked hard all this time to bury plays fresh through my mind, causing an explosion of emotions to shoot through me. Hurt, rage, sadness, grief. My heart painfully constricts, just as it did back then.

"Don't ever bring that up to me again," I clip out and try hard to keep the hurt out of my voice.

I don't mean to speak harshly to her. I know she means well and wants to see me as happy as my little brother. He's the reason we're going to the Bahamas in the first place. My father started the chain of resorts decades ago, and Elijah and his soon-to-be bride, Gabby, wanted to get married at one. My mother, lovely woman that she is, got it in her head that this would be the perfect time for a long-overdue family vacation.

We'll be spending the week leading up to the wedding there at the resort. Six whole days with my family, surrounded by happy couples so deep in love… I'd pay good money for someone to just shoot me now and put me out of my misery.

"Sweetie, I didn't bring it up to hurt you. I just want to see both my boys happy. I promise."

"I know." I run my hand over my freshly-shaven jaw again and peer up at the clock hanging on my wall. "I've got to go before I'm late for work. I'll call you tomorrow with my answer. I promise."

"Colt Alexander Rivers!" My name is a warning coming from her lips.

"Cross my heart, I'll call tomorrow." I can't help but laugh as I draw an X with my finger over my chest as if my mother's standing right in front of me. "Love you," I say before hanging up, not waiting for her to respond.

My shoulders drop as I shake my head clear of the conversation and the old feelings it brought to the surface. Feelings that I never want to experience again. Feelings that I wouldn't wish on my worst enemy. With that, I grab my keys and leave my house.

So far, Fuse and Einstein's bets are looking the most promising. The exhibition hasn't even been going for an hour, and I've already had four women slip me business cards with their personal numbers scribbled across the back. They'll all end up in the trash can before I leave.

I don't date. Thankfully, you don't have to date someone to sleep with them. But a huge rule of mine has always been that I don't mess around with married women. That doesn't mean I can't appreciate the very generous and not-so-subtle compliments they freely give. They do wonders for a man's ego.

After making a few more rounds around the gallery, I spot a woman who nearly steals my breath like a thief in the night. Her royal blue dress molds around her curves deliciously and pops against her slightly tanned skin. She's got her back to me, and the sight of her round ass covered in the thin, silky material goes straight to my groin.

She's got her arm looped through a man's as they discuss the painting in front of them. At least, I think they're discussing the art. I'm too far away to hear their conversation, but judging by the way they keep tilting their heads from side to side, I'm confident in my assumption. I glimpse the side profile of the man, and a grin shapes my lips.

My feet have me crossing the open space, and before I know it, I'm behind the couple. "I didn't expect to see you here tonight."

Jared Grayshaw turns, recognition sparking in his mossy gaze. Our families have been close for decades. His father was an attorney and had worked closely with my father any time he needed legal help or advice with his resorts. Unlike me, Jared had followed closely in his father's footsteps.

"Colt Rivers." His warm greeting causes his date to turn as well. "Long time no see."

I don't miss the way the woman's pale gray eyes widen slightly around the edges. Though she's about five feet from me, I can tell they're a shade I've never seen before. Like the thick clouds of a violent thunderstorm threatening to open up and drown the earth beneath. They only act to accentuate her slender, sharp features.

"They have you working security tonight?" he questions, observing the plastic earpiece that leads from my pierced ear and disappears beneath my shirt.

"Yep. Did they invite you in hopes of another large donation?" I tease.

"Of course." Jared snorts and practically rolls his eyes. "Sometimes I fear that's all people see when they look at me. Dollar signs."

I don't miss the hurt that flashes through his gaze, though it's gone just as quickly. It's my job to notice everything about my surroundings and trivial details that tend to go unnoticed, but also and probably most importantly, I understand *exactly* what he means.

"Who's your date?" I inquire, craving the subject change, and nodding my head toward the stunning woman at his side.

"This is Briella. Bri, this is Colt. Our fathers have known each other since before we were born."

"It's a pleasure to meet you, Colt." She gives me a timid smile and a slight dip of her head.

The sound of her soft voice alone does things to me I haven't felt in far too long. It has blood rushing to a certain extension of my body. And the sound of my name slipping past those full lips of hers…

Fuck, I groan inwardly.

I nod back and smile. "The pleasure's all mine."

Though I try very hard to resist, my gaze takes on a mind of its own, betraying me by slowly traveling down her front. Her chocolate hair is pulled tightly into a bun, leaving a few strands to frame her flawless face. The neckline of her dress dips between her breasts, showing off a modest amount of the curved, supple tissue. The silky material clings to her waist and hips before flowing elegantly to the floor.

Holy fuck… She's hands down one of the most beautiful women I've ever seen. The sight of her in that dress leaves little to the imagination of the treasure that lies beneath. An image flashes through my mind that has my groin twitching in my slacks. That thin dress of hers pooled around her feet. Her, standing before me completely naked, minus her heels that will only enhance her round ass and long legs.

I take a deep breath and force my mind to more appropriate thoughts. Thoughts that won't leave me having to explain the awkward bulge in my slacks in a room full of strangers. The sound of her addictive voice draws me out of my fantasy and back to reality.

"If you'll excuse me. I need to powder my nose," Briella says to Jared before she turns and heads toward the bathroom.

"Tell me you didn't find that one at a strip club too?" I laugh.

The last time I saw him at a business function, he had a stripper at his side. Not that she had looked like one. Far from it, actually. She was decked out in a name-brand dress that must've cost a few grand, jewelry that refracted the light with every movement, professional hair and makeup done elegantly, appearing like any other trophy wife at those types of events.

However, some of the men recognized her from the club, and word spread like wildfire. Once the news reached Jared's father, he threatened to revoke the law firm that had been passed down to him to run if he ever pulled another stunt like that again. Saying he didn't care who or what Jared did in his free time, but they had a reputation to uphold in public if they were to be respected.

Jared lives for moments like those, which made it so much fun growing up with him as a close friend. Jumping at any opportunity that would possibly give his old man a heart attack from his actions. It was playing with fire, but Jared was a skilled arsonist. Doing just enough to get under his old man's skin, but never enough to cause permanent damage to the family name.

"No." Jared laughs as if remembering too. "Bri is a hired plus-one." He must observe the look of confusion marring my features because he asks, "You've never heard of that?"

"No." I shake my head and ask hesitantly. "Is it like an escort?"

He throws his head back with laughter, gaining questionable looks from other guests as they pass by. "Almost, minus the sex. When men like us need arm candy for a night, we call someone like her. She attends the functions with us, smiles, and looks pretty, then we part ways after the event."

I purposefully ignore the way he says men like us. I chose not to follow in my father's footsteps for a reason. I chose to avoid anything upper-class related, and I plan on doing so for the rest of my life. Though I come from money, I don't act like it. I dress like a normal human, I have a modest job, work my ass off, and I keep my background and private life to myself.

Once people discover that you're rich, they're like fucking vultures or leeches, only hanging around you because of what you can offer them. I'm not interested in fake people.

Even my brothers at Red Sky Security know very little about my background. Not that they'd ever treat me any differently. They're good men. The best, actually, and I trust them with my life. They know I come from money, but they don't know how much or the details behind it, and they've never asked. Which tells me they're part of a very small pool of people who are to be cherished at all costs.

Scratch that. I'm sure Einstein knows. The little genius makes it his business to know everything about everyone. However, if he has uncovered the secret behind my family's fortune, he hasn't mentioned it to me or the others, which I'm beyond thankful for.

I quirk a brow. "And you pay her for it?"

"Yeah, but it's well worth it. Honestly, I hate attending events like these, so having someone at my side helps me endure it."

"Huh." I cock my head as an idea enters my mind. A very off-the-wall and completely idiotic idea that I should smother before it gets me into what I can only assume will be dangerous waters.

"Ah, man." Jared grins wickedly. "I know that look all too well. It got us in quite a bit of trouble as kids."

I watch as my friend removes his wallet from the pocket of his slacks and withdraws a business card before tucking away his wallet again. He retrieves the ink pen from the chest pocket of his tuxedo jacket and scribbles something across the back before handing it to me. I peer down to observe a series of numbers written in his neat script.

"That's Bri's number. In case you need a plus-one for any reason." He shrugs casually and slips his pen back into his pocket.

I slide the card into my pocket with the others. "Thanks." I chuckle and shake my head incredulously. "Enjoy the rest of your night."

"I'll try." Jared rolls his eyes again, but grins, though it radiates at half its usual brightness.

NOTE FROM THE AUTHOR

I wanted to start by saying that this book was by far the hardest to write. Not idea-wise, those flowed fluidly, but because of the darkness factor. The funeral and miscarriage scene hit a little too close to home. I grew up in a military family, and my husband joined the Marine Corps after we got married, so I'm no stranger to those types of funerals.

I also suffered from a miscarriage. I ugly cried while writing both scenes, but it was therapeutic in a way. I wish I could say it gets easier, but even though it's been over a decade since I lost a bundle of joy I'll meet in heaven one day, you merely learn to live with the pain a little better each day.

Just know that you, strong and beautiful women, are not to blame. No matter how much we curse ourselves for our bodies failing at the one job it's biologically designed to do, sometimes things go wrong, and it's nobody's fault. Know that you are not alone. Grief comes in many forms, and there are numerous resources available and ready to assist. Don't ever hesitate to ask for help, and don't ever suffer alone.

Matthew 5:4. "Blessed are those who mourn, for they will be comforted."

XOXO,
Maricca

FOR MY READERS

Thank you for reading Desire's End. I hope you enjoyed the final book in the Desire Series as much as I did. I would love to hear your thoughts about it, so please leave a review and follow me on social media to stay up to date on my latest writings.

Facebook: Maricca Wood - Author
Instagram: mariccawoodauthor
TikTok: mariccawoodauthor
Website: www.mariccawood.com
Newsletter: www.mariccawood.com/newsletter

ACKNOWLEDGMENTS

First, to the Most High—God, you are my rock and my foundation. Without you, darkness would've overtaken me. You were the light I followed when grief, heartache, and the struggles in life tried to swallow me. Psalm 34:18. "The Lord is close to the brokenhearted; he rescues those whose spirits are crushed."

To my amazing husband—Knowing that I have your unwavering support gives me the utmost motivation. It makes me feel like nothing is unattainable, and that is one of the greatest feelings in this world.

To my mother—Thank you! I was stuck on how I wanted to structure this book, and I was dragging my feet while writing it. I swear I wrote it at least four different ways and wasn't happy with any of them. However, over an amazing dinner and even better drinks, you helped me find the perfect way to tell this story.

To my beta readers—Thank you for the criticism, both good and bad, and for helping me spot any mistakes, plot holes, or areas where this story needed strengthening. I appreciate you more than you'll ever know.

To my editor, The Havoc Archives—Thank you for helping to polish this story so it can shine brighter than the sun!

To my designers, Books and Moods—Your ability to take words printed on boring paper and turn them into a visual work of art is something to be celebrated. Thank you for always making my books so pretty!

To my readers—Thank you for sticking with me for so long! It's always a bittersweet moment when you wrap up something that you've spent years of your life crafting. I created these stories to share with like-minded people who love 'love' just as much as I do. I can't wait to share more with you all.

ABOUT THE AUTHOR

Maricca Wood is a hopeless romantic who, believe it or not, used to loathe reading growing up. Now, she finds it hard to put books down. She writes contemporary romance, some darker than others, and fantasy, all with plenty of angst, relatable characters, and of course, spice!

She lives in Oklahoma with her family and possesses an associate degree in Entrepreneurship. She enjoys reading a wide range of genres, playing video games, watching anime, doing puzzles, and building Lego sets. She can count on one hand all the people who have ever pronounced her name correctly the first time. Good luck!

www.ingramcontent.com/pod-product-compliance
Lightning Source LLC
LaVergne TN
LVHW010308070526
838199LV00065B/5482